KU-676-965

This Stream
of Dreams

Roberta Latow

HEADLINE

First published in Great Britain in 1987
by Futura Publications
Reprinted in this edition in 1994
by HEADLINE BOOK PUBLISHING

Grateful acknowledgement is made to the following for permission
to reprint previously published material: Chatto and Windus Ltd:
Excerpt from 'Ithaka' by C. P. Cavafy from his *Collected Poems*,
edited by George Savidis, translated by Edmund Keeley and Philip
Sherrard. Reprinted by permission.

10 9 8 7 6 5 4 3

ISBN 0 7472 4392 1

Typeset by Keyboard Services, Luton
Printed and bound in Great Britain by
Cox & Wyman Ltd, Reading, Berkshire

HEADLINE BOOK PUBLISHING
A division of Hodder Headline PLC
338 Euston Road
London NW1 3BH

For
old friends
Adele and George and Senoe
and loyal helpers
Colin and Anita

The joy and essence of my life is the memory of the hours when I found and sustained sensual delight as I desired it. The joy and essence of my life for me, who abhorred every enjoyment of routine loves.

Cavafy

Chapter 1

Standing at the altar, his best man at his side, Adam Corey waited for Mirella Wingfield to walk down the aisle on the arm of her lover. Stark terror, an emotion Adam Corey had never before experienced, held him in thrall.

Tall and handsome, the forty-eight-year-old American multimillionaire was an adventurer, famous as an archaeologist and corporate executive. He had been a much sought-after bachelor, a man of the world who divided his exotic life between the West and his white marble palace on the shores of the Bosporus in Turkey. But more, he was a winner ... habitually. And he was his own man, remaining at all times loyal to himself, come what might.

How, then, was it possible for this man, this outsider, this nonconformist, this individualist, suddenly to take such fright? Adam was mystified by his terror. Outside there was warmth after rain. Sun splashed through the bright leaves of maple trees lining the deserted dirt road that ended at the white clapboard church set on a patch of green velvet grass against a clear blue sky. The short but proud steeple of the church was home for a single bronze bell that had arrived with the first of the Pilgrim Fathers.

Inside every pew was taken. The pristine white

1

interior was more like a meeting hall for the Puritan worthies who had arrived on the *Mayflower* than a place of Christian worship. Spartan, with no cross, no pious statue or sacrificial candles or golden gifts, the church's austerity contrasted greatly with the opulent clothes and jewels of the wedding-guests.

The guests were a cross section of celebrities that included high society, power players in the world of corporate finance and politics. Dazzlingly beautiful, chic women and magnificently self-possessed men mingled with a smattering of the less celebrated, the occasional academic, and a few exotic dark-skinned foreign guests. For the most part, they were family, close friends, and others who had played significant roles in the lives of the bride and groom before they met and fell deeply in love.

Deeply in love Adam most certainly was. And terrified. He did not fear that Mirella might change her mind at the last minute and choose Rashid Lala Mustapha, who was giving her away in marriage to him before God and the world. This was simply a gesture that had grown from the deep regard that still bound the three of them together, despite the rivalry in love of the two men for Mirella. Nor did his terror arise from his intuition that, although Mirella had chosen Adam to love, marry and share her life, Rashid would remain her lover for as long as they lived. He was sure that for the time being Mirella was unaware of the possibility. He guessed that if she knew the prospect was there, it was buried so deep in her subconscious that she had not yet come to terms with it. Adam was secure enough to accept that a *ménage à trois* was a distinct possibility and might suit the three of them admirably. It was implicit in their

2

characters and the lives they had led in the past. Confidence such as Adam's could never be shaken. He knew there was nothing in heaven or on earth that could change the deep love and ecstasy he shared with Mirella.

Was it then the act of getting married, the commitment to Mirella that suffused him with this profoundly unsettling emotion? Hardly. He had wanted to marry her, commit himself to her from the moment they met. He had walked away from her once, only to return. He had left her a second time, but only to wait for her to realize and to accept that theirs was the real, the rare, the true love. She had been the one to return then.

Estrangement had brought Adam no moment of terror, no fear of loss. Not when she had inherited the Oujie legacy which overnight made her one of the wealthiest, most powerful women in the world, nor when she became notorious for her much publicized affair with Rashid. He had always known Mirella was committed to him, and only him, for ever. Their passion for each other had been and still was a *fait accompli*. They both knew it then, and so did Rashid. The three of them knew it now.

Adam caught the angelic sound of a harp and a flute weaving their baroque harmonies through the building from the small gallery above the entrance. Because the musicians were hidden from view, the quivering chords of this exquisite music drifted down over the guests, soft and warm, drenching them in the sounds of romance and love.

His gaze swept across the sea of faces in the front pews. The expressions on those faces revealed how deeply lost to the music, how exquisitely rapt by the

3

romance of the occasion they were. The lone exception was an odd figure of a man, long in the torso and short in the leg, whose grey morning coat was impeccably tailored. He clenched a top hat and gloves in one hand. He was a handsome but pasty-faced man with thinning, steel-grey hair. His shiny forehead protruded like a slightly sinister child's and he kept wiping the corners of his mouth with a crooked finger.

The man was restless, his pale goat-like eyes darting nervously around the room. He fidgeted where he stood, looking over his shoulder on occasion, or out through the church windows, as if he were waiting for some disaster. No, not waiting, *willing* some intrusion upon this moment of bliss.

For a fleeting moment Adam sensed the negative chord vibrating from the man. It bothered him not in the least. 'It won't happen,' Adam thought. And at the moment he dismissed the man from his mind and his sight he knew what terrified him. It was not what any man on earth could do to him or his family. It was the naked power of a love that was real, and the one woman who could generate that in him that filled him with terror.

The doors into the church opened suddenly. In the sunlight spilling down the white carpeted aisle appeared Deena Weaver, Mirella's best friend and her maid of honour. Deena's long, amber-coloured, curly hair was loosely drawn and pinned by small yellow diamonds up and away from her face in tier upon tier to the top of her head, forming a soft crown of curls and jewels. From there it tumbled down her back like glistening splashes of honey.

She wore a gown narrowly cut, made of silk satin

with long, voluminous, transparent, silk-organza puffed sleeves. It was finished tight to the wrists in a narrow band of the same dress silk, that Yves Saint Laurent had ordained should be dyed to match the colour of her hair. It clung to her body enough to show her figure but not enough to be provocative. When she walked she shimmered in the sunlight like an angel and blended with the voluptuous yet heavenly music of the golden harp and the silver flute.

She smiled at Adam and at the man standing next to him, then gave an ever-so-slight curtsey to the seemingly ancient and frail Wingfield family minister. He stood at the altar, a handsome representative of God, dressed in elegant black robes and flanked by a pair of tall white azalea trees. Pruned in a luscious cascade from the top of their five-inch thick trunks like a great waterfall, they seemed to be weeping with joy at their own beauty. Deena took her place next to the best man, Brindley Ribblesdale, Mirella's English solicitor.

And then Adam almost gasped. She was there. His bride. Mirella. Standing alone, the sun from the open church doors pouring an aura of light behind her, Mirella's magnificence inspired sighs of admiration that rippled through the congregation. Deena had been a honey-gold angel heralding the arrival of a goddess.

Saint Laurent had chosen to dress her in heavy white lace that followed every contour of her body. From below the hips it miraculously and subtly flared into a bias-cut skirt that touched the floor. Its boat-shaped neckline lay just below the collar bone in the front, and low to the waist in the back, and was worn over a natural-coloured body stocking. Mirella's veil

5

was draped not over her face but over her breasts and across her shoulders, and was tied high up on the back of her neck. A hundred yards of the finest silk chiffon, mistily transparent, trailed down to veil her naked back and cascade in folds on to the church floor where it spread out into a train nearly thirty feet long.

She carried no flowers. The long sleeves of her gown ended in lace points deep on the backs of her hands, as she merely placed the tips of her fingers together in front of her. Her head, under a semi-soft, wide brimmed, nearly transparent, white horsehair hat with a cluster of fresh magnolias pinned to the side of the crown, was lowered in a shy, almost demure manner.

A pear-shaped diamond sparkled on her finger. It was an enormous gem, even by Harry Winston's standards. Adam had given it to her when for the first time they had taken each other, wholly and without reservation, on the banks of the Euphrates. At her throat gleamed the diamond bumble bee in the centre of the *collier* of magnificently lustrous, hazel-nut-sized oriental pearls that Rashid had given her. A pair of matching diamond chokers flanked the *collier* above and below. These were extraordinary for the size and flawless brilliance of each matching round stone.

Slowly, she raised her head, and a current of admiring sighs once again swept through the congregation. No such expression of admiration softened the clenched tight lips of the oddly-shaped, cold-hearted man, Ralph Werfel, who resisted the beauty and the passion of the moment affecting every other person in the church. But the sighs of delight swept over him and absorbed his resentment in a single wave of love and affection that added another dimension to the music and atmosphere – one that retrieved the occasion from the cool realm of the angels and gave it back to warm reality.

Adam, outwardly calm and in control, savoured each lovely nuance of the luscious Mirella and the power of beauty and love she radiated. But he remained inwardly terrified. And then, as she slowly raised her eyes and looked down the aisle directly into his, Adam understood his terror.

Mirella was the woman through whom he was at last able to make contact with feelings that until now had eluded him. Because of her, he was able to identify and cherish something new within the very core of his being and to see it as no longer dangerous and threatening. *She* completed his life, gave him greater value to himself, because she had brought him to yet another part of himself. His bride was the catalyst of his every feeling of identification, even in the feminine part of him – that part all men fear so much, thinking it dangerous and threatening to their manhood. For Adam it had become something beautiful and precious. It was Mirella who had plucked it from the very depths of his being, kissed it and handed it to him: a gift from a woman, a goddess, that completed his life.

Adam's terror dissolved for ever when, simultaneously across the church and for all there assembled to see, a smile of profound sweetness and light surfaced and broke forth from each of them to the other. It was at that very instant that he realized he was marrying Mirella Wingfield because she was always going to be for him *the one*, the perfect woman. The woman to whom he could expose himself totally and not lose his identity. In her he would find forever the profound intimacy that would allow him to abandon himself to her in the name of love and still remain his own man. She would never devour him, only love him the more for his open, raw vulnerability.

The irrational, unconscious fear that such a powerful love relationship as theirs threatened to annihilate him disappeared, leaving only an ever more prodigious love for Mirella, for himself, and for the marriage they were about to enter into.

The sound of the harp grew softer, then drifted slowly away, and the flute took over hauntingly. In every note there was a quivering beauty that penetrated the heart with a silvery sweetness.

Rashid appeared and took his place at Mirella's side. She slipped her arm through his and smiled. He raised up her hand and gently disengaged it from his arm where it rested lightly. He lowered his head and kissed it. Still holding her hand, he curled his fingers around hers and drew her arm forward, as if to take the first step of a minuet. But there was no minuet to dance, just a long, white-carpeted aisle for them to traverse. There was only the path ahead through the glittering group boxed in the church pews for the occasion, whose eyes and smiles were responding to their every move and gesture, down which Rashid would lead Mirella to the altar and give her away to the man for whom she left him: Adam Corey.

They looked at each other for a moment before they took the first step together – Mirella, smiling and radiant, Rashid appearing more dark and handsome, more mysterious and exotic, more magnetically sensual than ever she or anyone else in the church had seen him. He squeezed her hand lightly and said in a whisper for her ears only, 'Once more, my dear heart, I remind you that you may be marrying Adam, but you will have walked down the aisle with both of us this day. You have won Adam and me for life.' He smiled as he led her by the outstretched hand. They took their first step together into a new life neither one had ever envisaged for themselves.

Rashid was smitten with his role in the life of Mirella and Adam, amused by the edge their marriage gave to an affair with Mirella that he had every intention of continuing, no matter how emphatic she was that it was over and they should be good friends only. There was absolutely no doubt in Rashid's mind that she could not give him up for anyone or anything.

Rashid, too, was swept away by the romantic mood that permeated the church. In that, he was no different from the guests and everyone in the wedding party. He was filled with a sense of joy and happiness and not the least disturbed that he appeared to have lost Mirella to Adam and marriage. Rashid Lala Mustapha – handsome, millionaire Turkish playboy, hedonist, master of oriental eroticism, who captivated women with his seductive charm, behind which lay the menace of debauchery and sexual enslavement – was bound to Mirella. Their bond was strong because she was the only woman he had ever captivated who had not allowed him to destroy her. She alone had matched his lust for adventurous, sensual, sexual delights. She alone had allowed him to enslave her sexually, yet managed to get away and, astonishingly, with his blessing. She kept him as one of her closest friends, instilling in him a kind of love

9

that they both knew would never be allowed to die.

Theirs was unresolved love, the kind that bites deep and lasts forever; the kind of love that derives from pushing through every door of sex and debauchery and that emerges with neither a scar of guilt nor the mark of the devil, but with *joie de vivre*, creating a bond between two people which cannot be broken.

Mirella felt as if she were floating down the aisle on a cushion of air rather than walking. She looked neither left nor right, but straight at the man who was about to become her husband. She felt Rashid's old magnetism warming and exciting her, pulling her to him with every step she took, as he led her to marriage with the great love of her life.

How much she owed to Rashid, she mused. He had sought her out at the time when she was most vulnerable, when her superbly organized existence, including an important career as Assistant Director of Translations at the United Nations in New York, and a long-time love affair, had been disrupted by her amazing inheritance of the Oujie estate.

This mysterious Turkish legacy had been lost to the rightful heirs for generations. It was made up of huge land ownings, oil, gas, and mineral rights, houses, vineyards, a racing stable and farms, business of all kinds, even banks in England and France, art treasures and jewels. It produced an annual income in the area of forty million dollars. With it had come the discovery of a host of remarkable ancestors, including her benefactor, her maternal great-grandmother. And that had been only the first of the disruptions in her complacent and well-organized life. They had brought with them another disruption: her brief encounter with Adam Corey, that produced a taste of

10

real love, which, by her own stupidity, she had managed to lose.

Against her will, it was she who created the third cataclysmic disruption of the neat personal world she had spent years creating. She dissolved her fifteen-year liaison with her lover Paul, as a result of her encounter with Adam.

Alone, one life a shambles except for her work, another she had no idea of how to cope with looming before her, the cautious, one-time impoverished Massachusetts aristocrat Mirella Wingfield was a sleeping beauty. Raven haired and violet eyed she hid her voluptuous sensuality under grey-flannel suits and a hugely successful career until Rashid barged suavely into her life and gathered her up.

As one life crumbled for Mirella, Rashid had assembled the pieces and helped her to mould them into the other Mirella – the beautiful, sensuous, exciting woman she had been before she hid behind a facade of that vastly successful career and the part-time lover who evoked what she imagined to be love. Overnight she became one of the wealthiest, most powerful women in the world and Rashid's sublime mistress.

For him it had been a game, the same game he played with all women: sexual seduction, until the woman was mastered, and then sadistic abandonment of her. Only with Mirella there had been an added interest: the Oujie legacy.

For Mirella, it had been a most extravagant, carefree sexual affair with a disturbingly exotic, depraved man who pampered her at just the moment in her life when she needed it. The affair was even more wonderful by virtue of the fact that she saw it for

11

what it was, never fantasizing about it, and kept control over it. In the end her erotic sojourn with Rashid served as the catalyst that brought her back to Adam Corey and to where she stood right now. Oh yes, the bond between her and Rashid was very strong indeed.

Rashid offered Mirella's hand to Adam who received it and stepped to her side, and smiled at her.

'My life' Adam whispered just before he lowered his head and placed his lips gently on her hand.

Rigid with envy and anger, in the first row of pews close to the altar, Ralph Werfel heard Adam's words, 'My life'. He repeated them over and over to himself while he reflected on his years as Adam's friend and confidant, as a figure crucial to Adam's mega-million-dollar family business. The Corey Trust. And he savoured rejection of those roles. His mind spat the words he wished he could speak right there and then. He wiped the corners of his mouth with his hand again, as if he were salivating. A smile ruffled his lips and lit up his oddly attractive face.

The minister cleared his throat and brought the couple back to attention. Rashid took his place in the front pew next to the Princess Eirene, resplendent in a champagne-coloured silk dress and a small matching hat jauntily angled on her forehead, its more or less transparent, stiff, mesh-like net seductively veiling her eyes.

The flautist played his last notes almost imperceptibly, softer, softer, until they were gone, and with a mastery that left an echo of them interwoven with the murmured rites of the ceremony.

Adam slipped the wedding band on Mirella's finger and for a moment the bride and groom were mesmerized by the wide rock crystal band inset with long rectangular diamond baguettes, and by awe at what they had done. Finally, Adam lifted her hand to his lips, squeezed it lovingly and kissed her fingers with such deep emotion that she trembled. He then took her in his arms, and tilting her head up, he murmured, 'Thank you for marrying me. I promise to love you more profoundly than any woman ever dreamed possible.'

Then he kissed her long and passionately, in front of the minister, but hidden from the view of the wedding guests by her lovely large hat. The minister gently reclaimed their attention. Mirella and Adam smiled as they parted, and Adam shook the minister's hand.

There was a faint rippling of strings. And again, softly. Then, once more, just a bit louder. The notes of the enchanting flute mingled with the plucked strings of the angelic harp, and eighteenth-century music once more showered the church with gold and silver sound.

Chapter 2

The warm June breeze rippled Mirella's train as she stood with Adam on the steps greeting the people filing out of the church. The guests walked into the brilliant sunshine and mingled on a carpet of strewn peony petals. An occasional strong breeze lifted Mirella's diaphanous silk train up off the steps and into the air, creating a sensual aura around the couple as the silk danced on the soft current.

Two of Adam's friends, Helmut Newton and Terry O'Neill, dressed like Adam and the other male guests in grey morning-coats, surrendered to the unthinkable and took wedding photographs. And what wedding photographs! Taking them had to be more like creating exotic icons, so romantic, rich and opulent were their subjects, so perfectly American was the Puritan New England setting on this bright morning.

The occasion itself was pure enchantment – a wedding between two beautiful, adventurous public figures and the romantic, intriguing story of the Oujie legacy that brought them together and into the world's limelight. It was alluring material, irresistible to the two photographers – not least because of the underlying sensual charisma projected by the bride and groom, the international playboy, Rashid Lala

Mustapha, the famed courtesan Princess Eirene, and several other guests.

The subtle undercurrent of illicit passion and power tantalized Helmut. It was exciting, thrilling. He would ferret it out, and record the beauty of it in the powerful erotic portraits he was famous for, much the same way Terry would reach down to the very soul of the women present and record what he saw and wanted to evoke for others. He would add these perfect romantic beauties to his gallery of the most beautiful women in the world.

There wasn't the slightest possibility that anyone might believe this was just another wedding of two people in love. The presence of Massachusetts State Troopers patrolling the barriers that kept the world's press just out of sight of the church, and the ban on all air traffic within a ten mile radius of it, with the exception of the wedding party's helicopters and aeroplanes, broadcast that this was no ordinary event. And so did the obvious effect the couple's wedding had on their guests. They were touched deeply by it, reminded that true love and marriage could still happen to middle-aged voluptuaries with exciting careers and a penchant for freedom and adventure. It made them feel more courageous, more alive, instilled in them an energy to go forward and risk reaching yet again for the excitement of total love, commitment and marriage.

Most of them were well aware of the love affairs, romantic and scandalous, previously indulged in by the couple and their best man, Rashid. None of them believed Rashid would give Mirella up. They had expected a *ménage à trois*, or something more bizarre between these extraordinary people until they saw

16

and heard Adam and Mirella take their vows. Now they were not so sure. The couple's love was so obvious and powerful it embarrassed them for the doubts they had and served to give them hope, raise their passion, and to make them sense again the joy of love.

Princess Eirene felt that way. She had been an intimate friend and sometime lover for nearly thirty years to both men. She was Mirella's friend from the time Mirella had been brought to the Princess's *yalis*, a wooden palace on the banks of the Bosporus in Istanbul, little more than a month before.

So did Deena Weaver, Mirella's best friend since their Vassar days. And so did Brindley Ribblesdale, the young, handsome English solicitor who discovered, after years of investigation, that Mirella was the rightful heiress to the Oujie legacy. It had been Brindley who introduced her to Adam Corey, thus unwittingly changing her life. He was thinking about that when Deena placed her hand on his arm.

'Why do I think this is the most wonderful day of my life, Brindley?' Deena asked. 'I know that it's the most wonderful day in Mirella's life, and what we are seeing here is the Cinderella story emerge from the fairy-tale to burst into real life. And it makes me so happy! Happy, I can understand. The most wonderful day of my life, I can't.'

The pair were watching Mirella, enchantingly beautiful, walk down the church steps, Rashid on one side, Adam on the other, the three laughing and with arms linked, a puff of warm air billowing her misty silk train so as to nearly engulf them with it.

'Because that's the effect weddings have on you?' Brindley asked.

'No, I've been always the bridesmaid never the bride enough times to know it's not just being a participant in my best friend's wedding that is affecting me. Try again, Brindley.'

'Then it has to be Mirella and Adam and the energy they have to change their lives. It's infectious.'

'And thrilling, and wonderful,' she added. 'You call it energy. I call it love, real love, and if it is infectious, then maybe I've caught it – or a touch of it. No, it has to be something more than a smattering or a touch of anything. I have caught something from Mirella and Adam, and, whatever it is, it's a full dose of wonderful. Brindley, I think I may have been infected by their capability for real love. Do you think that could be it, Brindley?'

'Sounds too dramatic and fanciful for me. But, that being said, how would I know? I am an Englishman and we English, unlike you Americans, don't analyse our feelings to death. Nor do we have to rationalize what we do and how we feel – another of your Americanisms that is alien to us.'

Then, instead of becoming defensive as was the norm for Deena whenever anyone attacked or criticized the supposed ways of Americans, she smiled and spontaneously stood on tip-toe and kissed him on the cheek. 'Maybe you should analyse your feelings,' she said.

There was a tenderness in the kiss that surprised them both, and caught them off guard. Brindley reached out and touched one of her silky ringlets.

'Yes,' he said, 'maybe we should, but we don't have to. We have a built-in arrogance about who we are and what we are, a big history behind us that saves us from that sort of painful introspection. Since I have

18

met Adam, Mirella, and even Rashid, I have been affected in subtle ways and changed by the experience. It would be unthinkable for me to question or label it. Dare I suggest you simply enjoy feeling wonderful?'

'That may be easy for you. You're not an American over-achiever. Nor are you Jewish, nor first-generation, New York Jewish at that. *"Simply enjoy"* are not words in our vocabulary. Now, "Simply enjoy" hyphenated with guilt, is certainly in our vocabulary.' Then Deena began to laugh at herself, which was one of her many endearing charms. Brindley laughed with her.

Someone jostled them and Deena fell against Brindley, who reached out and caught her by the shoulders. He felt the firm flesh of her arms through the fine silk organza of her gown, her breasts against him. The feel of her skin and of her body scent mixed with the perfume of Egyptian jasmine, bluebells, wild thyme, lemon and garden roses, lit a passion in him.

At that moment the church bell tolled deep and rich. Brindley released Deena, their eyes met and silently the expression in his begged her not to say anything. Miraculously Deena understood, obeyed and smiled. What might have been an awkward moment for them was interrupted by Moses, Mirella's house-man, who spirited her away on an errand.

Brindley watched Deena make her way through the crowd of wedding guests milling around him, remembering the few times he had met her. Once he had been able to put aside the trendy, successful, New York career-woman image she was constantly projecting, she had always made him laugh and admire her quick wit. He found her extreme intelligence and the manner in which she asserted herself, so different from the upper-class English women he was inclined to meet, exciting. Deena Weaver had a feisty sexuality, and that too, he found new and interesting.

The church bell kept ringing and the party atmosphere began to take over as an effervescent, smiling and happy Mirella, her long wedding train draped partially over her arm and trailing in the peony petals, wandered among her guests towards Brindley. He watched her and was filled with admiration. He mused to himself at his inability to recognize what an extraordinary, sensual female she was when he had first met her and had been taken in by the liberated, executive facade she hid behind.

Big, black, handsome Moses, dressed in formal jacket and striped trousers, looked every inch the major domo he was – and more – to Mirella and had been to her great uncle Hyram from whom she had inherited him. Moses approached the guests, asking if they wanted to walk across the moor to the wedding brunch or wait for the cars to take them.

With the help of his huge Turkish man-servant, Turhan, who had been with him constantly since he was eighteen years old, Adam was putting the same choice before his Turkish guests. Assisting him and Turhan were Rashid's body-guards, a sinister-looking pair of retired, professional Turkish wrestlers, Daoud and Fuad. Bull necked, their faces dramatically scarred, they were incongruously dressed in the same manner as Moses.

Muhsine, a very pretty Turkish girl wearing a gold and silver embroidered *salvar*, was one of the young women Adam employed for his house on the Bosporus. She was attempting to encourage Adam's common-law wives and his five children to move along to the wedding brunch.

Lili Wingfield, Mirella's mother, looked stunning in an understated, softly draped dress of pearl-grey silk jersey, just the sort of dress its famous designer, Mme Gres, had been turning out for half a century. Lili wore a small hat on the crown of her head and its exquisite white egret feathers cascaded down the side of her cheek and curled towards the underpart of her chin. She stood with a few of the most senior and socially prominent members of the Wingfield clan. And she was seething, furious. She found it extremely difficult to maintain a civil manner towards Mirella or to feel any enthusiasm for the wedding. She could actually sense the shock and disapproval emanating from the Wingfields, could imagine them whispering to the other members of the family about 'the opulence and ostentation of the bride ... what a vulgar lot the guests were, dressed in expensive French couture, and bejewelled in the morning. And the foreigners. What a lot of foreigners!'

It was the foreigners who really bothered Lili. She knew the Wingfields would equate foreigners with those in her own background whom she tried so hard to bury in order to live up to her marriage into one of the first of the four hundred families, America's real and very exclusive aristocracy. Lili was not stupid. She knew very well that they would overlook Adam Corey's secret lifestyle and his illegitimate children because he was heir to one of the mid-west's great families and fortunes. To the Wingfields any person who was not a close relation or a member of their country club was a foreigner. To them any jewel weighing more than two carats was only to be worn on rare and formal occasions, and never in the daytime, or it was to be kept in the bank vault so as not to pay insurance. And, alas, Lili knew that unless a wedding followed Wingfield tradition, it would be judged a vulgar affair.

But Lili chose to put the blame on Mirella for inheriting a fortune from her side of the family that Lili considered should have been hers; for allowing herself to release her repressed sexuality for all the world to see and comment on; for allowing herself to become a public figure, and one with a good press, at that.

Lili was a woman who had spent her entire life seeking attention as the most beautiful woman concert-pianist in the world – something she had never come near achieving. What was infuriating now was that she had spent weeks with the charming Rashid planning this extraordinarily elegant and romantic wedding. And now her role was being eclipsed by the exciting aura of erotic sensual love emanating from the bride and bridegroom. Moreover, a game that she had reckoned was hers alone in her family she now found was being played by her daughter – bidding for the hearts of men with her sexuality. In these last few months a sense had crept up on her of being overshadowed by Mirella. She writhed now in terrible inner conflict because when she was able to put aside her self-centredness, her preoccupation with controlling everything and every-one around her, she loved her daughter.

Mirella and Adam held hands, and with the old Puritan bell still ringing, their friends and family surrounding them, they led the way up the peony-petalled road, away from the church and briefly across the moor to the timbered seaside hotel, Oceanside. The majority of their guests followed on foot.

The staff at the staid, exclusive Massachusetts spa thought that they had seen everything after working for a week with Rashid and the entourage of *chefs* and waiters flown in from Paris. The party-designers they glimpsed were from Rome, the florists from London and New York City, their flowers from every spot on the globe. By the hour, helicopters whirled down from the skies depositing celebrated musicians: an ebullient Spanish tenor and a black empress of a soprano from the Metropolitan, the Bee Gees, and Artie Shaw and his entire orchestra arriving with Peggy Lee. Then they saw the wedding party.

From the balconies facing the moor that stretched three quarters of a mile back to the church, and on either side of the hotel, until it ran into wild scrub bushes of blueberries and pine and then into sand and the Atlantic Ocean, they saw the bride walking along the only road to the century-old landmark of American architecture. Her husband was at her side, their entourage following them. The animated, smiling guests gathered petals and showered the couple with them. And among the party were strolling violinists who filled the air, already laden with the salt perfume of the ocean, midday sunshine, the scent of the moor and wild flowers, with the sound of Hungarian gypsy music. Vintage cars – Bugattis and Rolls-Royces, a Pierce Arrow, and a Lagonda, a De Dion Bouton – peeped and hooted their horns as they passed the strolling party, carrying more wedding guests to the reception.

They entered the nineteenth-century Pavilion courtyard, created by four circular projections, the ballroom, the tango room, the round-ended dining-room, and the sun parlour, the last two of which were on the sand and faced the crashing waves of the Atlantic Ocean. One of the long low sea breezes whipped Mirella's diaphanous train up and into the air. Several guests came to her rescue, playfully leaping up to catch it.

'Oohs' and 'Ahs' broke from the crisp line of uniformed hotel maids. 'Her gown is beautiful' one said.

'Magnificent,' corrected the Oceanside house-keeper. 'I've known her and her family since she was a little girl. One of the finest families in Massachusetts. Some say eccentric. No money, but real society. What *I* say is that money isn't everything. You see that man? That's her father, very famous, is Maxim Wesson Wingfield. A charming man, always has a kind word for me. You would never know he's a famous philosopher. World renowned, they say. People from all over go to see him at the family estate, Wingfield Park.'

'A real gentleman. And so is Mr Weinbaum, his right-hand man,' said Nathaniel Weeks, the manager of Oceanside's garages. 'That's Mr Weinbaum over there. Fixes everything for the Wingfields. Always lets me have the run of the estate, lets me help with the antique cars – those are only just a few of 'em. They must have fifty or more. Always been in the family, those cars. The Wingfields never throw anything out. I respect the Wingfields for that.' None of the girls was really listening. They were too engrossed with the glamour of the occasion.

24

'Look at her hat. Isn't it gorgeous, Mary? I've never seen anything like it. And with real flowers pinned to it. Now that's class,' said one chambermaid to another.

'And real horsehair, very fashionable in the Thirties. Mrs Astor used to wear hats like that. She even gave me one of her very own at the end of the season one year. It must be coming back into fashion,' said the ancient head-laundress.

Mirella reached up, removed her hat and tossed it to Deena, saying, 'Catch, the bride's bouquet,' and Deena did.

'Oh lord, will my mother be happy to hear I caught this! The last thing she said to me before I left New York was, "Deeny, for god's sake reach up, reach out – use your elbows if you have to – but for god's sake catch the bouquet. It's true, you know, that saying: if you catch the bouquet, it's your turn next up the aisle. It happened to Merna Pinsky's Sylvia. And if it could happen to her, it could happen to you. Make an effort, Deeny, make an effort." '

Mirella, who was trying to loosen her wedding veil and slip it off her shoulders and up over her head, broke into laughter, as did Adam, and even Rashid, who had come up behind Deena and put his arm around her. Brindley smiled. He didn't quite understand it all, but suddenly he began to laugh too. Deena always made him laugh. Moses and Muhsine came to Mirella's aid and gathered up the train of veiling. While they were busy fussing over Mirella, Deena walked up to her and placed the hat back into Mirella's hands.

'Here, Mirella, wear it at least until you cut the wedding cake. Just make sure you don't throw it

25

again to someone else. My mother would never forgive you.'

Mirella pinned her hat in place, Adam slipped his arm around her and shivered with excitement as he caressed her bare back. She was drawn to him with the same warmth and thrill she always felt whenever she was near him. Most of the guests were assembled in Oceanside's great hall, Lalique angel-stemmed champagne glasses charged and in their hands, waiting to toast the bride and groom when they entered.

'Have a happy life,' called down Kate and Trixi, two of the Spa's twenty junior vegetable cooks.

Mirella and Adam heard them and looked up: they smiled and waved. The balconies rang with the applause the regular staff gave them.

Mirella kept looking up at the Oceanside's bewildering *ad hoc* amalgam of tiled roof pitches, towers and verandahs, turrets and cupolas. A weatherbeaten wooden palace somewhat like a child's fabulous sand castle, the palace of every romantic fairy tale.

When Mirella turned her attention back to Adam there were tears of emotion in her eyes. He tilted her chin up and asked, 'Hey, what's this?' raising her hand and kissing it.

She gave a deep sigh, blinked back her tears and smiled. 'I feel happier now than those waves dancing from the depths out there. Walking up the stairs into Oceanside with you will complete so many of my childhood dreams. Just now, they suddenly came rushing back to me.

'Oceanside was my dream-castle, my play-castle. It represented gaiety and was exciting and dramatic, even mysterious, and always full of beautiful wealthy people wearing the latest fashions. People I equated with romance, intrigue, love, who, when they were not here, were travelling to far and exotic places, doing glamorous heroic things. Oh, how I wanted to be one of them.

'Because we lived so close by, during the season Oceanside was my second home. My family were *the day people*, who used it like a country club, and my dream was to be a guest, a resident, to sleep a whole night here and have breakfast in bed.

'From the age of five, I used to play "let's-pretend" games about Oceanside. As an adolescent I played romantic "let's-pretend" games and wished that we were not the cash-poor, property-rich, intellectual, eccentric arm of the family. I longed for lots of pretty, new ball-gowns, to replace the elegant family hand-me-downs I was obliged to wear. I believed that if I had them they would make me beautiful, and the Prince who lived in the dream-castle would come and take me to the Ball. But it never happened, and he never came, and so I abandoned my dreams, wiped them out of my mind, and settled for those that were possible.'

Adam placed his arm around her shoulder and together they walked slowly towards the wide, curved, wooden steps leading to the open verandah and the entrance. They were followed by their wedding attendants, Rashid, Deena and Brindley, who were walking arm in arm together, amidst the ringing of their own laughter.

'How strange the mind is,' Mirella continued. 'I'd forgotten those fantasies for so many years, and they have come back to me, just when at last I am going

27

into Oceanside to a grand reception, a Ball, in honour of us, with all my dreams fulfilled, and much more.'

Adam was extremely touched by what she told him. It was the sweetness, the innocence of Mirella the child, and her fantasies: the confession that she longed so passionately for them to come true, and that, when they hadn't, she gave them up and began making compromises, something he had never done. Aware of the nostalgic ache in her voice during the telling of her little story, he was now pained by it. He hurt for all the years they had not found each other, and he had not set her free. Now he would spend the remainder of his life loving her and giving her the world.

Mirella took her last awed look at the fairy tale castle facade of Oceanside with the eyes of a child, and then turned to her husband. Adam felt he was seeing the anguish of past unfulfilled dreams slip from her face, and the happy, passionate woman he knew so well come to the fore.

He gathered her in his arms, crushed her hard against him, and kissed her lustily. He could feel her fire, imagine her body under the white lace wedding gown dissolve like molten gold into his, feel her passion explode into the familiar tremors of ecstasy, and hear an almost imperceptible whimper of release.

The sound of the sea, and the distant music of Artie Shaw's sweet clarinet over his newest big band and the voice of Peggy Lee singing 'As Time Goes By' mingled with the applause, laughter and teasing from those above on the balconies. Mirella opened her eyes. She was still in Adam's arms, and from over his shoulder she could see Rashid watching her. Despite the deep and profound love and ruttishness she felt for her husband, something within her silently, invisibly reached out. She sensed a mad desire to touch Rashid, to be sexually enslaved once again by this dark devilish man. She blinked and it passed, but her mind and heart acknowledged for the first time that she and Rashid shared a kind of love that she was far from rid of.

Chapter 3

Since the day it had opened in the summer of 1893, Oceanside had beguiled all who had been privileged to enter. Its mellow luxury, reminiscent of Edwardian society at its most elegant and genteel, was modified by a delightful seaside informality. Nearly a hundred years later on Mirella's wedding day, the ambience was still the same.

The oakwood panelling of Oceanside's main rooms on the ground floor was as opulent as the furnishings, as grand as its arched and faceted ceilings, as spectacular as the view of sand and sea through its myriad windows. Soon the hundred breakfast guests would be seated in the extraordinary round-ended dining-room; later, nine hundred guests would assemble to dance and dine in the Ballroom and the Tango Room where Artie Shaw was playing his great rendition of the Forties hit, Frenesi.

Now these rooms were not so much transformed into gardens of Eden by the abundance of greenery and flowers filling them as they were decorated to enhance the contradictory elements that gave Oceanside its character. And these contradictory elements, oddly enough, imposed a light-hearted gaiety, an ease, on the ostentation and elegance of Mirella and Adam's wedding reception. It inspired a happy, lazy, holiday mood, in the hundred guests who were

31

invited to the church and the noon-day breakfast, while doing nothing to discourage their posing and preening.

When Adam and Mirella walked from the mid-day heat and the bright sunshine, into the cool, shady hall, they were greeted by a ringing chorus of good wishes and a shower of white flower petals – jasmine and rose, lily of the valley, apple blossom, carnation, honeysuckle, heather, and thousands of baby orchids. Mirella and Adam were soon separated by their guests' toasts and embraces.

Even Ralph Werfel was now swept up by the incredible style of this joyous occasion. When he shook Adam's hand, there was a tear in his eye and a tremor of emotion in his voice as he said, 'This day has been a long time coming for you, Adam, and I hope your marriage brings you all the happiness you deserve.'

He and Adam exchanged one of those hugs that men allow themselves when they're happy for each other before Ralph slithered away into the crowd. It was only when Adam, while being kissed on the cheek by one of the female guests, was wiping the palm of his hand with his white linen handkerchief that he realized he was trying to rid himself of the touch of Ralph's cold clammy hand. For the first time in all the years Adam had known and worked with Ralph, he suddenly found him repulsive, but he was too happy to linger on that thought and it vanished from his mind even before he replaced his handkerchief in his pocket.

When the fifty white-coated waiters finally stopped refilling glasses with Bollinger 'Spéciale Cuvée' '69 champagne, and began to usher the wedding party

32

into the dining-room, Mirella and Adam came together again and were surrounded by his family. There were his children – Joshua, Zhara, Alamya, Memett, and Alice – Alamya's mother, Giuliana, a Venetian Countess, and Memett's mother, Aysha, a young Turkish courtesan. There were several beautiful young girls, all now former mistresses of Adam who, he had explained to Mirella, were part of his household, and all considered to be his immediate family. The realization that these were *her* children now, *her* immediate family now, just as much as they were Adam's, shocked Mirella.

She always had thought of Adam as a big man, a solid man, but now she suddenly saw him as a powerfully loving man, a giant of a man. She saw she had taken him on not only with his unconventional family, but with all that living with a colossus and a rare human being might entail.

The mother of Joshua, Adam's eldest son, was the only other woman Adam had married. He had divorced her soon after Joshua's sister, Zhara, had been born, and she was not included in the immediate family. Joshua now put his arm around Mirella and hugged her.

'Do I see just a hint of concern about taking on our clan? We children, Marlo and Giuliana, Aysha, and the other ladies of the *yalis* household call ourselves a clan, you know. Not having second thoughts, are you?'

'Well, maybe just a little concern, Josh. You are a formidable group to take on. But certainly no second thoughts. Frankly, I am still so dazzled by your father's courtship, I haven't had much of a chance to think about you all, until this minute, when I realized the clan is my family now. Now you, for example,' she said as she snapped her fingers, 'in you I have a most attractive and intelligent 25-year-old son. It feels wonderful, exciting even – but strange. I know you all live separate lives away from Adam; that there are rooms for each of you in his house, the Peramabahçe Palace—'

'Correction,' Josh interrupted. 'Not *his* house: *our* house is what you must say now. I hope you don't mind my correcting you, but ever since we were all summoned to Istanbul to meet you, although it was only for one day, we've taken you to our hearts as Father's choice as wife, the newest member of our clan, the female head of the family. There's never been one before you. We've always been a closely bound family, loving and devoted to each other while loving and admiring Papa. We delight in the life he has chosen for himself, as well as the one he gives us, so we've never really missed his not having a wife. Now that Papa has selected you to stand by his side, we're all happy for him and for you too, and for ourselves as well. We want to love you the way Papa does. So don't feel strange. Welcome to the family. And now may I kiss the bride?'

Mirella was touched by Josh's sensitivity and grateful for his kind words. When he bent and kissed her on the lips, he had a similar warmth and appeal to that of Adam. Mirella knew instinctively that, in time, she would love him because he was every inch his father's son, love them all because they were a part of Adam.

'Yes, Mirella, welcome to the clan,' Zhara said. 'You're brave to take us all on. You're the loveliest bride I ever saw, and Papa looks so young and handsome, and happier and different than I can ever remember. I do hope you will love us, all of us. We already love you for making our papa so happy.' Then Zhara kissed Mirella.

Rashid was standing on the fringe of the Corey clan with Deena and Brindley. One of the waiters approached him and announced that the wedding guests were seated and waiting for the bride and groom. Adam heard him, went to Mirella and took her hand. 'Well,' he said, 'shall we go in alone, darling, or as a family, since all the clan is here? Well, almost all the clan is gathered; Marlo is missing. I can't understand it. She said she would be here.'

The disappointment on Adam's face surprised Mirella, even slightly worried her, since Marlo was the only member of the immediate family whom she had not yet met. Mirella had a gut instinct that here was the woman, possibly the only other woman who had ever got as close to Adam as she had. She felt not jealousy but rivalry – then put it out of her mind at once, because she knew she could not cope with even the thought of it. And, besides, she was too happy.

Marlo was Marlo Channing, a world-famous war-photographer, mother of Adam's youngest child, the seven-year-old Alice. And, Mirella knew from her first visit in Istanbul to the *yalis*, that Marlo was adored by all the children and women of Adam's household. That time, too, Marlo had announced she would be there, flying in from somewhere in the African bush where she was covering the side of the rebels in a Nigerian uprising against the current régime, to meet Adam's wife-to-be. They had all waited impatiently well into the night for her to arrive. Mirella remembered, as time wore on, how they had talked about her with such enthusiasm, love, and even adoration. Now, slipping her arm through Adam's, and taking Alice's hand in hers, Mirella announced, 'This is my wedding breakfast, and I'm famished.'

A chorus of 'This is *our* wedding breakfast' rose up from the clan, lead by Adam and Josh, 'and *we* are famished too.' It was followed by bursts of laughter and chatter, and a loving kiss from Adam. The children playfully pushed Adam and Mirella forward to follow Rashid, Deena and Brindley to breakfast.

The dining-room was enchanting. From the dome plunged great swags of fresh white lilacs entwined with lime green foliage and fashioned into large bows pinned to the walls ten feet above the floor. Dozens of delicate, clear glass birdcages, filled with white cooing doves, hung on varying lengths of vines braided with white daisies. They filled the ceiling, glistening above the guests like a giant crystal aviary.

One large table circled the room, forming a ring of snowy damask. The antique French silver, rare Galle crystal goblets, and Meissen dinner service that had been made especially for one of the more refined of the Baltic Kings were all wrested from the store of family treasures at Mirella's home, Wingfield Park.

Silver pedestal salvers punctuated the centre of the table every ten feet or so. Each salver held a tall slender cone of dark, rich chocolate mousse rising from a bed of fresh lilies of the valley and trailing small white roses with just a hint of pale peach colour to them. The cones were covered in whipped cream and decoratively frosted with sugar-icing lilies of the valley, blooming round and round up the sides; lovebirds of blown sugar perched on the tops. The wedding cakes were based on – but were not at all like – the traditional Scandinavian 'ring cakes' made by piling up rolls, in diminishing circumference, of almond paste dough, and were related more to the intricate *pièces montées* perfected by the famous and unsurpassed eighteenth-century chef, Antonin Carème.

The small, heavily-scented white roses trailed off the salvers prettily and were arranged in abundance, in twists and turns down the table's centre from one silver-pedestalled wedding cake to another and around the table, and hence around the room.

On a raised circular platform in the centre of the ring of tables, and directly under the centre of the dome and the crystal aviary, sat a musician at a seventeenth-century harpsichord of satinwood decorated with exquisite floral painting. A flautist stood and a viola player sat in front of intricately carved music stands of the same period, decorated with white satin bows and streamers, and bunches of fresh, sweet-scented lilies of the valley.

The concert of chamber music chosen by Lili was from the court of King Louis XIV of France; François Couperin's Air Contrafugue, Concert Royal No. 2. It was perfection; its grace and sweetness not cloying, but utterly charming.

They dined served by an army of liveried French waiters, one waiter standing behind every second high-backed chair, on souffle amalatta, filled with the finest shiny black beads of beluga caviar; lobster in aspic, dressed in a foamy yellow saffron sauce, and lychee sorbet. A perfectly chilled Bétard-Montrachet, 1971, a top white burgundy as rich in flavour as a dry white wine can be, accompanied these courses. They continued with Scotch woodcock, poached in a cream and anchovy sauce and served with spinach croquettes, followed by artichoke, and avocado salad, dressed in a lemon and raspberry vinaigrette; mango and lime sorbet (to clear the palate once more), and finally, for dessert the Chocolate Mousse wedding cake. The game birds in their cream sauce were served with an outstandingly fine and rare Bordeaux, a treasure of a wine whose bouquet resembled violets and raspberries, and whose colour glowed like liquid rubies and dark amethysts, the monumental 1945 Château Mouton-Rothschild. No other wines were served with the salad or the dessert: sacrilege to drink anything after the Mouton-Rothschild claret.

At one point during the meal, Adam looked around the wedding ring table and his eyes lingered for a moment on Rashid and Lili, who were seated next to each other. They had done Mirella and him proud – extravagantly and most elegantly proud. The beauty, detail and quality of everything they planned for this day were unsurpassable.

Adam knew it was Rashid who was the driving force and inspiration behind the wedding reception. He and Mirella had done little about their wedding except decide to exchange their marital vows in a simple ceremony, in one of God's houses. They had chosen the old-world, white Protestant spired church, not only because Mirella's paternal ancestors had founded it, but because it was a symbol of the visible heritage they wanted to add to. What pleased them more was that the white clapboard church still carried an air of meagre but sincere anarchy.

It was an original symbol of man's fight for religious freedom; of being pure in heart; of the kind of

America, the New World, that to this day represents New England on calendars and Christmas cards. For Mirella and Adam, whose religious faith had drifted from Puritanism through a Protestantism which faded into Unitarianism, and who had abandoned that and every religious 'ism' long ago for freedom to live and believe as they chose, there could have been no better site.

Adam, with his gaze still on Rashid, smiled to himself when he thought of the disappointment in Rashid's face when they had told him they wanted to be married in the simple white church on the small-town New England green.

Rashid had tried every sort of persuasion to entice them to a wedding in Istanbul's St Sophia. Or, he had offered, they could be wed in the Basilica San Marco, in Venice. When, time after time, they would not give in to his wishes, he gave way, reduced his aspirations for them, and suggested St Paul's Cathedral in London, and, with slightly down-cast eyes, Sir Christopher Wren's St James's in Piccadilly. Somewhat annoyed with them for rejecting even those noble buildings, he conceded, if it was a small place of worship they desired, there was always the Madeleine in Paris. His oriental mind simply could not understand that what they wanted was to make their vows to each other in a place restrained in adornment, a place whose spirit promised nothing but to allow their essential selves freedom to bathe in the inner light of one of God's houses. When Rashid did at last accept their choice and their guest list, there had been nothing more for them to do. Rashid simply took command of their wedding.

Adam was aware that he and Mirella never alluded

between themselves to Rashid's determination to be involved so completely in their wedding plans; nor to this being the first of many ways they would allow Rashid to take his place as the third person in their life together.

Sheer nectar, Adam thought, as he touched his glass to Mirella's and drank. Every morsel of food so far had been ambrosia as well. He touched Mirella on the shoulder, then caressed her back, raised her hand and kissed it.

He wanted her, more than ever now that she was his, now that he was hers. He became aroused at the very thought of their first coupling as man and wife. He bent forward and tucked his head under the brim of her hat and kissed her on the lips, bit her, none too lightly, wanting her to feel the pain of his desire. Then he kissed her mouth again with a tenderness that was as sweet as the nectar he imagined he drank.

There was an unmistakable air of sensuality in the dining-room; no one could possibly ignore it. It was everywhere, like the scent of an exotic perfume, and growing stronger, more exciting, as the breakfast continued. Rashid had done to perfection what he liked to do best – enchant, seduce, corrupt the senses, with beauty and pleasure. He was a master at it. No one in the room would dispute that. Every wedding guest was under his spell, and, methodically, as the afternoon wore on, he dazzled them with the joy of the occasion.

Mirella and Adam rose from their chairs and together cut a slice of the wedding cake in front of them with a Queen Anne silver cake-slicer. On its handle was a bunch of lilies of the valley tied with narrow white satin and lace ribbons in pretty bows

40

with long streamers. Their guests gave a seated ovation. Adam handed the dessert plate with the first slice of the cake to Mirella and put his arm around her shoulder. He picked up his dessert fork, cut into the mousse and fed it to her.

It was delectable. The rich, chocolate mousse, with its tang of orange and cointreau, covered with white, thick, whipped cream, was as light as air. The sensuous texture filled Mirella's mouth, its succulent flavours teasing her taste buds before it dissolved on her tongue, and she felt the crunch of a sugar-icing, lily of the valley blossom.

Ambrosia, yet again, Adam thought. It was a sweet conjured by the angels, a wedding cake like no other. Mirella took up the fork from the plate, sliced into the delicacy and fed it to him. 'Perfection,' was all he said.

Without a moment's hesitation, Mirella and Adam turned and presented their slice of wedding confection to Rashid, who had been sitting on Mirella's right. He stood up, clasped Adam's hand, hugged him affectionately, and kissed Mirella as she handed it to him. The couple watched him convey some of the cake-pudding to his mouth, and saw in his eyes the delight the rich chocolate afforded him, satisfying even his notorious craving for sweets, most especially chocolate. And they saw him savour the gesture of sharing their slice of wedding cake with him.

At that moment, without any manipulation or calculation on anyone's part, their instinctual beings came to the fore, and a pattern, along with an unspoken set of rules, was laid down for this extraordinary love-triangle, without their fully knowing it.

41

Without ever discussing their situation, they would treat one another with discretion, friendship, caring, mutual respect. This and much more was tacitly established as the three shared the symbolic first slice of wedding cake. And each sensed the pact thus silently, solemnly ratified.

Mirella and Adam stepped away from their places at the table. Two waiters trailed them, serving the cake Mirella and Adam had just cut to guests on either side of the sublime confection. The couple moved to the next cake and cut it, talking and laughing with their guests, then kissing before moving on.

The erotic tension between Mirella and Adam was building as they progressed around the room. And now, they had cut the last of the wedding cakes and had kissed. Mirella could think only of being naked and in his arms, of his marking every inch of her with his tongue; of his filling her again and again with his rich copious seed. She felt her face go very warm, and was embarrassed for the rush of ecstasy she was unable to hold back. Adam laughed.

'Mirella Corey,' he whispered in her ear, 'you are a lewd, carnal woman.' And he kissed her, this time on the side of her ear, and bit it very hard. She cringed from the pain and, flushing even more, whispered back, 'So what?'

'So, thank God for that. Upstairs, our suite, four o'clock, and don't be late. I'll be there waiting.' He took her hand and they started to return to their original places.

What joy, what bliss, she thought, but forced her voice to sound casual as she quipped, 'It's a date.'

They stopped so that Adam could exchange a few words with her father, Maxim. Mirella looked away from the men and across the room; her idle glance jolted to an abrupt halt at the entrance-way at the far end of the dining-room. There she was, leaning against the door jamb, casting an observant eye at the banquet and at Adam in particular. She was tall, deeply tanned, and had a handsome face with perfect bone structure. She wore no make up, and her long, messy chestnut-coloured hair looked mightily attractive, though dirty. She wore an old, stained Burberry raincoat that seemed to have had a long-time acquaintance with mud. She held back the raincoat with one hand that also held a tan, battered rain-hat. A pair of ill-fitting, very wrinkled men's tan trousers was cinched tight above her bony hips with some man's beige and brown old school tie whose ends dangled down her right side. She wore a beige silk man's shirt, open at the neck; one could tell it was new by the crispness of its creases where it had been folded and never pressed out. A pair of grubby, worn-out, once-white sneakers were on her feet below bare ankles.

On the floor next to her was a battered leather dufflebag. She was a mess ... but a stunningly beautiful mess. Mirella wondered how long she had been standing in the doorway. Odd how right the woman looked against the magnificent oak panelling, Mirella thought. Undoubtedly that accounted for why no one had taken any notice of her.

Mirella could not take her eyes off the woman. She kept thinking it was a young Katharine Hepburn, who had come for the tennis, or the golf, and had found Oceanside closed to the public for this wedding. But

Mirella knew better. The sudden pit she felt in her stomach told her she could only be one person: Marlo Channing.

The two women's gazes met across the room. They stared at one another. It would have been so easy for Mirella to draw Adam's attention to the woman in the doorway, but something stopped her. Finally it was Adam, putting his arm around her waist to walk with her to their seats, who broke her gaze. When Mirella was seated and looked up again to the entrance, the woman had vanished like some legendary apparition that breaks the good feast.

When she had begun to plan the wedding for her daughter with Rashid, Lili Wingfield had resented him and the lavish style with which he did everything. The vast sums of money he was able to spend so unconcernedly on aeroplanes was far beyond her conception of hospitality. He chartered a Concorde to fly the foreign guests in for the wedding, and a fleet of small jets to ferry them and others from New York to Oceanside.

Booking the entire hotel, so that the wedding guests might change their clothes there for the ball in the evening, or remain for a few nights to relax after the nuptial festivities, was an extravagance perpetrated by Rashid without Lili's blessing. The only positive point about that extravagance as far as she was concerned was the solution it provided her to the problem of what to do with all the foreigners and Mirella's new family. Lili found the so-called clan not only embarrassing but ridiculous.

Rashid's total disregard of what the wedding was costing made Lili stroppy, bitter, and reminded her of all her years of penny-pinching because her husband had an income incommensurate with his vast inheritance of treasures that he refused to sell and they could ill afford to maintain.

Again and again Rashid had cajoled, dazzled, teased Lili into giving in to his plans. She had never approved of his notion that the wedding should go on and on: the breakfast for intimate family and friends; the tea-dance to amuse the guests who remained for the evening festivities, and for those who were to arrive late in the day for the grand ball and buffet in the evening.

The grand ball and buffet indeed. How she fought Rashid over that. She fought over his allowing all Adam's children to invite their friends. She was furious at the number of people he was flying in, some of whom were the world's most acute minds: philosophers, writers, physicists, a group of Maxim's old friends who had been a part of Mirella's childhood and watched her grow up. The bride's friends, the groom's friends, anybody's friends, and family – Adam's family, Maxim's family. Too much, all too much for Lili.

It was the 'grande bouffe', as Rashid insisted on calling the food to be served at the ball, that finally made Lili stop fighting him and his party plans. She had listened to Rashid and his fleet of famous French chefs discuss the menu: oeufs en gelée, huge birds' nests filled with quails' eggs, gulls' eggs, plovers' eggs, seven chefs preparing individual omelettes for the guests in silver chafing-dishes, before their very eyes, fresh Perigord pâté de fois gras with truffles, chicken livers and mushrooms in sherry, pink grapefruit sorbet, elderflower sorbet, peach sorbet, lemon and lime sorbet, sides of Scottish smoked salmon cut paper-thin, and prepared in Danish-style, marinated with dill and cut in more chunky slices and served with a hot mustard. There was also to be fresh Alaskan poached salmon, served cold with a cream and horseradish sauce, Russian blini with beluga caviar, coquilles St Jacques, lobster thermidor, lobster salad, duck in aspic, cold grilled duck with brandied oranges, duck pâté with plum sauce, galantine of goose, layered pheasant terrine on a bed of corn kernels and served with a sauce verte, boned stuffed turkey in a madeira sauce, spiced kumquats, mango, banana, and lime chutneys, nine different green salads with vinaigrette dressings, the food for nine hundred people. Lili had listened in horror, numbed and deaf, to the list of the desserts and selection of vintage champagnes.

She hated it all, but gave in, always yielding to Rashid's plans, because he charmed her with his male beauty and sexuality, found her vulnerable point – vanity and pathological narcissism – and played on it, until she succumbed to all his wishes. But her resentment never wavered.

Now Rashid picked up her hand and kissed it. 'I think we have done ourselves proud this day, Lili. Who will ever forget this wedding breakfast, this room, the heavenly scent of an orchard of lilacs, the sound of such regal music? You have been wonderful in your selections. Have you forgiven me for all my extravagances, the spats we had working together for this day?'

Lili searched his charismatic face for some indication that his wooing of her had been for more than Mirella's wedding, more than just another of his pragmatic seductions. There was none. She had been

46

used. She knew it very well, having been the seducer enough times and of enough men in getting what *she* wanted.

The chief barker appeared, dressed in a red jacket, a sign for the musicians to close their concert of chamber music. The last strains gone, the barker struck the silver gong for silence and attention in the room, then announced, 'Thank you, my lords, ladies, and gentlemen. Coffee is being served on the verandah, if you please.'

Mirella and Adam rose from their chairs and led the way.

'I don't forgive easily,' Lili said to Rashid as one of the waiters standing behind her chair drew it back so she could rise. And, standing up, she continued, 'Your self-indulgence in this wedding has appalled me almost as much as the changes in Mirella since she inherited my family's estate. What's worse is the fact that I have nearly as much loathing for myself, because I have been seduced by your charm and excesses and have accepted them, enjoyed them even. You have not missed a thing, not a trick; you are the ultimate host, the ultimate seducer. Much as I hate to say it, you have teased us all into enjoying every minute of your extravaganza.

'Forgive you our "little spats", as you call them? Never! Do you really want to know how I feel? No, don't bother to answer that. I'll tell you: as if I am being led to the guillotine in the greatest of style. Not unlike every woman you are involved with, the obvious exception being my daughter.'

Rashid could only laugh at Lili. They stepped on to the verandah and took *demi-tasse* cups of Expresso from a waiter's heavy baroque silver tray. Lili turned her back on Rashid and started to move away. He subtly but firmly grasped her by the arm, and whispered in her ear, 'You are a bitch, Lili,' and walked her over to the wooden railings of the porch.

They stood together in silence for a few minutes. Up and down the timbered verandah guests sat in old-fashioned wooden rockers or stood casually leaning on the porch railings, drinking coffee. They watched some of the guests walk down to the water's edge, coffee cups in hand; others looked incongruous in their elegant clothes, seated on the sand under the bright afternoon sun, watching the heavy blue waves crash on to the beach.

'A jealous bitch, Lili,' Rashid murmured. 'You're angry and jealous and it's not over me or my self-indulgence. You're envious of your own daughter, because she has eclipsed you, because she has got it all: riches, monetary wealth, real hard currency, all her own. That makes her financially independent, a powerful woman, able to indulge herself in any way she pleases – something you have never had, or been able to do. I don't know what is most difficult for you. Her inheritance? Her success as one of the world's top executives, which she has achieved through a superior intelligence and sheer hard work? Or is it that she gave up hiding her sensuality, suppressing her needs and desires, allowed her sexuality to break out of the closet, and it brought her the one thing missing in her life, love? The one thing you have always beaten her at was a one-to-one love relationship with a remarkable man. Now she has even eclipsed you in that, because she has won, forever, the hearts of two remarkable men.

'Lili, you're filled with anger because she has

48

achieved success in her own right and is not living in the shadow of greatness as you have had to do all your life. First your mother, then your husband.'

Lili glared at Rashid, but remained silent.

'Don't you look at me that way, Lili. I repeat, first your mother, then your husband—'

Lili started to move away, but Rashid was too quick for her. She had one hand on the railings, and he pinned her to it by covering her hand with his own.

'And now, Mirella,' he went on.

Two people passed at that moment and congratulated Lili on the most wonderful wedding they had ever attended. What made it worse for Lili was that they were the most select of the Wingfields, and she knew they meant what they said.

Rashid slowly released the pressure on her hand as the couple walked away, but Lili did not leave his side. While she was trying to compose herself a waiter approached with a tray full of Leonides white chocolates and a huge box of Jamaican cigars. Rashid turned around, sat on the railing facing Lili, his back to the sea; he selected a chocolate and ate it while he chose a cigar.

The sound of the ocean hitting the beach, and the cry of seagulls following a schooner passing off shore, mingled with the chatter of replete, beautiful people lazing about on the verandah, and made a strange and exotic picture. One that might have been painted with sound as well as pigment. The scene could have been a nineteen-eighties Impressionist painting: a Manet, a Monet, a Cezanne, against a Norman Rockwell background painted by Andrew Wyeth. And, recognizing that aesthetic vision, Lili was calmed somewhat.

She watched Rashid in silence while a second waiter, having clipped the end of the cigar for him, bent down to him and held a flame to it while Rashid slowly, carefully turned the cigar between his fingers, puffed on it, and lit it evenly. Rashid selected several more chocolates and placed them on a small linen napkin on top of the railing next to him.

'You are an evil and cruel man Rashid,' said a now very controlled Lili.

'Yes, I readily admit that I can be both those things, and more often than not enjoy being evil and cruel. This, however, is not one of those times, Lili. I hope you understand how very serious I am when I tell you that what or how you think of me matters not in the least. Only one thing matters to me today, and that is Mirella, and the new life she began when I walked her down the aisle of that church this morning.

'If you give her one moment of anxiety, show her the slightest unkindness, withhold one fraction of the love she deserves from you, today or any other day for that matter, be warned: I will inflict such cruelties on you as you have never imagined.'

Lili was shocked by his words, the tone of his voice, the look in his eye. It was as if Rashid had said to her. 'I will entrap you in all that is vile. Brand you with the evil side of my nature, which will destroy your life; and, if it comes to that, I will enjoy every moment of your demise.'

'You would do well to heed my advice, Lili. Put away your pathological self-centredness, and allow yourself the privilege of loving and adoring Mirella in the same way you do yourself. You have a great deal to make up for, Lili, and your incentive can be that I have just made you no empty threat – simply a promise of what I will do to you if my advice is ignored.'

Rashid slowly slid off the verandah railing, picked Lili's hand up in his and noted with satisfaction that it had turned cold and was trembling. He bowed his head and placed his lips upon it in a kiss, then gently pulled Lili, who was rigid with fear, into his arms, and gave her a friendly, reassuring hug.

'Now you have an example of my kind of love,' he whispered in Lili's ear, 'and the lengths I will go to in order to protect what is mine. Make no mistake: Mirella may have married Adam, but she is mine.'

Chapter 4

Mirella exercised her prerogative as a woman and arrived a little after the designated time for her first assignation with her husband. She felt quite ridiculous when she hesitated in front of his door not knowing whether to knock on it or not.

It suddenly occurred to her that she had no idea of how a wife such as she approached her husband their first time alone together . . . or, indeed, on any other occasion.

'Ridiculous,' she said aloud, at the same time reaching up and touching the cluster of white moth orchids she had pinned in her raven black hair in place of her wedding hat. The seductive flowers seemed to reassure her, and she opened the door and walked in.

Adam was standing in front of the sitting-room fireplace opening a chilled bottle of Dom Pérignon. He looked up at Mirella as she came through the door. She was still dressed in the superb white lace wedding gown and her splendid jewels. The sensuous orchids in her hair were not wasted on him. They were a seductive sexual signal that made his bride even more ravishing to him.

He smiled at her as she walked towards him. His smile left her weak-kneed, as it always did when it was accompanied by an erotic twinkle in his eye. He poured the champagne into a pair of large

Lalique crystal *coupes* mounted on tall slender stems frosted with a pattern of hollyhocks. The *coupe* was etched with a scene of a couple lying in a field of tall grass and wild flowers making love under the soft warm rain of summer. He handed one to her and they touched the rims together. Only the faint ring of the crystal broke the silence between them. They sipped while looking into each other's eyes.

'Hello, my love,' Adam murmured

'Hello, my heart,' she answered. Simultaneously they placed their champagne *coupes* on the mantelpiece. Adam embraced Mirella. They kissed with passion, holding each other close. Their arousal was swift because this romantic liaison in the midst of their wedding celebrations ignited a sexual spark that flared into a sensual fire and engulfed them.

Reluctantly Adam released her, clapped his hands, and three violinists surprised Mirella by suddenly appearing from the bedroom to serenade her with a sweet, tender love song. Adam reached for their glasses of champagne and handed one to Mirella. They faced each other in the flower-filled room, its antique maple furniture covered in patterned glazed chintz, its Currier and Ives prints framed in birds-eye maple seeming to wink and smile at them, as they sipped champagne.

Adam's romantic gesture was perfect. With it, he blocked out the outside world and their new responsibilities as a husband and wife, and brought them back to their intimate selves. Almost before Mirella realized it, the music had stopped and the violinists were leaving, yet the atmosphere of promise spun in the air by their music lingered on.

Mirella thanked the men and watched Adam usher

the musicians to the door. Then she heard the click as he locked the door from the inside. Her heart skipped a beat in anticipation.

Adam went directly to her. He took another sip of his wine, and touched the blossoms in her hair with extreme tenderness, then kissed her fingers curled around the *coupe*. Mirella closed her eyes for a moment, savouring the touch of his lips upon her skin, wanting more, wanting to be taken by him, dissolved by him, drowned in their loving orgasms. She opened her eyes slowly and tried to bring herself under control.

'That was lovely. Crazy, romantic, lovely,' she said. 'Thank you,' and she kissed him, grazed his lips with hers, unable to take any more initiative with him for fear that his need for sexual release was not yet as great as hers. She continued somewhat nervously, 'And these champagne glasses . . .'

'I had them made for this day, one of my wedding gifts to you, and to me too. They are in memory of that first visit of mine to your house in Manhattan and the fantasy it inspired that came true. The very first time I saw you was when I was standing on your doorstep in the rain. I thought to myself then, "The last thing I expected to meet this evening was a woman I wanted to fuck in the soft, warm rain." I think I fell in love with you, or began to fall in love with you, at that moment, then and there. I have never stopped. When you served my drink in a glass like this one, my heart stood still. I shall never forget it.' Adam took Mirella's *coupe* from her hand and placed it along with his own on the table next to her. She had just enough time to say, 'Oh, Adam, I love you, I love you in ways that are utterly new to me.

55

This is like the first day of my life as a lover.'

And then she was in his arms and he was kissing her with a sweet tenderness that quickened to passion, and then, aroused by her sexual desire as well as his own, into something more wild and uncontrolled that erupted into more, much more. In between his kisses and caresses he whispered, in a voice unmistakably limbered with lust, 'After so much anticipation, so much waiting for this moment when I would possess you completely and forever as my wife, my friend, all that is eros, as the other side of myself, it's here. Only you have ever aroused both sexual desire and a real and deep love in me. Only with you am I over-whelmed with the power and delight of being both the dominant and the submissive man in love and in acts of sexual pain and pleasure.'

Adam's desire to kiss, caress, and experience everything conceivable associated with sexual desire and its infinite pleasures, spurred him on to assist Mirella to undress. In the church, he had revelled in the beauty of Mirella dressed as his bride. Mirella in her wedding gown and veil had felt deeply the role of the bride and what it would mean to their lives, but now they both found the white lace gown a symbolic burden in the bedroom. Silently, happily, they allowed their lust to direct their disrobing.

Less than ten minutes after she had entered their suite Mirella lay naked propped on one elbow enmeshed in Adam's heartfelt worship of her body with kisses and words of devotion and love.

Stripped of his wedding clothes, he stood with one foot flat on the bed, his hands resting on his hips, his large thick phallus, massively beautiful and erect, dominating their deeper feelings for each other.

The rhythmic crash of the deep blue, Atlantic waves on the beach below filled their ears. The salt air mingled with the scent of the flowers in the room and the raunchy perfume of lust. The natural aroma of pure, unadulterated sex subtly emanated from the pores of their skin. Soon it overwhelmed the other odours and captivated them further, sharpening the animal side of their sexual desire for each other.

Mirella's heart quickened, beating so hard she could feel it pulsating with the crashing waves. Mesmerized by the sounds, she imagined the crest of each wave as it broke and rushed across the beach in a torrent of white foam. And she took pleasure in Adam hovering over her in all his rampant maleness, the exquisite sensations of her own body inflamed by his hands, his mouth, his tongue.

Again and again she heard the waves hit the beach, and her one thought was of the rich delectable foam of Adam's orgasms breaking over her. She longed to feel all that force of life rushing down over her eyes, her lips, her breasts, and to see her erect nipples, flushed into painful sensitivity by the passion of his sucking lips, glisten with his come. She imagined herself glazed with his sperm from head to toe, and still she wanted more: the thrust behind *his* waves, *his* orgasms. She yearned to experience *his* need to take her, to fill her fully with himself. She longed to be the recipient of his desire to vanquish her, by probing her womb with his phallus again and again, and to have him explode inside her with a burst of his seed that she could draw up into the core of her being.

Mirella put the back of her hand to her lips, sucked the flesh into her mouth and bit hard, in the hope of holding back a cry for Adam to take her, fuck her into oblivion, wrench from her huge powerful orgasms to meet his own and to match the ocean waves, and then to bring her back into the world again with tender care and love.

But her need was too great, and tears of passion and love filled her eyes for the man she had just married, Adam, who always made her submission to him and to eros such a joy. She caught her breath, and a short quick sob escaped from her, behind the hand she clenched between her teeth. Slipping sensually and slowly on to her back, she drew her legs up and voluptuously, languidly spread them open, never taking her eyes from Adam's.

'How magnificent, how divine you are, my love,' said Adam, as he placed himself on his knees between her legs and sat back on his haunches and stroked the inside of her thighs.

Adam was clearly in awe of Mirella, her sensuality, the way she mobilized all her senses. He watched her intently, straining to catch every sound, scent and sight. He was all-seeing, all-hearing, wanting to miss nothing, wanting to take all of her into himself.

Because she had exposed herself totally physically to him, he knew that for the moment she had turned her self off mentally and emotionally, baring her body and her soul. Because of her and the way she was now before him, he felt himself stepping quickly out of his own defences and becoming vulnerable, felt himself give way to join her in that place she inhabited.

He stopped stroking Mirella, flattering her. Instead of pleading with her, he unexpectedly whispered commands, softly yet most firmly and authoritatively: how he wanted her to fondle herself for him, play with her breasts, suck on her own nipples, spread open her vaginal lips and play with her clitoris. She shivered with delight at her own orgasms and stroked his lips and tongue with her fingers covered with the sexual honey of her cunt. He never touched her while making his demands.

Mirella obeyed his every command because obeying Adam never failed to arouse her beyond all dreams, all fantasies.

Adam quite suddenly could not bear waiting any longer, and with passionate sexual violence he charged mightily with thrust after thrust into Mirella, at the same time lying on top of her and kissing her deeply. Lips and tongues, cunt and cock working together in a frenzy of lust.

It was what Mirella wanted: to be weighed down by Adam's body. To bear the heaviest burden simultaneously with one of life's most intense fulfilments. It was as if the weight of Adam upon her brought them, and their remarkable love and lust for each other, closer to the earth, made their mutual ecstasy more real and truthful.

Again and again Adam beat his cock deeply into Mirella. Her cries of acute pleasure, and the sometimes exquisite pain that can accompany erotic extremes, only extended his own carnal bliss and drove him on to lick, suck, fuck and devour her into himself. Pulsing through their bodies was pleasure beyond thoughts and manipulations. Adam and Mirella's orgasms were pure and perfect, on this their wedding day. It was a powerful physical pleasure that gave them a glimpse of infinity.

It was dusk. A hot, red sun, dulled by a curtain of heavy mist hovering several feet above the ocean, cast a milky grey aura tinged with pink all around Oceanside. Adam watched the waves, seductive and mysterious in the eerie light, gather momentum and roll heavily on to the shore. The ocean appeared to be more calm now than it had been earlier in the afternoon when he and Mirella had made love together.

The rich romantic music of the sea filled his ears and his heart, and he allowed the dramatic hour of dusk, and the fading of his wedding day to wrap itself around him like a seductive cape. Standing naked in the twilight at the doorway of the balcony he was warmed by memories of his wedding to Mirella, the most important day of his life. He looked away from the ocean to his wife lying naked in the shadows fast asleep, and he covered his face with his hands and wept. Tears streamed down his face and neck. He swallowed his sobs, and shuddered, so great and deep was the emotion that possessed him.

It was the closeness, the oneness he had with Mirella that was causing him all his tears of emotion. He knew that. He had always known that being too close to another human being can cause complications. That feelings, especially messy feelings that one would rather not deal with, were always brought to the surface when one accepted such closeness as his to Mirella.

The tears he shed were not for himself alone but for Mirella as well. They were far from tears of despair. Tears rather of joy, for being able to give himself up so totally to another human being, his wife, and not hate her because she possessed him, and knew him so intimately. It meant that he loved himself and could face himself as much as he could love and face her.

How many men were as lucky as he?

Adam lowered his hands from his face, and, wiping his tears away, stepped out onto the balcony. He liked the feel of the cool evening air against his nakedness. He ran his hands over his arms and across his chest, his hips, his stomach, as if he were washing himself with it. With one hand he lifted his flaccid phallus and gave that, too, to the evening breeze. He held it, cupped his testes in his other hand, felt the weight of them, and liked, as he always did, his masculinity, the sheer size and power of it. He smiled to himself. It was a smile not of cheap male vanity but one of appreciation of being a man, and most especially of being his own man. He bent down and cleansed his thighs and legs, in between his toes, then reached around his back and his tight, muscled bottom, and completed his strange almost ritualistic cleansing.

Adam watched dusk turning to nightfall, the pink pearly grey atmosphere changing to the frosted navy blue of evening. The mist being pushed inland by billowing puffs of thick fog rolled over the waves and muffled their sound. He walked quietly back into the darkened bedroom and found a cigar and his Zippo lighter. After going to the bed where Mirella lay, still sleeping, a tender smile on her face which he could not see but sensed in the darkness, he bent down and kissed her ever so lightly on the lips and one exposed pretty breast. He walked back to the balcony door, leaned against the jamb and, after wetting his lips with his tongue, placed the large Havana cigar between them. Slowly, meticulously, he rolled it between his fingers, then lighted it evenly. He was the happiest of men.

Adam thought about the lure of love. The fact that there was no defence against it. He had always loved women, truly loved them, and consequently knew a great deal about them. He enjoyed having women in love with him and therefore knew a great deal about that too. There had been women, so many women in his life, and he had loved them all and loved them well . . . but none as well as Mirella.

The muffled, mournful sound of a foghorn somewhere out on the ocean drew him back to the present. He stared out into the nothingness, that lonely space of no yesterdays and no tomorrows, and wondered about those women, some of whom were still part of his life. The mistresses of his bed and the mothers of his children, and *the* woman, his wife, who brought with her the half of himself he had lost long ago. He thought, too, about the incidental women of his life – the prostitutes he had enjoyed paying for, the casual insignificant women he had had sexual affairs with, the exotic mysterious women, and the dangerous women.

Ah, the dangerous women. Marlo sprang to mind. Where was Marlo? he wondered. It never occurred to him that she might not show up for his wedding. His thoughts flashed back ten years, to northern Nigeria and the second *Sallah* festival, after Ramadan, a high point in the Muslim year.

He first saw Marlo at the ancient city, the religious centre of Kano, riding a grey stallion whose saddle cloths of silk, velvet, and brocades were magnificently embroidered in gold and inset with diamonds, and whose bridle was of beaten silver. She was riding under the bright new moon at breakneck speed around the perimeter of the town, where stood the remnants of the once regal, fabled high walls. She rode surrounded by huge, black Muslim men dressed in their famed scarlet robes and turbans. The turbans draped around their heads with majestic style and in the legendary manner of the desert nomads, draped also around their faces and under their chins, some even covered their heads entirely, except for their eyes. They were the Emir's personal bodyguards.

They whooped and hollered and fired their rifles at the heavens. The air was acrid with gunpowder, because the multitudes of people who had gathered to see the procession and the slaughter of chosen sacrificial animals, and to hear the drumming and the blowing of horns, accompanied them with a barrage of rifle shots. Even the most suspect of muskets, no matter what its age or origin, was pressed into service.

Adam, who had just completed crossing the Sahara from north to south on an archaeological reconnaissance expedition, was, as the Emir's guest of honour, seated behind the mounted musicians, on a fine steed.

He was flanked by the Emir and the Sultan, resplendent in their Sudanese robes of coloured cotton and silk, over which the Emir wore a heavily embroidered green burnous and the Sultan, a cape of pure gold. Ivory and bejewelled handled scimitars hung from their waists. The rulers were mounted on extremely fine Tawati bred horses covered for the occasion with cloths of infinite beauty in silver and gold.

The conscious display of wealth and power recalled the splendours of the empire 180 years before, but it was also a reminder of the power of the Islamic faith in black Africa, of the Fulani nomads, possibly not

63

the most strict of Muslims, part pagan even, whose world is that of the *jihad*, the holy war.

Adam was getting the message loud and clear: that *jihad* was alive and well and waiting to sweep through Africa when the time was right. The magenta turban fell from Marlo's head and uncovered her face just as she rode past them. The Sultan burst into loud laughter, stood in his saddle and shouted out orders to a dozen of his bodyguards to bring the white woman rider to him, she must be made to ride behind him, not in front of him. Then, smiling at the Emir, the Sultan had thanked him for the gift, which had made the Emir look very unhappy. Adam was concerned for the courageous, foolish adventuress, whose beauty and style had instantly touched his heart. Then the Sultan had ordered the start of his procession.

Adam hadn't thought about that first meeting for years. It surprised him that time had not diminished the sensuous impression made by his first meeting with Marlo. How lovely she had been – a wild beauty, a mysterious woman with a reckless past as the mistress of a famous painter, and the main character in a love-triangle that caused the death of a poet laureate when she left him for a beautiful woman. A war-photographer with every news agency in the world after her work, Marlo had enough friends in high places to ensure her safety wherever she went.

In all their years together she had been a bewitching, sensual creature whom men and women alike fell hopelessly in love with. Theirs had been a volatile relationship because Marlo insisted she wanted a domestic life with Adam, which was not at all true. They both understood her restless energy, but in her perversity she both loved and hated Adam for his understanding.

In the end Adam had given her the most wonderful domestic life, one that suited her perfectly. A home of her own, shared with his other mistresses and his children, which he visited whenever he chose. It suited the lesbian side of her nature as well as her infinitesimal maternal yearnings. When she wanted a child, Adam's child, she was thrilled for a month and then resented every further minute of her pregnancy; she despised the pain, messiness and loss of dignity she experienced giving birth. Yet, when Alice was born, delivered at her insistence by Adam and a midwife in the *yalis*, on the Bosporus, she loved her.

Marlo loved her child and all Adam's other children, all the women in his life, and the *yalis* where they all lived, because they shared the burden of being mothers, domesticity, and Adam their lover and man of the house. Her capricious behaviour was never tamed: everyone loved her too much to try. Her many affairs were accepted and enjoyed by them all. Only war, that fast moving and unpredictable adventure of pain and destruction, thoroughly excited her. She used Adam, Alice and domesticity as others would use aspirin, for the relief of the pain or as a soldier would use R and R – rest and recreation. And then her questing nature would drive her on to the next experience, and the next.

She was one of the mainstays in the Corey Clan. Adam had no doubt that she would love Mirella just as much as the rest of the clan did, but thought it very mischievous of her not to be at Oceanside for the wedding festivities. And Marlo could be very mischievous.

Standing naked and alone in the swirls of fog now drifting past him into the bedroom, he enjoyed his cigar and had to admit to himself that, as many women as he might have loved, might still, he had never loved them as he did Mirella. He had never delivered himself up to any of them demand-free and asking for nothing more than their company, as he now did with her, and indeed as she did with him.

He could see now that both he and the women of his past had always asked questions of love. There had always been some degree of measuring, testing, probing, and saving it. And those were always the reasons it was cut short. No matter how subtle, there had always been the demand of love from one's partner.

Lost in memories, Adam had allowed his cigar to die. He snapped open the faithful old Zippo and re-lit it. He thought about that – the demands that kill love – and Beverley came to mind.

Beverley: mother of his first two children. How young, how naïve he had been when he was trapped into marriage by her. Twenty-two years old and determined to do the right thing by her, he had married her and endured the most unpleasant years of his life. That marriage was the first and last time he made a concession where his life and happiness were concerned. There had been nothing subtle about Beverley Winter's demands of love before he married her, and even less after she had become Beverley Corey. Yet he did love her, only not the way she wanted him to.

Until his marriage to her, Adam had never known deceit, had never understood envy and hatred, which were what she had had for him. Beverley was bourgeois, adored mediocrity and, though attracted to Adam sexually, resented everything else about him: his social position, his family, his intellectual and business acumen, his wealth, and most of all his large and loving heart. She had been unable to come to terms with Adam and his twin sister Jane, who had been moulded by a happy, privileged childhood and loving parents, and finely honed by their father, who became both parents to them after their mother's hideous death in a fire when the twins were sixteen.

Poor Beverley, Adam thought. It was beyond her to understand what he had always known – that if both partners in a relationship are to remain happy, sentimentality must never enter, and the partners must never make a claim on the life and freedom of each other. That was not something Adam learned from experience; it was something he had understood instinctively from childhood, as did his twin sister Jane. The Corey Twins often had been cited as hard and ruthless in their personal relationships. Their lovers especially were always amazed at what romantics the pair were, given the philosophy of love they believed in. The Corey Twins had been loved all their lives, but rarely understood.

Jane was the woman Adam loved next after his mother. He and Jane had loved each other always, since the cradle, and would do so until the grave. His sister, his best friend, his confidante, especially in those years just after the death of their mother. He smiled to himself when he remembered how he used to rush home to the Peramabahçe Palace where they were living with their father, and tell Jane about the beautiful older woman he was in love with and who was teaching him the wonders of sexual pleasure and the erotic life. He and the Princess Eirene had found the right man to do the same for Jane and she shared her experiences with him as generously as he had with her.

His smile faded when he remembered Jane, Zhara in her arms, Josh by the hand, as she burst into his office having saved the children from the blazing fire Beverley had set to their house. Never until he died would he ever forget her words.

'Adam, our hell is over.'

And it was. Beverley survived the fire, and he and the children never saw her again. She was committed to a private mental institution, where she was to this day living out her life in a twilight world between spurts of murderous violence. He no longer felt the pain of that episode in his life. It was long, long ago.

Jane, wonderful, eccentric Jane who fluctuated between being an earth mother and the grand patron of the arts, who was regrettably not with him on this day because she was where she had been for the last four months: up the Amazon, no one knew precisely where, collecting rare endangered orchids, which she propagated for posterity.

The first thing Mirella saw, when she opened her eyes and waded out from under the blanket of deep sleep into which she had slipped, was the small red glow of Adam's cigar in the dark. When her eyes adjusted to the darkness, she was able to make out Adam's naked silhouette framed by the balcony doorway. When he took a puff on his cigar, a rosy light lit up a portion of his face and Mirella was quite taken aback by the serene beauty she saw in it.

She had always been wildly attracted to Adam's

handsome, virile good looks. They held a fatal charm for most women, that combination of big rough-and-tumble, and the classical beauty of a Michelangelo sculpture. She even remembered telling Deena 'he's madly attractive, part Michelangelo's David and part John Wayne. His vigorous good looks remind me of America and every handsome movie hero who crossed the great plains on the screen to conquer the wild west.'

Suddenly, lamps down on the beach were turned on and they cast a milky white light, because of the fog, that allowed Mirella to see Adam clearly, naked and rampant framed against the light with an extraordinarily beautiful serenity in the long lines of his body, the way he held his head. She had never seen him so serene. Not for the first time, on this her wedding day, was she made aware of what a rare man she had married.

There were moments when she found the reality – not the idea – of being married to Adam daunting, and wondered if she was capable of being a wife to him, or any other man for that matter. Thirty-nine years of living on her own without a permanent live-in mate was a good basis for insecurity, she believed. But those moments were fleeting, made so by the power of Adam's love for her. Mirella had learned during the hours of the lust they shared that afternoon that she had not been the only partner in their relationship to have totally submitted herself for the first time to aphrodisia and another human being. Adam had done the same.

She sat up in the bed and called his name, but he didn't hear her. He appeared to be far, far away in his thoughts. Mirella called again just a little bit louder, and again there was no response. She stood up and was about to go to him, but she sensed it was not the moment, and stopped, ever cautious not to impinge on his space or interrupt what appeared to be a special private time for him.

Instead she walked across the room and went into the bathroom and very quietly closed the door. She ran the water into the tub and sprinkled half a bottle of Barynia into it and the scent of a wild and wonderful flower garden burst into the room. Then she climbed into the deep old-fashioned bath.

Mirella was surprised when, after her bath, wrapped in a full-length scarlet terrycloth robe, she opened the bathroom door and found the bedroom still in darkness, Adam standing exactly where she had left him. She could hear the faint sound of music drifting up from the Tango Room and knew that the first private hours of her married life with Adam were over. It was time for Mr and Mrs Corey to dress and receive their guests at the ball.

She walked through the path of light spilling out from the bathroom and across the hooked rag-rug of the bedroom floor and halted behind Adam. The scent of her perfume penetrated his thoughts and brought him back to the present, just as she slid her arms around his waist and up to his chest and caressed him.

'Remember me? I'm Mrs Corey,' she said, planting a kiss in the middle of his back, then another up on his shoulder blade. He covered her hands with his and pulled her tighter up against him.

Mirella rested her cheek against his naked back and asked, 'Where were you in your thoughts? You seemed light years away.'

'I wasn't that far, but I was a good distance away, in what seems like another life, because you weren't with me, because I didn't even know you then.'

He turned in her arms and kissed her, ran his fingers through her hair, smiled at her and then kissed her with infinite tenderness and caring again. He licked the back of her ear with his tongue.

'You smell like a flower-garden just after the rain,' he said, 'and you taste of almonds, and I love you, Mrs Corey, as I have never loved any other woman.'

'How I like hearing that, Adam. You have no idea how much. When I woke up and I saw you standing here naked and alone, you had the most wonderful look of serenity about you. You looked so beautiful, I don't mean handsome – beautiful. I called you, but you were lost in another world, the past, I thought. I left you in your past, not wanting to interrupt it, because I would have been a stranger there, and the last thing I want is to be a stranger in any part of your life.'

He put his arm around her waist and together they walked through the bedroom turning on lamps as they went.

'I wasn't lost in another world. I was thinking of all the other women in my life before you, and how I had loved them the best that I could, and love some of them now the best that I can. But I have never loved any of them as completely as I do you. It's important that you know and understand that, Mirella, my darling, my dearest.'

71

Chapter 5

Most of the nine-hundred-odd guests were milling around the public rooms of Oceanside when Mirella and Adam arrived for the ball. Turhan, Adam's manservant and bodyguard, followed closely behind, and Moses was in evidence as well. Although she had once considered the idea of the bodyguard – or minder, as she preferred to call such a servant – to be a paranoia of the rich, Mirella had changed her mind, learning not only to accept, but to enjoy the monumental convenience of having a constant attendant.

Only three months before, she had been determined not to let a legacy from a notorious great-grandmother she had never known change her life. She burst out laughing now. She could afford to laugh at herself: the legacy had made her not only one of the wealthiest women in the world, but a woman with considerable power in Turkey, the origin of her legacy and her maternal ancestors. Her corporate holdings in industry, communications, agriculture, strategic land and water were vast. Combined with her equally large liquid monetary reserves, her enormous wealth ensured that her power spread east across Asia Minor and into several of the Gulf States. It had also brought her love, real love, and an exceptional husband.

They were standing on the grand staircase that curved gracefully down from the mezzanine to the ground floor. Josh, who was at their side, began to introduce Adam and Mirella to a group of his friends.

'How about sharing your laughter with us?' Adam asked, putting an arm around her waist.

'I was just laughing at myself,' she answered, a blithe spirit in her voice. 'It's hard to believe that here stands a woman – correction, not just *a* woman, but one of the happiest of women, who only a few months ago stubbornly clung to her lifestyle and discounted change or intrusion of any form into her life. Look at me now!' And with that she did a childish little two-step, spun around and posed with her arms open. 'I'm a star.'

Adam, Josh and the circle of friends around them on the stairs were touched by her enchantment. They laughed with her. Deena watched her from the bottom of the staircase and thought she had never seen Mirella look so happy, so full of life, so sexy and enticing.

In direct contrast to the white of the gown she had worn for the wedding ceremony and breakfast, she now wore a strapless black satin gown with a long slit from the hem up to the middle of one thigh, that opened when she walked, allowing a seductive glimpse of thigh. The Gallanos creation hung just loose enough to ripple ever so slightly over her body, highlighting every sensuous curve – a more provocative look than a clinging gown could ever achieve. She wore no stockings over her long shapely legs, while on her feet were a pair of very high-heeled sandals of criss-crossed narrow strips of black satin. It appeared to be just a slip of a dress, but it was hardly that. It was one of those deadly expensive works of art where every cut was a masterful one, and every stitch in it invisible. A whisper of a dress that shouted out, 'This is elegance and sensuous beauty. This is female.' And, of course, the message cut and sewn into the dress exactly matched Mirella's feelings.

She wore her shoulder-length silky black hair loose and casual, brushed back off her face. Her large seductive violet eyes sparkled like the narrow ribbon of diamonds high up around her neck, that clipped to one side in a small bow of diamond baguettes, cut and faceted in a manner that made each of the fifty-two-carat stones in the platinum bow-setting a gem, and the necklace a unique treasure.

When Adam gave it to her while they were dressing for the ball, he had said, 'This is my wedding gift to you, with all my love, and in memory of the first time I touched you, on the evening we met. Remember, how I came to your rescue when you were on the verge of fainting from shock? Learning you were about to become the world's newest millionairess was more than you could take. I loosened the little red and white polka dot silk bow tied on the side of your throat, remember? I slipped it slowly from around your neck. And how fetchingly you wore the little scarf. It enchanted me then, it enchants me now. *You* enchanted me then, and I am still under your spell.'

The night before her wedding, when Adam was banned from seeing her until the ceremony the next morning, she and Rashid, who had dined with her immediate family, were walking alone together through Wingfield Park when he had presented her with a wedding gift: a pair of twenty-carat square-cut

75

diamonds that now twinkled on her ears. The wedding gifts from her husband and her lover set off her Gallanos gown more than admirably.

Looking down to the floor below, Mirella smiled and waved to Deena, then turned and said to Adam and all those standing with them, 'What an amazing ball! For years I have side-stepped grand occasions such as this for all sorts of inverted snobbish reasons – until I met Rashid, who swept me into the fast lane of glamorous international society, and taught me what fun an occasional bash like this can be.'

'If that's the case, then surely I have the right to claim the first dance,' said Rashid, who had made his way to Mirella and Adam through the throngs of beautiful people dressed in evening jackets and the dazzlingly pretty and extravagant collection of ball gowns and jewels.

Adam smiled, and the mischievous glint in his eye did not go unnoticed by Mirella as he said, 'We Coreys always pay our debts, don't we, darling?'

Before Mirella could answer, Rashid took her by the hand and moved quickly down the stairs, trailing her behind him. Mirella missed what happened next because she was still looking back at Adam, who had already been distracted by someone Mirella didn't know. But she did see Josh dash down the stairs behind them, felt him quite roughly grab her hand from Rashid's, and declare, rudely, half aggressively, 'Not so fast, Rashid. We Coreys do pay our debts, but we don't overpay them. If my father is going to share his bride this evening, old boy, you will have to get in line after me.'

And he almost ran down the remainder of the stairs with her in tow.

Mirella wanted to ask Josh why he was being so rude to Rashid and what made dancing with Rashid overpaying her debt to him? She held back, though, not wanting to make an issue of Josh's strange behaviour, and was encouraged not to by remembering the glint in Adam's eye, which she did not quite understand.

She looked up over her shoulder at Rashid, who was still standing on the stairs, and shrugged an 'I'm sorry'. He stood out from the other guests moving up and down the staircase. He was handsome, debonair and unruffled by the little scene, and Mirella's relief was edged with concern when she saw Rashid's expression slip for a second into coldness as he snapped his fingers and signalled to his man, Daoud.

Mirella was quite used to being watched over by Rashid's bodyguards, but she was taken aback to see that it was still going on. Had it not, then, ceased when she had run away from Rashid to Adam, and he had accepted her choice? And was not Adam the one responsible for her safety now?

But all thoughts about that quickly faded when, at the entrance to the ballroom, they were handed beautiful black silk eye-masks encrusted with jet-faceted beads and edged with rhinestones. The stunning Venetian masks were mounted on long slender rods wrapped in black satin and culminating at the base in streamers tipped with more rhinestones.

Both Mirella and Josh were overwhelmed by what they saw. From the thirty-five-foot dome of the circular ballroom hung dozens of crystal candelabras on ropes of white garden roses, their white candles filling the room with sensuous light. The wooden walls were encrusted with sconces holding hundreds of white candles all aglow as well. Couples dancing to the music of Artie Shaw, their twinkling masks twisting and turning around the room, lent an air of mystery and seduction, wantonness even, to the scene.

Mirella and her stepson held their masks up to their faces and danced on to the ballroom floor where instantly they became one with the swirling maskers. But not for long. There were barely half a dozen couples left dancing when Mirella realized that the others had gyrated gently one by one to the sidelines, relinquishing the floor to them.

Mirella began to lower her mask and Josh stopped her. 'No. Please! With your mask in place I can pretend you're all mine for a few minutes more. Without it, you're my stepmother, my father's wife.'

Mirella tightened a fraction at her stepson's boldness. She responded by lowering her mask again. Rashid and Deena, masks in place, danced past them, and Rashid adeptly whisked first Josh's mask and then Mirella's from their hands, and danced on to the edge of the floor where they joined all the other guests, who unmasked and gave the waltzing couple an ovation.

'This is all wrong somehow,' said Mirella blushing furiously. 'I should have had this dance with your father, and would have, had I known this was going to happen.'

Mirella could feel the blood rising in Josh, but he cut his anger short with, 'That fucking Rashid. He is a cunning bastard.' And they danced to the applause until the music stopped. When it began again with another song, Josh's young arms claimed her and they

78

danced towards Adam, who was standing on the fringe of the crowd as it formed into couples who were now eagerly filling the dance floor.

'Sorry about that, Papa. It was thoughtless of me. I guess you should have opened the ball with Mirella, not me.'

'Don't think twice about it, Josh. It doesn't matter who opened the ball. But if you feel you have to make an apology, maybe it should go to Rashid. He is, after all, the one you snatched Mirella from.' And, putting an arm around Mirella, Adam kissed her lightly on the lips.

'That won't be necessary, Josh,' said Rashid, who had walked up to them at that moment and handed Mirella and Josh their masks. He gave Adam's son an affectionate pat on the back, and there passed between Rashid and Adam a very private look of total understanding. 'Boys sometimes do strange and foolish things when they run up against overwhelming odds and beauty. And besides, it still leaves the Tango Room and its Latin American band, and the Beach Pavilion disco with the Bee Gees for your stepmother and I to conquer.'

Adam raised his arm from around Mirella's waist and with his hand discreetly caressed the side of the voluptuous swell of her breast. Then he stroked her cheek and kissed her again lightly on her lips, wanting secretly to reassure her that he understood he had to share her, even on this his wedding night, that he, as well as she, could handle it. And handle it they would – admirably. He knew that secretly was the operative word, for the three of them would never confront their relationship out in the open. Not unless it was over for them.

Adam knew too that when Rashid said 'Boys sometimes do strange and foolish things when they run up against overwhelming odds and beauty', he was indicating not only to Josh, but to Adam and Mirella, that anyone but Adam who ever tried to snatch Mirella from him would be exposed and eliminated as neatly as Josh had been.

'Perfect! Great timing for me, Rashid. While you are conquering the dance floor with the bride, I will, yet again, stake my claim on the groom,' said a huskily teasing voice belonging to someone behind Mirella.

Mirella turned around to see who it was, but the way her heart leapt at the mocking words, she knew it could only be Marlo Channing. The two women's eyes met. Before anyone could say a word, Marlo took over.

'The bride. Adam's wife, and flanked by her husband and her . . .' Marlo broke off deliberately, tilted her head to one side and raised an eyebrow a fraction of an inch, giving the three of them an arch look. Then her expression suddenly changed. Two mischievous eyes, and a personality exuding vitality and a vivid beauty replaced the look of hard, clean, sharp-edged bitchiness. She smiled at Mirella.

'Oh, hell and damnation, the clan failed to tell me you were such a beauty. I'm Marlo. Welcome to the family.' She stepped close up to Mirella and putting her hands on Mirella's bare shoulders, kissed her on the lips.

The kiss was calculated to rattle Mirella. Only once before had a woman kissed her on the lips. That was during one of Rashid's amazing erotic nights in Istanbul. She had found it very strange, disturbing, yet not unexciting. But that had been a sexual interlude and in private. This was in public, from a stranger, most certainly a rival of sorts, and quite possibly an enemy. Mirella's instinct was to wipe the kiss from her lips: it was distasteful to her. Lili, her own mother, had never kissed her like that. Nor had Deena, her closest friend. Nor had her beloved grandmother, Lili's mother, who loved and adored Mirella.

But Mirella controlled herself, knowing very well that to reveal her repugnance would not only be to hand the scene to Marlo, but to leave herself upstaged. It would be too, a subtle declaration of war with one of the clan – a dangerous indulgence for Mirella.

She tried to take up her poise again, by rationalizing the kiss and why she should not broadcast the revulsion she felt at being kissed intimately in public by a woman, the way a male lover would embrace her. They were, after all, two women, sisters under the skin. A quick summoning of feminist logic told her that she should accept it. According the kiss no response, she avoided the tawdry little scene that might have been. Marlo's determination to control her first meeting with Mirella was awesome, however, and Mirella watched her with fascination. She was clever, sharp, and bright, in every way a woman who rode her own temperament like a white stallion into battle, and deployed all her various tactics with great style and always as her own audacious self.

'Adam a groom! You do surprise me, darling,' she said. Slowly, seductively, slipping her arms around Adam's neck, she kissed him on the lips as she had kissed Mirella.

Unlike Mirella, Adam accepted Marlo's kiss and enjoyed it, and the feel of her long-legged, slim body pressed against him. Now his joy was complete: all the clan were there sharing this day with him and Mirella. He placed his hands around her waist and skilfully lifted the smiling Marlo six inches off the floor and returned her kiss. Then, setting her back down on her feet, he stepped back and took a long view of her.

What he saw this evening was not the glamorous American war photographer dressed in her famous Burberry trench coat and in bits and pieces of men's clothing she had pinched from her various male colleagues. She most certainly was not now the figure Mirella had seen leaning against the dining-room door during the wedding breakfast.

Instead of joining the festivities, Marlo had gone to the room reserved for her and spent the afternoon preparing herself for this meeting. She was dressed and groomed for her role as 'the other important woman in Adam Corey's life', played now to perfection and to a packed house.

Marlo, who always prided herself on 'travelling light', had the habit of packing her duffle bag with film, film, and more film, her favourite Hasal-blad, her Nike, a box of lenses, a wand of black mascara, one tube of bright red lipstick, a gingery pink blusher, a passport-case stuffed with credit cards, visas, letters of introduction, letters of credit, and money.

The other items she considered essential 'tools of her trade' were a large bottle of Mitsouka perfume, a pair of high-heeled evening shoes, an impressive long evening dress, and a handful of spectacular jewellery shoved into a small suede pouch stowed at the bottom of the lens box. Everything else she bought and disposed of on the way, or borrowed, took, or swapped, as was needed, with her male colleagues. They in turn used her and the contents of her duffle bag.

Marlo was notorious for it, as well as much else about her life. Mostly because with the contents of the bag she was able to get freely anywhere she wanted to be: war zones, *entrée* to generals, dictators, rebel leaders, the high echelons of governments, the poor and desperate, the spoiled, privileged and wealthy. She was not above using her bold and wily female mind or body to get what she wanted.

Many a female encountered during her dangerous travels would bitch her, claiming she attended wars dressed like a princess. But the men in her world of gore and violence knew better: she dressed in her costumes of the trade, sometimes their clothes, sometimes hers, and many were grateful because she and her duffle bag had got them out of many a tight spot – even saved a life, maybe, or a man from an unsought interview with torturers. Her duffle bag had as usual served her well on Adam's wedding day. She knew it, she could see in Adam's face that he knew it too, but it was still nice to hear him say it.

'You look like a million dollars, so beautiful, and you have made such an effort. It's most appreciated. Perfection would have been to have had you with us for the wedding ceremony and breakfast. But, alas, even we don't get perfection.'

Mirella had to agree with him. Marlo Channing, her hair smoothed back off her face and into a tight shiny twist at the nape of her neck, eye make-up so skilfully applied that only the long, thick black eyelashes attested to its use, the hint of ginger pink accentuating the handsome high cheek bones, looked beautiful. More, she looked exciting with a provocative slash of clear red across her thin, sensual lips, that when closed were like the form of two lovers closely entwined lying on their sides.

Mirella was certain that what made Marlo look especially thrilling was her one-shouldered evening dress of butter yellow silk taffeta, paper taffeta, so thin that the entire gown could be rolled up into a ball that would fit in the palm of the hand. A remarkable necklace of huge round cabochon emeralds, each encircled in diamonds, was at her neck to emphasize the deep tan of her skin. The matching earrings, whose green was the colour of her eyes, subtly softened the aura of a deep underlying drive towards self-determination, adventure, excitement and freedom.

Hers was a restless, masculine inner and outer beauty in a female form, worn this night with all the opulent decorations to enhance it. Mirella saw in Marlo a uniquely forceful style, the cut and thrust of her mind, and could well understand how she could be irresistible to men.

'Mirella, is this the first time you and Marlo have met?' Rashid asked. Marlo answered for her.

'No, not exactly.'

Mirella felt decidedly uncomfortable. It was such a little thing, her not telling Adam during the wedding reception that Marlo was at the entrance of the dining-room watching them. If Marlo were to mention it now, Mirella would find it embarrassing. She knew at the time she was wrong not to draw Adam's attention to the woman's presence, and now having met her, Mirella was certain it was an evasion that Marlo would make her pay dearly for . . . if not now, one day not far-off.

'We saw each other not long ago, across a crowded room. I can't speak for Mirella but I can for myself. When our eyes met I sort of knew we would meet again very soon, and then we would become friends.'

Here it came, she was going to tell him, Mirella thought. She did not enjoy one bit playing mouse to Marlo's cat. But Josh made a fuss over Marlo then, and Rashid stepped to her side and give her a big hug.

'You look ravishing,' Rashid said. 'Naughty, adventurous, mischievous – just ravishing in your Alice emeralds.' The Alice emeralds had been Adam's gift to Marlo in celebration of the birth of their daughter, Alice.

Marlo raised his hand and placed it on her flat breast, so as to cover her heart, and mocking him said, 'Words from the master of style and beauty. How you make my heart beat.' She laughed. 'Well, Mirella Corey, didn't you think we would swap glances again, and meet, as I thought we would? Or did you believe I was an apparition, and would just vanish?'

'When and where did you meet Marlo?' a puzzled Adam asked Mirella as he placed his arm around her shoulder and kissed her on the cheek.

'I haven't the slightest idea,' Mirella said promptly. 'I don't ever remember seeing Marlo, and if I did, I am afraid I have forgotten.' She could hardly believe she could stoop to such a trivial white lie and embroil herself in such a banal situation. All because of one moment of possessiveness, the fear of sharing her husband with someone he loved long before he ever met her. How stupid and pathetic, she thought, and asked herself if that was what marriage was going to do to her – trivialize her. She quickly answered her silent question with an equally silent 'Hell, no', and made the decision never to slide into such a ridiculous position again.

Marlo realized she had been outfoxed by Mirella with that fib. It would have been a real cheap shot on her part then to label Mirella a liar, and reveal that the two women had seen each other only hours before. She had the good grace to toss her head back and laugh, 'And now that we have met, Mirella, what next?'

'Oh that's easy. Our preordained relationship dictates the way. We, Marlo, are family. So I imagine you, Adam, and I will see a great deal of each other.'

'Pulling that old chestnut, family ties, out of the fire? No my dear Mirella, I doubt that. I will see Adam, and if you like, we'll see each other, but separately. Try to understand without being offended that I wouldn't want to see you as a couple. I don't care for the bonding that takes place in couples after they marry – that blanding, dulling sort of flattening of two personalities, who lose a part of themselves in each other's presence because they are so busy watching each other being a couple. I don't want to be bored by the people I love, or the friends I make. Now, that being said, Rashid has staked a claim to Mirella, so we know she won't be a wallflower, and I'm laying a claim on your Adam.'

Adam gave Mirella a quick peck on the cheek and said, as he put his arm around Marlo and they danced into the crowd, 'You are in good hands, darling, there's a lot of dancing for us all to do tonight.'

'And eating and drinking, and climbing up to highs, and making love. Come on, it's the Tango Room for us,' said Rashid, taking Mirella by her hand.

What was so amazing to Mirella was that the moment Marlo waltzed away in Adam's arms, the scene dissolved and along with it whatever fears she had. In Rashid's arms she thought of nothing beyond what was happening. They danced, and dined on the sumptuous buffet, and the old excitement was still there. He relinquished her to Adam and her father, and Brindley, and a few other guests for dances, always then reclaiming her for himself, and was delighted in the joy he sensed in her. The erotic bond between them was still very much alive.

The revellers behind their masks flirted with abandon, teased partners who were strangers to them, and, responding to the music and wine and food, and abundance of cocaine inhaled in the privacy of closed rooms, dropped all barriers and enjoyed the night without reservation.

Brindley leapt the three feet off the boardwalk on to the sand. Bared ankles felt good, and he was suddenly aware of all the bones in his feet. He dug his toes into the cool, clean, gritty sand, and enjoyed the texture, rolled his trousers up to the middle of his calves and then turned back to the boardwalk and Deena.

They were at the very end of Oceanside's beach, where they could look back at the hotel all ablaze with light. There were driftwood bonfires on the beach and a tripod was slung over each fire and held huge kettles of fresh New England lobster and clams. Small vats of warm melted lemon butter nestled in the embers along with old fashioned camping coffee pots whose contents mixed their scent with the salt air and the ears of corn buried in the white ashes. Beer and bottles of champagne were iced down together in huge copper tubs. Rashid had omitted nothing that would entertain his guests and keep the party going, not even this New England clambake.

Couples were dancing on the sand to the faint sound of the Bee Gees coming from the Beach Pavilion, or were stretched out on blankets making love in the firelighted shadows. The odd couple were chasing in and out to the surge and suck of the ocean's waves lapping onto the shore.

Everywhere in the moonlight and under a sky black but bright with stars men and women were coming together. Their senses, gratified but still not sated, yearned for sex, and it was there, everywhere around them, just waiting to be plucked, as if from the very air that embraced them.

Brindley looked up at Deena sitting on the boardwalk, her legs dangling over the edge, her seductive mask held in place, covering her eyes. She was silent, hardly able to contain the turmoil of passion, hot blood, unfettered sexual desire, churning within her.

She wanted what she had just seen, nothing less. If she were to die in the process of getting it, it didn't matter! In a secluded suite on the top floor of Oceanside, whose door was manned by Daoud and Fuad, Rashid's two bodyguards, she had seen a sexual performance that had inflamed her with a fire that she knew would burn for her for the remainder of her life. A fire that had to be fed.

She had seen, for the first time, a sexual slave. Not just *a* sexual slave but one who revelled in her own debauchery. She had seen a woman who was a beautiful and tantalizing sexual machine, who made Deena understand that, for all the sex she had had in her life, all the freedom she thought she displayed in her sexual encounters, she had never truly given in to her orgasms, died in them as Rashid's slave Humayun did. She had never really yielded herself totally to a man, handed her life over to him to do with it what he wanted. She had never reduced herself to nothing but a cunt, a mouth, an ass, the merest pleading receptacle for a man's penis and all his sexual and animal needs or whims.

Nor had she ever mastered the art of being both the sexual slave *and* the sexual-master of men. Humayun's golden red hair seemed not so much hair as erotic silk tresses with which to drape a naked body, the satin texture of her cream-coloured skin and her clever and seductive green eyes which were capable of changing in a flash into mean, punishing eyes were used as captivating instruments.

Everything about her was sensuous: the alluring face with its proud patrician nose and remarkable bone structure, the long slender neck that tapered into wide shoulders and a tall lean body dominated by extremely large, well-shaped breasts. The tantalizing nipples and their halo, tattooed, like her voluptuous hairless mound, in henna-dyed arabesque designs, acted as sirens for men's mouths. The narrow waist, slim hips, full round tight buttocks were instruments to torment males, or be used by men for their pleasure of torturing her.

The visions of sex Humayun had had that night with two handsome young men plus twenty or more of Rashid's male guests, who indulged themselves in any fashion they chose to – some bizarre, even frightening, and all of which were madly sexually stimulating – were the most thrilling pictures Deena had ever seen, and would stay with her for the remainder of her life. To taste a fraction of Humayun's pleasure, experience such boundless sensual delight, was to live and die in the same instant. Such an adventure as that was certain to enrich life, Deena understood now. She had to have that experience.

Brindley removed the silk sandals from Deena's feet. She watched his face in the moonlight and saw not one crack in the facade of English reserve he wore so well. Was the erotic passion there to satisfy her needs? He folded the skirt of her evening dress up on to her thighs, and raised first one leg then the other, unclipped her garters, and rolled each stocking down slowly, as if he were savouring the act. He tucked the stockings into the shoes and placed them neatly next to her, then he bent down and placed a kiss on her thigh.

He stood between her legs, spanned her waist under the skirt with his hands, then moving them down over her naked flesh adeptly unhooked the garter belt and slid it from around her and dropped it in the sand. How could this gentle Englishman take her where she wanted to go, through all the sexual portals that led through debauchery to depravity, all those places so foreign to Deena that Humayun had shown her glimpses of?

Brindley surprised her when he spread her legs further apart. She felt the strings of her bikini under-panties snap as he slid her off the boardwalk and the slip of silk from between her legs. Before the skirt of her gown could fall and cover her nakedness he tied it up around her waist.

The night air was warm and it caressed her exposed flesh, wrapping itself around her like a seductive lover. It thrilled her like the touch of Brindley's searching hands. She turned around and reached for his mask, abandoned on the boardwalk next to her, and broke it from its handle, while he was fondling and licking the luscious orbs of her bottom. Turning back to him again she pulled his tie. The bow dissolved and she slid it from around his neck and, placing his mask across his eyes, she clumsily tied it in place. He understood and smiled. When she held her own mask up to hide behind, he took it away from her and threw it on the sand, took her by the hand and pulled her along the dunes now cool underfoot, and over clumps of grass covered with dew that startled the feet.

Through the grass and shrubs he led her, leaving the beach and the bonfires and the people behind, and as the grasses grew higher and more abundant, the path of sand they were following grew more narrow, forcing them to walk along it in Indian-file, Brindley pushing her along from behind, slapping her bottom whenever she hesitated. He stripped himself of his clothes as they walked, dropping items along the path. And now whether the half-naked man in the mask was capable of taking Deena on the erotic road she was determined to travel seemed less doubtful.

In a small clearing, deep in the tall grasses, they found the old grey weatherbeaten boat house. Yellow candle light shone through the small uncovered window. They could see the shadow of two people moving about inside. The excitement of what was to

91

come was almost unbearable, unnervingly so.

Brindley put a hand on Deena's shoulder and she stopped. Still silent they stood in front of each other and their eyes met. Slowly he unzipped his fly and dropped his trousers. Deena fumbled with her dress unable to take her eyes from the wholly naked Brindley standing massively rampant in front of her. This tall, wiry, slim hipped, masked man appeared to be all cock and balls, and, frighteningly, an instrument of boundless sex. It was difficult to equate the mysterious stranger before her with the reserved English solicitor she liked and had imagined to be, if anything, somewhat naïve and merely adequate sexually.

He unknotted the skirt tied around her waist, and before it fell, covering her nudity, with one quick movement he tore the silver gossamer silk strapless gown open from the bodice to the hem. It made a frightening, alien noise against the night-sounds of crickets and toads, the faint rustle of tall grass in the intermittent soft summer breeze, then it drifted, silently, on to the sand around their bare feet.

Deena had been caught off guard by his action. The surprise and shock made her catch her breath. Brindley devoured her with his eyes. She was far more rounded and voluptuous than he had imagined. Visions of what he would do, shortly, to that willing body, the marks he would leave on it aroused him.

He took her in his arms, and a fistful of her long, honey-coloured curly hair in his hand, and he pulled hard on it while he kissed her deeply. He moved his mouth to her nipple which he sucked and ravished. Still holding her hair bunched in his hand, he pulled hard, tilted her head back and kissed her again bruising her lips with passion, and in a voice charged with emotion he spoke to her for the first time since they left Humayun's rooms.

'This is no midsummer-night's dream, this is our life we are playing with, our emotions, our most basic needs and desires. Trust me, I'm going to take you where you want to go. There's no turning back, all you have to do is submit. Obey me and your body, and remember, I too have the appetite for lust that Humayun has. Tonight you will experience the libertine in me as well as in yourself.'

Deena's heart pounded from the sexual excitement his words promised, his actions began to deliver, and the fear of what total submission might bring. Her mouth went dry, she couldn't speak. She felt a body change, a huge rush of orgasm. Her face and chest flushed and she trembled before her masked sybarite. He took both her hands, closed them around his raging penis and, lifting her up by the waist, wrapped her legs tight around his body. Swiftly, adeptly, he stretched open the lips of her silky-moist, lusciously fleshy cunt and in one sharp effort pushed, and she guided him in.

The silvery moon shone white upon them standing naked, the masked man in a frenzy, embedded as fully as the woman wrapped around him appeared able to receive him. With hands now on her shoulders he kept pushing down, determined to bury all of himself deep inside her. He felt his phallus sink to its fullest length, and her cry of ecstasy pierced the night.

'And now it begins for us,' he whispered, a tremor of unbridled passion in his words, his cheek against hers, his lips touching her ear. He kicked open the boat house door, and carried her in impaled upon his cock. The warmth of her vaginal clasp combined with her rush of orgasm, and it was as one that they joined the couple waiting to assist them in their quest.

Chapter 6

'He's not a fool, you know, not the born rich dilettante he pretends to be. Nor is he the absent-minded professor-type archaeologist, if that's what you're thinking,' Ralph Werfel said to Edward Osborne, one of the youngest of Wall Street's élite of deal-makers. 'It suits Adam to have people believe he's a blue-chip dividend man, playing it safe right down the line with his back up of stocks and bonds, just sitting in his palace on the Bosporus, cutting coupons to finance his interests. That's the image he prefers to give the world. The best thing he would want the general public to know is that he is the heart and guts behind The Corey Trust, a colossus he pretends is just a family business. The guy throws out a lot of red herrings, to make you think he's only a figurehead, dependent on his executive staff, who run the whole show for him. He has always been shrewd, using the most competent men to front for him. But make no mistake, they all know who's boss, who runs the show.'

'You're beginning to sweat, Ralph.'

'Listen, Ed! You wouldn't be the first to be taken in by that image he likes to project: tough handsome good looks, casual cool manner, solid and wealthy. All that healthy indifference to big bucks and power; and shy as a Quaker about dirty dealings in the boardroom. The best tip I can give you is to watch out. The sonovabitch may tread softly, but he touts a big stick all the time, even if you can't see it, and the bastard knows how to use it.'

'I get the message, Ralph. You've given it enough times for God's sake.'

'I don't think I can face him, Ed. Revenge is sweet, and I've got him by the balls. He'll have to cave in to this takeover bid for The Corey Trust. I've seen to that. But I wish I didn't have to eyeball him.'

'Oh, you'll face him, Ralph. You won't like it and I imagine you'll squirm a bit, but you'll face him. You've been setting him up for more than two decades. What surprises me is that you waited twenty-two years to get the knife between his shoulderblades and steal away his company. Correction. You can hardly call this a heist with the kind of money we're putting up to take over a multinational conglomerate, operating on three continents with annual sales of $5.4 billion.'

The signal sounded inside the sleek, stainless steel, self-service elevator warning them that it was about to stop. The floor number, 22, lit up on the band of numbers in front of them over the door. Automatically, like the door that soundlessly glided open, the two well-dressed, well-pressed business men fell silent. Two young, very pretty women, each carrying a stack of files in their arms, stepped in, pressed the button of the floor they wanted and rode up two floors with the men. They left the elevator, its doors again glided closed as if on a cushion of air. For the fourth time in less than two minutes, they whizzed smoothly upwards towards their destination, the boardroom of The Corey Trust.

'Great ass on the blonde one, just the kind I like to get into,' Ed said.

'I'm a leg-and-tit man myself,' said Ralph Werfel, The Corey Trust's number one man after its managing director and owner, Adam Corey. He put down his Mark Cross pigskin attaché case, took out a fine linen handkerchief from the breast pocket of his Armani jacket and wiped his sweaty hands before nervously replacing it.

'Jesus, Ralph, this isn't like you. Pull yourself together. You're not acting much like the man I have heard quite rightly called The Corey Trust's English predator. You've made as brilliant and gutsy a set of moves with aggressive takeovers and mergers in the last six months as I've ever seen you or the Trust make. There's no turning back now. Corey's set up, and in just about three minutes we're going to blast him out of the water.'

Ralph shook his head; perspiration beaded his upper lip.

'All that's new about this deal, Ralph, is that you're targeting your own company. Nobody in the world of finance is going to say boo to a goose over your role in this. Quite the contrary, and you know it. That is, after all, why you did it, isn't it? Those three p's: power, praise, and politics. And not wanting to be number two for another twenty-two years.'

'Adam isn't going to sit still for this, Ed.'

'Tough shit. Together you have created an amazing success story, and I can't see you shirking at your moment of glory. Your merger-mania has cost you a business friend. His reticence and peculiar business

97

morals have lost him his company and his best business associate. It's even-steven. And you're right and he's wrong in the financial climate of today. Now let's get this raid over with and our acquisitions in the bag.'

Ralph Werfel felt better and had to admit that that ruthless little shit of an upstart Ed Osborne was a hard case – smart and right.

The elevator doors opened. The two men, attaché cases in their hands and with all corporate knives at the ready for the kill, stepped out onto the white marble floor of the two-storey-high reception area with its wide, full-length windows fronting the New York skyline. White marble Greek sculptures were mounted on square bronze bases and placed most effectively around the room. The sun beamed through the bare windows, lending the gallery and its treasures an even more dramatic and electrifying ambience. With the bright blue sky and the skyscraper peaks replacing classical Athens, even Ed Osborne was affected by the power of the pieces . . . and their silence.

A larger-than-life-size nude man carved of white marble from the island of Paros, who appeared to be of considerable age, with fist clenched over heart, a protruding forehead and very little hair, a massive strong man still young in body and his sex, was the most eloquent piece. Senator? Philosopher? Had he spoken in the Forum?

Another piece, a life-size beautiful goddess with a crescent moon tiara worn in her white marble hair and a diaphanous marble gauze draped skimpily over her nakedness, with nipples like fresh cream rosebuds, smiled down upon them. Diana the huntress? Where was her bow? And how many stags had she slain?

And a third statue, again large as life, was a youth of infinite beauty and tenderness, with one arm raised as if beckoning the observer to him, the other held open and away from his body. How beautiful this virgin boy, this innocent youth, so open and sweet and vulnerable.

'Adam Corey's pieces?'

'Yes,' said Ralph.

'From his excavations?'

'Yes.'

'And all arranged here in this gallery by him, I presume?'

Ralph nodded his head in affirmation.

'This, I take it, is the waiting room before you enter the boardroom? No chairs, no tables, nothing but to stand around and contemplate the situation, whatever that situation might be. Not an easy place to consider treachery, but a great setting for the night of the long knives. I think I'm beginning to understand why you're sweating this one out. An unusual adversary, your Adam Corey.'

A pair of bronze doors at the far end of the gallery opened and one of Adam Corey's private secretaries came forward to usher the two men into The Corey Trust boardroom.

It was Ed Osborne who was taken aback at what he saw upon entering the room, although Ralph Werfel was not. The room was empty except for two men and a woman: Adam Corey, his faithful servant Turhan, and his private secretary Edelson.

Osborne had expected at least eighteen to twenty people. What was the guy playing at? He hoped Corey wasn't foolish enough to spin out the takeover in the hope of gaining time to work out tactics to prevent the raid. That was futile and Osborne was prepared to tell him so straight out.

Twenty-two years working with Adam had taught Ralph a great deal about the man. When he saw the boardroom empty except for Adam standing at the head of the famous Corey Trust boardroom table, an imposing thirty-foot long slab of six-inch-thick, petrified California redwood, Ralph guessed he had him – if not ready to sign, then certainly bloodied, bowed and on the run.

If he wasn't, then where was Josh, and where was Adam's sister and the other shareholders? And where were his executive board, The Corey Trust's lawyers, bankers, accountants? Ralph smiled and told himself, 'The sonovabitch has gone down without a fight because that sharp prick knows he can't win. We've made him an offer he really can't refuse.'

The table-end was wide enough to seat three people comfortably, and it was there that Adam chose to have placed Georgian wing-chairs for the three of them. Turhan was behind his employer, and the faithful Edelson, pad and pencil in hand, stood close by. It was evident to Ralph from the way the documents, pots of ink, containers of sharp pencils, carafes of iced water and glasses, stacks of blank white paper, and the portfolio on the takeover bid were laid out in front of each chair that Adam intended to sit between himself and Ed Osborne. Adam's place had in addition a cordless telephone. The other twenty chairs around the table were to remain empty: the places directly in front of them were not set for a meeting.

'Shrewd and cunning as ever,' thought Ralph.

'Divide and rule.' Ralph was annoyed: eye-contact with one's associate was always an asset in negotiations. Adam had blocked that.

Was Adam going to make the deal there and then, or announce that he was going to fight the takeover right down the line to the New York County Court House. Whatever the man had decided to do, he was well and truly in trouble. Ralph hoped that Adam would be sensible and take the easy option.

The two men approached Adam. Ralph was pleased to see that he looked beaten – the calm, cool facade was still intact, but beneath that the man had to be upset. It gave Ralph Werfel a great deal of satisfaction to see Adam that way, and the impetus to grind him further into the ground, if possible. After Ed Osborne had been introduced to Adam, it was a very aggressive Ralph Werfel who spoke.

'Delighted you've found the package we put together for this takeover well enough constructed to make a deal without the interference of our army of advisers, lawyers, and stockholders. You may not believe this, Adam, but I didn't want to fight you on this.'

'That's too bad because I would have enjoyed beating the shit out of you.'

And with that Adam hit him in the face with a succession of quick, sharp right-jabs, and one powerful punch to Ralph's belly. The Mark Cross, pigskin attaché case flew into the air and crashed to the floor. The buttons on his jacket popped and shot across the room. Winded, Ralph went down like a sack of flour. Amazement distorted his now painful and bruised face.

Ed Osborne went through several shades of white,

but he did not move to help his associate. He managed to stand fast. He watched Adam pull Ralph up off the floor by bunching his shirt and jacket together over the man's pained and bruised solar plexus with one hand, and by the scruff of his collar with the other.

'For Christ's sake,' Ed said, 'don't hit him again. Are you some kind of sadistic weirdo or just a thug? We came here to talk through a business deal, not to play out some cheap version of the shoot-out at the O.K. Corral. Now, you sonovabitch, we're talking assault and battery.'

Ralph, speechless and trying to get his breath back, was dangling from Adam's hands like a rag doll. Adam pulled him, rubbery legs and perfectly polished English hand-made shoes dragging along the pale marble floor, over to one of the wing chairs and shoved him into it, saying over his shoulder, 'Turhan, see to it that Mr Osborne stays seated. Either peaceably or otherwise.' With his hands under Ralph's arms, Adam pulled the moaning man up in the chair into a sitting position, took the handkerchief from Ralph's pocket, and pulling the man's head back by a handful of his hair, wiped the trickle of blood from just above his lip. He picked Ralph's hand up and, putting the handkerchief in it, placed the injured man's hand, none too gently, up to his nostrils.

'You had better keep that there, Ralph,' Adam said. 'I've broken your nose. "*Our* army of advisors, lawyers, and stockholders". No, not "*our*", "*your*" is how you should have put that. You and I share *nothing* anymore. You're fired.' Then to the devoted Mrs Edelson, who still stood with her back turned to the sordid scene, he said, 'You can turn around now,

102

Edelson. I think a snifter of my Napoleon Brandy might be in order. Always a favourite with Mr Werfel, and I would like him to leave this office with an agreeable taste on his tongue. Oh, you had better pour one for his accomplice as well.'

'I don't believe this,' Osborne said indignantly. 'What's going on? We're here to talk high finance, not play walk-on parts in your B-movie.'

The snifters were placed in front of the two men, and with trembling hands Ralph lifted his to his mouth and slowly drank.

'Ralph, are you able to get out of here?' asked Ed, bending forward and looking past Adam to the injured man. 'Oh Christ, your nose is coming up like an onion. Your face is one hell of a mess.'

Adam, too, looked at Ralph. 'Why, so it is. That's what happens when you get a broken nose. Always looks worse than it is. A small ice pack for Mr Werfel, Turhan.'

'You'll pay for this, Adam, and dearly. Shit, you've loosened my teeth. Dear God, will I make you pay for this!' Ralph winced as the brandy stung the cuts in his mouth.

'I figure I already have paid for my little punch-up with you, and heavily. Not only in monetary terms, but in the damage you have done behind my back. We've got eighty-five subsidiaries in this Trust. In any number of them, you've either shed labour or cut overheads or sold off surplus capacity to release cash for fresh acquisitions. And you have kept the board in the dark about all your manoeuvres.'

'The board? You mean you. The board never complained about the financial growth of The Corey Trust,' Ralph said.

'Because the other members of the board, like me, have had the facts of that growth concealed from them. You are not the man I once knew and trusted. And I reckon that one of my greater losses in this treacherous incident. You have become a sleazy asset-stripper with nothing on your mind but mergers and acquisitions and scant interest in what your target companies actually do. You – who profess in a raft of paperwork how intensely interested you are in their financial potential.

'If you wanted to emulate men like Slater and Hanson and a whole slew of operators who believe in management by numbers, you should have squared it with me, not stolen from me. We could have parted as gentlemen, not barbarians. Unless we resolve the situation you have placed The Corey Trust in, to my satisfaction, right now, here, at this table, I will fight you, Mr Osborne, American Agristar, and this takeover with such vigour that the air will be thick with writs and lawyers for as long as you live.

'I've got just one more thing to say to you both. You have chosen to try and merge my company with American Agristar—'

Ed cut in. 'Which means that The Corey Trust will double in size overnight. Those are high stakes you are up against. And the way we have you nobbled, unless you play our way your chances of winning are minimal and your chances of losing everything are as great as the megabuck deal we're offering. Cool down, Mr Corey, lie back and enjoy the rape is my best advice to you. You might even get to like it.'

Adam gave the man a look of complete disdain, but kept his clenched fists on the table and continued what he was saying.

'—Agristar, whose name is synonymous with about as many negative and questionable practices as constructive and good ones – the most negative of which is its connection with the CIA. You are attempting to drag my company into a situation I will never allow. Politics is not my game; my company is not political. We will never be involved in the politics of any nation, least of all my own country's. I've yet to find out what kind of politics you have wedged us into, but you can be sure that, before you men leave this room, we'll be out of it, along with your raid on my company. Now, shall we begin?'

'This is ridiculous. I'm in no shape to deal with this now, thanks to you, Adam. I need a doctor.'

'Edelson, would you be kind enough to give Mr Werfel two pain-killers and a glass of water. Turhan, look him over. See if he needs a doctor.'

The verdict was that he did not need a doctor until the swelling went down, by which time he might be ready for a plastic surgeon. With that announcement, Adam declared, 'Now, let's not have any more delays. The sooner I get what I want the sooner we will all be able to get out of this room.'

Ed Osborne rose from his seat and began to protest, muttering about hell freezing over. Without even looking at him, Adam reached out from his chair and pushed the man back into it. Ralph Werfel disposed of the ice pack that he had been holding to his bruised face and painfully sat forward. He asked for his briefcase, and removed a contract and tossed it on the table in front of Adam. He seemed to be bouncing back, and with miraculous energy. The shine of hate was in his eyes and on his voice when he spoke.

'Just sign on the dotted line, Adam. You've had your punch-up. Now it's my turn. I will simplify matters for you to save time, and tell you *why* you have to sign,' he said with relish.

Adam called for Turhan to bring a box of cigars, and, while he sat back and prepared the vintage Havana and lit it, he listened.

'The Corey Trust is crippled with debts. It is threatened by "excessive risk-taking", a result of the subsidiary companies financing takeovers with borrowed money. They are vulnerable now to an economic downturn. Come the slightest recession, these corporations could never meet their interest payments on those debts. Result? Loan defaults. At the moment, sixty-eight per cent of The Corey Trust's corporations are unable to make needed investments in their basic businesses. It's quite simple: their equity has been stripped away and replaced with high-cost debt.'

'There are all kinds of corporate debt. You are loaded with the worst kind,' said Ed Osborne, taking over from Ralph. 'Junk bonds, high-yielding IOUs with low credit-ratings that we frequently use to finance acquisitions. Your companies are so strapped for cash they can't pay interest to their bondholders. A matter of days, maybe a week in some cases, before they default. If you sell off, merge with us, and sign this contract, in a matter of hours the junk bonds will be paid off, and those corporations in trouble will be solvent, The Corey Trust will have more than doubled in value, and will flourish under American Agristar's umbrella.'

Adam puffed on his cigar, then scraped back his chair and walked across the polished marble floor to

106

the window. He stood there for a few minutes contemplating his situation. Far more disturbed than he could have ever imagined himself to be in this or any other business situation, he returned to his chair. The lack of ethics in the merger and takeover of industry got under his skin. More especially, the shoddy and nasty tactics used primarily by Ralph on The Corey Trust. He laid his cigar down in the large, square rock crystal ash-tray and pushed the contract away from him.

'I am not going to sign this document. I do not submit to blackmail.'

'Who said anything about blackmail?' shot back Ed Osborne. 'Christ, why are you taking this so personally? This is big business 1980s style. If you don't like it, you don't want to play, then here's your chance to get out.'

Ralph assessed the situation, surprised that Adam was going to fight on a loser's ticket. It was about as odd as Adam wading into him with his fists.

'You do understand, Adam, that it's too late for you to swallow the "poison pill",' Ralph said. 'The time's gone by when you could defend by the typical takeover defence of loading up The Corey Trust with new debt to save it from a takeover by American Agristar. We all know what the result of that would be: its credit rate would fall and the price of its existing bonds would decline. Okay, so the bond-holders would take a bath: it happens in nearly every takeover anyway. The deal is financed with huge borrowings that take a toll on the old bonds of The Corey Trust and American Agristar. It won't save you.'

'Neither one of you men seem to understand I don't

need saving. Edelson, please ask Carmel Colsen to come in.'

The moment Ralph Werfel heard the name, he knew something was going very wrong. Ed began to speak and Ralph stopped him.

'Ed, I think we have stated our position and we have said enough. It's best to wait for Miss Colsen and see what she has to say. Miss Colsen is—'

'You don't have to tell me who Miss Colsen is, Ralph, I have been in battle before with the lady. Not a happy experience. As a corporate lawyer, they don't come tougher or smarter, as a worthy opponent, more difficult and ruthless. You surprise me, Mr Corey. With due respect to the lady, you have chosen badly. You need a good negotiator. Carmel Colsen is an aggressor. She's best going for the jugular, not so good in the defensive position.'

Adam looked at the man next to him. He had nothing further to say to him. As far as Adam was concerned he had said the last word on the matter. The rest was up to Carmel Colsen. The men remained silent.

The room suddenly seemed hushed, except for the rapid click of Carmel Colsen's heels on the hard surface of the floor and the muffled whisper of Edelson reporting the events that had taken place between the three men, as she padded along in her sensible flat, rubber-soled shoes next to the attractive, sleek lawyer, dressed all in black. Her hair was shining and pulled back in a large elegant twist at the nape of her neck. She wore earrings of large priceless pearls set in a black enamel circle, a silk dress with a low V-neckline and cinched in tightly at the waist by a ten-inch wide belt of soft leather that shone like satin, stockings like smoke and shoes of patent leather.

Adam Corey eyed Carmel Colsen. It was always a delight to watch one whose looks and movements reminded him of a sleek black panther. Her rapier mind fascinated him, and her body like that of an amazon – huge breasts, tiny waist and wide pelvis – strong feline face – always excited him. He leaned back in the needlepoint wing chair, his arms crossed over his chest, his cigar between his fingers, and waited for her to cross the long room to him.

There was an awkward silence as Carmel Colsen placed her large, soft, Loewe leather envelope case on the conference table and began to remove several documents, stacking them neatly in front of her. She also took out a long slim Japanese lacquer box, opened it and retrieved fountain pens, three of them, which she laid out neatly one next to the other in front of her. Her movements were mesmerizing, and her actions somewhat like a ritualistic oriental preparation for battle. She had all three men's complete attention and she hadn't yet said a word. Then she turned to Ralph.

'Mr Werfel, was it a sporting accident?'

Ralph was decidedly uncomfortable. He was still in a good deal of pain. He removed the handkerchief from under his nose and tucked it into the inside pocket of his jacket. 'No,' he answered, 'very unsporting, I'd say. It was a cut-and-dried case of unprovoked assault and battery. With witnesses.'

Carmel chose to ignore that, and the insinuation that he had damages on his mind, and asked, 'Are you in much pain?'

Ralph lied. 'No, I have taken some pain-killers.'

Carmel shuffled through half a dozen papers,

found the one she was looking for, and walked the few feet that separated them. She placed the paper neatly in front of him and looked past Ralph directly into Adam's eyes. The look was calculated to tell Adam that she was in control and he should sit back and remain silent. Then, still standing above Ralph, she said, 'Good, that you took those pills. This will not be so painful for you.'

She returned to her seat, and while Ralph was reading the paper placed before him, she handed two copies to Edelson and said, 'Copies for Mr Corey and Mr Osborne, please.'

Ed Osborne spoke up. 'Look, Colsen, before a lot of paper starts getting passed around, I would like to know who you represent here? I was under the impression that the Trust's legal department were in charge of this merger. My offices have not been informed otherwise.'

Before she answered Ed, Carmel picked up one of the red enamel Dupont fountain pens, unscrewed the top, placed it on the end of the pen and again stood up and went to Ralph's side. She placed the tip of her long, red, polished fingernail on a dotted line and said, 'Just sign here Mr Werfel,' and placed the pen down on the table next to the paper. Looking not at Ralph but at Ed Osborne, she added, 'There is no merger, Osborne. There will be no takeover of The Corey Trust by American Agristar. Not today, not tomorrow, not ever.'

She returned to her chair. 'I have the shareholders of The Corey Trust and the Trust's legal advisers waiting in another conference room. I've afforded you the courtesy of not calling them in, at Mr Corey's request. He would like to keep what transpires here private, for the sake of all parties concerned. It is not his intention to ruin you, merely to save his company and undo the damage you have caused by your greed for power. And he intends to do it with or without your help. Preferably with. The degree of cooperation you give him is the deciding factor in the steps he will allow me to take in order to bring you before the Civil and Federal Courts, the Securities and Exchange Commission, and a Congressional committee where you will have to try to explain to them and the world's press what you have done.'

'Oh, you're good, Colsen, very good, but you haven't got a chance in hell of pulling that off.' Ed Osborne sat back laughing at the attorney, casually picking up the paper Edelson had put in front of him and starting to read it. His laughter trickled away and finally ceased entirely by the time he was just half way down the page. He stopped reading and shot an angry look across the table at the beautiful, threatening woman.

'A short and simple document, well to the point, don't you think?' Carmel Colsen asked. 'I have a similar sort of statement for you to sign too, Osborne. Edelson, this original to Mr Osborne, and the copies to Mr Corey and Mr Werfel.' She passed the papers to the secretary, who was looking a great deal happier.

'Colsen, you're crazy. Out of your mind. You have no basis for issuing such a statement as this for me to sign, no proof of what this statement insinuates. It's all a big bluff. You won't save The Corey Trust this way. Why, you couldn't – even if your allegations were true, which they are not,' said a furious and worried Ralph.

'Okay, that's it, Werfel,' said an equally fiery

111

Carmel, slamming the open flat of her hand on the conference table. A loud cracking sound pierced the air and all the pens and paper jumped.

'That statement I want you to sign says, in essence, that as the Vice President of The Corey Trust you have over-stepped your authority, and to such an extent that the managing director and shareholders ask for your immediate resignation, along with the return of all stock options. You must forfeit any and all contracts between you and other parties that directly or indirectly have anything to do with The Corey Trust, assigning them back to the Trust. Lastly, you must sell any and all of your personal stock in The Corey Trust back to the Trust at today's market price, and before you leave this conference room.

'Out of regard for your twenty-two years of devoted service to the Trust, they are prepared to give you a golden handshake of one million dollars, on the condition that you declare you have abused a basic tenet of US corporate law by not treating all shareholders of The Corey Trust equally and have withheld all the information that has affected the company's stock performance.

'If you have any sense whatsoever, you will sign that document as fast as you can, take the cashier's cheque for the million dollars and leave the country at once. The alternative is not pretty: Prison.

'It is patently clear that the major abuses by you as Vice President of The Corey Trust have come about because you chose to become nothing less than a professional trader acting upon information unavailable to the public about a pending takeover deal. Once you took that step you created a conflict of

112

interest for yourself. Acting as the trader rather than the protector of the Trust, you then, with inside information, and in collaboration with Mr Osborne, a well known raider, fixer of deals, armed with junk bonds, used your position with the Trust deliberately to drive The Corey Trust to merge.'

'You know that's libellous. Prove it, just try to prove it,' Ralph shouted as he jumped to his feet.

Ed Osborne was on his feet too. 'For Christ's sake, Colsen, the minute you walked into the room I knew you were the wrong counsel. You're playing "you've been bad-boys" games and we're talking mega-money deals here. Don't you grasp the situation? The junk bonds are The Corey Trust's death knell. This merger has got to take place. Unless of course you have a "white knight", to buy the Trust right out of this so-called corporate raid. Either put up or shut up.'

No one spoke. Osborne poured himself a glass of water, drank it and sat down. Once Ralph was seated again as well, Carmel Colsen rose and, palms of her hands on the table in front of her, leaned dramatically forward to face the three men, now seated before her. She said, very calmly, but with a voice that dripped disdain. 'I do not have to *prove* anything, not a single thing, to you men. You had your eyes on power and money. So you made such blatantly criminal moves that you have done all the work for me. Your rampant inside-trading has overshot. You had the gall to think you didn't need to cover your tracks. The cushy executive contract that was to be enforced once your merger was approved for instance. The "golden parachute" package you *gentlemen* awarded your-selves, for $32.8 million, stating that you will leave the company after it is taken over by American Agristar, is a prime example. Not bad profits, Osborne, for a man who was made an executive, illegally, I might add, just five days ago.'

Ralph Werfel, whose face, in addition to being so swollen now as to be unrecognizable, was ashen pale, was far from crushed. He made a vain attempt to rise and say something, but was stopped by the roar of Carmel's voice.

'Don't you move. Don't say a word. And especially not that as Vice President of The Corey Trust you had every legal right to do as you saw fit for the long term health of the Trust. That right was revoked when The Corey Trust needed to use a "shark repellent" and changed their bylaws to ward off predators. The bylaws of the Trust you protected yourself with have been null and void for some considerable time. If you should have any question about that, forget it. I have a civil court writ against you, a federal court writ against you, and a SEC subpoena for questioning, in the hands of three law officers. They're in the conference room waiting to be called in here to present them. You have no choice. Either of you.'

'You'll pay for this, Corey. You may have blown my deal, but no one dumps on American Agristar and gets away with it,' Ed Osborne said as he shoved papers into his Gucci case. 'They want some of your Trust's holdings and they will get them one way or another. You can bet your bottom dollar on that. You may be rid of us and our deal, buster, but you still haven't saved your company. Unless you do have a "white knight". And I doubt that.'

'Can't we talk about this alone, Adam?' asked a distraught and confused Ralph.

'No. It's all been said.'

'You wouldn't have come out so badly. Wealthier and more powerful than you have ever been or hoped to be. Is that so bad?'

Adam pushed back his chair and stood up looking down at the man he once trusted so completely. Ralph Werfel cowered in his chair, and put his arms up to his face as if to protect himself. Adam read the fear in the man's eyes, reached out and gently lowered Ralph's arms. Adam shook his head in disbelief.

'It's over, Ralph. You have nothing more to fear from me. For my part, we will keep this scandal as quiet as possible. I suggest you do the same. Not for my sake, for yours. Just go away. I don't ever want to see or hear from you again.'

Adam walked from the boardroom.

After Ed and Ralph had signed several documents, one a waiver of all rights to sue Adam Corey for assault and battery, Carmel Colsen passed the cashier's cheque to Ralph Werfel.

'Now, Mr Corey would like you to leave the building. Turhan, would you see these men to the street?'

Chapter 7

Josh found his father sitting on his favourite bench in Central Park. It was just inside the park, near the Plaza Hotel. From that particular bench Adam, surrounded by trees and grass and shrubs, could feel the buzz of the city and see the whizz of the traffic plying Fifth Avenue, hear the muffled sounds of the city and the water splashing in the fountain in The Grand Army Plaza to the side of the hotel.

There were other things Adam enjoyed from that vantage point: the scent of the fresh green of the park diffusing the exhaust fumes of the buses, taxis, and cars, the line of horse-drawn carriages waiting to drive romantics through the park, that zone of green within the steel and glass city that Marlo referred to as 'an adult's answer to Alice in Wonderland', or 'Decadent Disneyland'. Her occasional cablegram, 'Arriving Decadent Disneyland faster than March hare', meant she'd be in New York within hours. Then there were the joggers and the runners going by in the park, and the sleekly-groomed beauties of New York, clicking along the pavement in their high heels.

All kinds of women, luscious and less than luscious alike, rushed around the streets nearest the Plaza: into Bergdorfs, out of Bergdorfs; in and out of F.A.O. Shwarz, up and down Fifth Avenue they rushed. In for the hair, out for shopping. In for a facial, out for more shopping and another designer shopping bag. In for a pedicure, out for what? More shopping.

Delicious women, loaded with pretty boxes and shopping bags, taking only enough time out from New York's main occupation to go up the stairs of the Hotel Plaza for mid-day sex or lunch: a cheese souffle? a Caesar salad? Oysters Casino? If in season. Crab salad if not. Down the stairs to finish the day off. How? Shopping, of course.

An army of fast-moving, intelligent, interesting, clever survivors in Halstons and Tregers, and Calvin Kleins, and Ralph Laurens, and Saint Laurents, and Lagerfelds and whatever other label of *haute couture* was being thrust upon them by the '*treasure* of a saleslady'. Frequenting the *top* and most assuredly *right* Department Stores, the fashion cathedrals – Bergdorfs, Bendels, and Bonwits – where the faithful worshipped with their credit cards.

Adam never tired of watching the streets, dense with women and a smattering of his own sex. It had changed little in the twenty-five years he had enjoyed his bench; but the women had: they were more exciting. The vast platoon of attractive women around the Plaza were no longer just wealthy wives, mistresses, girlfriends. It was well peppered with successful lady executives, professional women, artists, secretaries with more power than their bosses, who carried themselves proudly twice over: first for being a woman, and second for not having to be *just* a woman.

Adam adored them. He smiled to himself thinking

of the many delightful women he had spotted and picked up over the years from his bench. Ah, there was nothing like the wonderful romantic interlude. It was irreplaceable. It encapsulated everything exciting about romance for a man: the courtship, the chase, immediacy, conquest, sexual involvement without emotional involvement; intimacy, without being intimate. Being understood without having to talk about your feelings. No threat of demands for honesty and openness that women are so fond of imposing. Freedom from having to open up and love. Most of all the thrill of the unexpected, and the brevity of an interlude.

Adam bought an iced yoghurt from a vendor peddling past the bench, leaned back and with his eyes followed a young beauty with blonde hair, tall and slender as a willow. In a thin white cotton dress with the sun behind it, her $5000 an hour *mannequin*'s body was revealed. When she turned around to apologize to a man she bumped into, Adam had a glimpse of that American-beauty type face, born, bred, and fed in the country's corn-belt, honed and tanned into the California calendar girl, who still, with or without her clothes, looked fresh from the fields. He registered her as perfect material for the romantic idyll, but that was all, because his eyes settled upon another candidate walking up the Avenue.

She was older, extremely well turned-out in a red linen jacket that hugged her every curve, and a black linen skirt that moulded itself around her. Her legs were a marvel – long, bare and shapely. She was sauntering along the Avenue, window-shopping, in a pair of tarty black, high-heeled sandals with an ankle-strap tied in a small leather bow.

Every step she took, every movement of her body was luscious and sensuous, and, when he caught a glimpse of her face, its beautiful features were bathed in a light of mingled liveliness and serenity. Or was it that contentment which comes from the depths of the soul? Yes, that was what made her stand out from the other women: she wore her rich soul like a second skin 'for the world's eyes'. She was fearless.

A mulatto youth was roller-skating past the bench, arms flailing about, for balance and speed. Adam reached out and grabbed his arm.

'Hey, Mister, watcha do that for? I ain't bothering no one. I got as much right here as you do. Let go!'

'I didn't mean to frighten you, fella. Do you want to make ten dollars?'

'You ain't gettin' dirty, are ya, Mister? Le'me go.'

'No, I'm not getting dirty, I'll pay you ten dollars to catch up with a woman across the street and give her this note.' Adam let go of the boy's arm and reached for the small Cartier note-pad and his pen in the breast pocket of his jacket.

'Which woman?'

Adam pointed her out and was not surprised when the boy spotted her immediately. He quickly scribbled out a note.

'Tha's all I gotta do for the tenner?'

'That's all for the tenner. But, for another twenty, after you give her the note, you skate like hell over to that flower shop' – he pointed to the florist's window – 'and give them this note. They'll give you a bunch of flowers. She'll be coming your way, so skate back and place them in her arms.'

'Listen, Mister, that's a lotta fast'n' fancy footwork for thirty bucks. Forty.'

Adam handed the boy two twenty-dollar bills. The lad snapped the money out of his hands with the notes and was off at high speed, now both legs and arms flailing, his bulging, satiny shorts in lime, and shocking pink trunk-top iridescent in the sun. Over his shoulder he shouted, 'My old man says there's a sucker born every minute. And my old man sure is right. I hope I never fall in love like you, Mister. It makes a real sucker of ya!'

Watching the encounter while walking towards his father, Josh took it all in with a grin. 'Do you think it's true, Papa, that love turns you into a sucker?' Then he sat down next to his father, laughing.

The pair of them avidly watched the young man's progress out of Central Park. With scant regard for the afternoon traffic and the screaming horns, he weaved across Fifth Avenue, answering the abusive drivers with a bang on their fenders or an elaborate hand, arm and elbow movement which read, fuck you.

'An afternoon idyll, Papa?'

'That's right.'

'Do you mind if I ask what you said in the note? You know how I pride myself on "like father, like son", and for that I need all the tips I can get.'

Adam took his eyes off the roller-skating messenger to look at his son with a smile. 'Is a father's work never done? From what I saw pass between you and Carmel over luncheon, I would say you need no tips from your dad. You seem to be doing quite well on your own. And anyway, let's just see if I score with the lady. If I do, then I promise you an introduction, and you can ask her to show you the note.'

They watched the boy approach his quarry. She was distracted by something in a window. He tapped her on the shoulder and spoke to her. With a courtly bow he handed her Adam's note, than took off as fast as he could across the crowded pavement towards the florist's shop.

The woman scanned the faces in the crowd, seeking the author before she opened the small folded piece of paper. Then she eyed the crowd once more, read it again and slipped it into her shoulder bag.

'He did that rather well, don't you think?' Adam asked his son.

'Rather well is an understatement. Sure as hell I thought he'd skate off with your money. How the heck did you know he would follow through, Papa?'

Adam laughed, 'Because everyone loves a lover, sucker or not. Because everyone goes for romance. In romance there is hope and escape. Because the romantic at work is a high-jumper, with his heart on his sleeve. And any half-black, half-white kid who dresses like that boy, doing New York City on rollerskates, is a romantic, full of spirit, who will try almost anything for fun and a bit of escape. No great gamble that.'

They continued to watch the woman and waited for further reactions from her. She resumed her walk up the avenue. It brought her past the Grand Army Plaza fountain and closer to Adam and his son. Suddenly all heads were turning around to catch a glance of the mulatto Mercury on skates, arms filled with dozens of long-stemmed white roses, zig-zagging his way around the pedestrians. He left a comet's tail of smiles lighting a path behind him.

Mirella, her arms filled with the flowers, threw her

head back and laughed. She buried her face in the roses and took in their exquisite sweet scent. She looked and felt radiant, and her joy spilled over to the waiting Mercury, and the passers-by who smiled at her. A few clapped their hands for the romantic gesture.

Mercury appeared to have shed the wings from his heels. He stood next to Mirella as if mesmerized. She chose one of the roses and handed it to the boy.

'A small gesture. My token of thanks to you, Mercury.' Mirella walked to the kerb, anxious to cross the street and meet her capricious lover at the fountain. The boy skated next to her and asked, 'Whyd'ja call me that funny name?'

'Because, he's the one who drops from the sky.'

Mirella stepped off the kerb, and a taxi which had jumped the light whizzed close by her. The boy took her by the elbow and together they hurried across the street. He insisted on accompanying her to the fountain and fussed sensuously around her.

Adam and Josh rose from the bench and started walking towards the fountain, too. Josh was completely admiring of his father.

'Lesson a million-and-I-don't-know-what', Josh said. 'How to keep a wife happy and a marriage new and fresh every day is the question. The answer? Be as much an imaginative lover as a husband.'

'And have a wife like Mirella,' Adam added.

Josh followed Mirella with his eyes, and thought her glorious, as he did whenever he saw her. Memories of when he whisked her away from Rashid and held her in his arms and they danced together, returned to him much too often. There was little he could do about that. He had fallen in love with her just as his father had, and he had come to terms with that, and the fact that he would love her the best way he could under the circumstances. He felt the same joy as his father, watching her hurry towards an afternoon assignation, and loved his father even more for having brought Mirella into the family. He would share her with Adam and the rest of the clan, because that was as it had to be. But he was secretly determined never to share her with another man, and most certainly not Rashid, who suddenly had become a constant presence in the lives of Adam and Mirella, something he could not understand.

They waited on the corner for the traffic lights to change, and Adam diverted his attention from Mirella and their Mercury to Josh.

'Josh, were you looking for me for any particular reason?'

'Yes, there has been a telex from Geneva. Your mysterious "white knight" has saved us. The money has been made available to the Trust, and our offices are picking up all the junk bonds as fast as they can, as per your instructions. Adam, who is this "white knight", and why have they come to The Corey Trust's rescue?'

Josh was astonished at the look that passed across his father's face. One of such relief that only then did Josh realize how much pressure his father had been under. Adam was so controlled, so well equipped to handle catastrophe, that it never occurred to Josh that the danger The Corey Trust had been through could affect his father as much as it apparently had. It puzzled Josh.

One of The Corey Trust's pet companies was a crisis-management group called Corey & Corey

International Industrial Consultants. Josh had taken over the company from Adam only a year before, when Josh had decided to work for The Corey Trust. CCIIC was a pioneer in the field of coping with catastrophe. They had been responsible for crisis management becoming the new corporate discipline. They were the developers of detailed planning to cope with crises from industrial accidents, product recalls, terrorist attacks to any natural disaster on any scale. And the creator, the compelling ideas man behind CCIIC had been Adam Corey.

Josh never worried about Adam when the raid on The Corey Trust came to light because he knew his father would practise what he had always preached: for an executive confronted by a sudden catastrophe, it is the element of surprise that is the most unsettling aspect; the wisest of executives is susceptible to paralysis when a crisis strikes. Adam would avoid those pitfalls.

Being unprepared was the worst part of a crisis: remove the unexpected, and the unnerving element is expelled with it. Josh had watched his father put that into effect, and learned much from the way Adam had communicated with all parties concerned, planning everything to the last detail in order to quash the attempted takeover. Adam, though emotionally involved, had the much-needed objectivity to win through. There had been no sitting on his hands waiting for the problems in the Trust to sort themselves out. He had taken charge. No evasion by Adam, no hiding from disaster. He had gone into action immediately and investigated in minute detail the causes. That and his White Knight had saved their huge conglomerate.

Whatever had passed across Adam's face that astonished Josh was now gone. Adam smiled, ran the fingers of his right hand through his hair, a gesture familiar to his son, who in fact had picked up the habit, and answered at last. 'The "white knight" is a Geneva-based holding company dealing mostly in agri-business all over the African continent. It's a multinational conglomerate, a private company not unlike ours. Why did they rescue us? What you should have asked is why and how were they able to warn us about an impending disaster before we ourselves were able to get wind of it, *and* rescue us. And on our terms – which were fair, but hardly as advantageous to them as they might have been. I'm not quite certain I have the answer to those questions, but I'm sure as hell going to find them out.'

The two men crossed the street and were walking in front of the Plaza Hotel.

'I can only guess some of the reasons. One is that my father, your grandfather, had always been a good friend to several of the companies held by our "white knight" in their early days when they were struggling to emerge from Africa into an international market-place. And so have I. We have funded them, have trouble-shot for them, made gifts to them, but not for a very long time, many years. As you well know, we still have close friends and retain strong ties with Egypt, the Sudan, Ethiopia, Somaliland, and deeper into Africa. Maybe they have just never forgotten us, and the fact that we were there for them when they needed us. Loyalty? Friendship? It's possible, even in this day and age. Rare, but possible.

'There is another reason, one that is very interesting and could explain it. But one that I like far less.

126

It's quite possible that both the raid on our company and our "white knight" were politically motivated. After all, one facet of the early tip-off from them was that CIA money was funding the takeover. With 2.5 million acres of land in Europe, Africa, Central America and the US owned by The Corey Trust and out of the hands of any government, our policy of remaining neutral and stubbornly independent from politics could be a very good reason for all our troubles. Interesting theory, don't you think, Josh?'

Josh nodded.

The two men were greeted by the doorman. Then they gave their attention back to Mirella and 'the boy with wings on his heels', who were by now coming around the fountain and were visible from the flight of stairs leading into the hotel. Adam's heart soared at the sight of them and he took the stairs two at a time into the hotel, Josh at his side. He booked a suite of rooms for the night and ordered flowers, champagne, caviar, and asked for the key, then walked through the lobby and re-emerged from the hotel.

Father and son stood on the top step looking at Mirella, who was standing at the edge of the fountain, a delectable lady carrying roses, the cascading water behind her, waiting for her lover to sweep her further into a romantic idyll. It was an image so out of context with the hustle-bustle of the steely city around her that it excited the senses, wiped out the world and made the heart sing for a split second.

The doorman looked up at the men, was about to ask them if they wanted a cab, but the look in their eyes told him a cab was not on their minds, and instead he followed their gaze. He saw Mirella, and suppressed a sigh of admiration and envy for the man who could remain romantic in New York and find time for love in the afternoon.

He was about to turn away and give his attentions to the queue of impatient people waiting for a cab, when he saw a boy on roller-skates close to Mrs Corey wheel around and approach her. Alarmed he put his whistle to his mouth, raised his arm to signal and stepped off the kerb into the street, ready to dash to her rescue. He felt a hand on his shoulder.

'Thanks, Jim,' Adam said, 'that won't be necessary. We know the boy.'

The three men watched as the boy stopped in front of Mirella, took her hand, bent to kiss it, then backed off with a gallant bow from the waist and slowly skated away, leaving Mirella aglow with laughter, waving goodbye after him.

'Josh, that's some special kid there. Do you think we could find a place for him in our organization?'

'Just what I was thinking, Papa. I'll go after him and see what he's all about.'

Adam shook his son's hand and patted him on the shoulder. 'You were terrific during our crisis, Josh. I could never have come through without you and Carmel. Thanks. I'll call you tomorrow,' and he walked out into the street towards his romantic *rendezvous*.

'Papa,' Josh called. 'The note. You said you would have Mirella show me the note, if you scored.'

'So I did, Josh.'

As Josh walked back to his father's side he saw a softness of erotic desire in his eyes as they sought out the woman waiting for him.

'Never mind, Papa. Not the right moment,' said Josh, who suddenly felt acutely embarrassed for

wanting to intrude into Mirella and Adam's masquer-
ade of seduction. It was the love that Josh sensed
vibrating between his father and Mirella, not the
passion, which ruffled Josh, made him feel an
intruder in his father's little make believe assignation.

The two men parted, Josh in one direction and
Adam in the direction of Mirella. Josh walked quickly
after Mercury, who was now poised at the corner as
the lights changed. He was disturbed. For the first
time Josh was deeply touched by the power of love
combined with passion. He had sensed something of
it at the wedding two weeks before, but had thought
he was being carried away by the excitement of the
occasion and two people committing themselves to
each other for all the days of their lives. But this was
something different. More profound. So personal,
private, intimate even, as to inspire a deep unease in
Josh. He realized for the first time that he might be
bypassing something rare and wonderful that should
be fundamental and yet for him was not.

When he had found his father on the bench cruising
the beautiful New York women, he was amused, but
not surprised. He knew his father well. Had grown
up, since the age of three, without his own mother,
yet among the women his father had loved. Over the
years, he had seen Adam, though loving those
women, drift into the odd romantic interlude, the
short liaison, the discreet one-night stand, which had
never affected his father's feelings for those women,
or the unconventional living-space he created with
them for himself and his children.

When Adam had, by chance, spied his own wife
Mirella among the crowds on the pavement and
selected her for his romantic interlude, Josh thought

it utterly charming of him. That should have told him something, but it didn't. It only amused Josh, who went along with the pretence that Mirella was a stranger his father was picking up.

Josh realized there was no place for him in their game only after he caught the look in his father's eyes, when Josh had demanded his father fulfil his promise and show him the note Mercury had delivered to Mirella. At first he had thought that husband and wife were playing the game, and as son and stepson, he could tease them about it. But he had been wrong.

They were two passionate strangers looking for the excitement of romance and an erotic coming-together, stealing away from their life as husband and wife for a few hours or days. Two people wanting to deliver themselves totally in sexual pleasure to each other, where nothing of who they were or what they were would come into it. Where they could in a sense die to their selves, and to their passion, and reincarnate again and again.

It was real and profound love that emanated from both Adam and Mirella: the joy of total submission to another that Josh glimpsed in his father's eyes, and was exhaled from every pore of Mirella's being, and it quite shocked him. He stole one last glance at the two lovers in the moment of their meeting at the fountain. He felt his chest tighten with the pain of never having experienced what he saw them now sharing.

The reality of their love and erotic passion had not only touched his deeper emotions, but also had illuminated the effect his father's commitment with Mirella had begun to stir in him. He was in love with his step-mother.

Words of Deena at the wedding about Adam,

Mirella and Rashid kept dimly nudging his memory. While he was talking to Mercury, he was trying to remember them exactly, but they still eluded him.

He could remember vividly standing with Deena and Brindley amongst the other guests in the road strewn with peony petals, in front of the white clapboard church. He was feeling happy, almost euphoric, as if high on some drug, better than that even. He kept glancing up at Mirella and his father, who were still on the landing in front of the entrance, accepting the good wishes of guests leaving the church.

Clear as the setting might be to Josh, Deena's words escaped him: they simply would not come into focus. They were there on the edge of his mind, on the edge of remembrance. He felt Mercury pull at his coat sleeve and say, 'D'ya mean it?'

Josh's attention was yanked back to Mercury,

'Mean what, Mercury?'

'Just as I thought. You're bullshitting me, man. There ain't no "opportunity to better myself" bullshit job waiting for me. My old man's right about three hundred and sixty-five suckers gettin' themselves born every goddam year. Every week, more like. And I'm sure as hell today's sucker. Ya had me goin' there for a minute, thinkin' this my lucky day, man. First yer old man's forty bucks and his romantic number, then you, spinnin' out that . . .'

'Hey, listen, I'm sorry, Mercury. Look, I was distracted for a minute, a long way off in my head. I do mean it. Come to my office tomorrow morning at eleven. We can talk better then. My father and I like you and the way you handle yourself. We have a big company and maybe we can find a place for you. We

131

have all kinds of programmes for young people wanting to get on in the world. Programmes where we pay to train you, and you come into the company later to work for us.'

Josh turned the boy around and used his back to support a notepad on which Josh jotted down how to contact The Corey Trust. Then he handed it to the young man. Josh smiled and patted him on the shoulder.

'You see, Mercury. Fathers get it wrong sometimes. It could just be your lucky day after all.'

Josh started walking away from him, and Mercury shifted on his skates and said, 'You gonna let me ask you a question?'

'Sure, one. The rest tomorrow, okay?'

'Right. Do I have to be called Mercury?'

Josh laughed, 'Well, it's not a bad name. But no, of course not. Not unless you want to. By the way, what do you call yourself?'

'Erasmus Luther Goldstein. But my friends call me Ras.'

'Well, Ras. Let's just say, with a name like that, you might consider it.'

Josh walked away, searching his memory for Deena's remark, which had suddenly come to seem terribly important to him.

All the way back to his office, Josh was obsessed with the idea that he had missed something, a vital something, and Deena's words that day at the wedding were the key to it.

He spoke to his secretary, double-checked that the vast staff of men assigned to roll over The Corey Trust's injection of new money furnished by the White Knight for the 'junk bonds' was moving swiftly and successfully, and went back to his office. He tried unsuccessfully to distract himself with work, then finally gave up.

His mind kept homing back in on Mirella and Adam on the stairs of the church, and then his memory would block. Mirella. To be made love to, sexually pampered by a woman like Mirella. A fantasy fulfilled. His father had it right. With the adrenalin still pumping from the drama of the takeover, what better release than an erotic duel? He dialled Carmel Colsen's office – her red telephone, the one she kept locked in the bottom drawer of her desk.

'Hello.'

'Hello, has anything gone wrong?' she asked.

'No, everything is going just as planned.'

'Then why are you calling on the hot line?'

'Because the heat's on. This is the kind of emergency the hot line was set up for.'

Carmel shed her authoritative lawyer's voice, as Josh's sexy tone got through to her. 'So how exactly are things hotting up, Joshua?'

'I want you to make love to me, Carmel, lots of love to me.'

'Oh!'

'Just, oh?'

'No, Joshua, not just Oh. How about, Oh, what a sizzling idea? Or, Oh, I've wanted to love you for a very long time? Or, Oh! how exactly would you like me to make love to you?'

'With total abandon. And that's only to begin with. I am prepared to be a selfish lover today, for you to spoil me, to spread me all over with cream, and caress and knead my slippery flesh with your slender sensuous fingers, then lick it off with your tongue. You can play with me like a cat, rather than the panther I imagine you can be. But if you are very good and would rather have the jungle, I'll take you as that panther and wrestle with you for your life. Then tame you with my cock and my lips so you're all kitten again.'

'Do you really think you can do that, Joshua? Play Tarzan, not Boy, today?'

'Oh, I *know* I can do that, that and much more. Carmel, there is never a time when I see you that I don't think, "She is a wild fierce animal in bed, one to both love and whip into submission. A woman I would like to wring orgasm after orgasm from. A rare species – to master and be mastered by." Shall we give it a go, Carmel?'

'Why not?' said a laughing Carmel, not mocking, but rather filled with sensuality and promise. 'My lair, or yours?' she asked, with a sparkle in her voice, 'and when?'

'Not my place, not your place. Partouz, the best, most discreet bordello in New York. I'll book a room, vodka and caviar, and we'll dine on lovely food, have two gorgeous hookers, skilled in what we want to do and where we want to get to, to excite us on our way. And you: another man? Would you like another man beside me?'

'No, I think not. You're big enough game for me tonight. In an hour?'

'No, that's too long. Now is better. I'll quit at once, and be right around for you by car. Wait at the Fifth Avenue entrance of your building, Carmel, I've wanted you for a long time too.'

Carmel listened briefly to the disconnected whine

134

of the receiver in her hand and then placed it back on its rocker, closed the drawer and locked it. She dropped the key in her open handbag and swung her chair around and faced the window and the New York skyline. Her body tingled with anticipation. She had wanted Adam's young son the first time she saw him; and then, a year later when they met again, she wanted him even more.

Of all the men at the wedding reception it had been Joshua Corey to whom Carmel was attracted. Ten years younger than herself, handsome, with the body of a quarter-back, and a sensitive, intelligent face, courtly European manners mixed on occasion with a mid-western reticence, all glossed over with macho sexuality, he was devastatingly attractive to her.

There was something else about Joshua. He had some of the characteristics of his father, a mystery, and an independence that could almost be called aloofness, a lively inner self and warmth beneath that cool, hard exterior that made them unusual men, and irresistible.

Carmel warmed to Joshua as an international socialite who like his father rarely hit the fast lane of the glamorous jet-setters. Young, fascinating, a man who lived and loved on his own terms and no one else's: Adam's son, and so much like him.

Carmel had suffered her attraction to Joshua in silence. Like the panther she had stalked her prey, bided her time, waited for him to appear at the right moment, in the right place. Until now there had been nothing she could do about it, because he had always managed to elude her. Now he seemed to have delivered himself to her.

She had a weakness for young male flesh, a passion

to be nourished by it, and had, till Josh came along, always known how to get the men she wanted. She was clever in her weakness, and few resisted her. But with Josh it had been different from the outset. She had a fatal attraction towards him, an obsessive infatuation. She wanted, exactly, the sexual life he had evoked for her on the telephone. To make love to him, voyage with him through an erotic land where she could do with him what she wanted, would be the ultimate bliss for her.

Naked, Joshua was a young Grecian god, the epitome of masculine beauty, flesh that cried out for loving. Carmel was tense with erotic ecstasy from the instant she laid her hands on his body, so young, so firm; his skin smooth and supple, vigorously alive, unblemished by time, acted as a drug on her.

He lay quite still on a marble dining table in the centre of the room, the heavy summer rain pounding on the skylight above, a crackling fire to warm him, a satin pillow for his head. Naked and magnificent, Carmel sat astride him, moving her warm moist cunt hungrily back and forth over his body. She was constantly caressing him, pawing him, playing with him, while she licked clean the almond cream with which she had garnished his skin until he was as radiant as live polished marble.

She was extraordinary. She used her tongue sometimes like a feather, other times like a whip, and amazed him when she turned it into a hard and erect instrument she used like a penis to penetrate him wherever she could. And her mouth -- she ate him, sucked up his flesh into her mouth and devoured him, leaving faint bruises and teeth-marks. No part of him escaped her passion.

136

She whimpered like a hurt beast with every orgasm, and, when in a frenzy of lust she plied his most personal orifice open with her tongue and readied him with licks and kisses, she came in an enormous orgasm whose come trickled between the cheeks of his bottom, while she groaned like a great jungle cat.

They were sexual animals, a panther and a tiger, in rut. Joshua had come three times and still she was able to excite him, bring him erect, and rampant. He selfishly wallowed in their mutual orgasms and drifted in and out of ecstasy, never touching her, or pleasuring her. He felt as if flayed by her tongue, as if very soon she would go for him, paralysing him with her lust so she could consume him alive and whole.

It was then that the quiescent animal in him died. Quite suddenly he felt the urge to dominate her with his body. His heart raced with the surging of hot blood through his veins, and his need to take over was acute. He was quite different now: his lustful desire was to bury himself deep inside this woman, this amazing animal, and fuck her slowly, hard and fully, calm her with his cock into passivity, and then bring her back into paroxysms of passion and pleasure his way.

Josh climbed down out of the strange and wonderful never-never land of lust, but only far enough and long enough to take command. He looked into Carmel's hard, passionate face, placed his hands on her shoulders and pushed her back on her haunches, to gain a longer look at the beautiful, wild, depraved woman astride him.

He buried his face between her huge full breasts and caressed them for the first time. His lips covered an erect nipple and he sucked it hard, taking as much flesh into his mouth as possible. And harder, more violently he sucked. She tried to withdraw and Josh slapped the side of her breast sharply, a warning to stay still, never removing his mouth from the exciting breast, his hands pinching, pulling. He released her, disliking her squirming and resistance. But, before she could move away, he grabbed her, crushed her to him and kissed her with a wildness she had not yet known.

He found her sublime. He rolled her over on her back, wanting to take her now more than he had wanted any of the women he had had for a very long time. She fought him, scratched and screamed at him, as if not wanting him to penetrate her. But he would not be put off. He was the tiger and he would take his panther, she would submit to him. He would have his pleasure of her until she liked it, loved it, and would beg for more.

And she did. All through the hours of the night, with their roles now reversed, he mastered her, penetrated her every orifice again and again and filled them with his seed. Josh was not much experienced in the act of sodomy, but while practising it with Carmel, he had never imagined it could be so thrilling, or a woman could want so much to be ravaged in that way. And ravaged she was, having driven him on to a wild frenzy of lust by her words, receptiveness, and reactions.

He was not in heaven and certainly not on earth, but somewhere in between. Nor was he a man. He was more like a beast, a tiger, while he sated her with sex. He only became himself and returned to earth when his orgasm burst forth with hers and she collapsed underneath him, enraptured with pleasure and tears of joy.

They lay like that for some time. Then, having regained his strength and his senses, Josh gently took her in his arms, wanting now to love her, care for her with a sweetness and tenderness he felt for this woman who took him on so sensuous a journey, and whom he had fought, pleasured and conquered.

It was only when they were lying on their sides, she with her back to him, and he kissed her lovingly on her shoulders, her neck, then down her strong feline back and he felt her freeze under his loving touch, that he spoke.

'Please,' he whispered, 'let me love you, hold you, show you tenderness.' And he placed a kiss on her hip.

She pulled away. He tried again, and again she pulled away.

'Leave me alone now, Josh,' she said, still with her back to him. 'I don't want you to be tender and loving, I only get pleasure from that if it comes from young beautiful women. I'm telling you now, because I have stronger feelings for you than I want to have, and I don't want to deceive you, not now after these exquisite hours with you, not ever, but that's the way I am.'

Josh was not shocked, but surprised and a bit sad, because he really did want to show her some tender loving. He was not by nature a selfish man. Spoiled by women all his life, yes, but himself generous and kind.

He rose from the blue-fox rug in front of the fire and went first to telephone for two young and very accomplished, beautiful Partouz ladies of the night.

Then he walked to the console table against the wall. While watching in the mirror above it the extra-ordinary Carmel, lying very still on the fur rug, the firelight dancing patterns over her naked supine body, he opened a fresh bottle of Dom Pérignon and poured two glasses.

The two girls entered the room. He whispered something to each of them and they walked with him to the fireplace. He squatted down facing Carmel, and placed a gentle hand on her shoulder and handed her one of the glasses. Their eyes met.

'You are a lovely lady, Carmel,' Josh said, 'and I want to give you what makes you happy. Otherwise why should two people be together even for one night?'

While he spoke, one of the girls, a seventeen-year-old blonde gamine, silently slithered down amongst the blue fox pelts tight up against Carmel's back and slid an arm around her and caressed her breasts, kissing her with the tenderness Josh had hoped he might show her. He saw a change in the expression of her eyes, one of thanks mixed with pleasure, and they each drank from their own glass.

Josh lay down on the low, white suede sofa close to the couple making love, with the other young woman. He kissed her and fondled her, showing her the affection he felt for women that he wanted to give to Carmel. Between sips of champagne, he watched the couple on the floor.

Josh was one of those men who enjoyed seeing two women make love. He found it very beautiful, and also very sensual. Most of all, he enjoyed it when he had, as he did now, a woman of his own to play with while he watched them – until the women were ready for one to take over the male role. Then Josh could become as inflamed as the women were, and the pleasure of observing ended for him. Participation usually with both women inevitably followed. But not this time.

The couple here remained as two women making love, and their orgasms were light and tender and sweet and filled with affection, just what Carmel wanted. In the relaxed and happy atmosphere, Josh drifted in and out of sleep.

He woke from one such moment with a start. It all came back to him now, what he had been trying to remember all afternoon, and clearly now.

It was on the wedding day. He was standing at the foot of the stairs looking up at the white steepled church from the petal-strewn road. Helmut Newton was standing nearby taking a photograph of Mirella – the enchanting, sensuous Mirella in her wedding gown and masses of sparkling diamonds that glittered in the sunshine, head thrown back in laughter at the world, her wedding veil swept up into the air, hovering like a voluptuous erotic mist around her and Adam, to whom she was linked with one arm, and Rashid to whom she was linked by the other. Each of the men was so distinct, yet similar in their dazzling handsomeness as they gazed at her. An awesome, voluptuous sight.

Then Deena, who was standing next to him, as moved by the scene and occasion as everyone else seemed to be, said softly, 'How extraordinary they are, how wonderful they are! I love them because what they have is so special. Have you noticed, the three of them look at each other with one set of eyes?'

The memory of Deena's words riddled him like a

spray of bullets. It was true. Here had been the same look that he saw in his father's eyes when he stood with Adam in front of the Plaza looking towards the fountain at Mirella, only hours ago. He hadn't understood then what he was seeing, nor Deena's words, but he did now, and he felt both jealous and angry. He was appalled at the prospect of having to share Mirella not only with his father but with Rashid. A vow shaped itself within him, then and there, that he would never share her in this way.

Chapter 8

Deena surveyed the short flight of steps to Mirella's front door. Like all the brownstone houses on the East 65th Street block, this one looked its best on a sunny summer's day. There were new flower-boxes bursting with red, pink and coral azaleas and dark trailing ivy, that lent colour, charm and a certain youthful elegance to the dull brown stone. The windows behind the boxes were open and the transparent silk chiffon curtains rippled in the light warm breeze.

A pyramid-sculpted bay tree growing in a bronze tub stood like a sentinel on either side of the polished mahogany front door. A gold-plated ram's head knocker, glistening in the sun, appeared to beckon the passerby to lift the butting horns and knock. The entrance looked handsome and hospitable.

Deena had always found it a romantic house, the type of New York town house one always thought of as turn-of-the-century, wealthy, the family home of city folk with country houses on Long Island or in upper-state New York. The kind of house that the Amberleys might have lived in, or the Forsythes, had they been New Yorkers. Or, in fact, one of the Wingfields – if he had been a renegade from Boston, as great uncle Hyram and his father before him were, as Mirella was.

That was exactly what it had always been and still was: a Wingfield family home. When great uncle Hyram sold it to Mirella, three years earlier, in order to keep a Wingfield in the house, he had been a dying man and, eccentric and wily as he was, he had used even that to press his advantage with Mirella. She was the only one in the family who could not say no to him. It had been Deena who held her hand all through the negotiations. Deena smiled to herself when she thought of those crazy days, and his crazy demands, and the reluctant Mirella, who had been perfectly content in her small apartment.

As she looked up at the house, Deena could not help wondering what great uncle Hyram would have thought, if he had still been around to see the vast changes in Mirella's life since she purchased the house from him. The bizarre arrangement, instigated by him, had included Moses, his major domo, who had worked for great uncle Hyram since the age of eight.

After Mirella had explained to Adam her obliga-tion to live in the house for at least five years before she could consider selling it, Adam had found the solution. When in New York, they would reside in her house and use Adam's own fifteen-room flat at the Sherry Netherlands as their auxiliary residence.

An excellent idea, Mirella, Adam, Brindley and Deena had all decided one night at dinner before the wedding. Extravagant, yes, for most, but not for multi-millionaires like Adam and Mirella. Shrewd, very. It did after all give them a place apart from Adam's family, who were quite capable of dropping in and out at will. No one had said it, but all had thought it to be the right solution for both Mirella and Adam. Much as they might love each other and want to live as a family, they assuredly would have problems in learning to live together after so many years of independence with no permanent mates to consider.

And the special challenge to Mirella of being the female head of Adam's family – a mother to Adam's illegitimate children, fulfilling an instinct once so alien to her, learning to relate to their natural mothers and some of the other women from her husband's past, whom Adam had proclaimed would remain part of his present, in spite of his commitment to her – could be put aside at the town house.

Deena had no worries about her best friend rising to these challenges, not after she had seen how Mirella, though reluctantly at first, was handling her legacy and all it entailed. The continuing changes and growth in Mirella produced by the legacy and the presence of Rashid and Adam in her life were thrilling for Deena. She was fascinated by the way lives get re-shaped – even the life of Mirella, who had always been content with her lot, no matter what it was and had always learned to live around it. This was an attribute Deena admired but had never herself been able to cultivate.

For Deena, Mirella had always been the brightest star that shines in the sky and everything Deena knew she was not. And Deena loved the oppositeness in them. As friends they had intriguingly separate sets of emotional problems to deal with, hangovers from family and backgrounds. Each faced the other with her problems, and together they outfaced them.

Mirella was not the overachiever that Deena was.

She did not have that innate middle-class Jewish ethic which dictated fight for survival. Hers was not a hostile world whose pain could be cushioned only by success, money, social acceptance. No edict instructed her that, having achieved survival, one must be generous, idealistic and a Democrat. Mirella was born a WASP, that rare breed of American who needs no stinger, because she is welcome wherever she goes and perceives the world as just as much hers as anyone's. No pushy Jewish mother set up Mirella as a Jewish American Princess, targeted by destiny onto a Jewish Prince – a plastic surgeon, at least. No, when they were passing out mothers in babyland they handed her Lili – who was as bad in her own way as Deena's mother, Miriam.

'Lili, oh God!' she said aloud. And then had to chuckle to herself because of both mothers' complaint that after twenty-five years of friendship Deena and Mirella were more like each other than themselves. And in truth, many times in the last ten years Deena had felt herself a star like her friend.

She stood on the pavement trying to decide whether to go up the stairs and ring the bell or not. She was early, and the prospect of having to spend time alone with Lili, if Mirella had not yet returned from her office at the UN, kept her right where she was. But if Lili had not yet arrived, while the Princess Eirene and Mirella had? Mobility was restored to Deena; their company before the luncheon Mirella was giving for the Princess would be just the right hors d'oeuvre. Deena found the Princess fascinating, but had not had the opportunity to spend much time with her.

Up the steps – no, Deena changed her mind. She

146

looked at her wristwatch. She was much too early for the Princess. The chance of the Princess being there at this hour was small. Back to the pavement. She looked down through the spiked railings of the fence to the areaway, planted with potted cypress trees and a weeping willow. Through the kitchen windows she spied Moses moving around, and her depressing thoughts of being cornered with Lili vanished.

She opened the gate and quickly skipped down the steps and into the heavy perfume of Moses' herb garden. The windows were open and the delectable scent of his cooking merged with that of the herbs in the little areaway. She pushed her head through the open window. 'Hi, Moses. Got a cup of coffee for an old friend?'

Moses looked at the kitchen clock on the wall and answered, 'You're early. Yes, come on in. The kitchen door is open.'

Entering the kitchen, Deena was enveloped by the charm of Moses' very special domain, a combination of a four-star chef's country kitchen somewhere in Provence in France, or Cajun country in America's deep south, and Moses' home, although he did have three other rooms off the kitchen to live in. She closed her eyes and inhaled deeply.

'Boy, if I could wear the scent of this kitchen, there is not a man alive I couldn't attract. Well, for a meal, anyway.' She opened her eyes slowly, as if savouring the perfume with them as well, and smiled at Moses.

He could not help smiling back at Deena: she always amused him. Her sense of humour, her self-deprecation which turned her often into the butt of her own jokes, combined with her timing, were for the most part irresistibly charming. Her intelligence,

147

her fierce loyalty, her deep affection for Mirella, and not least her very pretty golden good looks, made her always welcome in the Wingfield kitchen. Of course there was one other thing: she loved his cooking. Dieting apart, when Moses cooked, it was a joy to watch her eat.

Deena walked straight to the stove, touching everything she could en route: she grazed her hand briefly over bowls of fresh peaches, ducks' and quails' eggs, picked a shelled pecan and put it in her mouth, a dried apricot, reached up to familiarize herself with vintage Parmesan cheeses and smoked hams and the red Spanish onions and globes of white garlic hanging in bunches from hooks above the nine-foot-long scrubbed-pine work-table in the middle of the room. She lifted a lid and got her hand smartly smacked. 'None of that, madam', and was ushered to a chair at the end of the pine table.

'Now, you just sit right here, Miss Deena, and I'll fix some coffee.'

'You don't just happen to have a Danish, or a doughnut, to go with it, do you, Moses?' The look she received from Moses while he was pouring her coffee made her say, 'Oh dear, I meant a *croissant*? A *brioche*?' She watched him smiling and shaking his head in disapproval.

'No. A *spanicopitta*, a *tirropitta*, then?' He continued to shake his head in disapproval.

'No Greek eleven o'clock feeding either? I suppose a grilled cheese sandwich is out as well? Then I guess I will have to settle for one of your blueberry muffins.'

Moses placed the cup of coffee made from freshly ground beans in front of her and then scraped a dash of cinnamon stick on to the top of the steaming liquid from his tiny silver and ivory nutmeg scraper, a Christmas gift from Deena, who had found this collector's item in Brazil.

'No blueberry muffins. There are *croissants*, and *brioches* freshly made this morning, pecan and honey rolls, corn meal fingers, which I could warm for you and serve dripping in fresh, home-made butter, and a lick of Greek Hymettus honey, English crumpets and scones warm out of the oven an hour ago that I will serve with butter and home-made damson preserve. Then there's whipped cream and honey-dipped fresh strawberries to top the scones for tea this afternoon. None of which you may have now, because lunch will be coming through in an hour's time, and I don't want clapped-out appetites to greet it.'

Deena sipped the coffee, peeped out over the rim of the cup, and asked, 'A homemade Tollhouse cookie? Don't look at me that way, Moses, I'm not committing a crime. Just begging a morsel of food. Sorry I asked. OK, I give in. A Rye Crisp, no butter, no jelly, no jam.'

'Incorrigible, Miss Deena.' As Moses spoke, he reached into the centre of the table among the crocks, glass jars of all sizes and shapes filled with delicacies from the four corners of the culinary world, to extricate one of the many decorative tins, and offered Deena two of his home-made oatmeal cookies, which she placed on a French pottery plate from Provence that they used in the kitchen.

'I know I'm incorrigible, Moses, and frankly I'm beginning to worry about it.'

'That'll be the day,' Moses sniggered.

They smiled at each other, but Moses behind his smile was puzzled because, although they both made a joke of it, he had the distinct feeling she was telling a half-truth about herself. He knew Deena very well, almost as well as Mirella Wingfield, because Deena was so much a part of the Wingfield household. The two women had gradually become family to him in the three years since Mirella had taken over the house. He recognized subtle changes in Deena since Mirella's wedding night. Something was amiss, but not wanting to press her he went to the stove and poured himself another cup of coffee. Still with his back to Deena, he said, 'What are you doing down here drinking coffee in this kitchen? Why don't you wait in the library, or in the back garden where it's cool? You look very pretty, real fresh and summery, and you want to stay that way, don't you?'

Deena was wearing a short-sleeved, finely-woven, white linen Ralph Lauren dress, with four large patch-pockets, two at the breast and two on the skirt. A bright, red-and-white-check silk handkerchief flopped decoratively out of the pocket over her heart, and a sailor's small jaunty-looking hat, made by Adolpho in shiny white straw, perched prettily on top of her curly, honey-coloured hair. It was tilted at an ever-so-slight angle, insinuating mirth, and dictating to onlookers that they smile, show a little merriment in celebration of a pretty woman.

She had fussed about what outfit to wear in front of the mirror that morning and, after selecting the white high-heeled Maude Frizzon sandals of kid skin and a soft white leather Loewe handbag that was shaped like a sailor's duffle bag, had been satisfied that she looked good enough to dine with a Queen, but only *just* chic enough for luncheon with the Princess Eirene.

At Moses' words she touched the sailor hat, to check that it was still in place, and then stretched her arms out in front of her to check her hands for cleanliness and her long ruby-red finger nails for a chip in the polish. All was perfect. She ran her hand over her antique Indian ivory bracelets, toying momentarily with their stunning, large gold and diamond clasps, then played with the collection of slim ivory and diamond rings she wore on several of her fingers, and placed her hands in her lap.

Moses sat down in a chair opposite her to drink his coffee and carve white turnips, tinted by beetroot and spinach juices into blushing water-lilies and green lily pads, to garnish his star dish: sea-bass skinned and preened with fresh herbs, parcelled in a short pastry fashioned to look like the succulent fish enclosed in it.

'Is anyone upstairs?'

'Just Muhsine. When Mr Adam moved in, he moved her in too. She has become Miss Mirella's and Mr Adam's sort of lady's maid-companion until they return to Istanbul.'

'You're not upset, are you, Moses? I know you prefer running the house on your own.'

'No, not at all, quite the opposite in fact. Muhsine is so quiet and unobtrusive. Of course, there is a language problem. But that don't seem to matter much. She is discreet and helpful, stays out of my way, is willing and able to turn her hand to anything. In general, a great help to me now that Miss Mirella has married, and our routine is so changed. She's a delicate little thing, like another little flower in the house. She's upstairs now, putting the finishing touches to the dining-room table. I betcha it'll come out exactly the way I told her to do it.'

'Well, if you're sure she's the only one in the house, then I might go up after I've finished my coffee. Frankly, I came down here because I couldn't stand it if Lily were upstairs and I had to go solo with her for any time.'

'No worry about that. She won't arrive until the very last minute. She never arrives on time, and most especially if she knows it's a proper luncheon party.'

Moses rose and fetched from the marble-topped, French steel baker's rack, a baking-tin on which was laid the sea-bass. The pastry was already decorated with fin and tail scales. He sat down with a bowl of egg glaze and a pastry brush and began to paint the pastry with it.

'You are an amazing man, Moses. A marvel. That looks absolutely terrific. Only last night, I was telling the chef at *La Côte Basque* about your sea-bass, how the crust comes out of the oven in a shimmering shade of old gold. What sauces are you going to serve with it today?'

'I'm serving this on that French Baroque silver fish platter that the Princess Eirene gave to the Coreys as a wedding gift. I am going to put these water lilies and lily pads that I have just finished carving all around the bass to pretty it up. One of the fish-shaped silver sauce boats will be used for a hollandaise sauce spiked with tomato. The other will be filled with *concasse* of tomato flavoured with spices.'

'Oh, dear,' said Deena as she pushed the plate with the two untouched oatmeal cookies from her. 'You are right as always, Moses. I'll wait for lunch, I can't bear to spoil your meal. If Mirella wasn't my best friend, I would steal you from her. So help me, I would.'

'Oh, we all know that,' he said, a hint of a laugh tinged with pride in his voice.

'Do tell me the menu for today, you culinary genius.'

Moses laughed and put the pastry brush down. He leaned back in the Windsor chair and drank some coffee. Replacing the cup, he said, 'Such flattery. Don't you ever want to be surprised?'

'No, I really hate surprises. Well, I don't exactly hate them. Let's just say I like to enjoy the food twice: once in my imagination, and then on my tongue.'

'Well, actually, it's the kind of lunch you enjoy, because, like you, the Princess Eirene prefers fish to meat or game. So, for the first course, an appetizer – slivers of smoked salmon rolled around a mousseline of John Dory topped with fresh asparagus tips and a cream sauce.'

'Ah, shades of that archetypal maître chef, Louis Outhier.'

'I hope so,' said Moses. 'Then comes this fine seabass with its sauces, which I will serve with fresh-blanched French green beans and a purée of celeriac. For dessert, a cream of sweet chestnut, liqueurs, and a hint of praline set in a crispy pastry basket flecked with candied meringue.'

Deena could not utter a word. Her glazed-over eyes were compliment enough for Moses. While she was still recovering from these imagined fore-tastes, he said, 'I have a message for you, Miss Deena. Miss Mirella called and said, if you should arrive before she did, I was to put you properly in the picture.

'Miss Mirella and Mr Adam are flying out tonight on the Corey Trust's jet to Athens. Then they board

153

Mr Lala Mustapha's boat in Piraeus for a visit to the Greek Island of Delos. From there they take a helicopter and island-jump through the Aegean to Turkey. Or something like that. She says, please join them. Either tonight on the plane or in Istanbul. She said to tell you, sorry for the short notice, but they only decided on the plan two hours ago.'

'What about her work at the UN?'

'I don't know, but she must have it all planned. She mentioned something about taking the remainder of her holiday leave now, when she told me we wouldn't be returning till the opening session of the Security Council after the summer recess. I say "we", by the way, because I am closing up the house tomorrow and joining the Peramabahçe household in Istanbul in five days' time. Mr Adam insists upon it. Says he wants me to see Turkey, since we will be living there at least half the time. Wants me to find my place in the running of the palace there, to fit into his scheme of things. Same way some of his people will have to find theirs when they're working here in New York with me. And Mr Lala Mustapha has organized two weeks' holiday there for me, as a thank you for the help I gave him with the wedding preparations. Now, he didn't have to do that for me, but the two men and Miss Mirella insist that I accept. They are very generous to me, all three of them. But my arm didn't need twisting . . .'

'Christ, Moses, what a turn-up of affairs. And, I might add, you deserve it. Aren't you excited?'

'Yes.' He bit his lip, trying to be *blasé* about it, but delight radiated out of him. 'Quite an adventure for me. Mr Adam has certainly changed our lives, hasn't he?'

'More, I think, than any of us realizes,' Deena said pensively.

Although hesitating, Deena was enthusiastic about the prospect of seeing Turkey with Mirella, Adam and Rashid. Nothing had been said about Rashid being in Turkey, but Deena knew instinctively that he would be there.

'Where is Mirella? I'll have to talk to her before I can make a decision.'

'You'll probably have to wait until after lunch, because when she comes home it will be with the Princess and Mr Adam. She did say she tried to call you a couple of times this morning but couldn't reach you.'

'Well, where from? I can call her there.'

'The Plaza Hotel. But don't call. I've got an idea they're having a very private romantic two-day idyll, and don't want to be disturbed. They'll be here in only forty-five minutes. Now, shoo! Out of my kitchen, please. I have too much to do before lunch.'

Deena put her coffee cup down and was about to rise from her chair when Moses said, 'Oh, I almost forgot. One other thing. Mr Ribblesdale is arriving here from London in time for lunch.'

The furious flush of red to Deena's face was uncharacteristic enough for Moses to note and be puzzled by it. He picked up the pastry-brush and continued his task.

Silence hung heavy between the two, and Moses did not quite know how to break it. Deena tried desperately to still her heart. Surprise at the prospect of being with Brindley again rattled her feelings. Her mind was in a turmoil, trying to deal rationally with the present, while it thrilled again to the memory of

155

her sexual encounter with Brindley on Mirella's wedding night.

There followed for her an involuntary playback of the ecstasy they shared, their voyage of self-discovery and deep erotic release, overwhelming to them both. Memories of passion sated, and an intense new feeling of love were mixed with embarrassment – or was it guilt? – over so much freedom and self-indulgence. She recalled the contentment of feeling complete in herself and another human being at the same time. Of having it all.

It came rushing back to Deena, right there in Moses' kitchen, and she understood for the first time what she had missed that night and day when they were together, and again when she saw Brindley off to London ... and yet again all during their two weeks of separation and silence.

They had fallen in love: that's what she had not understood. Not, Deena had fallen in love. Not, Brindley had fallen in love. *They*, together, had done it. Hadn't they? She could hardly believe that in order to protect herself from a real and shared love and all the ramifications that it might entail, she had used a brilliant defence mechanism. She had labelled her night of bliss with Brindley as 'the greatest one-night stand'. She had even blocked out the expectation of a phone call, a letter, a card. And had received none. Not once since they parted had she thought of him. She now knew why. It had been too dangerous, the pain of losing him too great.

Moses' and Deena's awkward silence was broken by the appearance of the diminutive Turkish girl, Muhsine, so pretty and exotic-looking even when not dressed in her native *salvar*, but in a more western

156

version of the blousy pantaloons – more like wide trousers with a long tunic over them that hung to the middle of the calf and was slit up the sides.

Deena stood up and greeted the young woman. They hugged each other, all smiles at meeting again. The language barrier between them, and Muhsine's last-minute jobs before the guests arrived, separated them very quickly. Deena looked after Muhsine. Objects of wonder Muhsine and Mirella were to Deena. Each had reconciled herself to her exclusive role in Adam's household and in his heart: unique, yet perilously close to overlapping. Her admiration for Muhsine, who had stepped aside from Adam's bed and relinquished her role of favourite gracefully, embracing Mirella as Adam's wife, was enormous. Could she have confronted the emotional risks these two women took for Adam's love? For the love of any man?

Her mouth suddenly felt very dry, her tongue like cotton wool. She went to the old pine hutch at the far end of the kitchen and took a glass and filled it with Perrier. She drank it slowly and the throbbing on the roof of her mouth and at the temples of her head eased, but only slightly. Still with her back to Moses, she placed her hands on the hutch and leaned her weight on them, closed her eyes and took several deep breaths and let them out slowly. And it worked. The acute anxiety slowly dissolved.

She could hear Moses move from the table to the Aga, open the oven door and slip the baking tin onto its shelf. The clang of the oven door shut out the anxiety and the memories along with it. A burst of music from the kitchen radio brought her back to the here-and-now. She straightened up, took one more deep breath, and turned around.

Moses saw a subtle glow spread across Deena's face and the trace of an inner smile lying lightly on her lips. He placed a copper pot he had in his hand on the pine table and said, 'Ah, that's more like it. Not only do you look pretty, but suddenly you look happy.'

The smile broadened, and she walked around the table to Moses, kissed the big handsome man on the cheek, and said as she climbed the stairs, 'Oh, I am, Moses. I've just rediscovered love.'

Chapter 9

'Do you believe that fate governs our lives, Mrs Wingfield?' asked the Princess Eirene.

'Not at all,' Lili snapped back. 'But you obviously do.' A note of utter disdain for the woman and her question coloured Lili's voice.

'Oh, but I don't,' the Princess said.

'That surprises me. I would have thought that sort of thinking would be right up your alley,' Lili shot back.

'And why would you think that of me, someone whom you have only just met, and hardly know?'

The other three women in the room, Mirella, Deena and Muhsine, were aghast at Lili's manner towards the honoured guest. But before Mirella could say anything, Lili continued.

'Because you play the role of the orientalist. You are, after all, a Princess who has lived her entire life in a backward country. I don't suppose a woman of your age and background, steeped in a Turkish culture, and a privileged world can stop using fatalism as an excuse for everything. Come now, admit it, you do believe in fate.'

It was at this point that Muhsine, who was treated in the Corey household as more of a lady-in-waiting to Mirella than a maid or servant, rose from where she sat at a discreet distance from the other guests, and moved to stand behind the Princess' chair. It was a small gesture but a very powerful one, the more so because everyone in the room knew that Muhsine's English was not up to registering every nuance of Lili's rudeness.

Mirella was flushed with embarrassment. All through lunch, which had gone off perfectly, she had been worried about Lili. Lili had said barely a word, had hardly touched her food, had listened to them all laughing and talking and pretended that she wasn't there. Mirella had enjoyed herself enormously. Adam, Brindley, Rashid, the Princess, Deena, and she herself, had been in top form. But still she had been relieved when the men remained in the dining-room to drink port and the ladies had retreated to the living-room. Mirella stood up and was about to say something in defence of the Princess, when Eirene imperiously held up a hand to stop her.

'But, my dear Mrs Wingfield, I did not say that I don't believe in fate. What I said was that I don't believe that fate governs our lives. Quite a different thing, then what I asked you about.'

There was an awkward moment when all eyes were on Lili, who stared at the Princess, refusing to answer. The embarrassing silence was broken by a discreet knock at the pair of mahogany doors into Mirella's first-floor living-room. Moses pushed them open, and walked in carrying a large baroque silver tray with handsome English Jacobean glass decanters and small goblets of exquisite shapes in twinkling clear crystal.

The women remained silent while he placed the tray on the table between the two Chippendale settees in front of the fireplace. Their attention was diverted from the strained atmosphere by having to choose between two of the world's most celebrated white dessert wines.

The Princess chose Château d'Yquem, the Sauternes she called liquid sunshine. For over two hundred years the estate had been in the same family, and she often marvelled at that and the fact that she had sipped Château d'Yquem that had been up to a hundred years old and was still perfect nectar. She addressed Moses as he so very carefully poured one of the most expensive wines in the world.

'I would like to thank you for such a perfect meal, Chef. It was memorable, and to end it with Yquem, perfection.' Moses beamed. It was a joy for him to cook, and commendation from the Princess was a bonus.

'Thank you, ma'am,' he said, offering her the goblet from a small silver salver.

'Did you know,' asked the Princess, 'that it takes one whole vine to make a single glass of Château d'Yquem? Astonishing, is it not?'

They all agreed and chose the Yquem in preference to the Tokay in the second decanter on the tray. Except for Lili, who abstained, saying, 'I will have nothing, Moses. I know both these wines, but prefer to drink them only on very special occasions. But if I were to have one, it would have been the Tokay.'

'How interesting,' said the Princess, 'that is one of the things I remember about your mother: her preference for Tokay.'

Again there was a long silence, as the women sipped and savoured their wine. Moses left the tray, retreated through the double doors, turned and pulled them closed.

161

It was such a little thing, the Princess remembering that Lili's mother had a taste for Tokay, but it had a remarkable effect. The Princess had used a feather instead of a fist to punch her out and, like all bullies, Lili went down for the count, winded.

The tense, bitchy atmosphere Lili had created suddenly vanished. The relief felt by the younger women in the room was enormous.

The Princess stretched her arm over her shoulder and offered her hand to Muhsine, who took it in hers and kissed it, saying in Turkish, 'At your service, my Princess.'

The Princess asked, 'Please pour a glass of the Tokay for Mrs Wingfield.' And, while Muhsine was doing it, she said to Lili, 'Please, join us, at least in just a sip. Humour an old friend of your mother's, who loved and admired her, and who has spent many an afternoon not unlike this sipping Tokay among other women like ourselves, unhampered by the intrusive presence of men.'

Mirella watched Lili take a sip and close her eyes for a second, savouring the taste. A touch of the wand, and as if by magic, a hardness, a manic toughness slipped slowly from her mother's face.

Mirella looked around the room. Suddenly it seemed quite different. Yet it wasn't. Nothing had been changed for months, not since the night Adam had filled it with flowers and they made love together for the first time.

She caught a glimpse of the organized chaos of the room reflected in one of the several gilt Chippendale and Georgian mirrors, hanging on or leaning against the eighteenth-century pine panelling.

For the first time she realized how truly unique and enchanting the room was with its boxes and crates, half-opened, with straw and various art treasures spilling onto faded and worn antique Persian carpets. Her collection of Japanese prints: the finest Hokusais and Utamoros, in simple gold-leaf frames washed with silver, stacked one behind the other against the walls.

And everywhere flowers, potted shrubs: white daisies with rich, egg-yolk yellow centres; magenta, red, hot pink azaleas in full bloom, three, four, five-foot high, and umbrellas of even larger palms, and ficus benjaminas, and pandamus, and fig trees, heavy with luscious green leaves, rubbed shoulders with the large and beautiful Ming, Tang, and Han *objets d'art*. The large decorative Imari pots and vases, bases for lamps, with their handsome, but worn and tatty ivory-silk shades, askew or tilted dangerously to one side, were dotted around the room, standing on a wood slatted crate here, a table there, on the floor, and on a lovely, large Boule desk at the end of the room that overlooked the garden in the back. Overall was an air of elegant, depraved dishevelment.

Mirella gazed into the mirror, seeking what was different about the way the room appeared to her today. She felt herself melt into the mirror, disappear, as it were, into the reflection, and had a strange sense of *déjà vu*. Had she been there sometime in the past, in another life? If she had, it had been a different room, but its atmosphere and what it evoked must have been the same.

Then, quite suddenly, while enjoying every detail of the scene she was viewing – the books piled helter-skelter on Queen Anne wing-chairs covered in their original tattered and torn tapestry, on the end of a settee, the pale-mauve marble top (with a crack across it) of an impressive French Directoire table, whose legs were replaced by ormolu mounts of giant birds, wings flung back, adding a dash of what a French colleague of Mirella's from the UN described as typifying *le désordre britannique* – she found her answer.

What was different today was the beauty and utter femininity of the ladies languishing among cushions on the settee. She had never before seen her mother or her best friend, or the two Turkish women, or herself for that matter, as modern-day odalisques. But in this oddly sensuous room, with the sunlight dancing through the windows and playing shadows across the worn, white-satin Chippendale settees in the centre of the panelled room, that was how they revealed themselves.

The diminutive, delicate-looking Princess Eirene, still an exotic beauty looking no more than forty-five years old, half her age, was dressed in a pale-mauve linen and silk dress, over which was draped, across one shoulder, a dramatic black and white print of cabbage roses on a long length of lustrous silk. She wore her hat, a tiny pillbox of the same print, like a crown. The huge pearl studs on her ears, and a long strand around her neck that nearly reached to her waist lay half on the mauve and half on the black-and-white, softly draped scarf, and dazzled the eyes with their lustre. The scarf and the pearls were reminiscent of a sash of honour and the jewels of a Queen.

Muhsine, standing behind her, the youngest and most Oriental and sensuous looking of all the women in the room, might have posed for any of the famous Orientalist painters. Her brightly-coloured tunic of purples and reds would make a rich pattern for their pallets. Her dark honey-coloured skin and mysterious, slanted eyes like those of the Princess seemed still to hold the secrets of their past.

And, as she gazed past the two Turkish women, framed by the white satin of the settee where the Princess sat, and on through the flowers and trees, Mirella could just see two huge black Sudanese eunuchs of considerable age.

They were dressed in black suits and shirts, magnificent turbans wrapped around their heads. The Princess Eirene's coat of arms, emblazoned in black enamel on a gold disc, was pinned to their turbans, on one side, just above where an eyebrow might have been, had they not been deprived of hair on their body, by their unusual condition. They were the Princess Eirene's two devoted bodyguards, who never left her side night or day, and who had taken turns to sleep across her bedroom door for as long as either of them could remember. Their strangely bland features and womanish voices locked in the bodies of men, added a final touch of *harem* to Mirella's living room.

Deena, looking softer and more romantically pretty, exotic in her very own New York chic way, shimmered in the mirror with an innocence and a vulnerability that Mirella had never seen before in her. It surprised Mirella that there was a part of her best friend that she had never known.

Lili wore a Cacharel summer dress of sheer printed silk organza, in an all-over pattern of violets and pink and mauve pansies. It was a simple shirtwaist dress with a full skirt over a purple underslip. Round cabochon amethysts set in a circle of small diamonds were on her ears, and a black straw hat whose brim was pinned back framed her face.

For the first time in her life Mirella looked at her mother and understood what her father had seen in her that made him accept with a certain stoicism her petty, mean and often bitchy antics, and yet remain her devoted man, sometime slave, and lover.

Not only was she lovely to look at, but there was a fiery passion in her, tamed but present. It could be seen in the eyes, the full, pouting lower lip, the nervous energy that manifested itself in the way she fidgeted and moved. She was like a wild mare whom men enjoyed reining-in. To tame, and then to ride the voluptuous passion beneath the meanness and bitterness with which she pranced before the outside world, and more often than not her children, would be a tall order, and a thrilling one for any man.

Mirella watched Lili hold her small goblet up to the sunlight and smile, then slowly place it against her lips and sip. Her eyes showed how she savoured the taste. Then she said, 'Legend has it that Pope Leo XIII was kept alive for the last two weeks of his ninety-three years entirely on Eszencia, the best Tokay. My mother told me that. You are quite right, Princess Eirene, my mother was indeed partial to Eszencia Tokay. She used to wax lyrical about Hungary. She adored that country, and its people. They were a refined, and elegant people, she used to say, a people with taste as fine, as rare and as sweet as Tokay. And the Hungarians loved my mother. It seems that when she was a young girl, she was favoured by their King. But then, I imagine you would know more about that,

Princess, than I would have been told. To the end of her life, long after Kings were obsolete and two world wars ravaged the country, my mother still received high-ranking officials and ex-Hungarian Royals, and always had a supply of the best Tokay – Eszencia.'

'I always thought of your mother as a most romantic and elegant woman,' Deena interjected. 'I used to long for an invitation from Mirella to go with her for a visit to the Wesson-Cabots on Beacon Hill. I was always so in awe of their being Mirella's grandparents. I remember once promising myself that one day I too would drink a wine that came in a bottle so distinctive,' Deena said, a nostalgic smile on her face.

There was a moment of silence while the women in the room were half-lost in their separate memories of Lili's Turkish mother, Inje. It was broken by Mirella saying, 'It comes only from Hungary, and from rare vines that have grown there for more than a thousand years. The Furmint grape they use is virtually unknown in the vineyards of other wine countries. I know all that,' Mirella laughed, 'because Nama Inje used to tell me about grapes, all kinds of grapes, which she would feed me as a child. 'Now, I can tell you more about grapes, and much more about Tokay. For instance, are you aware that Eszencia is so rare because it is made by allowing the late-picked grapes' own weight to squeeze out the nectar-like juice? Aszu is the best grade of Tokay available today. Except of course in this house, as it was in my grandmother's house. Mother is able to drink Eszencia here today because she knows the owner of a vineyard, much as my grandmother must have.'

Lili looked both puzzled and somewhat wary.

Mirella walked from the *fleur de pêche* marble fireplace, where she had been standing, to the settee and sat down next to Lili.

'I own one of the few private vineyards in Hungary and it happens to produce the finest Tokay in the world. I found the vineyard on my list of acquisitions from the Oujie legacy, and have resisted selling it, because of sentimental loyalty to Nama Inje and her delight in the occasional sip of Tokay.'

Harsh lines appeared suddenly across Lili's face, her eyes seemed to harden. Very slowly and deliberately she placed the Jacobean glass on the table in front of her.

'And I suppose you think that's extraordinary? Princess Eirene will tell us that it's fate or some such nonsense. And I will tell you, poppycock. It's coincidence, Mirella. I simply no longer understand you. Sentimentality, multi-millionairess, a wife who acts more like a harlot, wealth, opulence, power – a great deal of power – a manipulator of men. I don't know you.'

Lili stood up and walked away from her daughter, to survey her from the fireplace.

'I look at you now,' she continued, 'and you are more like my mother every day. My mother, the centre of everyone's world. She had that ability always to make herself the centre for everyone she came in contact with. Everyone loved her, wanted her; even now long after her death, she is adored, revered – and for what? Being a cunning old whore, that's what. A selfish, self-centred old whore who destroyed my father, had not a shred of maternal instinct, and who still reaches out from the grave to touch us all, make us love her, admire her, respect

168

her. Yes, even me, and I hate myself for it. I loved her, but she was always a mystery to me. I never understood her, never.'

An embarrassing hush filled the room when Lili stopped talking. There were tears of frustration in her eyes, and no one quite knew what to do about the angry, unhappy woman. In a more controlled voice, but one still filled with anger and bitterness, she spoke to her daughter. 'Mirella, we never knew her. Not really. We only knew that part of herself she wanted us to know. In time, her foreign ways and even the fact that she destroyed one of Boston's favoured blue-bloods, were accepted. But that was mainly because your paternal grandfather was related to both the Cabots and the Wessons of Massachusetts. You have no idea what it is to be just barely accepted in society. To have buried a past. All those years of living down her vile past and her scandals. And what for? After a lifetime of making the world forget the origins of Inje Wesson-Cabot, to have you turn your back on me and embrace her ancestors and their wealth, emulate all that she was, love her. You are closer to her even in death than you have ever been to me in life.'

Mirella wanted very much to go to her mother, put her arms around her, but she knew better. Lili was proud; and pity was not what she was looking for. Mirella knew instinctively that the best thing to do was nothing.

'A sip of Tokay,' Lili went on, 'its bouquet, even its colour are enough to raise passions of one sort or another in all of us about my mother, so I make no excuse for my outburst. This oddly beautiful room, with its bad interior decor, that is more like a sort of spontaneous stage-setting, even this reminds me of her. I love it, but I don't understand it. I keep getting the distinct feeling of being thrown back in time, to her and her world, the world that my only daughter is being sucked into, a place and a life foreign to me. And, much as I hate it, there is nothing I can do about it. I suppose that's what you would call fate, Princess.'

'Yes, I think I would say that was fate, Mrs Wingfield,' answered the Princess.

The Princess Eirene rose from the settee and picked up her glass and Lili's as well. Mirella saw the two eunuchs at the far side of the room spring to attention and take a few steps towards her. The Princess stopped them with a word, went to Lili and handed her the tiny goblet of Tokay. For one moment these two women from contrasting worlds and different generations looked into each other's eyes, and were locked together in one world and in peace, Lili took a sip of the famed Tokay and sighed. The extraordinary Princess Eirene said, as she put her arm around Lili's waist, 'You have answered my question. You do believe that fate governs your life. You must, in as much as you have allowed it to do so all your life. But it needn't have been that way. Fate is like a great glorious wave: if one rolls with it one can have the ride of a lifetime and master it. You are very like your mother in looks and some mannerisms, but most unlike her in dealing with fate. She was a grand master at dealing with it, and to judge by the little I have seen of her, your daughter is learning to deal with it better every day.

'Come sit with me, Lili. I hope you will allow me to call you by your Christian name and you must call me Eirene. Together maybe we can lay a ghost, that will allow you to love Inje, yourself and your daughter.

170

For, after all is said and done, she was a most extraordinary woman, and the daughter of a clever and gifted woman.

'Your mother embodied the end of an era, as I embody the end of an era, as my bodyguards do. We were the last children of the court of the Ottoman Empire, all the splendour, cruelty, and intrigue that goes with a system rotten to the core. You would have to have known the life Inje led in the *harem* to have really known her and feel compassion for her. Clearly, and sadly for you, she never allowed you to know about that, or anything of her life before she married your father. I can understand her reasons. She had led a life which proper Bostonians would have hanged her for, which her husband's ancestors would have burned her at the stake for. She was very clever at deceiving you all, allowing rumour to make up a past for her. Yes, I can understand what she did, understand even your conflict about her, but it doesn't make it right. If she had not blocked out her life and abandoned her past before she arrived in America, I doubt that you would deal with her so harshly.'

The two women sat down together. Deena watched them in amazement, fascinated by Lili's outburst, enthralled by the power the Princess exercised over everyone in the room through her unique charm and beauty, and not least by her experience in the game of life and love, which shone in her face, her body, the way she moved, her every gesture. A formidably feminine woman. Deena was drawn to her by the aura of decadence around her respectability. The Princess had to be one of the most accomplished seducers of all time to have won Lili over. And clearly, she had.

More. Deena wanted the Princess to tell more about Mirella's Nama Inje, and their life in Turkey. For here was the first woman Deena had met whom she knew she would be able to talk to openly about her sexual desires, her fantasies, and the one night of her life when she had abjectly surrendered to eros in the arms of Brindley. And she knew the Princess would not only understand but rejoice for her.

Here, now, in this room, Deena was aware that all the women there could reveal themselves without embarrassment and even with a degree of love for each other, as sisters under the skin – each of them delicately subject to the charm of the Princess Eirene.

Deena thought of the *harem*, and the long hours the women must have spent together talking among themselves of love and sex, desire and power, the bond they had shared as victims and women. Her eyes roamed pensively over the women in the room, and she realized there was nothing about their being together that was vaguely like girl-talk, American-adult style. The Princess was a woman of the *harem*, the sort of woman Deena had always pitied for being treated like a thing, a chattel, a receptacle used by men.

Deena felt it no less deplorable now but understood it better, having submitted again and again, almost to the point of masochism, with Brindley. It was intriguing and unimaginable that Mirella's grandmother and the Princess had been part of that world.

The way things were shaping in Deena and Mirella's life, it had come as somewhat of a shock to Deena that Mirella was indeed the truly free spirit of the two. That, except for her night with Brindley, she had been ashamed of her desires, her wants, her needs. And not only sexually but emotionally as well. She had been merely aping the sexually-liberated woman all her life. Mirella had always given herself to the tide of things, sometimes resistant but never for long. In the months since Mirella inherited, Deena understood, as no one else did, that it was not change in Mirella that made her different, but a welling-up of something deep within her being that allowed her to flow with the tide of events, to crest the waves of her experience now.

The Princess must have sensed in Mirella the coursing of the blood that flowed from Inje through the maternal side of Mirella's family. Surely Mirella's relationships with Adam and Rashid must have reminded the Princess that this was not just another American heiress. And she might have warmed to the idea that the female line of the extraordinary Oujie women was not broken.

Then it all snapped into place for Deena: how important Mirella must be for the Princess and Adam and Rashid, who enjoyed a lifestyle that was dying out. They had found another human being who was rightfully a part of the world they could not let go of. In her, the past was not dead. Mirella, a direct descendant of the famed Kadin Roxellana Oujie, the great-grandmother she inherited the legacy from, was the closest they would ever get to having a rightful heir to their Turkish splendour and decadence. She was their Empress. Deena was deeply touched to think that the Princess had taken it upon herself to help Mirella and Lili by tending the wounds that had emotionally distanced mother from daughter and had scarred Lili's relationship with her own mother. Before the hateful Lili left the house that day, her life

173

would be richer, her pain less and her love for her mother and her daughter without conflict.

Deena would have liked to have shared in such a process of healing, but she felt compelled to extricate herself from revelations that could be embarrassing to Lili. It would have been quite different if Lili liked Deena, but Deena knew that was not so. Lili despised her, and had never made any secret of doing so for the twenty-five years she and Mirella had been friends. To hear Lili's family secrets could not possibly help their relationship; so Deena reluctantly took a last sip of the Yquem.

'Much as I would like to stay and learn more about the lives you and Mrs Wesson-Cabot lived in the last days of the Ottoman Empire, I think it best if I leave.' Deena rose.

'I knew it. I knew it would be you who would prod this conversation on. Always the one to push an issue, to exploit a situation, to interfere. The outsider trying to find a place inside. Well, I don't suppose you can do anything about it. It's in your people's blood. Jewish blood. Oh, do sit down, Deena. After twenty-five years of devoted friendship with my daughter, you have pushed your way into being part of my family. I suppose you have earned the right to stay, and learn that my maternal side of the family is probably as common as yours ever was. What must you be thinking? "That snob Boston socialite is about to get her come-uppance." '

'No. I was thinking, "Get stuffed, Mrs Wingfield." '

Lili stared right through Deena.

With that, Deena went to the Princess and the two women embraced and said goodbye. While Deena reached out to Muhsine and said her farewells,

174

Mirella asked her to stay and apologized yet again, as she had for so many years, for her mother's behaviour toward Deena.

'Don't, Mirella, please don't make excuses for your mother. We both know she has a viper's tongue. I've learned to live with that and the disdain she has always shown me. I have had to endure her when she tries genuinely to like me. And, believe me, that is far more upsetting and excruciating for both of us.'

Then she turned to Lili and said, 'You know, Mrs Wingfield, you are a miserable creature, but I have to give you your due. You're not always wrong. I never realized until just now that I did want to be part of your family. It never occurred to me that I had to belong to it, that living on the fringe of it was not enough for me, and was too much for you. I guess we both have been struck by a moment of truth. We just had both our souls hoovered.'

'Some exit, huh, Mirr?' said a not unhappy, smiling Deena as she slipped her arm through Mirella's and the two women walked from the room.

'Not bad,' Mirella answered.

'I bet the Princess would have done better. You will tell me all when next we meet, won't you?'

'Of course, every word. Tonight on the plane. You are coming with us. Oh, please, don't say no.'

'Can't help it. No.'

'Then you'll meet us in Istanbul?'

'Don't know, that depends.'

'On what?'

'This.'

And walking down the stairs, arms linked, Deena reached into one of the pockets on the skirt of her dress and handed Mirella a note written on a piece of foolscap torn in half and folded over once. Mirella read,

Deena,
    I think we're in love. I know I am. If we are, then come away with me to England. If the answer is yes, give me a sign, and we will make our plans tonight at your house.

                               Brindley

The two women stopped midway down the staircase and threw their arms around each other, their joy bursting and bubbling. They kissed and laughed, and for Deena, who had been holding back her happiness since she read the note, it all was suddenly very real and happening. She felt weak-kneed, and she drew Mirella down so that the two women sat midway down the staircase.

'Shush, shush,' she whispered, 'not so loud. I think we should keep this quiet. Well, sort of quiet between us. At least until I talk to Brindley.' Then they burst out laughing like school-girls.

'How? When? I had no idea. Why did you keep it a secret?'

'Why did I keep it a secret? That was simple, I didn't know, hadn't a clue. Not until this afternoon in your kitchen when Moses told me Brindley was coming to lunch. Suddenly the penny dropped. And what is so extraordinary is that when it did, I realized not that I was in love with him, but that we were in love with each other. Until that moment I thought that the night we spent together was the greatest one-night stand of my life, and that was it. The way we both behaved the day after, and when I dropped him

176

off at the airport, seemed to confirm it. Never heard from him again, not once, until this note. Nor did I expect to, I might add. When did we fall in love? I suppose that night. I haven't really talked to you about that night, but this isn't the moment to go into that.

'How? Because we like and trust each other, I guess, and the sex felt so right for us. I suspect neither of us ever gave ourselves so completely to anyone as we did to each other. But that's a guess. We never acknowledged it openly.'

'All right,' Mirella said. 'You've told me the how, the when and the why. But when did he pass you the note?'

'When he first came in and we were having our drinks before lunch. He gave me a big smile and a hug, slipped the note into my pocket and whispered in my ear, "I'm so very happy to see you." I went to powder my nose, and read his message, told myself: "Don't do a takeover on him, Deeny. Remember, he's an Englishman. So play it cool." And cool is how I played it, until now,' and she gave Mirella a tiny poke in the ribs, and the two women muffled their laughter with hands over their mouths.

'What was the sign you gave him? Are you sure he understood?' Mirella asked.

'What a question! You know me: cool I can play, but subtle I am not.'

'Oh God, what did you do?'

'When he pulled the chair out for me at the dining table I turned around, smiled, and said, "Yes". He smiled back and looked a bit squiffy and repeated, "Yes. How very nice." Then you saw the rest of it. He hardly gave me a glance or spoke to me through the whole meal. We were both playing it so cool I had to keep putting my hand in my pocket and feeling the paper to make sure I hadn't dreamed it.'

'I know Brindley. He is a serious man. As my solicitor, he has proven to me more than once that he gets what he goes after. He means to marry you, Deeny, I feel very sure of it.'

'Me too, but for God's sake don't tell my mother. She had her heart set on a plastic surgeon. A real mensch face-lifter.'

Chapter 10

Mirella entered the room, and it was as if the Princess had cast a spell on it. For a second, when she opened the door, that same powerful feeling of *dèja vu* returned. She wavered on her feet. Only the memory of Deena's joy and her absence from the room steadied her. Was life made up of just a series of memories?

Something was happening in the room and she wished that her oldest and best friend had stayed to be a part of it. As Mirella thought of Deena's revelation she had to hold back a tear of either joy or fear – she was not sure which. Deena, like herself, had found a man who would change her life and although the two women would remain friends and loyal to each other, to the end of their lives, they would no longer be able to share their happiness as they once had.

Mirella felt herself drift towards the centre of the room where the remaining three women were sitting. It was as though some force within was drawing her into the current, and the current was moving towards a centre. She sat down on the opposite end of the white satin settee from Lili, facing the Princess and Muhsine, who was now draped decoratively on the floor at the feet of the Princess, refilling the Jacobean goblets. The two black eunuchs moved discreetly to stand on either side of the pair of living-room doors.

Mirella felt as if she had been slowly circling the centre of a life foreign to her for a very long time, and now, as she swam with the current around this centre, created here and now by herself and Adam and enhanced by the presence of the Princess, for the last time, she wished Deena had chosen to stay in the room. She wanted Deena to hold her hand and slip with her into the void, to spiral down into a future that was ordained from Mirella's past and tunnel out into a new present in the land of her forefathers, Turkey.

But Deena hadn't chosen to remain and, though sad for her loss, Mirella knew her friend had been right to leave. She was not part of Mirella's new life with Adam and Rashid or Adam's clan, nor would she ever be. Distanced from it, Deena would never understand the legacy Mirella inherited over and above the Oujie estate. She had chosen always to be a welcome tourist in their lives, but not a part of them.

'I was sorry to see your friend leave. Was she very upset?' asked the Princess.

'No, she is quite used to my family and their behaviour.'

'Are you making excuses for me, Mirella? If so, please don't.'

'There is no excuse for you, Mother. I was trying to make a discreet apology to the Princess.'

'To apologise for my behaviour? If I felt it was necessary, I would do it myself.'

'You are quite right, Lili,' said the Princess. 'I need no apology, I know very well what women are like when they get together. You see, women like your mother and myself have lived a good part of our lives secluded in a woman's world, away from men. I am sorry Deena has left us, because women in seclusion are more interesting when there are many present. More intrigues, power-plays, petty jealousies, more love, more hate, to watch and learn from. Women need other women for friends, so they can love men.'

'You worry me, Eirene,' said Lili. 'In the same way that my mother worried me. You are women from an Eastern world, you think, you love, you manipulate people for your own ends and amusement, cleverly and successfully in a way I don't understand. You are a whole generation away from me. You have lived through amazing world changes. But you have relinquished nothing of yourself to those changes. You live in a world that is foreign to me and I find you dangerous because you are dragging me into the past and into an atmosphere so strong I feel we might be not in New York, but in one of Istanbul's famed *harems*.

'It is as if you and my daughter, Adam and Rashid are strong enough, powerful enough, to live against convention, purity. You can play with debauchery, depravity and evil, none of which I am able to cope with, nor want to. In that I am like my father, whom I loved and adored. He made one mistake – he bucked convention and married my mother. But he never made a second one. I have to give my mother her due, from the day she married my father she led an impeccable life. But you could always see in her eyes a decadence – beautiful, opulent, repressed. I envy you, Eirene, just as I envied my mother. You say you were friends, close friends, but I don't remember her ever mentioning your name.'

181

'That's not surprising. We never saw or spoke to each other for the last fifty-eight years of her life. Not since the night she ran away with your father.'

A look of amazement crossed Lili's face. She placed the goblet she had just sipped from on the table and asked in a more subdued manner than she had displayed all day, 'Then you knew my father?'

'Yes, it was my house they used for their assignations, my *yalis* on the Bosporus where the illicit lovers fled to, my *caique* they escaped in. He was so handsome and dashing, much younger than Inje, and completely besotted by her. He promised her the world, and he gave her Boston and love. That was not exactly the world.'

'He remained besotted by her to the end of her life. She ruined him, you know. He could think of nothing but her until the end of his life. He gave everything up for her and worried himself sick, for fear she wasn't happy,' added Lili.

'She gave up more,' said the Princess. 'She gave up her life, her heritage, went into isolation away from her friends, abandoned her country, her history, and threw away her identity. She left a life of luxury and wealth. She turned her back on her patrons, her very personal and secret sexual preferences. She fought her own nature to the end of her days, for your father's love, and for you. You see, she wanted you to have the security of a respectable name and a very American background. She fell in love with purity and innocence, kindness and caring, things she had never known or believed in until she met your father.

'She had her fling with him, fell in love with him and his fine qualities, and was bored with him before they even thought of running away together. It wasn't even a matter of being torn between her sensuous fickle nature and the only sweet and kindly love she had ever known. She knew what she was and which way of life satisfied her. She loved him and his noble nature, but was through with him. However, she had ruined your father and could not bear to desert him.

'The night they ran away, we parted after exchanging vows never to get in touch with each other again. She wanted to begin her life anew, in your father's world, and wanted no contact with Turkey and her past. If she had, Inje was afraid she would allow herself to desert him for the depraved life she led before she met him.'

A hush filled the room. Lili was very pink in the face, and for once looked embarrassed and very sad. Mirella, who had always been her grandmother's favourite, felt neither emotion, because Inje had always shared with Mirella what she could of her Turkish background without revealing too much of her past.

'Then she was a whore, just as I had imagined she had been,' said a very disturbed Lili.

'Rather a crude way of putting it, Lili. She was hardly a common whore. I would rather have described her as a very special lady of the night. A courtesan, a very beautiful clever courtesan, who had several devoted patrons and many lovers until your father came along. But that hardly tells her story.'

'Now I begin to understand why we just barely got along. Why she skipped over me with her love and landed it on Mirella. Why she was so close with her grandchild and not with her daughter. I can't understand why she wasn't satisfied with us.'

'How could you? Your life is black and white, your

mother's was full of colour, many shades of colour. You understand nothing, Lili. You were not born in a palace, part of an immense architectural miracle that for centuries was one of the most inaccessible buildings in the world, the most guarded and secret *harem* ever built. A labyrinth of rooms and staircases, alleys and corridors, courtyards and gardens where fountains played and flowers bloomed. A massive profusion of rooms in a mélange of decorative styles: Turkish and Persian, French, Italian, Austrian and even English. They opened one after the other, one above and below another, and revealed luxury beyond your imagination. Gold and silk, silver and brocade, velvet and jewels in abundance, draped and decorated, sparkled and charmed.

'Nor did you revel in the intrigues of the *harem* as your mother did. The intrigues of the Sultan, and his mother. Intrigues among concubines, between the black eunuchs and the white eunuchs: the most powerful people in the palace, whose bizarre machinations might lure their victims to their death. Murder and sexual depravity were talents they cultivated. It was a case of play the game and play it well, or die.

'And your mother was lucky. She had two things that ensured her survival. She was born a girl, not a boy, which saved her from the Princes' Cage – a place famous even outside Turkey for its cruelty, misery and bloodshed. It was where the Sultans, the royal Princes and the most powerful women of the court removed all rivals for the throne. They murdered less often in your mother's time, keeping their rivals locked up year after year with black eunuchs, sterile women and deaf mutes for companions.

'The second reason she was lucky was that she was

184

born to the Sultan's favourite, the *Kadin* Roxelana Oujie. The most powerful, clever and feared concubine in the court, Mirella's benefactress, her great-grandmother. So how could you have any idea, how could you understand your mother, Lili, if you were ignorant of all this?'

Although Mirella had learned a great deal about her benefactress and all the ancestors before her from the archives found by Adam during an excavation, she had no idea about the life her grandmother, whom she had known and loved, had lived before her arrival in Boston. Mother and daughter were speechless, trying to equate the Princess Eirene's revelations with the Inje Wesson-Cabot they knew.

The Princess rose from her chair and walked thoughtfully around the room. One of her guards detached himself from the door and followed a few paces behind her. She waved him away with a gesture and a word and he became a sentry once more. She smiled at Lili and Mirella, touched the top of Muhsine's head as she sat down again.

'I am not usually a woman to reminisce about the past. I like living for the moment too much. It keeps me young. One cannot become frail living every waking moment of one's life. I am reminded of how long I've lived by my guards, Hyacinth and Narcissus – silly names for men, but the black eunuchs of the *seraglio* always bear names of flowers as it links them with virginity and whiteness, which suits men who are constantly in the service of women. Hyacinth and Narcissus have cared for me nearly all my life. Inje had half-a-dozen such supports from the time she was five years old and was passed from the nursery in the *seraglio* to the Eunuchs.'

'Why are you telling me all this?' asked a still further subdued Lili. 'If you wanted me to know all this, why didn't you tell me when it could have done me some good? Why rake all this up now?'

'Because, until Adam Corey came to me and told me he was in love with Mirella and Rashid appeared with her at my picnic in Istanbul, I never knew you existed. I am telling you this remarkable story because it is part of Mirella's heritage and part of yours. She is one of the true heirs of a line that reaches to the Ottoman Empire, and it is my fervent hope that she will continue her Turkish heritage and perpetuate it as I have, as Rashid does. As Adam more than any of us does – and he is not even an Ottoman, only a Turkophile. There are very few of us left who have seen what I have, participated in the last days of an Empire. She is our chance to live on, after we are on the other side. For us, finding Mirella and the Oujie legacy is like the miracle that the White Russians needed: to find the royal Princess Anastasia and the Romanov treasures.

'I am not an unrealistic woman, Lili. I know you have been assimilated into an American culture so strong and powerful that you will never really understand Mirella any more than you did your mother. But you can appreciate that fate has dealt a hand, and your daughter has happily chosen to play it. She is more like Inje than you are.'

There was a discreet knock. Hyacinth opened the pair of doors and Moses entered carrying a heavy silver tray bearing a coffee service of silver-gilt and Sèvres *demi-tasse* cups and saucers.

'Shall I serve coffee now, Miss Mirella?'

'No, Moses, I think not. Just leave the tray and we'll help ourselves. Thanks.'

Moses' entrance was an interruption welcome to the Princess. She was finding her task of enlightening Mirella and Lili, especially Lili, hard-going. For them it was not Ottoman memories that she was evoking but family history, knowledge of which could only expand their lives and understanding.

The more she spoke of Inje, the greater her recall. Long-forgotten episodes came to mind, not all of them welcome. Telling Inje's story was very close in some ways to recounting her own, and she found retrospection exhausting rather than invigorating.

Princess Eirene Bibescu smiled to herself. She had outwitted and outlived most of the men and women of her past by dint of her intelligence, beauty and sensuality. And, even now, in her advanced years, she had no rival capable of taking from her what she wanted.

The lovers, much younger than herself, handsome and virile men from all walks of life who made love to her, adored her, could still be tortured by her game-playing and intrigues with them. They kept her sexually ageless, and some of the most interesting and powerful men in the world waited to be summoned by her, wanting only to please Eirene Bibescu. She still practised the persona she had learned growing up in the *seraglio* with Inje and was certain that her friend had done so as well – only Boston-fashion. Her exhaustion had come not from memories, but from sentimentality. When she detected that insidious feeling in herself, she mastered the exhaustion, took another sip of Yquem and allowed the memories to surface.

Lili surprised the Princess when she said, 'My mother was the most beautiful and fascinating woman in Boston, and remained that way until she died. She had no rival, she was unique, mysterious, enticing. But her true self she kept a secret. What was her life like before my father that she felt compelled to keep it a secret to the grave?'

Mirella, too, was surprised by her mother's interest, and again the women settled into a moment of silence. Mirella poured coffee, placed the cups in front of the women and sat down. She felt a sadness for Lili, and was concerned that what they were about to hear would shock Lili profoundly, as it would any Wesson-Cabot, or a Wingfield. Puritan New England has its lapses, but likes to see itself as pure.

The Princess took a small Fabergé powder-box of chased gold from her purse. The lid with its coat of arms emblazoned in diamonds caught the afternoon sunlight and showered prisms of colour over her dress. Mirella watched the Princess powder her nose and take a rather long look in the small mirror on the inside of the compact, snap it closed and put it away.

'Western poets, painters and travellers in the nineteenth century explored Turkey and described it to the world as a mythical East, a lascivious East, an astonishing exotic and erotic East. They were wrong about only one thing when they spoke like that: Turkey was Asia Minor then, as it is now, not the East,' said the Princess. She took a sip of her coffee and continued, 'They were telling tales of the Ottoman Empire and its sexual grip on the East as well as the West, and the hub and the centre of the Ottoman Empire was the Sultan, the *seraglio*, the

Constantinople, Turkey, of my childhood, of your mother Inje's childhood.

'The sexually-repressed, stiff and upright Victorians were titillated by news of a court designed to cater to the sexual penchants of men. I am quite sure, Lili, that both you and Mirella might be titillated by it, but like the suffragettes of their day, and what you call the women's-libbers of today, allow yourselves only to realize it as a rich male fantasy. One that should not be indulged in because of its domination over women and their human rights.

'There is no question that you are right to deplore female enslavement, but you would be very wrong to believe that it is only a male fantasy. It was very much a reality in your mother's day, Lili. I am here to attest to that, and to the fact it is a reality even today. It may be unlawful, more discreet and extremely rare in Turkey, but it lives on, as it does in the East and the Far East.'

The Princess made a point of looking directly into Mirella's eyes and observing a long pause before she resumed talking. Mirella blushed, aware that the Princess was reminding her of her recent erotic affair with Rashid, her near-enslavement to him that even in her marriage was not wholly broken, and of her night at Oda-Lala's, the *harem* maintained by Rashid and a few of his friends.

It was true that Mirella had put that part of her life on the back burner of her mind since the night she had run away from Rashid to Adam, love and marriage. And now with the Princess' words and the look she gave Mirella, her erotic life in Turkey with Rashid ceased simmering and began to bubble.

As usual, Lili got it wrong when she said, 'If you are

referring to the unorthodox household my son-in-law Adam maintains, I can assure you that now, having married Mirella, all that will change.'

'No, Lili. I most certainly was not referring to Adam. Adam has exactly what you described, an unorthodox household. He does not, however, keep it together by sexual slavery, but by the erotic delights he shares with its inhabitants. They are governed by love, affection, mutual respect and, above all, freedom. Quite the opposite of the things Inje and I were born to.'

'Born to! That brings us to my grandmother, Mirella's notorious benefactor. What sort of woman was she who would bring a child into the world she lived in? And did she not have any regard for my mother? I imagine she had as little maternal feeling for her daughter as my mother had for me.'

'I wouldn't presume to know about that, Lili. I only saw her once, when she came to visit Inje. It still remains a dazzling and unforgettable moment in my life – she was the most powerful and charismatic woman I have ever seen.

'The Sultan was sexually besotted and controlled by Roxelana Oujie. The court was used to that, but not used to a Turkish Sultan in love, as he was with Roxelana. In fact, Roxelana was not her real name but the name he gave her from an ancestor who became the most famous woman in the history of the Ottoman court, because he believed the wealthy, beautiful and clever Jewess surpassed that woman in every way.

'Inje was Roxelana and the Sultan's first-born. She was allowed to remain in the *seraglio* only because she was a girl. The boy who came later and another girl had been taken away in secret after the Sultan had seen them, hidden from the intrigue and murder the *seraglio* was famous for. Roxelana had powerful enemies and both she and the Sultan wanted them safe until they were mature and had grown powerful enough to return to the court and defend themselves. They never did return to the court, Roxelana saw to that. They were children fathered not by the Sultan but two of her lovers, and she was afraid that the Sultan might find out and take some cruel action against them. But I am digressing, and I mustn't.

'Inje was removed from her mother hours after her birth and placed with a wet nurse as most of us were in the *harem*. One thing is for certain, her mother was not a direct part of Inje's everyday life, although she did dominate it from afar. She grew up in the nursery, along with other children of the *harem*. And we led quite an ordinary everyday life surrounded by women and children, except that the men in our lives were eunuchs, whom we were guarded by, day and night. We played and learned to pray, and studied the rudiments of sewing, cooking and how to dance and sing. For our future was unknown, except for the fact that we would remain in seclusion in this *harem* or another all our lives until our death. Our father-figures were the black or white eunuchs who replaced the complete and virile men absent from our lives.

'It was a happy, colourful life where everyone visited each other. There was gossip and intrigue everywhere, plots and counter-plots, and many, many quarrels. But when you are five years old, you don't understand, and just accept the sometimes volatile atmosphere as normal. But it wasn't always like that. There was also the excitement of women in the *harem* giving birth and raising children, the endless arrangements and celebrations of marriages and deaths, and women consoling women on growing old, and being in and out of favour.

'The hatcheries and the nursery were extremely well organized, like the rest of the *harem*, which was a realm all on its own. A girl could remain there until way past nursery age, until the complicated ritual and protocol of the *harem*, which even the Sultan followed to the letter, allowed her to move on to one of the minor offices in the *harem* – unless of course she was lucky enough to catch the eye of the Sultan. Then she was called a *gozde* and given separate rooms, special attendants, and taught every aspect of erotica to please the Sultan. And there she would wait for the imperial summons, which might come at any time, or never at all.

'There was something else beside eunuchs that made life in a *harem* nursery different from a Boston nursery. We were never squawking, spoiled children. We were obedient little women, pampered and dressed in silks and satins and jewels, little dolls of flesh and blood, who from infancy were petted and fondled with oil of sandalwood, and jasmine, sexually aroused by the mouth, the hand, the nipple, by caressing fingers, lips and tongues, so that by the age of five we were sensual children, awake to erotic feelings.

'There were, after all, Sultans and Emirs and foreign Kings and Princes whose sexual preference was for children and, if not chosen for one of those, we were at least primed for the next step in sexual preparation.'

'And my grandmother condemned my mother to

that? How disgusting, how vile,' Lili said.

'Not disgusting and vile as far as they were concerned, at that time. Remember, your grandmother was a concubine, and her daughter, your mother, was born to a favoured concubine and a Sultan, and treated as such. For them the worst thing that could happen was that they should not have been taught the ways of erotica, not have been prepared to satisfy a master.

'How would Roxelana Oujie find Inje an important master, and hence an important position in life, one at least worthy of the daughter of Roxelana Oujie? One mustn't forget, Inje's mother was not only the most favoured concubine in the court, but she was also independently wealthy. She was the only daughter of the wealthiest Jew in the East, a Grand Vizier to the Sultan, who managed the Sultan's fortunes, and was given to the Sultan with her own fortune intact. Inje would go to a very important man, or no man at all.

'On one of the occasional visits of the Sultan and Roxelana to the *harem*, twenty of the Sultan's concubines were playing ball with some of the children in a courtyard trellised with roses, and cages of singing birds. Several of the women caught his eye and after conferring with Roxelana, he chose three of them for his bed. He was charmed by the beauty and manner in which Inje played with the women. From that day on she was called *gozde*, child of his or not. Any girl lucky enough to have caught the eye of the Sultan was called a *gozde*.'

'You are not going to tell me that my mother slept with her own father, Eirene? It is simply not possible. I will never believe that.'

'Well, that's good, Lili, because she didn't. He did, however, fall in love with her, and had her removed from the nursery that very day and placed in the hands of the eunuchs and attendants I spoke of before. She was adored by him. He could deny her nothing. He was besotted with her much as he had been by her mother. She was taught to read and to write and to speak four languages, but that was secondary to her erotic education. He was determined to have her as soon as she bled as a woman, and he made his intentions no secret. But the entire court knew it would never happen: Roxelana would never allow it. She did, however, titillate him with their daughter. There was no question about that.

'And as for Inje, well, by the time she was thirteen, between the women and the eunuchs who taught her everything there was to learn about the intrigues and pleasures of sex, all she wanted and waited for was her first bleeding, so that she could lie with a man and experience all she had learned.

'Don't look so shocked, Lili. We were all the same, you know. Remember, we had been turned into sexual playthings, and were looking for other sexual toys for ourselves. We were watched over night and day to make sure we remained virgins, but that never hindered us from getting our sexual satisfaction in one way or another, nor from falling in love.

'Both were very dangerous. Unbelievably cruel punishments were meted out for lesbian relationships, and the women who had been bedded by the Sultan and were no longer virgins and were long-forgotten, who resorted to sex with the eunuchs and were caught, suffered dreadful deaths. And a eunuch who had lost only half his masculinity, so that he could not only satisfy women but could do so enormously, since he had very large erections and could sustain very long performances, his fate was unspeakable.

'Inje knew all this and had no fear. She learned to intrigue and survived all her childhood transgressions. For us, she was as special as her mother, because not only was she *gozde* but she was the only one of us virgins who had actually been touched by a real man, and the Sultan at that. Who cared if he were her father? To us it was the greatest privilege in the world.'

'You were all corrupt, and corrupted,' said Lili looking very sad, 'and what's worse is that you didn't even know it.'

'Yes, that's true, Lili. Sad but true.'

'What happened to Inje?' asked Mirella, unable at that moment to think of Inje as her grandmother.

'Roxelana was, as I told you, a very clever woman. She knew that in time she would have only one serious rival for the place of power she held with the Sultan and the court, and so she removed Inje.'

'Please don't tell me she was cruel to her, did something physically violent to her. I couldn't bear it. If so, then clearly my grandmother was a monster,' said Lili.

The Princess looked at Lili and realized that indeed she would never be able to bear the sordid details of Inje's sexual life, or the niceties of depraved cruelty Roxelana was supposed to be capable of practising. Though never consummated with the Sultan, there had obviously been a strong sexual relationship between father and daughter. Lili would never be able to understand that any more than she would the sexual life Inje created with the elderly Balkan King who made her the first woman in his Kingdom – and a nymphomaniac.

Eirene had no intention of embarrassing Lili, only of making her understand where her mother came from and how remarkable she was. Because, aside from the sexual devil in Inje, she was in every way a kind and generous, elegant and charming woman. And as for Inje's own mother, Roxelana, although not a total monster, she certainly had some monstrous traits which she had been known to use from time to time. Eirene chose not to expose these intimacies to this very unhappy lady from Boston. There would be no point. She would not appreciate such knowledge. And so she said, 'No, Lili, not a monster exactly, just a product of her time and place in the wheel of fortune. And if you had ever seen her you would never call her monster, just utterly remarkable. An example of just how remarkable she was is Inje's departure from the court.

'Although steeped in the old régime of the Ottoman Empire to the end of her life, Roxelana saw the end coming for the corrupt, debauched and depraved Empire. Europe and the opinions of Europeans, their wars and their victories, their morals and their rules for western civilization had no room for the bizarre excesses of the Ottoman Empire.

'Europeans were advising the Sultan. All Europe, and even England and the United States, were working through diplomacy to moderate and mediate with Turkey. She saw the beginning of the end. Western civilization and the Ottoman Empire's own weakness and inner rot would destroy them.

'Through the years she cleverly convinced the Sultan that small reforms would keep the West quiet, and, by the time Inje bled as a woman, Roxelana had convinced the Sultan that the West would never deal with a man who openly had a sexual affair with his own daughter. He would be marked a barbarian, a depraved despot.

'Desperate to be the man to deflower his precious Inje, after years of ripening her for himself, yet convinced by Roxelana that he must not, he angrily refused to arrange a marriage for Inje. Instead he presented her to a King from the Balkans who had come to the Sultan to select an official mistress for himself.

'The arrangement was made on the condition that, when the King died, or if the King was displeased, Inje was to be returned to the Sultan. The King paid for Inje with a rock crystal cask with ormolu mounts, filled with fabulous diamonds, of all shapes and sizes, which he presented to the Sultan who promptly gave them to Roxelana. The Sultan banished Inje from his sight and her name from court because he could not bear another man to take her, secretly determined to bring her back when it was politically possible.'

Mirella had to cover her mouth with her hand to suppress a deep sigh that came from sharp surprise. The cask of diamonds was at this very moment in her possession, part of the three-pronged legacy she inherited. Mirella had actually scooped the diamonds up in her hand and let the gems fall through her open fingers, as if she were playing with pebbles on a beach.

'She was thirteen,' the Princess continued. 'The King was fifty-one. Six years later, he was dead, and

197

she returned to the *seraglio*. Within two years of her return, there was a new Sultan on the throne who made her his favourite. Roxelana Oujie, the last great concubine of the Ottoman Empire, was dead. The court was dissolving rapidly, a victim of reform after reform imposed to keep the West at bay. And your father, then a young, handsome and dashing United States diplomat, who had the ear of the Sultan and a considerable influence on him, was seduced by Inje.

'Your father's credentials were impeccable and it was because of that and his innocence, his loyalty to his country and the Sultan, that the lovers were not discovered. By the time rumours became rife in the *seraglio*, it was too late to give her up. He despised the deceit, the secrecy. He was riddled with guilt, and deeply in love. He believed her to be the same, and she was. Only for Inje it was a love affair that would run its course, and for your father that course was forever until death did them part. He would have her as his wife, or die.

'She did everything in her power to make him understand that they were playing a very dangerous game of love and that it had to stop. She was not free. But, as far as your father was concerned, she was unmarried and therefore free. He decided to go to the Sultan, because, remember, she was his favourite but not his wife, and ask permission to marry Inje. She tried to make him understand that, if he did so, she would be dead before he left the palace and he, before he arrived back at the American Embassy. Inje recruited me and my husband Prince Yorgos to talk with him, plead with him to give her up. It was useless. The French Ambassador and an English Admiral stationed at the palace to advise the Sultan

198

were friends of your father and were asked by my husband to intervene.

'Nothing would change his mind, and when it was evident that he preferred death to a life without the woman he loved, Inje saw no way out but to run away with him, because that was what they would have to do to save their lives. She made one stipulation: no goodbyes, no farewells to anyone. Just a *rendezvous* of two lovers was what those who knew about them must think. Inje trusted no one. And, once that was arranged, they must travel in haste from Turkey and not stop until they were safe in the United States.

'They met on a sunny afternoon at my *yalis* on the Bosporus. She was three hours late, having had great difficulty getting away from the Sultan, who was very suspicious. He questioned her endlessly about her recent movements and later interrogated her eunuchs, one of whom she had to bribe with a diamond necklace he had always coveted.

'She was extremely upset, frightened and barely able to cope. I had never seen her like that. Your father was admirable. From then on he had their escape planned as in a romance. They disguised themselves: both were dressed first as simple Turkish sailors, and boarded my *caique* and sailed down the Bosporus past the Golden Horn, directly along the shores of the *seraglio* and its gardens and trees that meandered down to the water's edge, the place where Inje was born and had lived most of her life, and into the Sea of Marmara.

'When night fell, under cover of darkness, they changed their clothes to those of English naval officers and the *caique* slipped alongside an English naval cruiser that took them aboard and to safety.

That was the last time I ever saw or heard from your mother. Your father was ruined. The Sultan realized she was gone when he called for her to his bed and she couldn't be found anywhere in Topkapi. He extracted all the answers he needed from the eunuch who had the diamond necklace.

'The entire palace was alerted. Troops were scouring Constantinople for the couple. But your mother and father eluded them. House-to-house searches were made everywhere, the waters of the Golden Horn, the Bosporus, the Black Sea, and the Sea of Marmara were plied with every class of boat in the Sultan's command.

'By midday, the Sultan was sure they had escaped his city, and were under the protection of one of the foreign governments in Constantinople. He called in the United States Ambassador, demanded the return of your father and mother to him for punishment, and required an immediate court martial from the Navy, to whom your father was attached. The scandal was out and an international incident was created between your country and mine, and Inje closed the book on the life she had led before your father and her arrival in Boston.'

No one in the room spoke. Each of the women was lost in her own reactions to the Princess' revelations. The Princess leaned back against the cushions and closed her eyes. Softly, almost inaudibly to those in the room, she said, 'So many memories, it was all so long ago, yet it is all present to my mind as I recall every detail of that day for you, as if it were only yesterday.'

Hyacinth approached the Princess, stood behind the settee where she sat and carefully, concernedly, adjusted the cushions behind her. Muhsine rose from where she had been sitting at the feet of the Princess and fetched her a crystal goblet filled with clear, sparkling Perrier.

The bright sunlight in the room had long since gone and was now replaced by the long shadows of afternoon. Lili sat silent and pensive, staring straight ahead at the Princess Eirene Bibescu. Very slowly, almost unconsciously, she reached out across the empty space on the settee between Mirella and herself and offered her hand to her daughter. She felt their fingers lock, the warmth of their clasped hands, and Lili Wingfield felt a closeness with her daughter that she had never known before.

Chapter 11

Rashid and Adam stood at the entrance of the living-room, watching the women for some seconds before they entered. Adam's enchantment with the room and his wife never wavered from the first time he saw them. But today, with the addition of the others who were reflected again and again in the mirrors around the panelled walls, he sensed more than enchantment. A depth, a sensual richness of events past and in the making shimmered in the shadows.

Rashid, too, seemed aware of it. When Adam walked to the nearest lamp and switched it on, he broke into the silence and the thoughts of the women who had been so lost in them and in Princess Eirene's story that they had been unaware of the men's presence.

The women came alive with the light and in that second of rebirth, Rashid could feel a passion, yet another small degree of submission, vibrate across the room to him from Mirella. Their eyes met, and he knew his patient waiting for Mirella to return to his bed was over. Their suspended erotic life together was about to begin again. He smiled at her, a smile filled with erotic promise and calculated to excite her, which it did.

Though it was not outwardly evident, Mirella felt flustered but only for a moment. She switched her gaze to Adam and with different eyes, eyes brimming with love, their hearts met. She wanted him, as she always wanted him when he walked into a room, and she warmed to his very being and was inflamed by his ready and rugged sexiness. Only for the moment she wanted sex with Rashid more.

For the first time since she was aware of loving and wanting both men, Mirella felt no conflict about it.

In the room that afternoon, sipping Château d'Yquem with the others, the Princess had made her point about fate. And it had not been lost on Mirella. She at last understood that fate had stepped in and had dealt her a magnificent hand. A new life, vastly changed from anything she had ever known, which included two men who were offering her different kinds of love and who made it quite clear by their actions, rather than words, that they both understood and accepted not only her fate, but theirs as well.

She would do as the Princess had implied she, the Princess had done, as Inje, Mirella's grandmother had done, and as Roxelana Oujie, her great-grandmother, had done: seized their fate with both hands, and run with it. Mirella made up her mind to do the same.

Rashid went to the Princess and kissed her hand, then to Lili, and repeated the gesture. He felt Lili stiffen when he touched her and was not displeased at her reaction to him. He sat down between Lili and Mirella and raised Mirella's hand and met it with his lips, then kissed her briefly on the cheek as old friends do.

Rashid could actually feel that old familiar sexual need she had for him pulling him like a magnet to her. They looked briefly at each other, and his mind exulted in their sexual bliss and in the paths he would guide her through to arrive there, before the day was out.

How, where, he had little idea, but he knew it would happen. She was ripe for him, ready to fall. Oh, how Rashid loved women when they needed to confirm their erotic natures with him. The upper hand with women was always thrilling; dominating their bliss, even more so. To tease and torture as foreplay. An *apéritif* to thrilling.

'Have you had a long amusing gossip over wine and coffee this afternoon, ladies?' asked Adam as he greeted the Princess with a friendly kiss on the cheek, touched Lili's shoulder in a kindly greeting and smiled warmly at Muhsine before seating himself on the arm of the settee next to his wife.

Tilting her chin up, he kissed her lips. Warm luscious lips, that neither parted sensually nor suggested the sexual excitement gnawing at Mirella at that moment, there only for Rashid. They were, however, loving lips, that satisfied Adam. Having confirmed their sexual joy and excess with one another during the past two-day tryst at the Plaza, he had no need for more.

'Yes, I guess you could call it that,' answered Lili, who stood up and declared that, much as she would like to stay on, she was most anxious to take the next train home to Boston. Everyone in the room politely stood up to say goodbye.

There was a distinct softness in Lili's manner, a degree of humility, which surprised the two men and made them aware that something profound had happened to Lili Wingfield in the few hours the women were left alone. But if they were surprised by her manner, they were doubly surprised by her when she thanked the Princess for an afternoon she would never forget and declared 'I am very sorry I have not had the privilege of knowing you all my life. I hope we will meet one day again.'

Where Adam sensed a profound change and sadness in Lili, Rashid sensed nothing of the sort, believing that a woman like Lili, with her self-centredness, pathological narcissism and bitterness, never changed.

'Please stay for tea and take a later train, Mother,' offered Mirella. But Lili was determined to leave.

Adam insisted on escorting her to Grand Central Station to see her onto the train. And, at the front door, before Lili left the house, mother and daughter kissed each other goodbye, a closeness and peace between them that delighted them both.

Watching her mother walk down the stairs and away from her, Mirella had the strange feeling that though they belonged to each other and loved each other, and peace and contentment now governed their interactions, it would always be a cautious relationship.

Having been set free by all she had learned from Rashid and Adam about love at once sexual and real, Mirella found that the contrast between tentative love with her mother and her natural inclinations to love freely and spontaneously, with passion and self-indulgence, felt not only unnatural but sad and wasteful. Princess Eirene's afternoon revelations of the fiery blood of her ancestors and the lives they led were only an added lesson to Mirella to live honestly, with her own code of morals, not anyone else's.

Adam's Rolls was pulling away from the kerb.

Mirella waved farewell and was about to close the door, when Adam called her name. The car stopped and he bounded out of it and up the stairs, leaving the car door open and the chauffeur and Lili waiting. He placed his arm around her waist and stepped into the front hall with her, leaving the front door wide open, and manoeuvred her behind it. Adam placed his hand on her breast, delighted to feel the weight, the soft curve of it in his hand, and rubbed his thumb across her nipple under the sensuous silk of her bodice. Looking down at her, he said, 'Would you mind terribly if I sent you along with Rashid and the Princess on his plane to Athens this evening? I have some unfinished business, an obligation to locate some people and thank them for their help and consideration in a business venture. If we were to change our arrangements slightly, I might just catch them in Geneva and be with you in time for dinner tomorrow evening on the yacht.'

Mirella was clearly flummoxed by his suggestion. It offered the way for her to be alone with Rashid, but was more than she had hoped for. And the surprise, the shock even, of his suddenly, without warning, leaving her, even for one day, took its toll on her feelings. Her heart pounded at the thought of a sexual encounter with her lover. Her nipples grew rigid under Adam's caressing thumb. She placed a hand to her forehead as if confused. 'Wouldn't you rather I went with you to Geneva so that we could go together to meet Rashid?' she asked.

'No, honestly, I think it best if I travel with Josh, who can be of help to me, since he is already involved. We can go at our own pace and I won't be concerned about your being bored waiting around. If you agree, then I'll dash upstairs and tell Rashid, who I am sure will be delighted to have you alone to himself for a change. I can say goodbye to Eirene, give some instructions to Turhan and tell Muhsine what to pack for me. Don't look so worried, I'm not deserting you. I promise you Josh and I will fly out sometime late this evening.'

'Well, it seems as if you have it all worked out. All right, of course, if that's what you want.'

He looked at the shape of her erect nipples showing through the silk and he pinched one between his fingers, then lowered his lips to it and kissed the nipple through the silk material. He tilted her chin up, kissed her on the tip of her nose and said, 'Wait here, I'll be right back.'

Mirella watched him mount the stairs three at a time, and tried to take stock of what was happening. In the last few days she had come to realize that Adam was a fast-mover, and it amazed her how clever he was at getting everyone to move with him or be left behind – not as if abandoned, but simply left standing because they couldn't keep up, and Adam waited for no one. But she knew that from experience. Had he not left her twice because she didn't recognizc his love for her fast enough?

She stood with her back to the door, looking up the empty staircase and waited patiently for him to reappear. When he did it was with Rashid by his side. She watched the two men talk for no more than a minute, but enough to remind her how very different they were.

For Adam, sex was not the most important thing in the world. Loving her was more important. Work was more important. A sense of life as somehow holy, no matter how abstract, was more important. Responsibility and loyalty were more important. The sexual life was some way down his list of priorities, but, once its turn arrived, of the greatest importance.

Rashid's priorities were quite different. His joy of life was completely dependent on his sexual mastery and manipulation of women and situations. All else in his life revolved around that. How could she be so frivolous as to love him for his sexual prowess, allow herself to succumb to a man who in some respects was no more than a sexual slave master, be inebriated by the sexual charisma and erotic charm he distilled around her? She didn't understand how, and didn't want to. She allowed it, and that seemed to be enough for her.

The two men shook hands, and Adam hurried down the stairs towards her. Rashid disappeared again behind the living-room doors.

Adam placed his arm around her shoulder and said, as they walked down the front stairs to the waiting car, 'It's all set. Rashid is delighted to take care of you. We'll be together for dinner somewhere on the Aegean Sea tomorrow night.'

As they stepped off the kerb Mirella began to ask a question, 'Adam, why are you pushing—'

But he cut off her words with a luscious, long kiss on the lips, then moved his lips caressingly along her cheek to her ear.

'We must all of us have our secret moments,' he whispered, 'and sex must always be a very private thing between two people, like yours and mine is. Privacy is quintessential, don't you agree?'

Then he moved his lips away from her ear and they looked deeply into each other's eyes, and a smile crept across the face of each. She nodded agreement, and fought back tears of overwhelming gratitude for the love and understanding he was showing her.

'I love you,' she said.

'Yes, I know. And I love you, and nothing either of us could ever do could disturb that.'

Mirella threw her arms around his neck and they kissed again, and this time lips parted and tongues met for a second to seal their kiss. One moment they were lost in their love and a kiss, and the next she was closing the car door and saying goodbye again to her mother. Then the Rolls slipped away from her into the centre of the road and sped down East 65th Street.

She sighed, feeling a rush of happiness, and hurried from the street up the front stairs into her house and to her lover.

Rashid put the key in the lock and turned it. He pushed the door to his suite in the Carlisle open and stepped back gallantly, allowing Mirella to enter first. She heard the door close behind her and the click of the double lock. It made her heart leap.

Mirella stood in the centre of the all-white living-room as if frozen in time and space. She fluctuated between a sense of desperate sexual desire, and a devastating fear of Rashid and of submitting to his erotic demands – demands she had found ecstasy in, had learned to yearn for, once they became part of her sexual life.

Sex with Rashid was total intimacy with Rashid, and only lasted as long as the sexual experience, and his desire for more. Therefore, sex with Rashid and the real Rashid were one and the same. Depraved sex, debauchery with Rashid, was thrilling. Ecstasy and more than ecstasy. Heroin to the addict. Only love, love with Adam, had saved her from addiction. That and her fear of complete submission to Rashid's sexual extremes, and of being enslaved by them, and consequently to him.

They had weathered all that. She had fought him masterfully to remain her own woman, while submitting, always submitting to his erotic demands and their mutual sexual bliss. And that had won her to his heart forever.

She felt a shiver of excitement pass through her body as he stepped up behind her. Where would he take her now? To what heights? On what paths would they climb in their sexual quest? He was a sorcerer: at the click of a lock he became a different man, she became a different woman. Only Eros was their god and could rule over them.

Rashid placed his hands on her shoulders. She jumped, so tense was she. He caressed them and then slipped his hands down her arms and around her waist, pulled her roughly back against him and buried his face in the silky hair at the nape of her neck.

There comes that time for two people when sexual chemistry takes over and no amount of plotting and planning, loving or game-playing, is of any significance. All thought disappears, and the sensual elements mix and meld, interchange and take command. That was how it was at that moment for Rashid.

His passion, their passion, inflamed and burned them, seared their flesh. They clung together, tongues silent, bodies screaming.

Mirella trial to cool the fire by distracting herself with the details of the room, but that was impossible because the whites were all texture: silk and velvet, suede and alligator and pig-skin, deep white wool underfoot, and ermine-coloured wood, and white marble, tactile instruments to caress and excite the naked flesh.

A virginal-white chamber, with a huge Stuben crystal vase filled with eight dozen, deep-red, long-stemmed roses on a table in the centre of the room. The red roses, an aggressive and stunning blow to the purity of the room, made a sacrificial bowl of blood, to be drunk from, to be marked by. A sinister, sensual touch, extravagantly erotic and beautiful. A room calculated to tease the senses. The room was so much like a woman and the slash of red was the cunt, the heart of it.

Rashid pulled her down where they stood, onto her knees. Still with her back to him, he gently pushed her forward so that she rested on her elbows, and slowly he slid her silk skirt up over her bottom, leaving it in neat folds around her waist. He caressed the luscious rounds, more sensuously defined by the nylon stockings, whose tops were high up on her thighs, and the garter belt worn low on the hips. The white garters against her rounded firm flesh, and the provocative, submissive position he had placed her in, left her exposed, vulnerable, just the way he liked her best.

He toyed with her, teased her with gentle hands and ranging fingers, and could feel her giving in to him, slipping, falling under his spell. Her need for more, much more than caresses, was evident to him in the way she arched her back, gently rocked her pelvis teasingly towards him, moved her knees further apart.

Rashid's heartbeat accelerated. His erection now demanded. He slid his black lizard belt from the loops on his trousers, and teased Mirella's flesh with it, slowly, lightly, stroking the leather across her yielding orbs and between the cheeks of her bottom down to the lips of her cunt. Her sign of pleasure and excitement mixed with fear was the tribute he sought and received.

He smacked her hard, and kissed the place he marked with his hand, and his kisses continued, his tongue searched out reactions he wanted. The hugely well-endowed Rashid teased Mirella with his cock, using it on the surface and at the entrance of her most intimate orifices like a gentle probing kiss. She whispered huskily, 'Now, Rashid. Now.'

And for the first time, in all the sex and outrageous sexual antics they had shared together in the past, he obeyed her demand, wanting to please her on her terms. Swiftly, without any further thought or tenderness, he slipped his arms under hers and in front of her, his hands over her shoulders, mounted her and pulled her roughly back onto him while thrusting ruthlessly into her. He fucked her hard, again and again, with seemingly endless deep strokes, until he had wrung several huge shattering orgasms from her. When he finally withdrew and had released her, she collapsed on the floor, face down in the deep white carpet, whimpering from the sheer force of ecstasy she achieved with him.

He stood over her: she was a compelling sight, raven black hair spread wildly on the carpet, just a hint of the beautiful erotic face showing its finely-etched profile, arms and legs reminiscent of alabaster, flung lasciviously apart. The sensuous silk of her dress was draped carelessly over the top half of her torso, the bottom half naked and exposed, raped and ravaged, still looking desirable – more than desirable, tantalizing, and his to do with as he wished.

While watching her, he slowly undressed until stark naked. Then he gathered her up in his arms. While he carried her across the room to the bedroom, she loosened her dress and raised it over her head and dropped it to the floor. Then she kissed him. He stopped before they entered the bedroom and spoke to her for the first time since they arrived in his rooms.

'You do know that there is no running away from me a second time, don't you?'

'Yes.'

'Good.'

Mirella ran her fingers through his hair, trembled at the feel of his skin under her hand, their naked bodies touching. She lowered her mouth to his nipple, kissed it, opened her mouth wider and sucked.

Still holding her in his arms, he shifted her, wrapped her legs around him and, smiling, knocked at the bedroom door. It opened at a touch from Humayun and he carried Mirella to bed.

It was midnight when Rashid's long black Daimler pulled up to the waiting Boeing 747 revving its engines at Kennedy Airport, and four stewards rushed down the stairs with huge bouquets of flowers.

'Mr Lala Mustapha welcomes you aboard his plane with this bouquet,' each said to Mirella as he presented her with the flowers.

She looked up at Rashid standing next to her and smiled. Her heart leaped. He was as ever a most beautiful, depraved and sensual-looking man. Then

214

she laughed openly, because her heart was full, because she was happy, because she knew what she would never dare to suggest to Rashid, that he was as enslaved by her as she was by him.

'You do spoil me terribly,' she said.

'I adore spoiling you. It's the devil in me ruining you. I like a woman who can be ruined as well by a flower as by a jewel.' Then he began to laugh, as she touched the handcuff around her wrist. He slipped his arm through hers and together they hurried up the staircase into the aircraft.

On the movable staircase landing, before they entered the plane, he reached beneath the flowers she carried and grabbed both her wrists in his hands. The pair of inch-wide, diamond cuffs, securely clasped by a lock cleverly hidden under the large, blue-white, hand-polished diamond, bit into her skin. His last words to her before they left New York were shouted above the roar of the engines.

'These cuffs were made without a key. I once gave you a slave collar of priceless pearls and allowed you to remove it. Not a second time, Mirella. When I bound you to me this time with these diamond chains, it was for now and for ever. Swear to me before we enter the plane, you will never ask to be released again. Swear to me you will never have them cut away.'

'You're hurting me,' she shouted. But he did not release the pressure on her wrists. Tears came into her eyes from the pain, and then she shocked him with her answer.

'You have forgotten. It is not I, but you who offered to release me from the pearl collar. You who placed the key on a chain around my neck. You who were just as afraid of sharing your sexual excesses with me as I was. And maybe you even more than me. Now, please let go of my wrists – you are really hurting me – and move aside. You and I need no promises. Just like my *painfully* gorgeous bracelets, we are linked together for life.'

Then simultaneously they smiled and as he pulled her by the wrists tight up against him they kissed passionately, crushing the flowers between them.

When Rashid yanked her into the aircraft cabin they were laughing, and when he released her wrists, several drops of bright red blood fell onto his white jacket lapel.

'You bleed like a red rose,' he said, and kissed the tiny wound on her wrist so that he licked the last droplet of blood.

Chapter 12

Deena lost no time walking. Not far from Mirella's front door she hailed a cab and got in.

'Do you know where Ralph Lauren's shop is?' she asked.

'Yeah.'

'Terrific. Take me there, the fastest, the quickest way you know how.'

'You got it. Hey, you must be going to England?' asked the puffy faced driver chomping on a dead cigar.

'How did you know that?' asked an astonished Deena. 'I haven't even told my mother yet.'

''Cause that's Ralph Lauren's big number this season. The Country English look, or is it the English Country look? Well, whatever.'

'How amazing that you should know that.'

'*Women's Wear Daily.* I read it every morning over coffee at the H and O Luncheonette. Ain't I seen you there talking to Hymie? Well, maybe not.'

'Well, maybe yes,' she said laughing, picking up his New York dialect.

'Thought so. Small world, isn't it? That's supposed to be a cliché, but believe you me, it's true. Here you got a case in point.'

'God help me, another cabbie philosopher, Brooklyn?' she asked, trying to pinpoint which borough he came from.

217

'Yonkers, kid, Yonkers.'

'Don't "kid" me. That's Brooklyn I hear coming through.'

'Pretty smart. I moved to Yonkers from Brooklyn twenty years ago. You?'

'Riverside Drive, by way of a Bronx father and a Brooklyn mother.'

'So where'dja get the fancy accent?'

'Listen' – she looked at the name on his licence, prominently displayed in the taxi – 'Abe Kimball, we have no time for the story of my life.'

'You should try Loehman's in the Bronx. Some bargains, if you can stand the crowds and the pressure. They're a tough lot, those Loehman customers, shuffling through the racks.'

'Thanks a lot, Abe, but no thanks. One of the greatest perks in being successful and financially comfortable is not having to go to Loehman's. My Loehman's days are over, thank God.'

'Bendel's has got some great-looking cruise wear in the window. But your choice of Lauren, and especially if you're going to England, has got to be better. That's some shop he's got. A lotta taste has Ralph Lauren. Come up like a mushroom he has, and good luck to him. A nice Jewish boy made good. I always like to see that and especially in the rag trade. You gotta give him credit, he's class. A class-A act. Stole the whole idea from the English. You know, elegance, simplicity, country chic—'

Deena interrupted. 'What is it with you, Abe? How do you know so much about fashion, and high fashion at that? You New York cabbies kill me, always a mine of information.'

218

'I've been running a couple of regular fares to and from Seventh Avenue for thirty-seven years. I've got a wife and four daughters who grew up knowing when polka dots were in and stripes were out, the skirts above the knee, the skirts below the knee, before the fashion magazines even knew. Some cabbies get stock market tips. With my luck, all I got was fashion tips – and wholesale. But, believe me, with four daughters, wholesale can be as good as the stock market.'

Deena began to laugh. She sat back and her laughter fed on itself and she could not stop. Abe the cabbie watched her through his windscreen mirror, and couldn't help smiling: she was so pretty and happy and friendly.

'Laugh, kid. *Zei gezunt*. What do I care if you're laughing at me? I'm funny, my life's hilarious. So would yours be if you'd married-off four daughters—'

'Four well-dressed daughters,' Deena corrected him, and began to laugh again.

Abe Kimball got caught up in her laughter. 'That's right, kiddo. Four well-dressed daughters, and married them off after each of 'em had a college degree. NYU, City College, Columbia and Hunter. In the meantime, remember, he who laughs last laughs longest. I see you're single.'

'Yeah, *touché*, Abe, I sure am. Who knows, it might have been different if my father had been a Brooklyn-Yonkers cabbie fashion-freak, who reads *Women's Wear Daily*, instead of a rare-book dealer.'

They pulled up in front of the Ralph Lauren Shop and Abe turned around to look over his shoulder and speak to Deena, as she fished through her bag for her wallet.

'Just look at the cut of those clothes, the fabric, handkerchief linen. I ask you, who but Lauren would cut white handkerchief linen on the bias in this day and age? Only a genius with a vision and a lot of *chutzpah*. But, remember what I always told my girls, you buy linen, you buy a licence for wrinkles and to stand on your feet and iron all day. Look at that jacket, a miracle of tailoring in khaki poplin, did you ever hear of such a thing?'

Deena slid across the seat of the taxi to open the door, 'Stop! Stop Abe! I can't stand it, you're terrific but I've got to go. You've missed your vocation. You should do a column for *Women's Wear Daily*, not read it.'

She paid him through the window, and was hurrying towards the entrance when she heard him shout out to her, 'Miss, oh, miss!' At the sound of his voice, she stopped where she stood and turned.

'You might get something with top stitching,' he called after her. 'The way he uses top stitching is a kind of poetry.' Then, before she could say anything, he shot off into the traffic, waving away potential passengers.

Deena pushed the door open and put aside her laughter because buying clothes in New York is no laughing matter. It's a very serious business. You don't achieve that sleek, immaculate, New York Look, so discreetly up-to-date, without mastering the art of buying. And for that you have to be serious.

Deena, arms full of boxes and shopping bags, was doing a balancing act while she struggled to open the door of her Central Park West duplex apartment.

Once in, she dumped her shopping unceremoniously onto one of the khaki hand-woven covered sofas. Balancing herself on one foot, she kicked a shoe up into the air and sighed with relief as it plummeted to the floor. She shifted her weight and did it again with the other shoe, then collapsed into a chair facing the huge picture-window overlooking the park. Deena massaged her feet and moaned with the joy of easing out the aches and pains. Where had that Abe the taxi driver been in her hour of need? She had had to walk all the way home because it was the rush hour and she couldn't find a taxi.

She removed her hat, placed it on a table, delighted with it. It had done her well, had even been admired by the Princess Eirene earlier in the day. She made herself a cup of tea and was looking forward to having it, quietly, while she relived Mirella's lunch party.

She looked at her watch. She would have just enough time before Brindley arrived to do that, and to enjoy the best part of shopping: opening your purchases in the quiet of your own home, without your favourite saleslady telling you you look 'drop dead' – meaning drop-dead chic.

She was approaching a large dress box, when the telephone began to ring.

'Oh, you're there. I am free now. If it isn't inconvenient, I would like to come round at once.'

'Brindley, where are you?'

'At a call box on the corner of your street.'

'Oh, of course. Come right up.'

He said no goodbye, simply hanging up. It occurred to Deena that he sounded awfully remote, not at all like the man who had asked her to go away

221

with him only hours before. Suddenly it seemed to her that all that shopping possibly had been premature. She rushed about picking up her purchases and all but fled up the stairs to her bedroom where she stuffed them helter skelter into her closet. She was brushing her hair and repairing her makeup when the doorman buzzed to announce that Mr Ribblesdale was on his way up. Then Brindley was knocking on her door.

Deena was surprised at herself. She was not nervous, nor was she anxious, but simply joyful that he was there and about to enter her life. She opened the door.

'Hello,' he said.

'Hello,' she answered.

He stepped into her living-room and, smiling at her, presented her with a box of Godiva chocolates.

'Didn't know what else to bring you. Flowers didn't seem right because we will be gone by morning.' He opened the lid of the box and two aeroplane tickets lay across the tissue protecting the Belgian confections. She picked up the tickets, looked at them. Then she placed the box and the pair of tickets on a table nearby. He took her in his arms and they kissed passionately.

He removed his jacket and lay it on a chair, loosened his tie and asked, 'Where's the bedroom?' Together they walked up the staircase that curved against the two-storey glass wall of window with a spectacular view over Central Park and the upper East side of Manhattan, undressing themselves and dropping their clothes as they went.

There was something so special and wonderful about Brindley and the way she felt with him, Deena thought. Something she had never experienced with any of the other men before him. Deena had always been aware of coming from a certain background and culture that held her back from finding the kind of love she wanted. Suddenly, walking naked up these last few stairs with Brindley, she knew that was over, and, although he had never said so, it had been the same for him.

On Mirella's wedding night, the first and only night Brindley and she had ever been together, each of them had worked out fears and inhibitions. That night had given them the courage to go forward and change their lives. Although they had not known it then, they both knew it now. There was little doubt they had been influenced by the love affair of Adam and Mirella and their marriage, and that they wanted an emotional bond such as Adam and Mirella had, such as Rashid and Mirella had.

In the bedroom Deena felt really wicked. She stood back a few steps so that Brindley could take a good, long look at her. With her legs wide apart, she ran her hands over her breasts, squeezing them, pulling on her nipples. She arched her back and then slid her hands over her beautiful mound covered in golden pubic hair. Brindley was entranced by the lascivious beauty she was showing him, and to him it seemed that the pussy offered was begging to be opened and probed.

Deena rubbed herself roughly up against Brindley like a cat on heat. Feeling and seeing the full, throbbing penis of her lover, she let out a little gasp of joy. She dropped to her knees and on her way down she briefly rubbed her face around his cock.

Brindley stroked his fingers through her hair again and again. She hungered for his penis throbbing against her lips, but she held back. Hungrily, greedily, she rose and placed her arms around his neck, and they both kissed with open mouths to the deepest part of their being. Deena was swallowed up by that mouth that had made love to her so many times in so many ways on the one night they had had together. Their tongues played with each other and all the time she felt him pressing, pressing up against her cunt.

Deena moved away from his lips, kissing him now on his chest, and ran her tongue down and down, then around the inside of his navel, filling it with her saliva. Her lips left a wet trail down to the patch of dark-brown hair between his legs. She sighed, her heart filled with lust for this tall, slender, quiet Englishman who came alive and wildly passionate in her hands. She rubbed her lips across the patch of short curly hair, and then her face, back and forth, and inhaled his raunchy male scent. She could hold back no longer. All she wanted was to love him, give him pleasure. She opened her mouth and licked.

She kissed the base of his penis and, taking his rampant hardness in both her hands, caressed it and lipped and tongued the underpart. He was wonderful, and she adored him. Physically, they were perfect together, and it felt natural and right. She took him fully in her mouth and began sucking, making love to that part of him she longed to be hers for all of their lives.

Together they made sexual love. Sometimes he delighted her with sweet and tender sex, at other times he used his cock ruthlessly to wring powerful and copious orgasms from her. And with each sexual act, each orgasm, the couple confirmed to each other what they already knew when he appeared at her door – that for them sex would always be new and fresh and sometimes bizarre and extreme, sometimes just simple and loving. All sexual and emotional barriers were down for them as a couple, and what they had together they could never hope to find in different mates, nor would they ever seek it.

Deena lay exhausted and replete on top of Brindley, his arms locked around her, flesh against flesh, only their lust blanketing them against the world. She opened her eyes, and Brindley read their message of love. With gentle hands he caressingly pushed back the strands of luscious golden, silky hair falling about her face. Then he held her face in his hands and touched her lowered eyelids with his lips. Choked with emotion, she managed to tell him, 'I love you, Brinn. Oh, God, how I love you! It's heaven when you abandon yourself and take me with you. It's a miracle of emotion I have never known before, this allowing our natures, whether sweet or base, to flow from us in an act of love.'

Deena's eyes shone with tears of emotion, her voice merely a whisper with a tremor in it. So touched by her words, her love, and her ability to express her feelings towards him, he caught up at the corner of her eye with the tip of his little finger the tear that fell on it and carried it to his lips, where he took it on the tip of his tongue.

'I love you too, Deena. I adored your humour and the way you made me laugh from the first moment we met. It's easy to abandon myself with you. You're beautiful and clever, open-hearted and courageous, sensuous and vital. The thrill of knowing there are no limits for us sexually, of going always that little bit further together, makes you an aphrodisiac for me. Each orgasm becomes a voyage of discovery. I want to live and love, and laugh and cry, the rest of my life with you. Tell me it's the same for you.'

'It's the same for me,' she whispered.

He kissed her now, not once but several times, hugging her and rocking her gently in his arms. And he asked, 'Then you'll marry me?'

'Oh yes. Yes, I'll marry you.'

It was after they had made love once more and were lying on their sides facing each other, that Brindley said,

'I've made a reservation for us at Le Cirque for nine o'clock. The best French food and the finest champagne in celebration. Good idea?'

'Great idea.'

Brindley patted her naked bottom and then jumped out of bed. He showered while she bathed. As Deena watched his blurred silhouette through the glass shower walls, her happiness suddenly lost its sharp outline too. Brindley was much younger than she was. He was still a young man, she was thirty-eight.

He stepped from the shower and dried himself with a huge, fluffy bath towel, and, walking up to the bath, laughingly said, 'You will miss towels like this in England. And showers like that simply do not exist.'

'I'll bring my own towels. Even the shower,' she said rather flatly.

'How clever you are, a simple solution. An Englishman would never think of importing his towels from the States, let alone a shower.'

'What would an Englishman do?' she asked, again in that same rather flat voice.

Brindley caught her tone and eyed her with prompt concern. Something was wrong, and he didn't know what or how to respond. He dropped the bath sheet onto the bathroom carpet, took a smaller towel and wrapped it around him, tying it at his waist. Then he went directly to her and sat on the edge of the bath.

'An Englishman would go to Harrods and buy the best towels he could find there. That is, if he were an extravagant Englishman. But most of them would do as I would: forget about it and use a rough old towel that has seen better days but is not yet tatty enough to throw away. We English are not so much mean about money as frugal.'

'But I'm extravagant,' she all but wailed.

'So? I'm not marrying you to change you. I'm only telling you the English are frugal and not consumption-crazy like the Americans. You have the courage to be extravagant, to change all the time. We English prefer less change. You and I are very different – our backgrounds, our culture, our religions even. But I embrace that difference in you. It adds to my life. You expand my life.'

He bent forward to kiss Deena, but her hand on his arm stopped him. 'Brinn, how old are you?'

'Thirty. And you?'

'Brinn, I am much older than you are. I'm thirty-eight.'

Deena watched for a sign, any sign, no matter how slight, of shock or retreat. She saw nothing but a smile break across his face.

'Brinn, I love you, I want to marry you, but if that makes a difference to you, please, I beg you, let's finish it, call it off, right now before it's too late, and the pain of losing you too great for me to cope with. I will understand.'

'You are not too old, just too dramatic. Don't be so stupid, it's too late for us even now.'

Then he leaned over the tub from where he sat on the edge and pulled her up to him, and they kissed, as he slipped slowly over the edge into the hot, foamy water beside her.

Deena sat staring across the table at Brindley, who was busy reading the menu to her. Never had she been so sure of anything as she was that they were going to have a wonderful life together. Her moment of anxiety over their age difference would be the first and last insecurity she would allow herself where she and Brindley were concerned. Once that decision was made she reverted to her own happy, positive self, and vowed never to look back.

'*Raviolis De Homard Et Son Jus Tagliatelles De Légumes*. That's raviolis of lobster served with its juices, scented with caraway seeds and set on a bed of juliennes of vegetables. That sounds delicious, don't you think? Or would you rather have something else?'

'No, nothing else. That sound's perfect.'

'All right,' he said, passing the menu on to Deena. 'Now you choose the main course and I'll choose the wine.'

Deena chose for them both a dish of sweetbreads roasted and served with their juices enriched with a hazelnut butter spiked with almonds, pine kernels and pistachios, called *Pomme De Ris De Veau Roti Aux Amandes Pistaches Et Pignons De Pin*.

Over the superb meal and two bottles of an exquisite Richebourg '69, Burgundy's best, the lovers began to get to know each other. The overwhelming delight at being in love gave them the courage they needed to face the enormous changes they were about to confront.

'I want you to promise me something, Deena,' Brindley asked. But not in a way that showed concern. It was more in the manner of a solicitor cautioning a client. It amused Deena and she answered, 'Yes, dear.' They both smiled because they were a little tipsy and because the endearment, though new to them, charmed.

'If you are ever unhappy, even for one day in England, or lonely – and I am sure you will be for a long while after a life in New York – you will tell me, so that we can work it out together.'

Deena agreed. She wanted to tell Brindley that for her this was like a new life, a great adventure, a chance to have love, and marriage, and children, and a partner to share it with, all the things she had missed while climbing up the success ladder – what's a little loneliness in exchange for all that? But she said nothing.

She scrutinized his handsome, still boyish face, listened closely to his educated upper-class accent, thinking he could not be anything but English. The cut of his hair, and his Savile Row clothes, the highly polished shoes, the navy-blue-and-white silk polka-dot hanky cascading decoratively from his jacket pocket. The old-fashioned pocket watch he carried. His quiet, calm control in public. And she loved all of it and all of him and for once in her life she had the answer to the question she secretly asked herself time and again. What was it all about, this struggle to be alive, and for what? For love. To love. To be loved. That was what it was for.

Chapter 13

Adam had not been successful in Geneva. His timing had been off. The person he wanted to see was in an all-day meeting at the Swiss Credit Bank in Zug. He took a helicopter to Zug, only to miss his elusive White Knight yet again. The Sudan. He might find the person he was after in Khartoum in a week's time, he was told. After that, in Addis Ababa until the end of August.

From Zug, Adam called Mirella aboard Rashid's yacht – not the *Azziz*, his schooner, but his ocean-going cruiser *Topkapi*. He was surprised at how much the sound of Mirella's voice dissolved the frustrations of his day and warmed his heart. He felt joyful rather than sentimental about her.

'Is Rashid treating you well?'

'Yes, very well. He's being his usual extravagant self, lavishing attention on me – flowers, extravagant gifts, a pair of diamond bracelets. I hope you like them, because I am pledged to wear them always in the name of our friendship,' she said bravely to her husband, the man she loved.

Adam smiled to himself and answered, 'Rashid has impeccable taste. Of course I will like them, and a pledge is a pledge.'

Their conversation was brief because Adam wanted to be on his way. Rashid was put on the line, then the

Captain, who gave Adam the course the *Topkapi* was taking through the Aegean Sea to Mykonos and Dilos. He replaced the telephone receiver on its rocker, pleased and proud of the way Mirella had handled the call.

He was relieved to think that the three of them could cope with this unusual and delicate relationship with an unspoken truthfulness, respect for one another, and above all discretion. The guidelines have been drawn, he thought, and we will not breach them. He knew that was true from the way each of them had handled this first and most important separation. No side of their triangle had suffered or broken.

In Athens he said goodbye to Josh, who took the company plane on to Istanbul. Adam boarded his small helicopter and the pilot and he whirled up into the hot, smog-bound atmosphere that hung low over Athens.

Permission granted, they flew low across the sprawling white city that roasted under the hot sun, over the Nekrotafeion, Athens' cemetery, dotted with white marble monuments and shaded by tall, elegant cypresses. Over the remains of the Olympieion, still overwhelming in size with its Corinthian capitals and enormous columns, the vast column-drums lying on the ground. Adam's heart began to race in anticipation of what was to come. And there it was as they flew over Hadrian's arch – the Acropolis.

They circled once, twice, a third time before the pilot was allowed to dip down over the Odeion of Herodes Atticus. They hovered there for a few minutes. Even empty and silent, the excavated ruins of the huge, ancient, open-air theatre once so splendiferous with its walls of dressed poros covered in marble slabs, with its floors, staircases, and anterooms of mosaic. Its facade alone which had stood ninety-two feet high stirred a sense of the wonders of Greece. And then the pilot whirled off to the Agora, where they lingered for several minutes before swinging away from the ancient Greek architectural treasures, across the city and out over the sea, heading for a *rendezvous* with the *Topkapi* somewhere among the Cycladic islands.

They hugged close to the mainland as far as Sunion, circled the temple once, and then made out to sea. They crossed the tip of the island of Kea, and as dusk was approaching followed the coastline around the island of Syros, where they began searching the sea for the *Topkapi*.

The sun was just dropping below the horizon – a flaming orange disc driving into the glorious blue Aegean and pulling darkness down behind her – when they spotted the yacht several miles ahead of them, sailing towards Mykonos.

Adam took over the controls. They were about five miles from the *Topkapi* when the circle of lights around the landing pad on the uppermost aft deck was switched on. They made radio contact. The Captain cut the yacht's motors, and Adam landed the 'copter just as the last drop of light turned the day into night.

Mirella's and Adam's reunion could not have gone more smoothly. Rashid cleverly busied himself with the dozen or so other guests on board, after welcoming Adam on the helicopter pad and leading him to Mirella. He even made a joke about it.

'It seems to me, Adam, I am always leading you to your wife when I am not leading your wife to you.' They both laughed, and then Adam and Mirella were together.

Dinner that evening was very elegant: black tie for the men, and the women in long dresses and dazzling jewels. The food was sublime, an all-Greek cuisine, but the chef was French, which turned the food into a gourmet miracle. The wines were impeccable, and the people all at their conversationally brilliant best.

The wind was down and the sea unusually calm for Mykonos. The party took their after-dinner drinks on deck to watch the twinkling lights on shore.

'It has been a wonderful evening, Rashid, and your yacht most elegant, dinner and the company the same,' complimented Mirella.

'Well, at last a Corey who doesn't think the *Topkapi* is – to quote your husband, dear lady – a vulgar floating gin-palace.'

'Adam, oh, please, you couldn't have been so rude.'

'I could be, can be, and have been. And had you been in Greece last year for Rashid's birthday celebrations, you might very well have agreed.'

There were complimentary words said about the notorious birthday party by some guests, blushing embarrassment from others. Rashid only laughed.

'It was a one-off, I grant you,' he said, adding archly, 'more what I think you would expect from a Greek millionaire ship-owner than a sophisticated Turk like myself. But, one must not always take to heart Adam's opinions. He has always preferred the *Azziz*. He simply likes sailing ships and small parties better. But indeed, Mirella, I do wish I had known you then and you had been to it. It was my birthday party cruise through the Greek and Turkish islands. The cruise guests arrived from various parts of the world and took up residence aboard *Topkapi*. All the fifteen double staterooms were occupied, with a varied cross-section of old friends, and business acquaintances. The other guests, who were invited only to my birthday celebrations, were put up for three days at the Astir Palace Hotel. The plan was to spend three days with the hundred-odd invited friends in and around Athens, ending with a spectacular birthday party for five hundred guests.

'There were daytime excursions to Delphi and Sunion and Epidaros. The evenings were spent dining at exquisite parties given in my honour by a couple of Greek ship-owners, friends of mine since my Oxford days. But all that was just the prelude to the gala reception I arranged on board the *Topkapi* as my official birthday party.

'It began at midnight, or to be more accurate, one minute into the day I was born. The hundred guests were all brought on board from *Topkapi*'s private dock near the hotel for a sit-down dinner. As we sailed away, we were treated to a spectacular firework display, set off from hundreds of small craft lining the water's edge all along the coast for miles. The *Topkapi* anchored two miles off shore at Vouligmeni, and we watched the display, which went on for an hour.

'Afterwards, the black-tied men and bejewelled women sat down to a sumptuous feast organized by Madame Point, the famous restauratrice, who had flown in her entire staff for the occasion from

Restaurant de la Pyramide at Vienne. After the gourmet delicacies and a feast of after-dinner wit in the speeches, the guests danced to two orchestras playing near the swimming pools on the fore and aft decks of the *Topkapi*.

'Oh, Mirella, I wish you could have seen it. The *Topkapi* was transformed into a floating paradise of flowers, its lights pouring over the water turned the Aegean to silver, and the twinkling lanterns on the dozens of boats – *caiques* and row-boats and motor launches constantly circling the cruiser – was a sight to see. It looked more like a constellation of stars, bright against a black sky, than a yacht with a cordon of security boats.

'At three in the morning a signal of three loud blasts was sounded from the *Topkapi*, and a flotilla of small speedboats set out from shore for the yacht bringing four hundred guests. Dazzlingly pretty girls in glorious gowns and handsome men in formal dress, arrived to dance and drink champagne, eat birthday cake – ah, and what a birthday cake it was – and to watch the sun rise. They stayed for a breakfast of scrambled eggs and caviar and croissants, served until eight in the morning when the *Topkapi* was set to sail on its cruise.

'Of course, Adam didn't like it. It was the sort of evening he rarely attends. It was too jet-set, Greek millionaireish for him. Or, to put it bluntly, too Turkish playboyish for him – which is, of course, what I am. It was a larger than life extravaganza that could turn great hospitality into sensational vulgarity, not at all your husband's style. He is much too grand for that. Not me, my dear Mirella, I enjoy a touch of the base, the common, the crude – even the animal – in

236

me and in others. A touch of the vulgar can be diverting, even exciting.'

Rashid wanted to add, 'But you know that, don't you? It is, after all, one of the things that you find attractive about me.'

It was true. Had she not admitted the very night before to loving that part of him, of herself, and to being attracted to Rashid for some of those very qualities. She liked rubbing up against his rough edge. Yet, as soon as Adam appeared, any feeling she had for Rashid, other than as a close friend who adored and desired her erotically as she did him, seemed to melt away. Adam's presence had always done that for her. When with Adam, she simply wanted no one but him. Rashid saw no point in hinting anything of that to her and so he continued telling her about his party.

'It was a jet-set party like all the other jet-set parties described by all the gossip columnists in the world. The kind of party the papparazzi make fortunes stealing photographs of. I gave them their pictures. I designed it like a cinema production of a mega-millionaire's birthday party. The sort of party young, would-be actresses try to gatecrash, or handsome gigolos have to swing an invitation to in order to hook themselves a wealthy, middle-aged lady for the season. I made it a show that businessmen needed to be seen at because it could be good for future deals; that politicians needed for the vote; society for obvious reasons, friends because friends are after all friends, and family out of respect. Has-been actresses and actors, because that was what was left for them. The odd opera star, ballet-dancer, for that illusion of culture. The painter, the sculptor, the odd academic because they enjoy my patronage – and I am not altogether frivolous, as you very well know.

'In spite of all the vulgarity, the noise and intrigues, there did remain an air of class, that comes not only from money but from good taste, style and fun. Even you have to admit that, Adam. If I remember correctly, you got caught up in the enjoyment with your family and friends who were there for the evening.'

'You are quite right, Rashid. No one can make more of a splash with a party than you. There is something agreeably abandoned about the parties you give, and I have to admit that your birthday bash was one of your best, only surpassed by the one you threw for our wedding. But, you will admit, old boy, the evening had its dramatic moments. The pappa-razzo who skipped through the security net and got picked up by one of your bodyguards and thrown overboard, camera and all.'

'I detest having my privacy infringed,' said Rashid defensively, and everyone laughed.

'And what about that unfortunate public scene,' Adam asked, 'between the Greek lady, her husband and his baby-faced mistress, that turned into a screaming match?' The memory raised smiles. One of the female guests sitting near Adam said to Mirella, 'After the party-crashers arrived the silly young men began throwing the silly young women into swimming pools all over the yacht. The orgy discovered during the security check, to make sure everyone was ashore who was supposed to be before we set sail for the cruise, was made even more dramatic because all the participants were male, and their clothes had been thrown out of the portholes.'

238

'What went a trifle beyond the norm,' said Adam, 'was the famous, expensive French hooker who had to be rushed ashore to hospital under very tight wraps after an Arab prince had bitten off her nipple.'

'True, and a little unfortunate,' said Rashid, 'but accidents like that do happen, Adam. However you must admit there were other things to make that night memorable. Touching things, sentimental moments, that did not go unnoticed.'

'No, that's quite true, Rashid. I remember the old Cretan dressed in his traditional clothes who climbed aboard from one of the launches, carrying a huge country basket whose contents were covered in white cloth stitched neatly all around the rim. Olives from his grove, a gift to you, Rashid, for your birthday from a man whose son's life you had saved. The six little school-girls and their headmistress who arrived with the mayor of their village from the south of France, carrying baskets filled with rose and heather, geranium and carnation petals with which they showered the guests like confetti. Their way of wishing Rashid a happy birthday and thanking him for the village school and the endowment he made. That was one of the nicer moments at the party, Mirella.' Rashid winced with embarrassment, at having been caught out being the good guy.

'I remember the fisherman from Kos who arrived with a whole basket of *octopodi*, a man from Samos with a crate of his best wine, and the rumpus caused by a shepherd who had travelled for days to bring Rashid two live black sheep. All of them wanting to say thank you for this man's past favours. A stream of old-timers kept arriving, not only from Greece, which

239

is compliment enough to a Turk, because their hatred of Turkey has never diminished, nor ever will. But there were also the poor Turkish peasants who came from different parts of his country to pay homage to their fellow countryman who had owned their villages and had helped them all his adult life, bearing their simple gifts proudly. You have to remember, darling, to them Rashid is their number-one glamour-son. To them he signifies international fame and fortune.'

'And remember your kids, Adam? The whole clan was invited and they all came, but their gift to me was brought by Joshua and Zhara. They arrived in time for dinner, bringing with them Oscar Peterson to play the piano and Pearl Bailey to sing 'Happy Birthday', Stan Getz and Charlie Byrd for a little Bossanova. Eric Clapton and the Bee Gees. Their gift alone made my party memorable. Oscar Peterson and Pearl Bailey stayed on for the entire cruise.'

'I did hear about some of it,' said Mirella. 'A great deal of what you told me and much more hit every gossip column around the world. I remember seeing many photographs of your glittering party and cruise.'

'That was, of course, not much to my liking. We did everything humanly possible to keep it private, but they used telescopic lenses from boats and tried to break the security ring around the *Topkapi*. Most photographers were satisfied with snapping the honoured guests as they climbed in and out of the speedboats making the continual run to and from the yacht, but not all of them.

'The official reportage of the party and the cover stories I agreed to, came out in *Newsweek* and *Time* magazine with me on the cover. All the world loves to

240

read about a rich man, especially if he owns a shipping line. Greek, Turkish, Arab – it's all the same, as long as he has the right friends and throws glamorous parties. I suppose we can thank Niarchos and Onassis for that.

'The fact that I am only a mini-shipowner, and more an international businessman, hardly matters to the media. I am better media-fodder if I have a fleet of ships, it makes a more glamorous label. Of course, as I am single, the spotlight is turned as much on my parties in bed as in business. It ups my appeal no end.

'I learned a long time ago to accept that, even if the press doesn't like me, I'm news and so the press decrees that the public does like me. I have made for them an escape into a world far from their own. Maybe for no longer than it takes to skim through the article, but I serve as an escape for them nevertheless.

'Enough talk about my enviable sufferings! The night is young and there is still fun to be had. How about us all going ashore for some music? There are a couple of good places here in Mykonos, disco and bouzouki, a few amusing bars.'

Rashid was not surprised when Adam and Mirella declined; Adam was tired from all the travelling, and Mirella wanted a good night's sleep before starting their island-hopping.

'Okay, my lovely,' said Rashid, giving Mirella a friendly hug and a kiss. 'Until the morning then, you two. We'll have a wonderful day on Dilos. A picnic lunch under the hot sun among the marbles, surrounded by ancient ghosts and the sea.' He patted Adam on the back. The two men shook hands and Rashid happily joined his waiting guests in the launch.

Mirella and Adam waved Rashid and his dozen

guests off, as one of the *Topkapi* motor launches bumped across the water towards the picturesque port twinkling in the darkness of the night.

Chapter 14

The Mykonos winds came up just after dawn. There was a rough sea, much too rough for the tourist boats to come out from the port, and much too rough for the other guests on the *Topkapi* to leave their cabins, especially after a long night of drinking and dancing on shore.

Rashid was delighted. Except for the guardians of the island, he would be alone with Adam and Mirella to enjoy the archaeological wonders of Dilos.

The sun was bright, high in the sky, and though there was a strong wind, it was a hot summer day. The helicopter landed and the three were joyously welcomed. The pilot handed the two guards a large box of wine and provisions, a gift from Rashid for allowing them to land, and a large wicker picnic-basket containing their lunch.

The two men made a great fuss over Rashid, who was delighted with his reception and obviously overjoyed to be there. He gave orders to Taki, one of the guards, where he wanted the table and chairs placed for their picnic. Then, the island theirs, they set off to explore, yet again, this place so dear to each of them.

The uninhabited island of Naxian marble was gleaming in the sun and surrounded by the white caps

243

of the rough, blue, Aegean Sea. Dilos, overpowering even in its ruins, still combined the effects of the material and the supernatural. And why not? In ancient times, it was the great centre of trading between the Dardanelles and Crete, as well as a great religious centre. A reminder that religion and trade often flourished together. Dilos had that and more: it had myth as well.

Here, supposedly, Apollo was born which reminded the three of them of the role that handsome god had played in their lives. It was a statue of Apollo that had brought Adam and Mirella together, ending their final estrangement, and it was the same statue of Apollo that Mirella gave to Rashid in thanks for all they had been to each other. That same Apollo sculpture had been coveted by both men for years before Mirella had materialized to decide who should possess it. And here they were, the three of them, on the island where Apollo's mother Leto took refuge from the wrath of Hera.

And so, for Rashid and Adam, minor deities in their way of the modern world, Dilos held great mystery and wonder. They loved the island and the stories of its ancient beauty, successes, and fate, and sensed a power still remaining amid its debris.

More than for Rashid, the sheer splendour of the island was a wonder to Adam as an archaeologist, an ancient world that was a part of his life.

There had been a lake, now dried up. There was still the Mount Cynthus, looking almost man-made in the sunshine. At night, under the full moon, it looked anything but that. In its cold, mysterious beauty it was charming, magical.

Adam had been on the island years before. His schooner had landed one winter night when the moon was full and lit the island as if by a great floodlight. He and Marlo managed to break the law. With the help of the guardians of the island, they were allowed in to experience another wonder of the world – Dilos by moonlight.

In the ancient cisterns running beneath what were once great buildings and temples they heard the croak of green frogs and winds whispering like so many ghosts surrounding them. Today in the sunshine Mirella, Rashid and Adam walked over the stones and were amazed that, every time they visited the island, it revealed itself anew to them.

They saw huge, emerald-green lizards roaming in the hot sun with them. They watched the creatures strut and slither over the stones with such propriety. Near the site of the Temple that was Apollo's, they saw a snake weave across his part of the island. In the Agora, near the ancient port, they could feel still the richness and success that had demanded such authoritative building. The lay-out of everything to the last detail was so elegant, impressive, and grand, that it must have had a magnificence almost beyond the imagination. To think of it with all the statues complete and upright made one's imagination soar in response to what the life of the island must have truly been like.

In reality there is hardly anything upright on the island. It is, for the most part, extreme, ancient rubble of an island city of great importance. And then they appear, the five remaining Mycenaean lions, lean and slinky in their archaic style, ready to pounce as you invade their premises, their privacy. In fact, all the poetry and mystery of the place is heightened and you are put on your guard by them.

Rashid and the Coreys walked over the stones, broken marbles and treasures of they knew not what. But the treasures were there, of that there was no doubt.

Dilos, the dry island. No water left, it is spotted with dry brown grass that shivers in the hot wind. Lovely sounds, whispers everywhere. The more you walk into the centre and are swallowed up by the battered and broken civilization, the more you feel the ghosts. There are so many mysteries to Dilos, you cannot help trying to discover what they are, what they mean. There are facts, too, about Dilos that always creep in and are remembered, such as that anything connected with birth or death was removed from the island, officially banished from the place. Dilos was like a place of immortality outside time. Whatever happened in ancient days in Dilos, the reinforced magic of the place is still strong and very powerful.

It did not seem strange to Adam and Mirella that Rashid should love Dilos so much and go there so often. The whole of the Levant had traded there, banked there, worshipped, and felt protected there by the shrines, gods and myths. There was much of Rashid Lala Mustapha in Dilos.

The three walked in silence and let their thoughts merge with the ghosts of so many souls who walked with them. Mirella watched a huge red snake slither over some stones, stretch and turn in the sun, while she listened to Adam.

'All you ghosts of Dilos, you bring into my mind that poem of Cavafy called 'The City'.

'You said, "I will go to another land, I will go to another sea.

Another city will be found, a better one than this.

Every effort of mine is a condemnation of fate; and my heart – the corpse – buried.

How long will my mind remain in this wasteland.

Wherever I turn my eyes, wherever I may look I see black ruins of my life there, where I spent so many years destroying and wasting.

"You will find no lands, you will find no other seas.

The city will follow you. You will roam in the same streets. And you will age in the same neighbourhoods; and you will grow grey in these same houses. Always you will arrive in this city. Do not hope for any other—

There is no ship for you, there is no road.

As you have destroyed your life here in this little corner, you have ruined it in the entire world."'

No one spoke for a few minutes. The hint of a tear glistened in Rashid's eyes when he looked at Adam and said, 'You could have been a Turk, or a Greek for that matter. To know Cavafy, to feel Cavafy as you do, shows me that you have the heart and soul of the Levant in you.'

The poem, the place, her lovers, left Mirella unable to say anything. Adam sighed and smiled, feeling contentment with himself and the world.

Rashid put his hand out to Mirella and helped her by swinging her up a few feet to the level where he was standing. He put his arm around her and they walked up to a lone statue still standing upright. Adam on her other side walked with them. The figure was headless and armless: feminine and draped in the softest folds of marble. It was larger-than-life-size and might have been a statue of Cleopatra, who had once visited the island, and lived there for a time with Antony.

Adam and Mirella sat at the feet of the astonishingly heroic lady, holding hands and looking across the ruined city out to sea, while Rashid stood back and recited to them. He chose a poem of his old acquaintance George Seferis, and, when finished, he sat down with his friends. After a short silent interlude where the only sounds were those of the island, he said,

'Ah, to be a Turk and understand a Greek is to be king.'

A smile broke across his face and he laughed loudly, and it echoed through the precious stones of the island and rolled out across the water. He stood up, and with outstretched hands he pulled Mirella to her feet.

'Come,' he said, 'I am famished, and we have a delightful lunch waiting for us.'

They worked their way among the ruins against the wind, under the hot sun, and then descended to what once must have been a grand house in ancient Dilos. The floor of the room they walked across had been excavated and restored. The mosaics were magnificent, and on them Taki had set a table and three chairs. The silver plates and crystal glasses on white linen gleamed and sparkled among the marble ruins.

'We'll dine now with the ancients, drink with the gods and laugh with the wind. May it be like this for the three of us always,' was the toast Adam gave. The three rose from their chairs, raised their glasses high to the gods, and drank.

Mirella and Adam left Rashid and Adam's pilot on Dilos to be picked up by the *Topkapi*'s helicopter. The last they saw of Rashid was when Adam piloted his 'copter across Dilos for one last look from the air, and there was Rashid standing almost exactly in the centre of the island waving farewell. They could just hear him shouting, 'Dinner, in Istanbul, in four days' time.'

He looked like a living Apollo.

Mirella and Adam flew from one glorious island to another, the white villages sparkling in the sun. Once they left the wind behind them, from the sky the green islands looked like emeralds, the barren ones like yellow diamonds, and all the villages like lustrous pearls dropped on a shimmering, blue satin sea.

First to Paros, where they slept in a valley of butterflies, and then to Andiparos, where they climbed the barren hills on donkeys while waiting for their fish, fresh from the sea, to be cooked. They swam naked in deserted coves whenever and wherever it took their fancy.

In Naxos they landed on a high hill and walked through a grove of twisting, turning olive trees, where they could see below what was once the ancient quarry of Ston Apollonas, and the half-completed marble blocks, thirty three feet long, of an unfinished Kouros from the seventh century BC.

It was hot, and very quiet. Too hot even for the birds to sing, but not the cicadas clicking their constant Grecian tune. Hand in hand the Coreys wove their way between the trees, trying to stay in the shade of the silvery green leaves, and slipped and slid down the hill.

Perspiring and breathless with the heat, yet feeling high on happiness and drunk with the passion and beauty of the Greek Islands, their past and their present, and their very personal and private tour, Adam felt randy for Mirella all the time.

He was acutely aware that he was living through that excruciating, exciting time in one's life that happens to most of us at least once for a long time, or several times for short periods. That delicious, self-indulgent period when you and your partner are oblivious to anything but yourselves. A superbly egocentric time when the woman in a man's life is his world, his goddess, and he would do anything and everything not to lose her. That gorgeous 'in-love' state when he thinks his partner is the most marvellous creature, the most exciting woman in the world. That obsessive time when she never leaves his mind, travelling with him every minute of the day and night wherever he goes.

Everything they did and everything they saw, from the moment they left Rashid in Dilos, was an adventure in love, togetherness, oneness.

As if reading Adam's mind, Mirella, still holding his hand, stopped, put her arms around his neck and placed her head on his shoulder and rested against him, wanting to feel his strength, his love for her through her body.

He gently pushed her away and looked deeply into her eyes and, taking her hand again, he led her to a tree and stood her against it. Both her hands in one of his, he lifted her arms above her head and pressed them hard against the tree-trunk. With his free hand he undid the buttons of her cream silk shirt, exposing her naked breasts.

She said nothing, she did nothing. She felt a burning sensation in her wrists from his tight grip, and Rashid's diamond bracelets rubbing against her skin, but she remained silent, pinioned by him to the rough bark.

He held her that way and took a step backwards, better to absorb the sight of her naked, heavy breasts. Beads of perspiration on them glistened in the sun, only making them look more voluptuous, beautiful and desirable. He roughly pulled her shirt further away from her body, and watched her nipples harden and become erect. Then he raised his eyes to hers and said, 'I love you.'

He kissed her wildly, passionately. There was an animal sexuality about him at that moment. Mirella saw it and said, 'What if someone sees us?'

He laughed and ordered, 'Take your clothes off,' as he began to undress himself. Mirella did not protest.

He felt wild, desperate to take her: she could see that in his eyes, the way he moved. They were both naked when he took her in his arms roughly, trying to blot out that 'in-love' state he felt for her. In that, he was like most men who suffer the condition: he could enjoy it, but preferred to keep it secret and under control.

He fucked her standing against the tree. He was hard, almost crude with his cock, but quite tender and passionate with his lips and his mouth. For Mirella it was wonderful, wild and crazily abandoned, being made love to naked in the bright, open sunlight, in an olive grove on a Greek island, the legendary haunt of Dionysus, the god of wine. Where the beautiful

Ariadne was abandoned as a bride by Theseus, prince of Athens; and while looking down into the valley where lay a colossus, the incomplete Kouros in the tall grass.

She kissed and bit him with a wild passion of her own, dug her long red fingernails into his back and gasped when he pulled her away from the tree, bent her over and took her from behind. Neither could hold back their passion any longer, it exploded in the untamed setting of the Naxian landscape under the burning sun and seared their naked bodies. They came together, only this time with all passion out of control. They screamed ecstasy to the mythical gods and the glorious day.

Long after their orgasm mixed his seed with her come and glistened in the sunlight, Adam remained hard and continued to pleasure her, again and again until he quickly came once more. Withdrawing from Mirella he spun her around in his arms and pulled her to the ground. There, in the grass, under the olive tree, their bodies splattered with patterns of sunlight filtering through the leaves, Adam kissed Mirella tenderly, so softly and sweetly, as if she were a child. They dozed off, appearing on the side of the hill like two naked innocents in nature's green embrace.

When, later, they reached the bottom of the hill, they were greeted effusively by the farmer-caretaker, an old acquaintance of Adam. They ate succulent, purple figs and watermelon, sitting on rickety wooden chairs at a wobbly old wooden table, on a make-shift stone patio, overlooking the Kouros that lay in the tall grass. There was retsina, the Greek resinated wine. Then more retsina, as others from the surrounding area arrived and word spread that the man who landed in the helicopter on top of the hill was the archaeologist Adam, and that he had brought a wife.

It was a long, dazzlingly beautiful hop in the late afternoon sun to fly low across the Aegean from the Cyclades to the Dodecanese Islands which lay close to mainland Turkey. In a beat-up Chevrolet of indeterminate age, loaded with tins of fuel, two men waited nervously, at a point on Leros designated by Adam, for sight of the 'copter.

Mirella and Adam landed safely. It was dark when they arrived at a deserted back street parallel to the harbour, having been driven some distance over the fertile and varied landscape to transfer into a waiting *caique* on one of Leros' numerous bays.

The hotel was up a steep flight of stairs that ran along the outside of an old building at one end of the crescent-shaped port. The ground floor was a large restaurant whose tables and chairs spilled out on to the street under a bright green canopy with yellow lettering.

The Papoulies was a shock. The small entrance served as lobby as well. There was a desk of no age, no style, no quality, stained muddy brown. Behind it, a wooden plank hung on the wall with half a dozen keys dangling from it. There were three cheap modern chairs with wooden arms and legs which shone with shellac in some places, and were dirty and dull in others. The foam-rubber cushions were covered in glossy, worn, powder-blue plastic, whose gashes had been patched with Band-aid in several places. A much-too-dim light bulb drooped from the ceiling.

When the plump hotelier came out from the back room, Mirella understood why they had no choice but to stay at the Papoulies. They were greeted with tears of joy from Stavros, hugs, even kisses for Adam. When he rushed away to find his wife, Adam explained, 'It would have been impossible to stay elsewhere, Mirella; he would have been so offended.'

'I do understand, and you're not to worry about it,' she replied.

'I knew this man in the early days of the Junta. I was staying here in 1967, doing some archaeological work inland. It was such a dreadful time for the Greeks and Greek democracy.

'I used to sit at a long table with the local expatriate group who live here in the port, and some of the Leros Greeks. They were all anti-Junta, but virtually gagged by fear of prison, torture and, worst of all, expulsion from the country.

'There were exceptions who were for the Junta, and spoke of Papadopoulos as if he were the Second Coming. They praised those murderous Colonels like they were the angel Gabriel teamed up with Gandhi. For me, those lunchtime exchanges were heavy with the reality of fascism. It felt like a hideous rebirth of something tragically known already.

'I watched and listened, day after day, to those few people distort terms like freedom, truth and democracy into an ingenious defence of fascism, downright Hitlerism. Listening, you could learn a whole lot about what a corrupt system does to well-meaning individuals. Some of the guys who defended the regime could convince themselves by their own words that they were firmly behind it. But, for all their loud-mouthing for their corrupt rulers, they were two-faced enough to sicken you. They would hedge their bets when they dealt with officials – in case the fence they were so carefully sitting astride came tumbling right over on top of them and they went down along with the Junta in a counter-coup.

'I can frankly say I was mesmerized by their ability to hang together an acceptable case for fascism. Shades of Mussolini and Hitler. I watched with fascination and horror how the Greeks themselves whispered against the regime only out in open spaces and with close friends. Walled in, they were jumpy as cats about being overheard. They learned to trust no one, and blamed the U.S. and the CIA for everything.

'Where were the heroes? The real life Zorbas? The old man Papandreou? Some were dead, others were alive and suffering, sometimes making an effort, but where was their support? Where were the freedom-loving Greeks whom they represented? Those who would fight and die for their freedom, where were they? There were Greeks by the thousand under arrest but there were hundreds of thousands who were not.

'The coffee shops were filled with gossip of those anti and those pro the regime – the arrested and the beaten, the tortured; those who escaped the country and those who were caught. The Colonels censored the newspapers, tried unsuccessfully to censor the tongues. Everyone waited for the change to come and wondered who would bring it about. But no change came in the days I lived here in the Papoulies and dined downstairs at Paradisos.

'I found myself in Greece at a pivotal moment in its long history. I was fascinated, vaguely concerned and yet indolent about it, like the majority of the western world. But my indolence passed because I also found myself under the same roof as a great patriot, a very courageous man. I helped Stavros in any little way I could. He used Leros and its many harbours as an escape route for those on the run from the Junta. He is a remarkable man, the best of the Greeks. He may be a poor hotelier but I see him as a Kazantzakis, a Zorba, a Katsimbilis. A giant among men, who gave his all in those days and asked for nothing in return, and is the same even now in these times of freedom and peace. That's why we must stay the night here, and consider it a privilege to do so.'

As Adam spoke to her of Stavros, Mirella caught the echoes of a deeper comradeship in the minor epic of those times than any Adam would lay claim to. Now she understood the genuine concern displayed by the men who met them at the remote promontory where they landed, low on fuel, and why one of them slapped Adam on the back and said, 'You still take big chances, *but* very carefully, my friend.' And why he insisted on guarding the 'copter all night until their return, with a loaded shot-gun over his shoulder. The affectionate, jovial greeting they had from the men on the *caique*, that too had been more than just Greek expansiveness. Yes, Adam had done more, much more, than help Stavros in little ways.

Mirella began to feel she might have married an unsung hero, a man to admire, who had a profound effect on everyone he came in contact with. She had glimpsed it in Turkey, she now saw it in Greece; her sense of the potential in this man she had taken as her husband slightly overwhelmed her. It suddenly occurred to her, standing in that sad little lobby under a dim light, that she really knew very little about her husband.

Chapter 15

Shabby, the ultimate in shabbiness, but clean, very clean, was what kept going through Mirella's mind. But what could she say – 'I miss my beautiful stateroom on board Rashid's yacht'? Hardly. And the fact of the matter was she missed not the yacht, nor Rashid, only the luxury, beauty, and comfort he insisted upon.

Stavros returned with his wife, and there were kisses, hugs and tears from Adam again. Then 'ooh's and 'ah's over Mirella, and another round of hugs and kisses for her. Stavros took their passports so he could register them with the police, the usual procedure, and Mirella's dress was produced for pressing from her Louis Vuitton mini-duffle bag.

Mirella saw the smile on Adam's face when Stavros' wife, Aliki, shook it out and kept clucking away in Greek about its beauty.

'That damned Rashid. He talked me into taking that dress and my jewellery, and now I'm going to be overdressed because that's the only dress I brought with me. That's why you're smiling, isn't it?'

His smile broadened. 'On the contrary, you couldn't have chosen better. They will expect you to look glamorous. And it is Saturday night, their big night in the port.'

'Marlo Channing would have gone to dinner

257

dressed in her rag-bag fashion, and everyone would have loved her and her clothes. A few years back, I would have done the same. I think I'm becoming a frivolous fashion-plate.'

Adam laughed at her. They were walking down the dingy dark corridor to their room behind Stavros, who was chattering over his shoulder at them.

'Well, you're not Marlo, are you? And she is not my wife, is she? Now does that settle your Marlo-problem?' Putting an arm around her shoulder and kissing her on the cheek, he added, 'Oh, and just for the record, Marlo is a tremendous clothes-horse, mad about high fashion, much worse than you could ever be. But for her it's all a big game, lots of fun. She loves to use it and play with it. If it had amused her, she would have worn a ball-gown for dinner in the port of a remote Greek island.'

Mirella was, for the first time, relieved that it was so dark and dim at the Papoulies. She really did not want Adam to see her embarrassment, and registered once more in her mind that Adam missed very little. She had after all not mentioned to him her concern that Marlo might be a rival in her love for Adam.

Stavros opened the door to the room. It was enormous. He set down Mirella's duffle bag and the Purdey canvas shooting bag Adam used as an overnight case on jaunts such as this one. Stavros walked through the dark room and opened the shutter doors leading onto a small balcony. He beckoned them. It was magic.

Spread out before them was three-quarters of the crescent-shaped fishing port. It was dark and the port twinkled with lights. Fishing boats bobbed up and down on the black water. Dim yellowish lights pinpointed the houses and the restaurants and cafes were lit by white neon and masses of fluorescent tubes. It was full of movement. The port was readying itself for the town's nightlife.

The exhilarating Mediterranean sight of waiters carrying tables to the water's edge; the flash of white paper tablecloths covering worn wooden tables, held down at the corners by rubberbands or string. Shopkeepers closing up, restaurants opening for business. That short time between work and play for the hundreds of big and little ports in Greece.

Adam loved this time of day, the simplicity and purity of it, along with its sheer vitality.

Stavros knew what he had in his small, simple hotel. He placed his hand on Mirella's shoulder and said, '*Oreha, poli oreha, eh?* Beautiful, very beautiful, no?'

'Oh yes, extremely,' she replied.

Stavros switched on the light. The small, naked bulb hung on a long black wire from the ceiling. Then he left them alone for a siesta.

For what must have been half an hour, Mirella and Adam watched the port come slowly to life, saying barely a word to each other, simply allowing themselves to be absorbed by it. They turned away finally from the magic and leaned against the rusted wrought-iron rail to look into the room.

It was large, clean and white, but bare. There was a double bed with a thin, too-soft mattress that sagged in the middle. It was made up with sparkling clean, rough cotton sheets and what looked like a khaki army-blanket. There was a table of dark wood next to the bed and a minute table-lamp on it, probably useless for reading. Across from the bed was a small, square wooden table, and two chairs with worn rush seats. There was a large and particularly ugly chest of drawers with a white crocheted scarf on it. Above it, a small mirror with a wavy surface. On one of the otherwise bare walls was a large black and white photograph – a badly-tinted family portrait of a man, a woman and a child. From their dress and hairstyles, the picture might be eighty years old. They were really ugly, all three, and very stiff and formal, desperately serious-looking. Tucked behind the picture frame was an arrangement of dried flowers, proudly portraying itself as a cartouche of some sort. There was something awfully sad, even ghoulish about the people in the portrait. They did not even look proud-poor.

The floorboards were wide planks, dark with age and polish. The only rug – hand-woven, diminutive – was placed next to the bed. Mirella looked up at the ceiling and was surprised. It was wooden, carved and painted. The room was not otherwise pretty or interesting. Just a large space in an old port house with a view that was everything magical: a scene like a carousel, with its movement, colours and lights, that whirls one round and into its enchantment, a kind of make-believe sorcery.

There was something so sad and pitiful: the bare room, yet, outside the window, the crazy carousel. It was schizophrenic: the carousel juxtaposed with the loneliness.

Then Adam put his arm around her, as if he knew what she was thinking. His warmth and love led them to the bed, where they undressed and lay down in that lonely room and naked they fell asleep as one in each other's arms.

At ten o'clock in the evening the port was in full swing. It was bright now, with its tables and chairs set out along the waterfront. People were eating and drinking, talking and laughing. Greek music was carried across the harbour from the far side. Waiters dashed back and forth from the tables to the kitchens of the dozen restaurants all along the crescent.

The delicious aroma of lamb and rosemary, roasting pig and grilled fish, floated up to fill the room. Greek perfume. The happy, hospitable sights and smells drove Mirella and Adam to bathe and dress as quickly as possible, so that they might lose no time in joining this waterside carousel.

Every eye was drawn to Mirella when she and Adam appeared at the restaurant, even those of Aliki and Stavros from a balcony above. Adam waved to the owners of Paradisos, Manos and Despina, who were overseeing from in front of the restaurant's entrance, arms folded across chests, serious looks on their faces. Seeing Adam wiped away their intensity.

Manos threaded his way through the crowded tables to fling yet another welcoming arm around Adam, and pointed to where he had a table reserved for them. The Coreys wove their way among the diners and were stopped half a dozen times by old acquaintances of Adam's who asked the couple to join them.

Mirella was wearing a cream silk dress with a halter top that bared her back to the waist and plunged as far down in the front in a V-neckline. It had a cream silk ribbon-knit jacket, but that was draped over Adam's arm. Her hair was swept back and pinned in several places with fresh, cream-coloured flowers that were

261

waxy looking, brought to her by Aliki as a welcoming gift.

She wore the diamond earrings and bracelets that Rashid had given her, and her diamond engagement and wedding rings, so that she sparkled with luscious elegance. Yet she worried that she looked bold and vulgar.

The men, young and old alike, were devouring her with their eyes as she walked past them, her breasts moving freely under the silk. She had the half-flattering impression the men were willing one of them to slip free from her halter top. The gossipy women were stunned into silence: they had never seen anything like her outside magazines and the movies.

'God,' she whispered to Adam, 'you would think I was a piece of meat they want to sink their teeth into.'

'You are a tempting morsel, my dear. Watching you from the back, I can feel my own teeth start to grind a little.'

She shook her head, surprised that he teased her, misunderstanding how she felt. Finally they made it to their table. Its position allowed them to see and hear the water lapping on the stones of the beach. A barefooted boy of eight stood sentry at the table, fighting off anyone who tried to grab it. Adam gave him fifty drachmas and the child danced away happily. The table the boy had guarded for them was filled with dirty dishes, piled two and three high.

Miracle of miracles, a waiter appeared immediately and swept them away with a symphony of chat and clatter. He crumpled up the stained paper tablecloth and pitched it above Mirella's head and over the sea wall onto the stones below.

With an elaborate flourish, he shook out a clean one, slammed it on the table and snapped its corners under the rubber bands. Then, like a conjuror, he produced the inevitable lime-green plastic salt and pepper pots, the thin, hard-pressed, three-cornered, shiny paper napkins that absorbed nothing, the green and yellow plastic woven basket stacked with thick slices of white doughy bread, and a handful of bendable knives and forks, all slightly out of shape. Mirella and Adam watched his performance. No matter how many times they had seen it, the Greek waiter provided a mesmerizing sight.

He disappeared, to return in a moment and slam down a copper measure mug of retsina, which slopped on to the paper cloth and melted it before Mirella's eyes. From his pockets he produced two small squat glasses as thick as jelly-jars and about as attractive, which he crashed down on the table before them. Then he rushed away before they had a chance to order their food.

From then on, it was all go. The Greeks were quite used to tourists and foreign residents. Liking especially a pretty one who did not look or act like a hippie, and a tall handsome man straight out of a Marlboro ad, they were open and gregarious with Adam and Mirella.

A young man from the table next to theirs politely invited himself over to talk with them in rather good English. Where were they from? What were they doing there? How long would they be in Leros? Where were they staying? On and on, and all questions – most of them personal – that were very typical of the extroverted, inquisitive Greek. He left them only when his food arrived at his table and his friends called him.

Mirella was amused at how much Adam enjoyed himself with the young man, the gusto with which he answered all the young man's questions. They looked at each other across the table, and smiled lovingly and affectionately.

'Come on, darling, we will have to run the gauntlet again and go choose our meal ourselves, or we'll never dine tonight.'

And so they did. At every other table they passed, someone stood up and called '*Adaam, ela,* come,' asking Adam and Mirella to join them. They sat at one table for a few minutes, then another, and another. Morsels of food were fed to them on forks as glasses clinked sharply, as ouzos were downed. Only Adam's charm allowed them to get away without offence.

At last, after crossing the road between the quay and the pavement cluttered with people dining at tables close together in front of Paradisos, they pushed their way through to the huge, ugly, aluminium, charcoal-fed rotisserie, with its clanking chains and revolving spits. Huge skewers were arranged one above the other. Row upon row of roasting animal. The top skewer had half a dozen sheep's heads, skeletons with eyes sizzling in their sockets, slowly going round and round. Then came the *kokoretsi*, the sheep's innards seasoned and stuffed in a casing of the animal's intestine, looking like one long, fat sausage. Under that, turning slowly, along with the other skewers, a whole lamb partially cut away. As it turned and roasted, slowly dripping fat onto the hot glowing coals, waiters hacked at it. Fresh rosemary and

264

cooking meat made a heady perfume that billowed over them in puffs of cooking-smoke.

The skulls turning round and round had Mirella hypnotized. She wondered, if they look as barbaric as this on the spit, what they would look like on the plate. Later, returning to her table after selecting their food, she would be shocked to see several on a platter: the skulls split down the centre and half a dozen diners digging around, gobbling up the delicacy. Adam would see the look of horror on Mirella's face and say, 'The cheeks are the best part.'

Manos and Despina pulled them away from the rotisserie on the pavement under the canopy and into the back of the restaurant.

They stood in the middle of the busy kitchen where again Adam was received ebulliently. Two men in filthy aprons, shirt sleeves rolled up, were cooking over the cast-iron wood-burning stove. On a large wooden table there were a number of round aluminium pans filled with different Greek specialities: stuffed peppers, and fried aubergines, and a red-coloured stew of rabbit and onions, rich and succulent. The fried courgettes, and *pastichio*, a kind of noodle pudding, the *moussaka*, and fried potatoes, a bowl as large as any Mirella had ever seen, filled with red tomatoes, quartered and dressed with olive oil and fresh oregano, tempted the palate.

Two women, again in soiled aprons, their hair under white scarves, beads of sweat on their foreheads, dished out large portions on small, white, shop-worn porcelain plates, quickly handing them to busy waiters. There was shouting back and forth across the kitchen, and spurts of temper, and more than the necessary clanking of pots and pans.

The waiters hovered around Mirella and Adam as they looked into the bubbling saucepans and skillets to see what else was on offer, a custom of the restaurant that replaced a menu. Amid the kitchen clatter, cooking chips, frying fish and squid, the smoke and heat, and the smells, they selected their dinner.

They pushed their way past the conveyor-belt of waiters and food trailing in and out, and through the restaurant. It was almost bare because its tables had been set out in the street and across the road on the quay. The white neon light picked out starkly the odd chair or table left in the featureless restaurant.

They dined on the lamb and the *kokoretsi*, which were in fact delicious. And, while they ate, they were offered an endless choice of Greek dishes from the hot kitchens in the back of the restaurant. Glasses of ouzo and retsina were sent over with the compliments of many of the Greeks, who waved to them, lifted glasses and drank to their health.

By the time they had finished their meal few Greek males had missed a furtive eyeing of Mirella, their eyes lowered out of deference to Adam, and not wanting to offend. In fantasy they actively undressed Adam's wife, caressed her breasts, her bare back and naked arms.

And he was not offended. Adam had a strong friendship with these men, based on shared experience of trust and loyalty, and a common perception even now in the present. There was a kind of power and magic in sharing his beautiful wife with them and their coarse fantasies.

Adam raised his glass and silently gave a toast to his wife. He knew that Mirella would understand that what these men shared with Adam, he could never fully share with a woman. Some base, unspoken bond of sexual desire roused him. He desired his wife even as they did now.

It was camaraderie, devotion between friends. Adam always enjoyed close friendships with men: it was more selfless, more intimate. His relationships with men had always been more enduring than with women, and he knew it was the same with most men. These men were here at their table now because men seek companionship with another man, no matter how much they want and desire a woman. In an unforgiving world, and when the struggle of life is too unrelenting, men seek out men because women are just another responsibility. With other men they know freedom.

Yet he watched and listened to the conversation going on between Mirella and the men, and understood so clearly that his only real friend was his wife. It was Mirella who would give him the emotional support he needed, not these or any other male friends. Adam knew that men don't make real friends, that the closeness he felt with men was not that of mutual interest or shared emotions, but a solidarity in the face of danger. That kind of closeness, an arbitrary and discriminating one, had little to do with real friendship. Adam had always been drawn to male friendships by common experience of loneliness or danger. Accidents of association offering no basis in personal sameness for an alliance of love. When he had sought a caring regard for another, there always had to be a woman.

Adam felt content, delighted with his wife and their Greek admirers. There was something else that added an exhilaration to the evening, an edge of competition.

It was late and the tables began to empty. Mirella and Adam sat looking out across the black water to the boats rocking at anchor under the moonlight and stars. There was a stillness that seemed to settle upon the port, like an invisible blanket and there were sudden holes of blackness in the distance, where lights went out, all around the crescent-shaped harbour. The only sounds were the lapping of the water and the bark of a dog far off. The carousel had whirled to a halt, the people had gone home, and suddenly the magic of the island embraced them again.

Adam smiled to himself in the dark. Here was the Greece that he loved best: sensate, creative, sensual and complex. In the hot, sultry and romantic night, Mirella and he walked through the dark silent port and on past the end of town to the deserted beach, where there was a soft, warm wind under the moonlight. There he sat on the sand and pulled Mirella down into his lap and cradled her. She felt to him like the other side of his deepest self.

They walked back towards the Papoulies across the port. They didn't speak. Dawn coming up over the horizon was sheer poetry and they saw another kind of magic about the place.

The sound of their shoes clicking over the cobble-stones; dark forms turning into the outlines of boats or buildings. The black water was transformed to burnished silver and there was the smell of an early morning sea, and the faint scent of dew-freshened flowers . . . and silence. Heavy silence, on which the sounds of foot on stone or water upon shingle scarcely impinged. Yes, and there was mystery, strange and distant mystery there and in their lives. God or hell was at hand. It was like a walk on the edge of a crater.

It was a very different town that Mirella and Adam woke up to. The sun and the heat poured in through the shuttered balcony door. They bathed and dressed and went out to meet it. A morning freshness and sunshine had revitalized the old port. The *caiques* bobbed up and down in a luscious blue Aegean that sparkled as if sequins had been scattered on the waves. The carnival atmosphere of the night before had vanished with the dark.

By day it was a colourfully lazy town. Everything seemed to move in slow motion, even though it was a working port. They meandered through it discovering the grocer, the butcher, the postmaster, the baker. At Adam's favourite coffee shop, they sat in the sun to drink coffee and eat warm fresh bread smeared with sweet butter and honey. It was a simple enough breakfast, yet flavoured in its setting with a specialness that they both acknowledged. They sat and enjoyed the laid-back atmosphere that was seeping into their bones, while a bee alighted on the rim of the cracked white saucer to share their honey.

People walked back and forth in front of their table on their way to work or on daily errands and greeted the now-famous couple with, 'Kalimera.' But there was no chit-chat. It was business as usual, even though it was Sunday.

The port had a daytime vitality quite distinct from its nocturnal enchantment. They sat there, husband and wife, absorbing the magic of it all but silent lest they break the spell.

Finally Adam reached out his hand to Mirella.

'The spell these Greek islands cast will always be here for us, but now we must be on our way. Just one quick look around the town, then back to the 'copter and Patmos.'

They wandered through the back streets, dirt lanes that twisted and turned, and briefly became cobble-stone roads before reverting to mere tracks with an occasional large stone pounded into them. Old, white houses bordered each street, immaculately attended by women in loose black dresses, their hair covered with black cotton scarves twisted under their chins and tied with a knot on top of their heads. The women seemed to peck away at their chores like black crows. They looked tough and brutal in what little femininity they had, and Mirella could not but think it was their men who had caged them in this hard and sexless domesticity. It depressed her.

They came upon an old white-domed church. The wooden doors were open and the thin, white, cotton-embroidered curtain hanging in the doorway was pulled back. A cool, incense-laden breeze wafted from the church and seemed to beckon them in from the hot, glaring sun and the dusty street.

Inside, thick walls washed in bright white lime enclosed them. There was a screen of intricately-carved wood that divided the church and led to a small sanctuary. The wooden lace-work of birds, trees, flowers, even primitive-looking mermaids was well but naïvely carved. They could see candles burning behind the frieze. The two arched openings in it were hung with worn, dark velvet cloth, too short and not quite wide enough for the opening.

There were thick bees-wax candles and heavy brass

and copper candlesticks, ponderous with piety. The polished surfaces and the silver votives, old embossed silver dishes and intricate silver covers over the icons, glowed mysteriously in the glimmering candlelight. The Byzantine holiness was overwhelming, so great was the power of the ancient and magnificent icons placed reverently there. Dozens of slim candles were burning and dried flowers disintegrated everywhere.

The church was cool and damp but the orthodoxy was rich, exotic and all-powerful. It seemed to Mirella that the essence of this little sanctuary would imprint itself upon her senses and her being forever. She left Adam inside and stumbled out into the light and leaned against the building, tears trickling down her cheeks.

She could not understand her anxiety, the tears she was shedding, the deep loneliness that had engulfed her soul. Never had she been so close to another human being as she was to Adam, yet on this remarkably happy island voyage where she felt a strong oneness with him, she felt him drifting away from her. The islands were too powerful, too overwhelming. Now she acknowledged two serious rivals for Adam's love: his unspoken desire to remain the solitary man on some adventurous quest she did not yet understand . . . and Marlo Channing.

Chapter 16

Their world changed into something ethereal for the next two days. They were somewhere between heaven and earth, between living in the present and experiencing the past in the same moment. There was no Mirella, no Adam.

They were angels who flew in the sun, dolphins who swam and played in the sea. They were the first and the last man and woman God created. They were all the gods and goddesses of mystery and myth. They were of an earthly delicacy of substance that changed its form to fit the elements, to satisfy and be satisfied by nature – the nature God created, and their own natures. They felt they were two of the luckiest people in the world, chosen people.

They flew between the blue of the sky and the blue of the sea, so dangerously low at times that they felt the spray off the top of the waves they clipped. At other times so high as to see the chain of islands between Leros and Samos as so many beads broken from a necklace and scattered on the sea.

They dropped out of the sky onto a dot of an island between Lipsoi and Aykathonisi, uninhabited except for a few birds. A dry rocky place, with one large and luxurious tree growing from the side of a crevice that split the island nearly in half, shaping it to look from the air like a heart or a voluptuously-cleft feminine bottom. The heat waves shimmied and shivered off the whole diameter of the mile-wide rock island.

Mirella and Adam left their clothes in the 'copter, and, naked except for sandals, scampered down the crevice where the waves rushed in six feet below the tree to form a sort of narrow lagoon. And there, to cool off, they swam and played like dolphins, and watched the huge waves roll towards them, slow down and dissolve as they were forced through the crevice.

Cool and wet, naked, they clambered back up the side of the crevice and over the rocks, one below the other, Adam occasionally helping her with a push from underneath. They dried off, spread-eagled under the sun. Adam quenched his erotic thirst for Mirella at her cunt. The taste was exquisite: he delighted in her orgasms. They were for him like an aphrodisiac on the tongue. His tastebuds came alive, and his tongue probed her constantly for more.

He watched her writhe in ecstasy on the hot stones. Her clitoris became swollen with pleasure; her outer and inner labia, luscious and pink from his lips and his nibbling mouth, glistened with her come and his saliva, and lay open and exposed under the sky and the sun and the sea breezes. She was like a glorious sacrifice to the gods, and she revelled in this stream of dreams he wrought from her, again and again.

She tried to stifle her cries of ecstasy by placing the back of her hand over her mouth and biting into it, but Adam gently moved it away and her cries travelled on the wind and dispersed with the sound of the pounding sea all around the tiny island. Her joy flowed and filled his mouth.

274

He swallowed, and as her nectar trickled down his throat, it threw him into a licentious, untamed passion. It was the taste of her combined with the sexual power he possessed that enabled him to wring so much joy from this beautiful, proud and independent wife of his. In desire he wanted to reach in further, where his tongue could not go, to caress her womb, fill his cupped hand with her delectable juices – to him an elixir of life – and drink her from his own palm.

Soon. Soon. Before nightfall, in the little white house covered in magenta bougainvillaea, on his private island, not very far from where they were, he would do just that.

Adam knew when he scooped her up in his arms, kissed her deeply, and filled her mouth with her own delicious elixir, that she could not stop, she was not sated. He could feel it in her body as she tensed and then shivered with the release of another orgasm, while he carried her to the 'copter. They never bothered with their clothing, just covered their nakedness, he with his white cotton shirt, she with the silk one she had been wearing. He could see it in her eyes, how she wanted to stay in his arms, how she wanted him, and he said, 'Soon, on another island not far from here. I know a place.' And they climbed into the helicopter, and he swung off the rock at a sharp right angle and into the sun.

But, if Mirella wanted more, Adam out-reached even her desire. He could not keep his hands off her. He piloted the 'copter to his Aegean hideaway, yet continued to fondle her, to bury his hand between her legs and play with her cunt until it was wet with her

275

pleasure. He stole glimpses of her where she slumped back in the seat, her cream silk shirt flung open, her head thrown back, erotic violet eyes searching the heavens and the seas, hands placed over her mouth, as if sealing her lips so as not to break the spell. She was beautiful in her lust.

Finally dazzled and dazed with sexual delight, swooping over the mythical playground of the Greek gods and goddesses like some licentious winged lady from Hades, Mirella dissolved into this magical place that was part world, part heaven. She reached down, removed Adam's hand and covered it with her mouth and licked it clean. Then, placing his arm around her shoulder, she leaned over and collapsed on him.

Neither of them spoke. There was no need. Words were for mere mortal communication. What need had they for words? They were saying it all with their bodies, and their souls, in this mysterious, magical place.

Adam caught at the dream within the real. It was part of the excitement, the unreality of it all. But he found it was the real that almost eluded him. It was so difficult to step out of the dreamworld he was sharing with Mirella.

This island, like the other, was uninhabited rock, except for a hidden, horseshoe-shaped cove. He carried Mirella from the 'copter, kissing her face, her breasts, down a sweep of steps carved in the rock to the house below.

It had been made ready for them. All the faded blue shutters that dotted the stark white of the villa protruding romantically from the rock on the water's edge were flung open. It was baking hot, but a strong breeze blew through the one-room house so that the diaphanous white curtains of the enormous four-poster Indian ivory bed in the middle of the room danced voluptuously.

Mirella was aware of nothing but Adam. Not the outstanding beauty of the white marble floors, not the collection of Hellenic marbles standing in pools of sunshine from the skylights set in the series of domes on the roof. Not the walls of rare books, the garnet-coloured porphyry chairs and chaise longue. Not even the ten-foot-square sunken bath whose white marble steps, leading down into it on all four sides, formed bases for the occasional Minoan amphora excavated from the sea. The Byzantine mosaic of dolphins and mermaids that formed the floor of the bath was covered with cool, scented waters, and an enormous bowl of jasper was filled with fresh white rose petals, whose perfume hardly affected Mirella.

Adam pushed the bed curtains away with his elbow, and laid Mirella on the white, silky, lynx-furs among the huge, soft feather cushions covered in antique white Persian embroidery. He slipped the silk shirt from her shoulders and dropped it with his to the floor. He kissed and licked and fondled her. He searched out her lips, her mouth, caressed and sucked her breasts until she squirmed with the sharpness of ecstasy. He buried his face between her legs and sucked her passion-swollen genitals into his mouth until she came. Then he left her, only to return with a small ivory table which he placed next to the bed. On it were objects of art: a silver, baroque Italian ewer filled with fresh peach nectar, two golden Grecian cups of great antiquity, and boxes and covered jars beautifully carved from blocks of semi-precious stones – malachite, jade, jasper and rock crystal.

He lay down next to Mirella among the cushions and together they drank from one cup. And with one passion they made love. From a covered box of malachite he smothered and kneaded her body with an ointment of musk and honeysuckle. Her breasts assumed the sheen of marble, and before he was done with her she gleamed all over, silk to his touch. Her swollen nipples and her genitals he coloured with an ointment of henna, alum, and honey that made them feel suddenly tight and soft, and inflamed her lust beyond passion. When he entered her with his caressing fingers and massaged the ointment round and round, deeper, always deeper into her cunt, she cried out helplessly as the ointment and his fondling sensitized her into an untameable pleasure.

Adam had done it for love of her, for his erotic desire to both give and take pleasure in her, and he was rewarded tenfold. The musk had done its work on both their senses. And now the sight and scent and feel of unimpeded sexuality enveloped him, and focused all his desires in one: to take her, bury himself inside her, fill her full of himself and his seed, and to dissolve her in their orgasms.

And he did. The ointments made her perform as a wanton, and yet at the same time made her cunt feel like that of an untouched virgin. When Adam entered her with his erect and throbbing penis, he experienced anew the joy of slowly, methodically deflowering that tight and mysterious place.

Again and again he pressed deeper, and fucked Mirella until at last she could take him into herself entirely. And then the rhythm changed. Her orgasms began to come in rapid succession, until he moved in and out of her with ease, assisted by the silky smoothness of these copious orgasms. He left nothing inside her untouched by his thrusts and caresses, and after he burst forth and filled her with his seed, he entered her again with almond cream as smooth and cooling as a shaded grove, its scent as heavy as the trees in blossom.

He soothed her with it and created more sensuous sensations, added another handful and fondled her with fingers that entered deeper, deeper, till with one final, painful thrust he was inside her up to his wrist. The pain was short and sharp, but nothing to the pleasures eased from her with the almond cream and his caressing of even the tiny opening at the neck of her womb. He used his hand and his fist as he had his penis, again and again. The sight of his arm sinking into her brought their mutual lust to a kind of madness, so untamed and out of control was their passion.

They had lost their identities, and now their separateness. They were sexually as one, and Mirella's orgasms were his, just as his were hers. His hand and her womb were of the same body. They shared one mouth, one heart. And only after Mirella had lost all control over her orgasms and had come until she had actually swooned from exhaustion, was Adam able to harness again his violent passion to tenderness and love.

They gave each other everything there was to give, and never had demand been made for such giving, for such rewards. Adam had planned this voyage carefully, wanted Mirella to understand that they were solid, with no bonds to hold them either in some unreal and dreamlike world or in the real world. They were as one, and yet individuals, their own true selves, and nothing could ever change that.

At midnight, they bathed together by candlelight and oil lamp, in the soothing, scented water, washing each other with oil of lemon and mint until their skin tingled with a cool revitalized freshness. As they walked together up the steps out of the water, Adam flung handfuls of white rose petals from the jasper bowl and dried her with them by rubbing them against her skin until they absorbed all the water and left her blooming with the perfume of a rose garden.

They dined by the romantic light of the candles and oil lamps on huge fresh peaches and glorious black grapes, and cold roasted quail stuffed with apricots. They drank a bottle of Bonnes Mares '66 Grand Cru, the colour of garnets and rubies, while reclining on the bed, surrounded by its thin, misty curtains, with only the soft sound of ivory curtain rings dancing on the ivory rod and the far crashing of the waves outside in the blackness and otherwise utter silence of the night. And then they slept.

It was very strange. There seemed no explanation for it, but from the moment Mirella saw the luscious green island of Samos rising out of the sea, she knew she was leaving one world for another. As they whirled over the island thick with lemon and orange trees scattered among all the other trees, leafy and laden with fruit, she touched Adam's knee affectionately. He turned for a moment and their smiles merged.

Adam put the 'copter down at the end of a dock where the *caique* boat-builders worked. As Mirella's feet touched the ground, a moment of sadness passed through her. She thought she sensed that feeling she had heard about, but never understood – as if someone had walked on her grave.

She watched Adam as he shook hands with two men who were to stand watch over the 'copter, protecting it from inquisitive hands. When he walked back to her their eyes met and the silence between them was understood immediately by both. They broke it together, trying to speak at the same moment. They laughed and he placed his arm around her shoulder and together they started their walk into town.

Their happiness with each other vibrated, like a perfect burst of song from the best tenor and the best contralto. And they began to talk to each other, something they had not done in days. As they chattered on, Adam was acutely aware that they had made a heavenly journey together with nothing but their bodies and their souls. On earth it was good, great even, but being earthbound had to be inferior. Such was the nature of things.

'And what about Patmos? I loved Patmos – even if it is where the apostle John wrote the Apocalypse. I want to go back one day when we have time to stay. But even from the air I knew how special it was,' she said.

'I have a marvellous house there at the top, *Khora*, with a panoramic view across the Bay of Grikou. It's magic. It's our house now, and we'll go to it one day.'

'There has been so much. Remember the valley of the butterflies, and Andiparos, and that view when we flew from Leros to—' She stopped in mid-sentence. That part of the journey was too personal, too ethereal, to attach words to.

281

Adam stopped and pulled her up to him by her arm, and looked into her eyes. They seemed more beautiful, more violet. Then he abruptly let go of her arm and put a hand in his pocket. When he withdrew it, he had something in his clenched fist. He dropped her duffle bag on the ground and, taking her other hand by the wrist, he held it in front of her and opened her palm.

'I bought these for you on my last day in New York. Take them now in celebration of our voyage through the Greek Islands. I was going to give them to you in Dilos at the beginning of our island-hopping, and then several times during it. Now seems the right time, so that they'll always serve as the words that we'll never utter about those days between Leros and Samos.'

He opened his fist in her palm and removed his hand. A pair of cabochon, pigeon-blood rubies the size of a quail's egg lay in her palm, each of them set in a circle of square cut diamonds. She gasped, the jewels dazzled her, so powerful was the allure of the gems. Adam began to laugh.

'They do rather leave one speechless,' he said. 'Once I saw them I had to have them for you. Van Cleef and Arpels assure me they were once worn by an Empress. A Russian Empress. I can only assume it was Catharine.'

Adam lowered his voice and added, 'Not even thank you. That would be too trite. It would spoil it, trivialize the gesture, not to mention the jewels, not to mention what we share in each other.'

'I love you,' she said her eyes still riveted to the rubies.

'That'll do, that'll do just fine,' he said with a smile

in his voice, as he plucked them from her hand and clipped one on each of her ears.

He handed her the duffle bag and she fished out a fair-sized tortoise-shell hand-mirror. Even she was struck by how beautiful she looked with them on. So was Adam. She attempted a joke about them to cover her vanity. 'I am beginning to think I was born to wear great jewels.'

'That's what Rashid always says about you. That's one of the reasons he adores buying them for you. And, you know, that devil is right.' Then he slipped his arm though hers and they took great long happy strides towards town.

They were a glorious sight, the two deeply-tanned people dressed all in white. She wore a silk shirt tied at midriff and hip-hugging fine, wide, cotton trousers with turn-ups that moved provocatively with every step she took. Her raven-black hair was loose, casually brushed back, held in place with black enamel combs. The blood-red rubies and diamonds lit up her sensuous face. The stunning diamond hand-cuffs were on her tanned wrists, of course, and her bright finger- and toe-nails flashed scarlet sunshine with every movement of her hands and feet. She looked great, she looked rich, and most of all she looked beautiful, intelligent, witty, and imaginative.

Adam wore fine white cotton Oxford bags, a paper-thin, white cotton shirt, sleeves rolled up; he held his Dougie Heywood white poplin jacket suspended from his shoulder together with Mirella's duffle bag. His dark blond hair had turned the colour of ash, and the normally white streaks shone silver against his deeply-tanned face. His bigness, his broad shoulders, his carriage, his sure stride, all seemed godlike to

Mirella – her Zeus or Poseidon. To the average, short, dark and hairy Greek, though, he looked like a movie star.

They walked to the back of the port and into town. It appeared to Mirella that every shop was a speciality shop – the tyre shop, the used-tyre shop, the electrical shop, the electrician's repair shop, the plumber's, the carpenter's. They all had minute premises filled with thousands of used parts. The tinsmith, the black-smith, and shoe-repair shops by the dozen. Endless shoe-stores with dusty window displays and dated styles, and all selling the same models at the same prices. Shirt shops and blanket shops, trouser shops and jewellery shops. A town where you could shop for everything, and be lucky in the end to buy anything.

The town was a mad scramble of work and people. There was a constant noise of machines, powerful automatic drills digging somewhere. A pump gasped and gurgled water into the street from somewhere. Hammers, saws and shouted instructions every-where. There was a traffic jam of two cars and a lorry, a donkey and a flat cart pulled by a man.

A modern concrete building shooting up five storeys sounded the death-knell for the old, the run-down and the beautiful. Around the corner from the five-storey building was a narrow street full on either side with bright blue, red, orange and yellow plastic buckets and tubs, hoses and dishes, pots, pans and ladders, yards and yards of cloth, the best plastic, the glossiest money could buy.

At last they found the post office. It was closed. The whole town was open for trade, and the post office was closed. Adam had wanted to send a cable.

He gave up, and the Coreys fled back towards the old port of Pythagorion and the more primitive shopkeepers.

'Not wars, not pestilence, not poverty, nor politics, is murdering Greece. It's plastic. They're being corrupted by primary-coloured plastic. And just you wait – they'll find a way to blame even that on the CIA,' said Adam, a note of amused despair in his voice.

They left the freezer and the fridge shops behind, and turning onto a small street with bookshops and stationers came as a relief to both. Under a scorching midday sun they got lost in a maze of winding streets that flattened out at the back of the port. They were tired because of the humidity that accompanied the heat, and they were hungry and looking forward to a shaded table near the water.

They turned a corner and then, suddenly, the ugliness was behind them. Spread out in front of them was the dusty old picturesque port, a few unimpressive *caiques* bobbing up and down in the water. They looked straight out across to the Mykale foothills on the coast of Asia Minor. Adam's face shone with pleasure.

'Look, over there! That's home, our real home: Turkey.' He placed his arm round Mirella's shoulder. 'Where once the women of your family ruled their men and were clever and beautiful and held great power. We're going home where you can take your place among them.'

It was only then, in the quiet old port of Pythagorion, within sight of Asia Minor that Mirella realized Adam meant what he said. He was not just taking her home to his beloved Peramabahçe palace for a few months. He expected her to put her power and position to use as her ancestors had in their lives and their family and their country. In Mirella's case, not country,' but countries: the USA *and* Turkey. She had a station in life she would no longer be able to shrink from when she chose, as she had in her situation at the UN as Assistant Director of Translations in New York.

Of the few people in the port, some were busy eating their lunches at tables crowded together under the faded blue awning in front of the restaurant. She watched and listened to Adam instructing a waiter to place a table and two chairs under a gnarled tree. Behind the vast trunk of the port's solitary tree, someone sat at the only other table, engrossed in a newspaper.

Money, power, love, she had them all, and more – she had famous ancestors to live up to. And she had Adam and Rashid to support her. And it had all come in the prime of her life. It was as if fate had issued its challenge. Mirella Wingfield Corey knew one thing for certain: as long as she had the love of her husband, she could take it up. Take up the challenge, indeed! she thought. She would take it up and shake it for all the world to see. Her spirit expanded and she sensed excitement at the prospect of all she was going to do with her life.

When Adam returned to her side, she was laughing to herself, reminded of the party she had gone to for a middle-eastern King and his American consort at the UN a few months before. She remembered looking around the room with a degree of inverted snobbery at Nancy Reagan, Betsy Bloomingdale, Wynn Taggert, and all those stunning American women with rich and powerful husbands, who were invading the world and terrorising ladies who had less.

Mirella suddenly felt a sympathy for all those New York-rich, Washington-rich, Dallas-rich ladies with their reserves of hard-earned knowledge worn like bullet-proof vests under their Ungaros, Blasses, Galanoses, and de la Rentas. The Nans and the Annes, the Lynns and the Judys, the Pats and the Jackies. They too had it all in their prime; and maybe she had something to learn from them of how not to live her life. They chose their way, she would choose hers. She would opt for more than a wrinkle-proof life in society. In her life there would be time for sexual ecstasy and dying to the world as she had the past few days with Adam, as she had with Rashid. Her own sensuality and theirs was part of her future, and she would, as her oriental ancestors had, weave it into the high-wrought tapestry of her life.

They sat down at the table, and Adam said. 'I've ordered for us, I'm famished and I'm sure you are. Lots of different local dishes and some *kahlah-mahree*, because I know you like squid and some freshly caught *bahrboonee*. I know red mullet is not one of your favourite things in life, but, never mind, we'll dine better tonight in Istanbul.'

Mirella heard the voice before she recognized its source. Then, when she did, she could hardly believe it possible.

'I wouldn't bet on that if I were you, Mirella,' said Marlo, as she lowered the newspaper to reveal her face and tilted her rickety wooden chair at a precarious angle so she could lean from behind the tree to see Adam and Mirella.

Before either of the Coreys could say anything,

287

Marlo pointed and continued, 'Adam, Mirella, meet my friend. You are going to love her. In some circles she gets called a white knight.'

The phrase altered Adam's business self. He rose, instantly the courteous company man, only to confront a vision of feminine beauty beyond even his experience. Having emerged from behind the tree, she stood before him, silent and proud, no greeting on her lips but a passionate fire in her large black-brown eyes. The six-foot-tall woman locked her gaze into his. Her long, ultra-slim body matched arms and legs that appeared to go on forever. Her hips and breasts and belly were straight, flat, as if non-existent, except for nipples that protruded beneath the loose, bright red, fine woven cotton shift.

She was part-animal, he thought. A gazelle, an impala. No, not quite. An oryx, yes – that black hair pulled tight to her head and coiled on the top. And all female, ruthlessly female. He was right: she was all that and more. Her bearing was regal. She was more like a female King than a Queen.

Mirella sensed Adam's response to this presence. The woman's skin glowed like dark-brown satin catching the sun. Her dramatically handsome Semitic features declared profound intelligence. Mirella directed her mesmerized attention from the dusky royal of the upper Nile to her husband,

Adam and the woman stood silently taking each other in. They were as if locked into a trance, not saying a word. Mirella herself seemed more shocked than surprised by the appearance of the woman standing before her. She wanted to rise from her chair and break the spell between the lady and Adam, but she was unable to move. The heat reverberated to the cicadas' mid-day symphony and the tide lapping the stones on the beach. She felt the sun burning one arm not shaded by the tree. There was a tension in the air that immobilized her. Her gaze drifted from the table top and some flies stalking across it, to the boats in the harbour, to the women standing on either side of the tree. But she could not look at her husband – she was both frightened and embarrassed at what she might see.

She ignored them and fixed her gaze on Marlo, her antagonist. She wondered why Marlo had done this to her. Marlo was dressed in her attractive rag-bag fashion. Today her hair was tucked under a wide-brimmed, man's white panama hat with a slim black band around the crown. Her ears bore handsome, big gold hoops from Senegal. A white cotton jump-suit was cinched at her waist with a bright blue silk embroidered shawl from China worn like a wide sash, its fine silk fringe dangling decoratively to her knee. Something about the sash thankfully distracted Mirella into thinking of Gainsborough's The Boy Blue. The hat, Somerset Maughamish, evoked the South Seas. Her eyes met Marlo's, smiling and mischievous.

It was Marlo who made the move, not Mirella. She rose, placed a hand on Adam's shoulder for a minute and patted it affectionately. She passed behind him and walked directly to Mirella. She took Mirella by her elbow and kindly but firmly pulled her up out of her chair, and in a low voice said, 'I think you and I might go for a little walk.'

Mirella followed Marlo towards the end of the quay and, when they were out of earshot, Marlo looked at Mirella. Mirella saw a change in her face: the smiling eyes turned sad and just a little frightened.

'Try not to think or worry about it,' Marlo said. 'They have something to resolve. Remember, I want her back no less than you want him. In spite of what you might think, I'm not your rival, she is. Look, Mirella, we don't have much time, so I'll be brief. Her name is Tana Dabra Ras Magdala Makoum. She is the brains behind a Geneva-based conglomerate at work in the Third World. She has just saved Adam's skin and The Corey Trust from a disastrous takeover by becoming what is called in the financial world his 'white knight'. She is a red-hot Ethiopian Marxist who controls all the money syphoned off from the treasury for foreign investment. It was important that she and Adam meet and talk and, for her, essential that it be in secret, since she is under constant government surveillance, and as of late not completely trusted. They track her every move. I was able to organize this meeting because I am officially travelling back to Ethiopia with her on an assignment for her government.'

'How did you know we would be here?'

'Oh, shit, Mirella, never mind all that, it's not important. What is important is that they have met, and Adam will not pursue her in the open. They'll be making plans for future secret meetings, which it's best that neither of us know anything about. Now I must go. We came over from Kusadarsi by fast motor boat, supposedly for lunch, after conveniently losing her bodyguards somewhere among the ruins of Ephesus. That was hours ago. We must go back and reclaim and chastise them for their inefficiency.'

The two women started back towards the table under the tree – anger just spurting within Mirella at

Marlo for being far too dramatic, and talking down to her. Then, as was typical of Marlo, she did something to charm and endear herself. She placed her hand on Mirella's arm and said, 'Adam and I adore our little girl Alice. Please love her too, Mirella. She loves you; she thinks of you as a glamorous princess in the castle since the wedding. Every day she asks when you're coming home. She loves you. Take good care of her for me. The whole clan is waiting for you in Istanbul. But put Alice first. Saddled with a mother like me she needs you most.'

Mirella did not see Tana Dabra Ras Magdala Makoum again because the table was empty and Adam's shrill whistle pierced the air. Marlo pulled her hat from her head and ran down to the beach. By the time Mirella reached Adam, the speed-boat was a good distance from the shore. All Mirella could see of the two women was a white hat waving in the air, and a red-hooded figure standing in the boat, her gaze fixed upon Africa.

Chapter 17

'I think I'm suffering from culture shock.'

Brindley began to laugh. 'That's very amusing, because that's what I say to myself half a dozen times a day in New York.'

'What do you do about it, Brinn?'

'Much what I expect you will do about it. Sit back and enjoy it, and not pretend I'm going to join the natives, because I know I am not. I'm too British to be anything else.'

Deena took his point. 'And I'm too American to be anything else, is that what you're saying?'

'Yes. The best you can hope for is to be an Anglophile with a British husband and bi-lingual children, meaning they will speak English-English and American-English.'

'And tolerate the subtle English put-down like the one you have just delivered? I have learned this past four days to recognize it as a work of art. But for the rest of my life?'

'I would hope so. I shall, after all, have to suffer the "poor little England" put-down for the rest of mine.'

'Oh dear, do we have a problem, Brindley?'

'I have no problem, Deena. Do you?'

Deena came back with greater precision, 'I didn't ask if you had a problem, Brinn. I asked if *we*, you and me together, have a problem.'

'I stand corrected. No, I don't believe *we* do. What's this all about, Deena?'

'Whether you still love me, want to marry me.'

Brindley began to protest, and she looked away from the lake with the majestic white swans gliding on the mirror surface of the water, and into Brindley's eyes. That was difficult, because Deena was enchanted by Lyttleton Park, the Ribblesdale house in the green English countryside. Its nine hundred acres of parkland that Capability Brown had addressed his genius to held working farms, idyllic gardens, and a forty-two-room Tudor Manor House. On a sultry summer day the estate made a less than ideal site for a confrontation. It was, therefore, with a heavy heart that Deena confronted Brindley with that question.

She placed a hand gently over his mouth. 'No, please, Brindley, don't say anything. Just hear me out.'

He looked at Deena, so pretty. His golden girl, as he christened her in bed. And here, at Lyttleton Park, he found her even prettier, more vital, more sensuous if possible than in New York. He applauded the way she slipped into the pattern in English country life and without even trying, brought new energy to his family home, and laughter and a freshness he savoured.

In his ancestral home she appeared softer, more at ease with life. Yet still she exuded for him that feisty sexuality he had been seduced by. He was so proud of her, so proud that she would soon be his wife, the mother of his children, and one day the mistress of Lyttleton Park ... and she would be his mate for eternity in their secret sexual debauchery. It puzzled him that she could even suggest that he might not love her, not want to marry her.

He reached out and tucked a golden curl under the white chiffon scarf she had tied in a wide band around her head and into a soft floppy bow just off centre of her face, in order to keep her long hair pulled back. She looked so romantic with her white handkerchief-linen dress rippling in the soft, warm breeze, and the straw garden-hat held in her hand with its wide brim and peach-satin band and streamers. He took her by the arm and silently walked with her to a three hundred year old elm tree and spread his coloured blazer on the grass for them to sit upon.

After some minutes of silence, Deena said, 'Brindley, my dearest love, please be patient and hear me out. In all, since we became lovers we have spent less than a week together. We fell in love under the influence of two enormously charismatic people and their inspiring love affair. We calculatingly used each other to gather up our courage to go forward and change our lives, wanting to fulfil ourselves in an emotional relationship as strong and binding as Mirella's and Adam's.

'You saw my life in New York, you met my mother and father, and saw very clearly what my background is. Now I have experienced your family and your background. We are no longer under the influence of someone else's romance. We are out here on our own. I think it's important for us to face squarely how we feel about each other now, not when you asked me to marry you in New York. Don't get me wrong. I am not discounting how we felt for each other then. I am just saying that in the four days I have been with you, your family and friends at Lyttleton Park, I scarcely have seen you between the village fêtes, and the cricket field, and the lawn tennis, and the luncheons, and the dinner parties, and the ball – not to mention your mother's greenhouses, and her walled garden, and her fruit gardens and orchards, and vegetable gardens, and her glorious flower gardens, and tea parties on the lawn . . . and our separate bedrooms.

'I have met the vicar, your old cricket chums, all those Binkies and Bonkies, and Henrys and Jeremys and Percys, the fast bowlers and wicket-keepers and batsmen of your life. I've picked up their private language of cherries and prunes and boxes, which have nothing to do with fruit and everything to do with balls and cricket.

'I have made sandwiches unacceptable in your musty-smelling club house because I made them too thick. That is, with more than a smidge of butter or cucumber, fish paste, or one of the other pastes that tint the bread and disguise themselves as sandwich-filler. I have been on the receiving end of embar-rassed silences and blank gazes and abrupt changes of subject when I've missed the point with your chums or their wives or girlfriends.

'I have sat on the edge of conversations with the Babses and the Carolines and the Dianas, the Tamsins and the Camillas. I've been dazzled by the English beauty who has never heard of a nose-job, has encountered cosmetics but has no need to use them, whose hair is rarely combed but stays clean and shines as if by moon beam. I've seen skins and complexions that carry that English-beauty lifelong guarantee that ignores wrinkles.

'They're terribly nice girls, with classy voices and feet shoved into green wellies, or riding boots, and bespoke brogues and Charles Jourdain dancing pumps. Lovely girls with cracked fingernails, who can ride, hunt, shoot, fish, and still outshine any woman at a Grand Ball. Those cool-looking girls with their quiescent smouldering sexuality – in old age, when they get to be seventy, will they still be gaily answering to schmucky nicknames like Piggy and Froggie and Bunty, Poo or Koo, Poppet and Midge?

'And I have been aware of your mother's confusion about me. We have had a freaky dialogue going with each other: "Oh, please, Miss Weaver, you simply cannot go on calling me Mrs Ribblesdale. Do call me Lady Margaret, and I will call you Deena, if you don't mind."

'"Oh, Brindley, Miss Weaver is our first American guest in Lyttleton Park, in my lifetime at any rate. I think she must have the State Bedroom, next to mine. Don't you agree, dear?"

'"Is Deena a friend of Fiona's? No. Oh. You will get on well with Fiona, my dear. Fiona and Brindley have been friends all their lives. She once flew over North America. I believe she even went hunting in Virginia once with her father when she was a little girl. Is that the near coast or the far one, Deena?"

'I seem to have communicated with your mother entirely through what I was "just in time for": the first of the new potatoes, the runner beans, her garden roses, her delphiniums, the Bagshots' ball, the Tetbury fête, the Sherston flower festival, the Oaksey bazaar.

'Or it has been what I have just missed: Royal Ascot for the racing, Badminton for the horse trials, Wimbledon for the tennis, Henley for the rowing. Or it's been the strawberries, the spring greens, the baby carrots, the first of the lettuce, the Spring opening of the gardens to the public, the wild daffodils, narcissi, bluebells and forty thousand tulips.

'Then, of course, if I were to stay on awhile, there were wonderful things just about to happen: the glorious twelfth – that's the twelfth of August and the opening of the grouse season – the pheasant shoots, the deer stalking in Scotland and the salmon fishing. Couldn't I hang on for the raspberries – they were coming on but not ready – her tomatoes and her rhubarb, her artichokes and her prize-winning dahlias, the field of oriental poppies? And wasn't it a pity I had not been in time for the rhododendrons, four acres of them?

'Not once in the four days has your mother spoken directly to me, on a personal level, nor asked me one question about myself, myself and her son. And why should she, since neither her son nor I have appeared together as anything but casual good friends? We haven't had sex, made love, had a personal conversation, since we arrived in England. With every mile of the road from Heathrow airport you became more reserved, more remote. And from the moment you changed into your cricket whites and took up your stance among your family and friends, if it hadn't been for the occasional time when our eyes met, I might have forgotten that you said you loved me once.

'Brindley, in New York when you said you loved me I suddenly knew I was in love with you too. Now, together, here at Lyttleton Park, I appreciate you and our differences even more than I did in the States. I have fallen far more deeply in love with you than I did before, something I never expected and our families never, I suspect, wanted to happen. If it's not the same with you, I want to leave today, this very afternoon.'

'"Creams", not cricket "whites". Some of the locals prefer to call cricketers' trousers "creams", darling. And that's the colour they are, really,' said Brindley, fending off her outburst. He smiled, stood up and pulled Deena to her feet, and holding her hands in his, continued. 'I am by nature a very conservative man. I function by habit and tradition. No woman has ever aroused my sexual passion as you do. You have made my heart laugh, you've lit up my life. I never gave myself to a woman as I gave myself to you that night in Massachusetts. Between our meetings I did nothing but think about you, and about bringing you home here to be mine, and about sharing Lyttleton Park with you one day. I've been a fool. Once I had you here, I reverted to type, took it for granted that you understood. It hardly occurred to me to talk to you about it. Every day I saw you slipping into place and enjoying Lyttleton I fell more deeply in love with you. It's too late for you to leave: I couldn't bear the loss.'

Then Brindley pulled Deena roughly to him and kissed her passionately. They hugged each other and he untied the scarf from around her hair and wiped the tears from her eyes and cheeks, delighted when she explained they were tears of joy and relief that he loved her and would never let her go.

'We'll go right now to my mother and tell her we want to marry as soon as possible. Then we'll deal with your parents.'

'What about the cricket match this afternoon?'

'Quite right. Priorities. We'll tell her after the game.'

It was grey and pouring with rain. Lady Margaret and Deena got caught in it at the fête. Rain stopped play, so the cricketers were disappointed, disgruntled with the weather. Not Deena. One more tombola, one more prize-giving award for the most succulent marrow, the biggest onion, the weightiest tomato, the best flower arrangement, the most perfect English rose; one more visit to the beer tent, or innings at cricket, would have tried her nerves to breaking point.

Yes, Deena's very un-British nerves were fraying and would continue to do so until Brindley and she confronted their parents with their intention to marry. She watched the cricketers in their 'creams' walking dejectedly off the pitch, as she and Lady Margaret drove past in Lady Margaret's vintage Bristol. In the pouring rain several old men with passive faces gave the players a round of applause from canvas folding-chairs.

'Mrs Houghton's chocolate cakes were gone before anyone else's. They always are. Cook's pork pies and scones, I never did see them. She will be pleased they were such a success. I did manage to get some ginger cake for tea,' said Lady Margaret as she swung the car around a sharp bend and through the open gates of Lyttleton Park.

'And I managed to grab one of Mary Jane Jones' French apple tarts,' said Deena, hardly believing the enthusiasm of her own words.

'Oh, that was clever, dear, her tarts are excellent. I never seem to get there in time to buy one.'

There was one sharp blast on a horn and, in a flash of ruby red, Brindley passed them on the drive in his open MG, a 1954 TF, and sped up the avenue of lopsidedly-pruned lime trees that led to the house.

'Oh my, Brindley is driving in a temper. The cricket is finally rained off, I expect. He was looking to score his first fifty of the season, you know. A game so completely at the mercy of the weather makes him very frustrated, and I sometimes wish he would occupy his time here more fruitfully. It is a little silly. Well, we'll make him a lovely cup of tea and that will cheer him up. Oh, by the way, Deena, we'll dress for dinner this evening, I've invited guests.'

They had tea in the sitting room. A room of beige and peach and aquamarine roses on cream-coloured, glazed chintz, overstuffed chairs, and soft sofas and Queen Anne furniture. The tea table was set in an Oriel window, one of the four in the house, that overlooked the rose garden. The room was damp and chilly, and a wind had come up and was beating the rain against the huge leaded window, criss-crossed with stone mullions. Brindley lit a fire and turned on lamps. He walked around nervously looking at the Augustus John paintings, the Singer Sargent of his great-grandmother, picked up a book, a magazine, several of the dozen family photographs in silver frames, but nothing could hold his attention.

Lady Margaret whispered to Deena as she poured the tea from a Victorian silver service, 'He has something quite serious on his mind, I can tell because he behaves just as his father did when he had something to say and didn't know how to say it.'

Then she raised her voice and said, 'Brindley, my dear, do say what you have to say, and come and have a cup of tea.'

'Mother, Deena and I are going to get married.'

It was Deena, not Lady Margaret, who fumbled with her cup and saucer; Deena whose colour faded from her face. The clicking of a grandfather clock sounded to her like a time bomb, so quiet was the room. Lady Margaret took Deena's cup, which was swimming in a saucer of spilled tea, from her hands and placed it on the silver tray and put a fresh cup on the table before her future daughter-in-law.

'That's nice, dear,' Lady Margaret said. 'Now come and have a cup of tea. China or Indian?'

Brindley smiled at his mother, the sort of smile that said 'thank you mother for never making a fuss, never letting me down.' 'China,' he answered, and went directly to the tea table, taking his place between the two women.

He looked at Deena, surprised to see how tense she was, smiled at her and took her hand in his and kissed it. Lady Margaret passed the cup of tea to him and asked, 'Ginger cake or Mrs Jones' French apple tart, children?'

Deena was awed by the civility, the composure. Where were the screams, the tears, the hysterics, the expected objections. 'But, she's Jewish, my dear. She's too old for you, Brindley. It is out of the question, she's not English, Brindley. Are you sure about this, my boy? She is not one of us, how will she get on with your chums? You hardly know her. We rather expected you would marry Fiona. I will move to the Dower House as soon as possible so as not to be in your way.' She found herself mentally translating into British the reaction she would have expected from her family in New York.

But what she heard was, 'Under the circumstances, I think we might splash out just a little on the wine at dinner this evening. Will you take care of it, Brindley? Do check with Cook, but not until after I have seen her and made a few adjustments to the menu. Who is going to tell Nanny, you or I?' asked Lady Margaret.

'I will, Mother.'

'What a relief. Nanny Wilkins will be asking you some rather personal questions, Deena. I am sorry, but it can't be helped. She is ninety-three years old and, having been here at Lyttleton for seventy-three years, rules us all, as you have already seen. I hope you won't mind. I remember the first time I came to this house and my husband broke the news to Nanny that we were going to marry. We were sitting around this very same tea table and she replied, "Naughty Waffles" – she always called him Waffles – "teasing Nanny like that, and embarrassing the young lady." Then she slapped him sharply on the knuckles with the silver cake-slicer, and looked very black indeed when she said, "Marry, humph. Elbows off the table, Waffles, or Nanny will be very angry."'

Lady Margaret's little story seemed to break the ice and at once all three were laughing.

Deena could hardly believe what she was saying when she turned to Brindley and exclaimed. 'Fiona. Someone is going to have to break the news to Fiona, and if it is to be you, Brindley, I hope you are a little less abrupt about it than you were with your mother.'

For a moment, mother and son looked uneasy, and Deena almost wished she had said nothing. Brindley's mother stood up and excused herself on the grounds of having to see Cook and call on the vicar. Her last words for Deena that tea-time were, 'How very thoughtful of you, my dear. Then you did understand that it was expected Brindley would choose Fiona as his wife?'

Later, Deena stood in front of the long mirror in the dark, wood-panelled and red damasked State Bedroom. She was trying to decide what jewellery to wear with the Ralph Lauren, peach-silk, dinner-dress cut on the bias and held up by shoulder straps as thin as shoestrings, and its transparent bolero-jacket of stiff, pale, lemon yellow, silk organza with huge puffed sleeves. There was a knock on the door, and, to her surprise, Lady Margaret entered the room.

Her snow-white hair was fashioned at the nape of her neck in a beautiful twist, and she was so lovely to look at in her long dress of lavender silk chiffon, with a small shoulder cape of the same material. She wore the family sapphires on her ears and around her neck, and diamond and sapphire rings on most of her fingers.

She carried a worn jeweller's necklace box and two enormous roses, each of which had been made from the petals of half a dozen of her prize white roses.

'How lovely you look, Deena,' she said, 'I thought we might wear these. My gardener learned to make the cabbage rose from Constance Spry herself. I always wear one on very special occasions.' Then together they decided where to pin it on Deena's dress, at the waist just below the bottom of the jacket. Lady Margaret secured it for her and said. 'Perfect, my dear.'

Then from the dressing table she picked up the jeweller's box and presented it to Deena.

'My mother-in-law gave me this in honour of my coming marriage. It's traditional in the family. I know you will be happy with Brindley, Deena. He is a very good man.'

Deena was so nervous she simply could not open the catch on the box, and Lady Margaret did it for her. When Deena saw the necklace she gasped. It was magnificent: a four-strand pearl choker with an oval opal as long as her thumb and as wide as three fingers with such fire in it that it seemed to dance before her eyes.

Once Lady Margaret had clasped it around Deena's slender neck, Deena's composure seemed to return. The two women smiled at each other and Lady Margaret handed her the other rose which Deena positioned beautifully on Lady Margaret's dress.

'I will make Brindley very happy, Lady Margaret, I can promise you that.'

'I know you will, my dear, otherwise my son would never have chosen you. He inherited his title only a short time ago and is very proud of it, of the family and of Lyttleton Park. He would never share his life and position with anyone who would not add to it. He must love you very much. Many is the young woman who would have liked to be the next Lady Ribblesdale.'

In Brindley, evidently, the gift of understatement amounted to silence. He had never revealed that he was a Lord, nor that he presided over a magnificent manor where once Kings and Queens had dined. Deena looked down at Brindley, who was waiting for them in the great hall, and she realized that about the only thing Brindley had told her was that he loved her. The rest had seemed unimportant to him. She understood that she might spend the rest of her life discovering her husband. How was she going to tell her mother that she had found the man she wanted to marry, and face the fuss her mother would make of something so simple yet exciting?

She was thinking about that when, as they were walking down the staircase, the maid opened the front door to admit the vicar and his wife into the hall. Seeing him in his white dog-collar triggered something in Deena. She stopped and, touching Lady Margaret's arm, said, 'Lady Margaret, I have something very serious to tell you. I am Jewish, very Jewish.'

'Oh, how interesting, dear. You must tell me all about it sometime. But come along now, we must greet our guests.'

When Brindley claimed her at the bottom of the stairs and took her to the library where he presented her with another family heirloom, a ten-carat, square-cut emerald engagement ring, they kissed, and she forgot about being Jewish. But only for a moment, because, when he offered to place a call to her parents to tell them their happy news, she remembered, and said, 'Brindley, I told your mother I'm Jewish, and I don't think she understands we have religious differences.'

'No, I don't imagine she does. And so what if we do? You keep your faith and I'll keep mine, and we'll both keep each other's. Fair enough?'

Deena began to laugh. The Ribblesdales simply never allowed anything to become a problem. Oh, God, she thought, how sweet life must be when you are one of them. She suggested to Brindley that they put off calling her parents until the morning.

There were twenty for dinner: the vicar and his

wife, Fiona and her parents, an uncle, and, from what Deena could gather, a few of the more select neighbours, all old family friends. Deena could hardly fail to notice that they recognized the emerald on her finger and the opal and pearls around her neck. But nothing was said. She didn't see how it could be when neither mother nor son made an announcement.

Everyone was now walking towards the dining-room. The vicar took Lady Margaret on his arm and they led the way, the others drifting in, a genial and pleasant group. At the entrance to the dining-room Deena, if she had not already understood it, realized how remarkable a hostess Brindley's mother was. She had obviously done more than 'just have a word with Cook'.

The guests looked perfect for the setting, the men dressed in black ties, and the ladies looking casual yet elegant in their summer evening dresses, at ease in their English manor-house habitat. They could have stepped out of one of Ralph Lauren's photo advertisements. Deena had to ask herself, 'Was it really only six days ago that clothes-freak New York cab driver drove me to Ralph Lauren's shop, where it was all the vogue to look as if you were on your way to a dinner party such as this one?' She smiled to herself and mumbled under her breath, 'God bless Ralph Lauren.' But she was uneasily conscious that wearing the English Country Look he was pushing this season did not constitute belonging to the English Country set.

The guests gathered around the table revealed discreet delight at the beauty of the dining-room and dinner table. The room perhaps merited more admiration than their restraint allowed.

The dark, seventeenth-century, oak-panelled walls were hung with Turner paintings. The long mahogany table gleamed with Georgian silver, Baccarat crystal, and an antique Meissen dinner service. Candelabras of silver-gilt sparkled down the centre of the table amid sprays of full-blown garden roses mixed with freesia, their colours a combination of washed-out tints combined with vibrant pigment, like the passionate Turner paintings on the walls. The scent: a rose-garden, candle-wax, and centuries of furniture polish.

Charles II heavy silver serving-dishes and Queen Anne silver pieces were filled with exquisite food and the service was unostentatious but perfect. Village girls disguised in crisp black uniforms and white starched aprons assisted two elderly butlers. Lady Margaret had shrewdly arranged the seating of her guests to maximize their potential for vivacious witty conversation. The wines caressed the palate and were plentiful.

Between each place-setting, lying on the table, Deena noted a feature she had never encountered before. There were Queen Anne silver menu-slates. As charming as they were rare, the slates measured between four and five inches, some oval, some square. The thin, pale-green slates were framed in heavy embossed silver. The elegant, tapered handles were not only embossed with flowers and birds, but, where space permitted, they were engraved with leaves and baroque monograms. Neatly written with exquisite penmanship – the staid exterior of an English butler, she reflected, concealed some exotic skills – the menu read:

Aperitif: Champagne Rose
Pol Roget 1978

*

Jellied truffle consommé garnished with quails
eggs

*

Savoury pancake roll of fresh wild salmon with
seaweed, garnished with fresh uncooked tomato
sauce and basil butter

*

Batard-Montrachet 1978 (M. Guyot)

*

Kiwi and lime sorbet

*

Saddle of lamb with a forcemeat of broad beans
Soufflé of aubergine with a sauce of new garlic

*

Château Ausone 1961, Premier Cru St Emilion

*

Belgian Endive with sauce vinaigrette

*

Stilton Cheese served with celery hearts

*

Bavarian crème of apricots with apricot purée

*

Château d'Yquem 1976

*

Coffee – Petit Fours
Porto 1961

*

Bas-Armagnac 1948

Deena became thoughtful. This was a grand, elegant dinner party, a celebration by anyone's standards, and it had been accomplished with a minimum of fuss. It surpassed anything Deena had expected, having seen the *sang froid* with which Lady Margaret took the news of her son's forthcoming marriage. It was a lesson to her, not only about Lady Margaret and Brindley, but about the tribal standards to be lived up to by the English lady when she played the hostess.

After the guests had been served the Château d'Yquem, Lady Margaret rose from her chair and addressed her guests. 'This is the big moment,' thought Deena, 'the announcement of our marriage.' She steeled herself for surprised faces and shocked congratulations. However, the only one who was surprised was Deena.

'My dear friends and neighbours,' Lady Margaret said, 'will you raise your glass in welcome to our friend from overseas, Deena?'

They drank and smiled, and conversation calmly reverted to cricket and the Royals. It was only after the port was being passed for the third time around the table and Lady Margaret had asked the ladies to retire with her from the room while the gentlemen lit cigars, when the mixed bag of beauties were powdering their noses in Lady Margaret's suite of rooms, that each of the women beginning with Fiona said how happy she hoped Deena would be in her coming marriage. Deena could see that, despite the English reticence, the message had been passed through the undergrowth and the elders of the tribe were not dissatisfied. She breathed more freely.

They were all gathered in the drawing-room before an uneasy feeling again crept over Deena. This time she contemplated slipping from the room as quietly and unobtrusively as possible. And then, suddenly, the unease evaporated. She, Deena Weaver, an American, a woman about to marry the man she loved, to become a lady, perhaps a millionairess – what need did she have to tremble at the feast? She had it all.

Chapter 18

Dawn was just breaking over the Bosporus. The river
came slowly to life with the advent of light. It was
rough and choppy. The heavy downpour of rain
drummed a dangerous beat on the broken surface.
Gusts of wind skimmed the crests and swept a fine
mist off the river onto the Peramabahçe dock and
across the garden. It smashed into the windows,
dissolved once more to river water and ran in huge
streams down the glass intermittently with the driving
rain.

The night, cut into by a single beam of light,
rose slowly like a heavy velvet curtain, and Mirella
watched the prologue to another day. Through the
morning storm and the half light, exotic silhouet-
tes of ships and boats from the four corners of the
world that plied the river beyond her garden
appeared, making their way to or from the Golden
Horn and the Sea of Marmara. She watched the light
rise higher in the sky. It seemed to absorb the rain and
the wind. A stream of yellow light announced the
advent of the sun and another glorious hot summer's
day.

But the day loomed less glorious to Mirella for
being the day Adam was to leave for Africa – without
her. Cradled in his arms, she felt the warmth of his
body up against her back, the rise and fall of his chest

as he slept deeply and peacefully, his lips brushing the nape of her neck.

For five days now she had known that this was the day he would leave. Although she would miss him and would rather have had him stay with her, it had not bothered her unduly that they were to be parted for a few days, possibly weeks. Not till now, when the light broke on the day of his departure.

Mirella lay on her side, mesmerized by the receding storm beating against the window panes and by the coming of the day. She tried to fathom her sudden unease at Adam's departure.

They had both been asleep when, in the small hours, five days before, the telephone next to their bed had shattered the stillness of the night and cut into their sleep. It had been Mirella who answered it.

'Adam.'

Just one word. That was all the woman had said. Mirella knew at once who it was.

Her reaction had been natural, instinctive. She had turned on the light, woken Adam, handed him the telephone and said. 'It's your African princess,' then turned over, and drifted back to sleep.

In the morning, after they had made love, Adam had announced he was travelling to Ethiopia on business, and that his trip would include a safari with some of his big-game-hunting buddies, if they were available. They would leave in five days' time.

Uninvolved in the plan herself, Mirella had thought no more of his departure. Once again she had acted naturally, and from an inner instinct. She made plans to get on with her own work and life in Istanbul. Part of which was to arrange to see more of Adam's family, the clan, and get to know them and their lifestyle, and how she could fit them into her life. And, of course, there was Rashid: more time with Rashid.

That Mirella would miss Adam was, well, natural. She loved her husband and valued every minute they spent together. However missing him was not, in itself, something to disturb her sleep.

One of the things she had found most attractive about marrying Adam was that they would live full lives of their own outside their marriage. Their work, their business and social positions, Adam's family and his projects, his obvious need for space and time to be alone decreed that. Her own singular life until they had married, and her attachment to Rashid were the basis of her understanding.

Why was she so disturbed then? Tana Dabra Ras Magdala Makoum, the dusky princess of the Blue Nile, summoning Adam in the middle of the night? No. She could hardly be jealous of that exquisite black goddess. Not after the way Adam declared himself in love to Mirella all through the night, confirming each declaration with renewed ingenuity in making love to her.

Suddenly she understood. It was her husband's genuine love, his devotion and adoration of her that dissolved all barriers between them. It was so strong, the love they shared. It enabled Adam to give himself totally to her, as she did to him, all through the past night, and every other night when they came together in body and soul.

It was that: wild and passionate lust combined with real love that ran the gamut of affection, trust and tenderness. This she possessed with her husband, in contrast to an unreined loveless lust she shared with her lover, Rashid. The thought had robbed her of her sleep. For this morning heralded separation from the most perfect love she had ever known.

Mirella listened to the wind change its tune as it abated, and she watched the cascades of water thin out upon the window panes as the rain dissolved from a downpour to a summer shower of large drops that pitter-pattered on the glass.

In her memory Mirella re-ran something she had seen earlier in the day, when she had been with Rashid.

A beautiful mature woman with raven hair and white-white skin. A voluptuous naked body with huge magnificent breasts that stood firm and proud. Hanging by wrists bound tightly with a heavy purple silken cord from the rafters in the centre of a circular room, around, around she swung, slowly, two feet from the floor, like some famous acrobat under the big top of a circus.

Mirella, hidden by a screen so no one would recognize her, watched the woman charm, entice, cajole, the circle of men watching her into using her as she demanded. She dominated them with her desires, her wants and needs, and they complied.

One after the other the men gave in. They climbed upon her and ravished her breasts, wrapped their legs about her and fucked her again and again, applied a whip as she demanded.

Mirella watched the woman: a man, bound to her back by inch-thick jute rope that dug deeply into her lustrous marble-like flesh where the bonds crossed between her breasts, sodomised her with multiple thrusts, while they slowly spun around together dangling from the thick, purple silk cord. She called out erotic obscenities, cried, moaned with ecstasy.

The couple in the throes of sexual bliss were steadied only long enough for other men to mount the woman and suck her breasts, drink from her vagina wave after wave of copious orgasms. A penis, thick as a woman's wrist, would displace a tongue and she would be fucked from the front and the back at the same time, while always spinning, spinning in the air.

The beautiful, trussed-up woman, lost in her licentiousness, being used as nothing more than a tranche of female flesh, frightened Mirella. She had never seen anything so debauched, so depraved, so obscene. Yet she had been riveted by the depravity of it, disturbed by the rank sexual excess, as had been every other person in the room.

Excitement, mixed with revulsion at the thought of men using women as inhuman objects of sexual desire, became a blur in her mind when she saw the pleasure both the men and most especially the woman derived from the orgy. Mirella had been further confused by the warmth and moistness of her own vaginal lips, and her own need to be ravaged by her lover. How was she to appraise, to reconcile the conflict within herself between desire and revulsion?

There came a point of no return, a moment when depravity was breaking all boundaries, when Mirella had thought the woman's sexual playmates might devour her with their lust, might even snuff out her life. It was then Mirella had felt she could bear to watch no more and had begged Rashid to take her away.

Together, for the remainder of the afternoon Rashid and Mirella had played out their own sexual drama, a magnificent few hours, trying to assuage the flame of sexual lust the exhibition had ignited.

The rain had stopped now. The sun was shining, and the garden, drenched from the storm, sparkled under its rays. Mirella marvelled at the garden's recuperative powers, knowing full well, that by the time the house awakened, Adam's Eden on the shores of the Bosporus would have absorbed its drenching: it would be fresh and green, each flower crisply bursting with revived colour.

Rashid and she sharing in a pure sexual love after the exhibition was not the picture she conjured up now, no matter how she tried. It was wiped out, replaced by visions of Adam's erotic prowess with her and his words of love. Of two people indulging each other, satisfying each other with every fleshly act conjured by their fantasy. All night they had used and shared and loved each other, and now, reliving those moments of bliss, she rolled over in the cradle of Adam's arms, and facing him, their naked bodies caressing, she laid her lips upon his in the most tender and loving kiss, and finally fell asleep.

Under a brilliant, burning sun, the speedboat, its bow riding high above the surface of the water, sped over the no-longer choppy waves, as it swung away from the Peramabahçe palace and towards the clan's wooden *yalis* further along the river, going towards the Black Sea and away from Istanbul.

Wearing a bright yellow linen backless sun-dress, held upon her shoulders by shoestring straps of the same material, with the brooch she found lying in a white velvet box upon Adam's pillow when she woke, pinned upon her breast, Mirella sat in the stern of the boat, grateful for the coolness of the river.

It was particularly hot and humid after the dawn storm, and she was feeling the oppressive heat more than she would have liked to admit. Her eye caught the twinkle and sparkle of her brooch. The Cartier leopard cast in gold, with its spots of inky-blue sapphires, held her attention, and she smiled. She placed her hand over the stunning four-inch-long leopard and caressed it, remembering every word of the note that had accompanied it. She repeated them aloud now.

'I leave you while you are fast asleep because goodbyes are not for us. Not now, not ever. I'll be home to you as soon as possible, but until then you will hear from me every day in one way or another.'

'What did you say? I can't hear you with this engine carryin' on and an ear full of water. You're gonna have to speak louder,' shouted Moses, who was sitting next to Mirella.

The two bodyguards, Daoud and Fuad, seated in front of them, jumped up and turned around to shout through the din as well. What did she want? Was something wrong?

Finally, with her large-brimmed white straw hat still in one hand, her white piquet bolero jacket in the other, Mirella waved her arms. She crossed them in front of her several times, indicating to them all was well, while she shouted for the men to sit down.

Then suddenly the wind swirled and snatched her Adolpho hat from her hand and spun it over her head, depositing it somewhere behind the speedboat on the water. It happened so fast that the four just watched it fly through the air, amused disbelief freezing any effort to grab for it.

Mirella laughed gaily, she could not stop. Daoud

ordered the driver to swing the boat around so they could go back and retrieve the elegant sun hat, now nothing more than a dot of straw bobbing up and down on the waves far behind the motor boat.

She tried to tell them not to bother, to make them all understand that it was too late, the hat now belonged to yesterday. But it was impossible. Her laughter drowned out her words, and in the end she just let them do as they pleased and sat there laughing at her own carelessness. Her amusement softened to an inward smile at finding herself now, all dressed up, in a speedboat en route to spend the day with her stepchildren and their mothers.

Only a month ago, all she had thought about them was that they represented quite a turn of events in her life, and she would, of course, take them in her stride, for Adam's sake, for the sake of their marriage.

After Mirella and Adam's return from the Greek Islands, she still fought their acceptance of her as head of the family after Adam, and all the love and respect that went along with her new position in their lives.

'They're *too* good to be true. *Too* quick to take me to their hearts, *too* interfering on my time. It's all *too much* family, *too much* loving. The household of women, past lovers of my husband, and their children – my husband's children – are suddenly becoming a very natural, normal household to me.' And indeed it was true. She was finding their lifestyle as comfortable as it was unique and at some level she resented this new perception. It would have been less challenging to have stuck with her original view – that it was all just ridiculously bizarre.

She began to laugh again, and tried to hide it from

the four men clumped together, bending over the side of the boat trying earnestly to haul in her hat. Any laughter now must seem to them ungracious. Which she most assuredly was not. She was laughing on two very different levels: the men might at any moment topple the boat into the river and soak them all. And then there was herself, looking forward to spending the day in the bosom of the clan, being part of their life.

Mirella shook her head from side to side in disbelief at her now-pathetic Adolpho creation, retrieved, but only as a floppy, soggy affair of clumps of white paint shrivelling away from straw. Hardly less misshapen now, though, was her former image of herself. For she, Mirella Wingfield Corey, found she wanted nothing more at this moment than to reach her destination, the *yalis*, and play with the clan, be a part of their loving and caring, be just one of the family.

Suddenly the UN and her work there seemed less than the most important thing in her life. So did the business side of her legacy, and her obsessional sexual love for Rashid. Loving and learning how to live with and relate to the children and their mothers, her new-found sisters seemed far more significant, and far more enjoyable to her. Remarkably, it seemed natural, more human than the life she had lived before her legacy wrought havoc with the tight little world she had created for herself.

Three short wails from the speedboat's siren announced Mirella's arrival. Women and children seemed to pour out from different entrances of the stunningly romantic wooden palace whose arched marble foundations were lapped by the Bosporus.

The clan took Mirella's breath away. A smile broke

like sunlight within her heart as she waved. They were magnificent, all colour and shimmering opulence as they ran and danced, skipped and walked through the gardens, followed by a four-piece Turkish music-ensemble playing Anatolian folk music.

They lined up on the dock as the speedboat cut a large arc in the water and pulled alongside the waving, welcoming family dressed in fabulous antique Turkish *salvar*, and robes and vests and scarves and *yashmaks*, all sorts of period clothes.

Everyone seemed to talk at once, hug, kiss, touch, as the two gardeners secured the boat. Mirella, inundated with so much extroverted affection, stiffened, hardly knowing how to behave. But it didn't matter; her reaction was barely noticed. And so boisterous and amusing was the clan's behaviour that, before Mirella reached the house, her reticence melted away.

Alice, Marlo and Adam's child, the youngest at seven years, and Memett, Aysha and Adam's ten-year-old son, kissed Mirella sweetly on the lips, Giuliana and her daughter Alamya hugged Mirella affectionately, giving her a kiss on each cheek. Mirella was dazzled yet again by the resemblance of Alamya to Adam.

Muhsine patted Mirella on the back and crowded in with the others for Mirella's attention, surprising Mirella with a kiss on her bare arm. Aysha presented Mirella with several hibiscus blossoms, tied together, with long narrow streamers of red satin ribbon, which she pinned in Mirella's hair. Her greeting was a smile and yet another kiss on the cheek. Zhara clapped her hands for attention and blew her stepmother a kiss. Only Josh and Marlo were missing.

322

'Come to my room, come to my room first. We can play with my toys, I will dance for you. I study ballet. Then I'll take you to Mummy's room. Mummy's not home just now, she's in Africa, but I can show you her room and all her pictures,' said Alice, who was delighted by Mirella's arrival and was bursting with enthusiasm.

'No, no, Alice,' chided Memett, 'we must take Mirella to the surprise-room first. Remember, first the surprise, then the party, and after that I will take her to visit my zoo, and then there's the wrestling match, and *then* she can go with you and play with your toys, and you can dance for us all at tea time. Remember the plan we all agreed on?'

'Oh, I do remember,' said a disappointed Alice, who frowned as she removed her hand from Mirella's and slipped it into Memett's, at the same time shoving the thumb of her other hand firmly between her lips.

The little girl looked up at her half-brother adoringly. The dark handsome boy reached out and adjusted the flower-embroidered pillbox hat Alice wore over a rosy-pink silk scarf studded with more embroidered flowers that draped to her ankles over her *salvar*. Bending down, he whispered, 'Alice, you're forgetting little sisters who visit their brothers at Eton don't suck their thumb.' Then looking at Mirella and giving her a glance that asked for her support, added, 'Do they, Mirella?'

Mirella charmed by the obviously loving relationship between the children was delighted to be drawn into their private little world. She bent down and kissed Alice on the cheek and gently patted the little thumbless fist clamped over the child's mouth.

'No little girl I ever met who loved her brother would ever go to Eton to visit him with a thumb stuck in her mouth. That's quite true, Memett.'

Slowly and most reluctantly, while listening to Mirella, the child took several long luscious sucks on the precious thumb and then withdrew it.

'There's your friend Moses, Alice. He's brought you and Memett and all the others some things from Papa and me. Why not go and say hello to him, too?'

Mirella saw clearly how quick and free and fickle a child's heart can be. She watched Alice's disappointment at not being able to sweep Mirella away to play with her in her room fade from her face, and her eyes sparkle with delight at the thought of another playmate, Moses. She curtsied politely to Mirella, and pulling Memett by the hand tried to drag him toward the men unloading packages from the boat.

Memett shrugged his shoulders and made a not-too-convincing grimace as he stood his ground long enough to say to Mirella, 'I had better go with her. As you see, we are the best of friends, and she does depend on me.' And with that he allowed himself to be pulled away.

The lessons. So many lessons to be learned from this unique family, thought Mirella dozens of times all through the day. What kind of love was this maternal love all these women seem to have and she knew nothing about? Would she ever experience such a love as maternal love? And, more to the point, did she need to, or even want to?

And, slowly, slowly, all through the day, revelations were made to her about the women and the children of the *yalis*. Revelations Mirella thought she would rather not have heard. Intimate details of their relationships with her husband and his emotional bond with them, individually, and as a family. Instead of feeling jealousy and envy, those vile emotions she detested and feared might possess her, Mirella was relieved to find she felt nothing but admiration and no little respect for them all.

Of all the surprises – many of which were charming, warm gestures delivered with nothing less than affection and a deep regard for Mirella's position in their lives – surely the one that affected her most was the 'surprise-room' Memett had referred to.

Once their greeting on the dock was over, the entourage, the Anatolian quartet still playing, had made their way into the house, Alice riding on Moses' shoulders, Memett trying to wrestle Daoud and Fuad en route. There she had been led to what had once been Adam's private rooms for whenever he chose to stay in the *yalis* with the clan. Giuliana and Muhsine flung open the pair of doors, and Aysha had said, 'From all of us to you.'

The rooms had been redecorated and were utterly exquisite, as were the clothes they had laid out on the bed. Period Turkish pieces in silver and gold embroidery and white silk, more elegant and impressive than any of the other women's clothes. Once again Mirella had been handed a role she had never envisaged for herself. As Adam's wife the clan had not only accepted her joyously but expected her to be the matriarch no one of them had been chosen to be.

If there had been any doubt in her mind about that, it vanished when, alone with the women after dinner that evening, she listened to them confess their love for Adam, their devotion, their gratitude to him for allowing them to remain in his life, not as cast-off

325

mistresses but as friends and lovers.

She listened to them tell how Adam's taking a wife had resolved many things for them. Not the least of which was that, once their children were of age, they would then exercise the freedom and security Adam had given them and go out into the world and create new lives for themselves, maybe even marry. But, they assured Mirella, they would always remain one united family.

She studied them closely now, one beautiful and intriguing young woman after the other. Each one of them at least ten years her junior, a hundred years her senior when it came to understanding and practising different kinds of loving.

They humbled Mirella with their honesty about being in love with her husband and the life they had all created together. They were candid about the discretion they used when satisfying their erotic needs beyond those they were able to share with Adam. How, with an unspoken sanction Adam had accorded them, they worked other love affairs into their lives. Where was the bitterness, the disappointment she had anticipated from the women of the clan? She felt ashamed at having expected it.

It was very late when the women walked with her through the gardens under a black sky studded with lustrous stars, and up the steep path between the pines and cypresses to the road where one of the *yali*'s vintage Bentleys waited to take her home. The speedboat had long since returned to her house with Moses and Daoud. Fuad opened the car door for Mirella and the women kissed each other farewell.

At the end of the three-quarter-mile drive through the *yalis*' private park, the Bentley stopped and Fuad pushed open the huge ornate iron gates and the car drove through them.

All the way home Mirella kept feeling the warmth, the affection and joy of the day, the women and the children slipping away from her, and she surprised herself because she minded so very much.

In the darkness and comfort of the back seat of the Bentley, Mirella slipped her hand under the bodice of her dress and fondled her naked breast, teased and thumbed her nipple until it was erect, felt a slight flush of excitement and wondered what it was like to suckle a baby.

Chapter 19

'Welcome to Addis Ababa, Mr Corey. It's a long time since we have seen you here.'

'That's true, Mr Minister. You do us an honour to receive me at such short notice, and to permit our company jet to fly over Ethiopian territory. I did not, however, expect Ethiopian MIGs as escorts. It makes me feel far more important than I am. May I present my son Joshua, sir, and my attorney, Miss Colsen?'

The minister all but ignored the introduction, his gaze fixed on Adam. Adam was aware of trouble. Such calculated disdain was unusual . . . and ominous.

The MIGs had certainly been an unpleasant reminder of military paranoia. But sabre-rattling of that sort threatened him personally no more than did the armed military in the streets and along the wide avenues of the city, who almost outnumbered the civilians. Routine, perhaps, since the revolution. But tanks were parked on the soft shoulder of the motorway from the airport to the suburbs of Addis. Armed soldiers, looking dangerously bored and trigger-happy, lolled all over them. Heavy armour at the ready signalled military unease. Clearly the revolutionary government had big trouble, real or imagined. But what link was there between civil unrest and an Ethiopian Minister of Commerce deliberately being rude to Adam when he was normally so friendly and charming? Adam had to establish the connection promptly.

'To what do we owe the pleasure of your visit to our part of the world, Mr Corey? How might we be able to assist you?' the minister asked, civilly but coldly.

'I have come to reassess our holdings here, study our successes for myself. And to see a few old friends, such as yourself, sir. I'd like also to take on some big-game shooting and some archaeological research in the highlands, if you will permit me to do so.'

'And Mr Werfel? Does he not accompany you on this visit, Mr Corey?'

Adam shook his head. Ah, there was the rub: Werfel. The tone of the minister's question cut through his manner of studied eloquence. Was Adam right to detect a more-than-diplomatic slyness in the man's eyes and on the faces of the two aides flanking him? Alerted, Adam deduced that the minister knew something more about Ralph Werfel and the raid on The Corey Trust than Adam would have liked. His immediate anxiety was for Tana Desta Ras Mangasha Seyoum. He hoped for her sake that she had covered her tracks well when she became his white knight by exposing Werfel and Agristar to save his company. Had their meeting in Samos perhaps been found out?

'I found Mr Werfel to be disloyal, Mr Minister. He has been disposed of. I tolerate no traitors. That is something you should understand, sir.'

Josh and Carmel exchanged a glance that registered shock at Adam's new tone and the brashness of his words. Tension crackled and bounced off the walls like a broken electric cable. Adam kept a cool gaze fixed on the minister.

The Ethiopian's fist coming down on his desk resounded in the bare, modern room. His chair scraped as he stood up. Then, leaning on the desk he bent forward and asked, 'What did you do, Adam? Throw him in prison, torture him for his disloyalty? Stand him against a wall and shoot him?' Then the ruthless eyes softened their threat and the minister began to laugh. 'No, not you, Adam. A golden handshake of a million dollars is not dispersing with a traitor. One can hardly equate that with a bullet between the eyes, or a knife thrust through the heart. He deserves worse. Myself, I would have thrown him into a concrete cage and let him rot. Even that would have been too good for him. You would make a very inadequate revolutionary. Too soft. Too civilized. That comes from lack of political faith, the American over-estimation of the individual, and its paranoid fear of communism. How like a capitalist society to kill off a traitor with American hard currency. You reward them for treachery. We punish ruthlessly as an example, and demand total loyalty to the cause.'

The moment the minister put himself on first-name terms with Adam, Adam sensed that he was safe. He would be able to play macho money games with the minister. But then he saw the eyes change again, become mean, nasty even, when the man warned, 'Watch your back, Adam. You have dangerous enemies.'

Enemies! The plural carried a special menace. Too many innuendos without clear accusations. Tough it out, that would be all the Sandhurst-educated colonel-minister would understand. Tough it out, and pay up. That's how Adam would get what he had come to Ethiopia for. No doubt about it.

The minister walked to the window. He looked up the wide Avenue, deserted except for the occasional car and a tall, elegant, black figure dressed in rags he wore proudly as if they were a cape of gold. The man walked on bare feet, a long, bent walking-stick shoved under his armpits and across his back, his hands gripping it over the top. A poverty-stricken peasant who walked like a king. Several cocoa-coloured ladies with pure Semitic features hurried across the street draped in traditional white cotton, banded with coloured embroidery, large silver coptic crosses swinging freely across their breasts. A shepherd driving a few sheep up the Avenue was accosted by two soldiers who pushed him ruthlessly to the ground. They drove him and his flock off the Avenue and on to a side street.

The minister beckoned Adam to the window, where they stood together and silently watched for several minutes what was going on below. 'You used to love my country, my people,' he said. 'Ralph Werfel would have us believe that has changed. Those holdings you have come to look over – The Corey Trust has almost bled them dry. You know it, I know it. We depend on our share of your profits from those holdings. We do not intend to share your losses. You should have cut Werfel's balls off long ago and pushed them down his throat and let him choke to death on them. But you didn't. You gave him a million dollars instead. How do you think that looks to us?'

The minister returned to the desk, angry once again, and shouted as he pounded on its metal top. He swiped a stack of documents off it and they flew up into the air and fluttered to the floor.

'You stripped the assets of your companies in our

country mercilessly. We consider that to be robbery. You have caused thousands of my kinsmen along with my government hardship they can ill afford. And you profess to love my country, my people?

'The takeover by American Agristar would have solved all your business problems and all my country's arms problems with the money they proposed to pump into industry here in Ethiopia, and the interest-free loans they offered against the country's future profits acquired through an advantageous profit-sharing scheme. Wars and insurrections are eating up fifty per cent of our annual budget. An end must be made to these petty wars that are destroying the country. This government intends to do that.'

Adam started to speak, but the minister angrily waved him silent.

'A million of our peasantry have died in the droughts of recent years. We have to resettle the survivors of that disaster. We intend to combat centuries of poverty and famine with a programme of villagization. Can you tell me, Adam Corey, how we can carry out our plan to re-locate and re-house virtually the entire rural population without the legitimate profits gained from our own investments here and abroad? We depend on that money. It is my country's life blood. Without it, we are at the mercy of world charity, and the world's criticism for negligence and being poor. The world condemns a Marxist government which has to shop around for assistance from regimes the West deems dangerous because our political affiliations are compatible.

'In the space of less than a decade we want to uproot thirty-three million people, and settle them in villages with running water, electricity, schools, clinics and post offices, give them services they have never had before. But our critics claim all that is nothing but a smoke-screen to herd the masses into centralized communities where the army can keep them under control and Marxist cadres can indoctrinate them.

'The money Agristar promised us after the merger could have aided our cause and silenced our critics. That dedicated, brash, simplistic Mr Bob Geldof rushed in screaming, "I'll help". And he did. But what is that compared to what the final solution must be?'

A less single-minded man would have avoided the phrase, thought Adam. But even to think in terms of creating 'final solutions', genocidal or not, was a sign of the ruthlessness with which these men might pursue their goals.

With every word the minister uttered Adam was rapidly understanding why Tana Dabra Ras Magdala Makoum had sought such secrecy in becoming his 'white knight'. All that CIA money backing Agristar – and indeed Agristar itself would give the regime total political power ruthlessly to drag this noble, but backward nation, the world's poorest and most desperate people, into the twentieth century. Money is power. And too much money, too fast, like too much power, might wipe out a country that had changed little since Biblical times. It would, under this regime, turn it into a Marxist state and curtail the basic freedoms of the people – the very future so infuriatingly predicted by the critics of the regime.

Adam's admiration for the acute corporate mind of Tana Dabra soared. She had saved The Corey Trust, tied up vast sums of her country's hard currency where she knew it was safe. And she had made deals that

334

would produce an annual income of hard foreign currency and commodities within the country, while it stimulated industrial expansion. It would yield sums large enough to allow a transition to modernity and the reconstruction of a poor and desperately illiterate society as rapidly as was possible under the circumstances, yet slowly enough to allow the people time to adjust to a new world and freedom of choice.

'Mr Geldof is a humanitarian who has opened the world's eyes to my country's plight, not a businessman like you,' the minister continued. 'Though dedicated in the same way you are to not getting involved in politics but only with people, he does what he can. Now I want to hear what you're going to do. And before you answer that, let's remember that Agristar is not going to come here to take over, and from our point of view it should have. We are not very happy with Mr Werfel or Agristar for failing in that takeover bid. It has caused much trouble. But most of all we are not happy with you. We trusted you. Yet, according to Ralph Werfel, who, as your number-one man for years, presumably has had all the figures of The Corey Trust, you are unable to pay out the trust's yearly dividends. There are no profits, only debts, and this condition will exist over the next seven years at least. His reports say all you were able to do was to save The Corey Trust from going under. You haven't been too clever, Adam. Now, I ask you for the last time, what are you going to do about it?'

Adam walked slowly from the window where he had remained during the minister's tirade. He reached inside his jacket and withdrew his cigar case, and offered one to the minister and to the minister's hitherto silent henchmen. Then, towering above the three seated army officers dressed in their combat fatigues, revolvers worn menacingly on their hips, as if ready for hostilities to erupt any moment, Adam lit his cigar, turning it between his fingers until it burned evenly.

The silence in the room was deafening. All waited for Adam to answer the minister. He seemed in no hurry. He walked back to the window, sought permission to open it, and got a nodded assent. He returned to his chair directly in front of the minister. Before taking his seat he removed the cigar from his mouth, stared into the minister's eyes, and said, in a voice stiff with anger, 'Nothing. I shall do nothing out of the ordinary. As far as I and The Corey Trust are concerned, it's business as usual.'

The minister started to rise out of his chair, his face contorted with rage, his breathing laboured with anxiety. He was shocked back into his seat by Adam's booming voice.

'Sit down. You had better listen to me and listen well. If you or anyone in your government ever accuses me, as you have done today, of being a thief, ready to exploit not only my own companies but my partners, I will close down all our operations in your country so fast you won't even have time to sequester them.'

One of the minister's colleagues tried to rise from his chair, but Adam stopped him by slamming Carmel's brief-case on the desk. He propelled it along on the desk towards the seated men, shoving their papers and pads into their laps, clearing a place for himself on his side of the desk. Then Adam sat down and scrutinized them with an air of disdain.

'Don't you move,' he ordered the aide who had attempted to rise in support of his superior. Then directing his gaze back to the military trio, he added, 'Not one of you, until you hear me out.'

The men kept their seats. Then Adam too sat down, and smoked his cigar in silence. Josh followed his father's example and placed his attaché case on the table, but quietly.

Finally Adam spoke. 'Abebe, I have no concern for you, or your regime any more than I did for the former government of Emperor Haile Selassie. I have *never*, I repeat *never*, left you in any doubt about that. I am a merchant, albeit a high-powered corporate executive, a man who lives by trading. I obtain ingredients, I put them to work. I live by taking profit. You, Abebe, and your regime are gentlemen warriors who master the virtue of weapons. You are strategists and appreciate the role of weaponry. I do not ask you to sympathize with my job, and I insist you never attack me for not sympathizing with yours.

'You're a lucky bastard, Abebe, that the Agristar takeover failed, because like you, those people try to mix politics with big business. The best you will ever get out of that arrangement is a banana republic, African-style.

'You suffer from an ambition for power to impose sociological success on your people, rather than survival and slow, consistent growth with stability and freedom as a foundation. And your desperation to legitimize your political ideology before the world has blocked out your memory of who and what The Corey Trust is. You forget that it is a vast network of corporations under the umbrella of the parent company. It is spread across forty per cent of the world. What made you think it would submit to a takeover without a fight that would go on for years? By

337

God, that fight never even got out of the boardroom.

'You have material on our portfolio. You know very well that within The Corey Trust's empire is housed an enormous private agricultural development programme whose economic growth and contributions to progressive agriculture are unmatched.

'You have benefited from that as well as its energy divisions in oil, gas, solar and water power. And you know they are influential enough to control more than a few countries. One of which is yours. And if we don't, it's because we are not interested in that kind of power. We are merchants, interested in the profits and passing them on to our investors.

'Who do you think keeps you on the road? You know very well our airline companies and shipping networks are among the largest in the world. And what about our smaller organizations, such as railroads, autobuses, and lorries that keep lines open in remote parts of this country? Where would you be without them?

'Oh, shit, Abebe, I could go on about its communications divisions: computers, telephone and telex companies that keep you in touch with the world. But what would be the point? It will only make me more angry and you more embarrassed, and that, after all, is not our purpose.

'Josh. Please get out a copy of The Corey Trust Manufacturers World Wide, and The Property Development Divisions of The Corey Trust, and give them to the minister.'

Josh opened his attaché case and placed the papers on the desk in front of the minister. They all watched him thumb through the information and lists of the corporate manufacturing holdings, without looking at them, never taking his icy glare from Adam's face. The volume on property holdings was half as thick as the Boston Telephone Directory.

Adam was aware that he had crushed the immediate danger. Now his strategy was to grind the minister into the ground without giving him space to breathe. He had to be flattened all at once. Adam dared not let Abebe recover his position even a little.

Adam had three things to protect: The Corey Trust's twenty-five-year contracts with Ethiopia, the Trust's investments in the country, and Tana Desta, his 'white knight'. It was essential that Adam, Josh, and Carmel walk out of that room leaving the minister satisfied enough not to delve further into The Corey Trust's affairs. He dealt his two final blows.

'You're a shrewd and competent, more than competent, minister, Abebe. You do your homework. You know as well as I do that I don't have to pay you a fucking dime, not a grain of rice, a kernel of wheat. I don't in fact *have* to do anything, because the way our contracts read, I am not in breach of one of them. I don't pay out profits that are not there, not for you, not for anyone. That would be bad business.'

The minister had clearly had enough. He appeared shattered. All the punch and the menace was gone. Like a weak and beaten man, he slowly rose from his chair; his two aides, all pomposity shrivelled from their faces, followed suit. Adam remained seated. He changed the tone of his words, they were hard and firm, but friendly now.

'I am here today, gentlemen, because I want to introduce my son to you. He will assist me, replacing Ralph Werfel, until he is ready to take over the Trust's business dealings in this part of the world. Otherwise I

339

could have sent any number of other competent people in our Corporation. Please be good enough to hear him out.'

Josh rose from his chair and began. 'Mr Minister, gentlemen, every year, according to our contracts – Miss Colsen copies for the gentlemen, please.' Joshua waited until Carmel had placed a copy in each of the men's hands and then he continued. 'We, The Corey Trust, are always pleased to pay to the Ethiopian Government twenty-three per cent of the profits of all the business we conduct in Ethiopia, in a commodity-package of coffee, tea, rice, wheat and sugar, and the same amount from the communication and transportation corporations. This year, however, owing to unforeseen circumstances there are no profits, only deficits. An unfortunate situation for all concerned. The Trust, however, is very much aware of how dependent Ethiopia is on the profits rendered from her contracts with The Corey Trust. It has therefore devised a method in which the hardship of this loss can be spread across twenty-five years, the length of the contracts. Fifty years, if the contracts are renewed for another twenty-five years, which we on our part are prepared to do.

'In order to alleviate any further hardship caused by these losses, The Corey Trust will make the expected payments for this year in the way of an interest-free loan, rendered against future profits. In addition, The Corey Trust is willing to increase its holdings in this country by fifty per cent, under the same contractual agreement we have in our present investments here in Ethiopia. The additional revenue the Ethiopian government should receive through the years should be effective in wiping out this one year's losses. Our increase in holdings here will come from capital designated for investment in other Third World Countries; these actions can be taken as soon as contracts are signed.'

Carmel Colsen took over by handing the new contractual agreements to each of the men. They accepted them and sat down to study the documents. Joshua returned to his chair. Adam re-lit his cigar and studied Abebe's face, which was a picture of relief mixed with exhaustion, yet not without a glimmer of enthusiasm for the future. Carmel was doing her stuff, answering all the legal questions raised by the three Ethiopians. Joshua was summoned by one of the aides to answer questions about a time-frame for the deliveries of the pay-off.

Adam began to relax, enjoy the taste of tobacco in his mouth, and the excitement of wheeling and dealing and winning. His mind drifted back to the telephone conversation that had brought him from the Peramabahçe palace to Addis Ababa.

She had said few words. 'You must be in Addis in five days' time, with a solution for the losses. Speak forcefully to the Minister of Commerce. You must win him over, and not only maintain but better your corporate image with the regime. No one must know I was the 'white knight', or that we ever met; I must see you, we have business, but my position has become vulnerable. Go hunting, with a party of foreigners. Plan a secondary exit through the Sudan. It may not be necessary, but, then again, it may be. Don't look for me, I will find you.'

The sound of her soft, something akin to a whispering voice, with its well-educated English accent, except for her rrr's which she trilled, and an occasional guttural sound on some letters of the alphabet, lingered in his ears. He was doing as she had bid, and so far it was going well. Why, he wondered, why had she done it?

All he had managed to learn in their fifteen minutes together in Samos was that she was indeed his 'white knight'. That she made the journey to Samos explicitly to tell him to stop chasing around trying to find her, as he had done in Switzerland. He was compromising her and putting her in great danger. She had made it plain to him that the identity of the 'white knight' who came to the rescue of The Corey Trust had to remain a secret as long as possible. Yes, they had to meet, and they would. She would tell him how and where, and he was to stand by and wait for word. It niggled at him, that 'why' behind her rescue of his organization. And, Marlo. What did Marlo have to do with Tana Dabra? Something else niggled: her regal, animal sexuality.

Adam directed his attention back to the discussions going on in front of him. Excitement was building with every question to Josh and Carmel. Two other men had been called in. Adam could read the Ethiopians' faces like a book. He had won them back, probably saved their skins and gotten them promotions. There would be a great many unhappy businessmen from the eastern bloc rushing into Addis Ababa's hotel bars, and trying to get flights out of the country in the next twenty-four hours, when those contracts were signed and the news got out. The Americans could see it as a coup, the Russians as a threat, and some mid-east madman, furious, would probably blow up an aeroplane somewhere in the world.

'I think we must have time to renegotiate the contracts, Adam, but I believe we have an interesting and workable package here,' said the minister, all smiles now.

'I think you misunderstood Josh, Abebe. He stated clearly that you could *renew*, not renegotiate, the contracts for another twenty-five years. Now that's the deal, and the only deal you are going to get out of The Corey Trust. Take it or leave it.'

The smiles dissolved. The minister, with all eyes on him, said, 'You're not the only merchant looking to invest in my country, Adam.'

'Then negotiate with the others, Abebe. Competition is always good for business. But you and I, we don't negotiate. Not with an honourable and fair deal such as we have presented to you. It's sign, or goodbye.' Adam looked at his watch, and then added, 'an hour, that should be long enough to explain it to your Chairman.'

'You are very sure of yourself, Adam.'

'Yes, very.'

Abebe returned to his office one hour and forty minutes after he had left, flanked by two of the three top men of the government. Introductions were made, and there was a formal signing of the contracts with several rubber stamps applied, two red wax seals over red and purple satin ribbons, and some billion-dollar happy faces on each side of the desk.

Adam accepted an invitation to dine with the Chairman that evening, and the room cleared except for Abebe, Josh, and Carmel.

'You are a hard businessman, Adam, but an honourable one. This deal of ours will help my country and our people, now and for a long time to come. But you do not help our regime and its image, its cause.

'We understand that like Armand Hammer you are an international businessman who deals in profit and capitalism, and will respect you for it, for what you have done today. But you have to understand that what Agristar offered us was irresistible – The Corey Trust, plus a heavy commitment to this regime in arms and worldwide recognition for our political causes. Now every penny of our capital investments abroad will have to be used for military armaments.'

That was it! Of course, that was why Tana Dabra wanted her role as 'white knight' kept a secret. She was dumping liquid funds meant for arms into long-term investments they would never be able to get their hands on. Smart, very smart, but very dangerous for her when they found out. Now he knew why she did it. But why choose Adam?

Adam could not help but smile. What a game. What a woman. She was courageous and dangerous, and that excited him. He looked forward to their next meeting with sharp relish.

'You smile, Adam. There is a joke?'

Adam switched off all thought of Tana Dabra and returned his attention to the minister. 'No, Abebe,' he answered, 'not a joke, my old friend. A curiosity. Ralph Werfel. It turns out that, by his failure to destroy me, he has in fact been a traitor to your cause. And we know how you treat traitors.'

The eyes of the two men met unsmilingly.

Chapter 20

Adam stood in the shadows of a crumbling stone wall and he crushed out his cigar against it. The glow might have given him away. He swore under his breath. He hated ruining a good cigar. But he hated more the idea of getting caught in the muddy alley while trying to get into a house that looked empty and abandoned. An open American jeep, with a machine gun mounted next to the driver's seat and manned by a professional killer, was making a sweep through the neighbourhood. The authorities were searching for anything subversive: leaflets, people of the old regime, weapons.

To be picked up could do no good for his friends inside, once members of the Emperor's court, and certainly no good for him. He would be abusing an official authorization, received earlier in the evening, to roam freely through the country with his hunting party, or to fly his Cessna anywhere through Ethiopian air-space.

When the jeep shone its swivelling spotlight down the alley, the guide next to him was trembling so much Adam was afraid the man would give them away. None too gently, Adam clamped his hand over the Ethiopian's mouth, while flattening him against the wall. He could feel the man's heart pounding, but his violent shaking did subside, and his breathing grew more calm.

They had a clear view of the radio-man sitting in the back of the jeep taking orders over a blaring crackling radio that issued jumpy-sounding instructions. The expressionless, ebony faces of his cohorts, the driver and the machine gunner, were partially obscured by motorcycle goggles and heavy metal helmets caked with dust. Sinister, beetle-like, the trio belonged to the night.

There was a burst of gunfire not very far off, followed by hoarse screams. Commands crackled and wheezed from the radio. And Adam watched the spotlight inch its way down the alley. Suddenly the alley went dark.

The jeep backed into a high-speed turn, throwing its headlights down the centre of the alley, but remained blocking it at the head. Dogs were barking everywhere. Then, without warning, the armed vehicle streaked at full speed through the mud. It was going to pass right by them.

Adam was furious. They were sure to catch him and his guide. With a screech of brakes, the jeep stopped twenty feet from where they stood. Shouts among the three monsters in the jeep, a rending of the gears, a burst from the radio, and they were reversing out of the alley, headlights striping across the houses on the back street. Another high-speed turn and the jeep kicked up mud and disappeared in bursts of machine-gun fire.

Adam and his guide stayed frozen in place, not passing a word between them. They heard the wild dogs of Addis Ababa, a population of pedigree dogs riddled with vermin and malaria, with filthy tangled hair, left abandoned to run free through the streets of the city at the time of the revolution. Poodles and griffons, airedales and boxers, greyhounds and shih-tzus, red setters and dobermans, after losing their pampered homes, had made the city theirs. Adam prayed they would deem the alley unworthy of them and look for their scraps elsewhere.

Their barking and howling reminded him of a time just after the revolution when one of the managers at The Corey Trust's wheat-depot told him a story of a man who'd come in asking for work. His last job, he told the manager nervously, was in the palace. He had worked for the Emperor. His Majesty had a Japanese dog, Lulu, the man had said. The Emperor's great bed was where Lulu slept, His Majesty's lap was where Lulu sat. When the Emperor held court the dog would sometimes leap from His Majesty's lap and run around peeing on the shoes of the dignitaries. The venerable gentlemen, though they felt their feet getting wet, were never allowed to flinch, or show displeasure. The man's job for ten years had been to walk among the dignitaries from all over the world, wiping urine from their shoes with a satin cloth.

Adam felt the guide's hand gently cover his, and he removed it. The Ethiopian patted it in thanks. And again they stood very still and silent. Adam had no idea how long they remained that way in the foul-smelling alley. Addis Ababa was a dust bowl, and he had had to get stuck in the one alley with an open and running water pipe. He detached himself from his present predicament by wondering how long the water had been running. Days? Weeks? A month? Two months?

As a man claiming he never played politics, Adam

wondered what in hell he was doing in that alley at four o'clock in the morning. But he knew the answer: friendship and loyalty. He knew he could locate some of his friends in hiding and bring them out safely. The Chairman gave him his word it would be safe, that there was no need for anyone in the country to hide. Trapped still in the alley, pinned down by fear of a bullet through the darkness, Adam had to question that guarantee.

The sun was coming up when he returned to the Italian Embassy compound where he left the two friends from the old regime. He knew they would be safe there until Josh could establish them in their new positions as top executives in The Corey Trust. Those jobs would protect them from their past associations with the Emperor and give them a chance to re-build a life in their homeland.

Coffee in the embassy was spiced with accounts he had heard before of the last days of the Emperor. For some reason he had not perceived then the cruelty of the way Mengistu Haile-Mariam had treated the Emperor. Mengistu's relentlessness struck him now.

It was eight o'clock in the morning when Adam left the Embassy and began his walk back to the Addis Ababa Hilton across from the National Palace, the embassy's black Fiat a hundred yards behind in case he preferred to ride.

Adam had a genuine fondness for Addis Ababa, the city built on hills amid eucalyptus groves, born when he first saw it with his father thirty years before. He always thought of it as a vast village pretending to be a city, a folly of the Emperor's. He liked the strange mélange of embassies and houses, walled-in compounds that blocked out the primitive city peasantry in their ramshackle tin-roofed hovels. He was amused by the huge ghost-like city with its enormous buildings and wide avenues, where cows and sheep grazed the main streets amid Haile Selassie's concrete dream that housed almost no one. As late as 1963, the nomads driving their herds of frightened camels across the streets had right of way. He enjoyed enormously the tall eucalyptus trees, pungently-scented, swaying in the wind, and the excitement of the high plateau on which the city was built. Only minutes away in the surrounding country-side were cheetah and baboons, lions roaming the hills, hippopotami in the river. Adam's heart still raced at the thought of going down to the source of the Blue Nile.

And the church, the glorious Coptic church and its special Christianity, so pagan and so pure. Still one of the great sights in the world for Adam was to walk through the streets of Addis and see the faithful making a hundred genuflections, standing, dropping to the knees, arms outstretched and forehead to the earth. And this they did all over the city, because the Ethiopian Copt will only go into or as close to the church as he feels himself worthy to.

Addis never impressed Adam as a happy city, but it was a fascinating, exotic one ruled by a tiny despot who charmed the world with his vanity, his country's poverty, and his wily, ruthless control of his people amid spurts of mad opulence.

Having just spoken about the last days of the Emperor's life with Admassu Lemma and Assefa Wajo, the two men he had brought in from hiding after so many years, their recollections occupied Adam's mind. How Mengistu Haile-Mariam in those early days in August 1974, was a slight, tense, but controlled Army officer who knew the structure of the court because his mother had been a servant in that court. His secret had been to know who was who, whom to arrest, how to cripple the palace so that it no longer functioned. And he had acted on his knowledge, paralysing the staff, turning the system into an ineffectual shadow of itself, then abandoning it to deteriotate into the thing it was now.

Early one August, the military committee, the Dergue, had decided to arrest gradually the five hundred dignitaries and courtiers who surrounded the Emperor. One by one they were removed by the Dergue. They disappeared from the court, never to be seen or heard of again. A slow, sinking loneliness surrounded the Emperor, until finally His Most Extraordinary Majesty occupied the palace in the company of a single servant.

And still they did not touch the Emperor. They had good reason: for that, they had to prepare public opinion. Addis Ababa had to be made to understand why its monarch was being removed. And so he was left to wander in solitude from empty room to functionless office.

Adam saw Haile Selassie at the end as a figure like King Lear – a vain autocrat who selected an entourage from men who were mean and servile. Favourites rewarded with privileges. No step would be taken, no word said, without his knowledge and consent. If everyone spoke with his voice, that suited him perfectly. There was only one condition for remaining in the Emperor's private circle: to practise the cult of the Emperor. 'They flattered me like a dog,' he admitted. If you didn't play that game, you lost your place. You were stripped of your power, you disappeared. Haile Selassie tolerated only shadows of himself. Men made in his image alone could satisfy his vanity, give body to the gestures that kept him aloft on a pedestal for the world to see.

When, like King Lear, he let go his power, they whittled away his retinue. Doomed, as it seemed, to re-enact Lear's fate to the end, the Emperor was abandoned to the mockery of a single attendant. And what an end, an Emperor alone with his valet.

With a grim smile, Adam conjured for himself a further vignette of that time: the officers of the revolution asking His Benevolent Majesty to give back the money supposedly concealed in his fifteen palaces, in the homes of his devoted dignitaries, or deposited in secret foreign bank accounts. How naïve they must have been to think he would surrender one penny.

Adam could not help wishing he had been there when the officers, frustrated by the Emperor's denials that he had any hard currency anywhere, in desperation even rolled back the great Persian carpet. Astounded, they came upon an underlay of rolls of dollar bills stuck together, one next to the other, a thick under-carpet of green money. And when the officers raided the bookshelves and dollar bills fluttered from between the leaves of holy books, how the wily old despot must have laughed up his sleeve at the pittance they were getting.

And what of the great riches he had amassed himself? He had become greedy in his dotage, and he had it all buried somewhere. They might nationalize his palaces, but they could never repatriate his bank accounts in countries all over the world. The Dergue claimed billions, but it was more like hundreds of millions of dollars that he never returned to the state. There it languished in foreign banks even as Adam mused about it.

Adam had to admire his pathological vanity. For here was a man who kept saying to the end that the army had never disappointed him, and that if the revolution was good for the people, then he too would support the revolution, would not oppose even dethronement. Yet he gave them nothing.

Adam thought about the egocentricity of the Emperor who, after being systematically stripped of his power and prestige, isolated from his court, his family, his friends, deprived of his retinue of servants, and left to wander through the empty rooms of a palace no longer his, bridled when he was made to get into the back seat of a green Volkswagen. It was his only gesture of protest, before he was driven away from his palace and his world, and through the gates of the Fourth Division barracks.

Adam called the black Fiat forward and climbed into the back seat. The last days of His Royal Highness, 'the King of Kings', seemed terribly ugly and sad to Adam, and he was suddenly anxious to get back to the hotel and call Mirella. His spirit lifted, thinking of her in his house on the Bosporus, working in her office on the Oujie legacy and archives, organizing her department's annual programme at the UN, and getting to know his children and Istanbul. The lovely Mirella, his wife. Adam's heart sang for the other side of his soul.

Abebe was waiting for him at the hotel surrounded by a dozen aides. Gone were the battle fatigues, replaced by pale grey business suits expensively tailored on Savile Row, ties and shoes from Jermyn Street in London. There wasn't a hip holster or gun in sight. Josh and Carmel and Adam's faithful man-servant, Turhan, all looked peeved at having been given the slip by Adam the night before, but relieved to see him safe and sound.

Adam looked away from them out through the entrance of the hotel. He focused on what had seemed so different to him walking through the streets or riding in the back of the Fiat: the streets suddenly lacked soldiers. They had simply evaporated, trans-formed themselves into well-dressed civilians. Their crisis was over – over for the moment anyway.

Their greeting was friendly, and while Abebe and his aides spoke of a press and TV conference due at ten o'clock in the ballroom of the hotel, Adam drew Abebe and Josh to one side.

'Abebe, your propaganda wheels may be in motion. That's okay with me, but I have a team of The Corey Trust's top executives flying in from all over the world to play that game with you. You can have them for as long as you like. But not me. Nor Josh. One still photograph with you and your Mr Big, and that's all you get. I'm going hunting. How about joining us? It'll be like old times.'

Abebe's eyes twinkled, revealing his yearning to take off for the interior of the country that he loved so well. And then Adam saw it pass, as he'd imagined it would, as he'd *depended* on the knowledge it would. It was a calculated gamble that had to be, because somewhere out there he would meet up with Tana

353

Dabra. The invitation was another insurance policy of Adam against Abebe's suspecting he would be doing anything in the country but hunting. It appeared to have paid off.

Adam drove the lead jeep with his favourite hunting-guide sitting next to him, Turhan and Jock Warren-Williams, Adam's companion, in the back. The second jeep was driven by Macalister Whittington, Kenya-trained, and a man with a reputation as the sort one liked to have at one's side when things went wrong in the bush. Next to him was Rex Walker, a life-long friend from New York. The other two jeeps were driven by Jock and Mac's men, Sudanese hunters and trackers.

By the time the hunt had stretched into its second week, news of the exploits and expertise of Adam's party had travelled through the highlands preceding their arrival. They had shot hippo, and rhino, cheetah, leopard, lion, and any number of smaller animals, all of which they offered as food to the peasants. But first they had taken their trophies and sent them back by a relay of walking messengers, who appeared as if from nowhere, to agents in key towns in the highlands who were ready to fly them to the taxidermist in Addis.

Adam was beginning to be concerned. Tana Dabra had not appeared. He had half expected her in Lalibela, one of Ethiopia's main tourist centres, because she could have concealed herself in its crowds or in the surrounding chaos of mountains and gorges, where the men had trekked and hunted on mules and foot across cliffs and ridges that plunged a thousand feet below. He imagined she'd catch up

354

with him in a jungle-like area where the hunters had frolicked with baboons they found sitting in a semi-circle around one of the dominant males of the troop. The beast had chattered and squealed and screamed incessantly to his family of simians. Adam knew Tana would be safe among the nomads of the highlands, far from the world of finance and politics. He had even lingered, under a white, nearly full moon, within the eleven famed churches sculpted out of living rock, a wondrous place that was the heart and soul of Christian Abyssinia. Adam realized he had made nothing but bad guesses.

One night, they had been camped on the banks of the Blue Nile, far off the track, in an unpeopled flatness of man-high thistles that flowered like giant foxgloves, and surrounded by heavily-wooded country inhabited by innumerable small monkeys. Adam had woken in the night, certain that she was in the tent, or had been. Could he have been simply wrong? In the morning they had found a scrap of bright red cloth.

By six forty-five, the convoy of jeeps was tearing out of a settlement on a mountain near Gondar. They would go as far as they could before abandoning the jeeps to switch to mule and pack horse, heading for higher mountains and other settlements, an area well-known for leopard.

The jeeps had made their last, breathtaking, hair-pin turn up curving tracks of hard dirt roads, and bounced in and out of holes for the last time because the track was no longer wide enough for the jeeps' four wheels.

From nowhere they appeared, two slender, bare-foot Ethiopian nomads, their hair shiny and curled with rancid butter, dressed in tatters worn as elegantly as Brooks Brothers suits. They loped along like gazelles towards the jeep, rifles slung over their shoulders. Before Adam could pull on the hand brake, they had slung their rifles off their shoulders and fired shots into the air.

She had sent them, he knew that instinctively. The hunting party made camp where the nomads suggested, in a wooded area clinging to the side of the mountain, the Blue Nile flowing lazily far below, where bathed a herd of hippopotami.

In the setting sun the men watched the mountains turn from green to red. The four of them stood together searching the mountain range through their binoculars, and absorbing the jungle, the birds and wild life. They were in their element.

Jock touched Adam's arm, and silently each man alerted another. They detected a leopard ten feet away from Mac. The handsome creature lay asleep along the branch of a tree. Delight was edged with excitement and fear. No one moved a muscle. Eyes transmitted their instructions. Slowly Rex pulled out the magnum he always carried tucked under his trouser belt, Adam put his hand around the barrel of the Purdey rifle leaning against his thigh, ready to yank it into action. The scent of fear was in the air.

What wind there was shifted – not much, but enough for a still-hot breeze to bring a sharp scent of the animal, and its smell was not repulsive. There was a latent savagery about it, and great power and beauty. The leopard opened its eyes and looked into Adam's. Man and beast, the hunter and the hunted locked together in a trance that immobilized them both. A footstep disturbed it. It growled and the glorious beast was still growling when it sprang to another tree, grazed over a branch, and slid in one sinuous movement into the undergrowth.

Each man had sprung into action at the first movement the leopard made. All weapons were cocked and held at the ready to fire. But no bullet shattered the leopard's grace. Their action was one of self protection. Since the beast had not attacked, for hunters such as they were, to kill the leopard would have been a cheap shot, not sport. Unthinkable. They relaxed as it slunk away.

'Hello, hello. Not Mr Livingstone, I presume.' Jock Warren-Williams's words broke the tension. All eyes followed his to where Tana Dabra stood. Adam stepped forward, raised her hand and kissed it.

'To come between me and the predators in my life, be they human or animal, seems a role you are fated to play, Tana Dabra.'

When Adam had hastily organized the hunting party at Tana Dabra's request, he had felt it necessary to tell his friends only the outline without the details of the safari. Until Tana Dabra's appearance in the bush, the men knew only that they were invited for good sport as Adam's guests. They might also be asked to assist Adam in a possibly dangerous exit from the country with an additional person in the party. All had accepted, and no questions had been asked.

For them, romantic names such as Prester John, Rasselas, the Queen of Sheba and the Lion of Judah linked the present-day Ethiopia with the land that had been Abyssinia. The appearance now of Tana Dabra, though a surprise, was a delight. The men still clung to the romance of the country. They identified her at once, without knowing who she was, as a new romantic figure whose name might rank with the great names of the imagined past.

Macalister was the first to step forward after Adam, doff his wide-brimmed, tiger-banded hat, ddrop to one knee and kiss the hem of her dress. In Kenya there were still old movies that taught this sort of routine.

'Madam, your servant, your slave,' he quipped, a smile forming under his bushy, ginger-coloured moustache.

'Rex Walker, at your service, ma'am,' the next hunter said, as he mimicked Macalister's expansive gesture, gallantly sweeping his New York Yankees baseball-cap from his black, curly hair, while giving her a knowing smile. Clark Gable was hovering in the wings, Adam thought with amusement.

Jock Warren-Williams removed his worn safari hat, famous for its supposedly-lucky white leopard band, and after running his fingers through his hair, smiled at Tana Dabra. He had spent less of his childhood at the movies.

'Princess,' he said and bowed his head in respect. Then looking into her eyes, silently he held out his hat and she touched the band, aware of the legend associated with it.

Tana Dabra by that time was surrounded by her escort: two Amharas and two Tigreans, true-blooded Abyssinians like herself and most of the population of the six highland provinces.

Adam could barely take his eyes from Tana Dabra. He felt that nowhere in the world could there be more stunningly beautiful examples of the human being than he found in her and the people of this vast

358

fissured plateau that lay between the Upper Nile valley and the Somaliland desert. The ebony satin skin stretched taut over the tall slender body of the Princess with pure Semitic features. Pride and the power of keen intelligence emanated from her. The rich spiritual quality of her special Christianity that vied with her still savage paganism was unique and thrilling. It tortured his senses.

Her hair was pulled away from her face and plaited in one long braid wound on top of her head into a small sturdy crown. Over it was draped a cloth of thin, hand-woven, indigo blue cotton, which stayed in place because of the manner in which she draped it over one shoulder. Her dress was of the same indigo blue, a loose shift that finished at the ankle. Around her neck she wore a circle of antique ivory matching the ones around her wrists.

He wanted her. The erotic side of his nature demanded he vanquish this woman. His desire for her was a physical urge that rose from his baser nature. It was a fleshly appetite shared with the animals he stalked.

He watched her talking to his friends, and all the time she spoke there was a silence about her. Her mouth was framing words, and yet also this incredible silence. It was a sort of silence of the soul.

He and his hunting friends often claimed that one of the reasons for the great beauty of the Ethiopian people was their stoicism, their deep silence, their mistrust of the outside world. They might be poverty-stricken and suffering famine but they were not beggars. Rex had the habit of calling them the Chinese of Africa because he found them inscrutable.

Adam was amused because he could see erotic lust

in the eyes of his hunting-companions, every one of them, and it perfectly mirrored what they might detect in his.

'You are very gallant, gentlemen,' Tana Dabra said. 'And all across this region of the Highlands the people talk about your hunting exploits. A mile further up this escarpment there is a small settlement of *tukuls* and there the people have prepared a feast of *injara* and *wat* in your honour. They wait to drink *talla* with you. There are several fine hunters there who know the game and hope to take you out at sunrise for some special hunting.'

There had not been much initial enthusiasm in Adam's companions over the idea of drinking pints of *talla*, the cloudy, home-brewed highland beer, while sitting within a circle of *tukuls*, the round thatched huts clumsily constructed of stakes and mud. But their spirits lifted over thoughts of a meal of the fermented bread, *injara*, made from *teff* – the cereal grain that only grows in the highlands.

The bread came in sheets two foot in diameter, half an inch thick, bitter-tasting and gritty-textured. It looked like damp foam rubber, served double-folded beside plates of the highly-spiced stew of meat or chicken, *wat*. It was a dish unique to Ethiopia – an ethnic meal not to be missed for its strange and exotic combination of fiery flavours.

The invitation was instantly accepted by the men. Stomaching this stuff was the price of the opportunity to hunt with the local men. It seemed a fair exchange. They were busily assembling their gear for a three-day trek from the base-camp, together with gifts for their hosts, boxes of candles, quinine, bags of sugar and powdered milk, and salt, when Tana Dabra announced, 'Mr Corey and I will join you at the settlement as soon as we complete our business. I hope that will be before you set out hunting, but if not, we will find you.'

The men said nothing, but did hesitate and look towards Adam. Their eyebrows declared them unsatisfied with the walk-on parts apparently now allotted them. It was Tana Dabra who spoke, and it was not to the men but to Adam, 'Please, Mr Corey, it's essential your hunting party carries on. It is a wonderful cover for us, and news of your movements and your exploits keeps us all safe. Please do it my way until tomorrow.'

'You heard the lady, guys. I'll follow as soon as I can.' Adam grinned as they marched off the set.

In a short time they were gone and the camp was very quiet. All Adam's men except Turhan were sent with two of Tana Dabra's escorts into the bush, a few hundred yards from the camp, for their evening meal and to sleep. Before going, Tana Dabra's men pulled from under their shirts two packets of documents wrapped carefully in oil-skin cloths and handed them to her. The three spoke in Amharic for some time, and finally, much to Adam's surprise, both men dropped to their knees, spread their arms in front of them and bowed their foreheads to the ground. They rose only when she touched each of them on the head, and, from the little Amharic that he understood, seemed to bless and thank them.

His own surprise wasn't readily understandable to him, because there was nothing unusual about the act. In the days when Haile Selassie reigned as Emperor, the people of the country considered him a living god and paid homage in that manner to him or to any man, white or black, whom they thought superior and god-like.

Tana stood alone now facing him, and suddenly he understood the source of his wonder. Tana Dabra Ras Magdala Makoum was both the old regime and the new. He saw in her Ethiopia's past, its present and its future, in the guise of the existing Marxist regime. She was breaking away from her commitment to them. She had control of all their foreign currency. She no longer trusted their methods, but she still believed in their ideals. A pattern was beginning to form in Adam's mind about her activities and ambitions.

They gazed into each other's eyes. Adam absorbed the sounds of the jungle chattering away the end of the day. The monkeys with their laughing screams, the birds fluting their last calls, the rustle and crack of movement throughout the bush made by animals of all sorts on the move. Tana Dabra kept her silence. Adam broke the spell between them when he very gently removed the indigo cloth from her hair. She spoke then.

'You, Adam Corey, and I have things to resolve. Shall we take them one at a time?'

Her words brought him back to the reality of the moment. 'Yes, but of course.'

He led her to the four staves that had been pounded into the earth, a canvas stretched across them to form a canopy. They sat on comfortable canvas and wood safari chairs in a small clearing ringed by a semi-circle of sleeping tents.

'I think we need a table of sorts and a lamp for when the sun dies,' she said.

Turhan placed a series of wooden boxes, one butted against the other, in front of them. He covered it with a black and white batik of a handsome, bold design. Lower than a standard dining-table or a desk, the assemblage of boxes did serve to satisfy their needs. Turhan returned with a dozen or more fat white candles of varying heights that needed no holders and placed them on the table with a box of matches.

'I said that we have things to resolve,' said Tana Dabra, 'and we would take them one at a time, and we will, Mr Corey.'

'Adam, please, not Mr Corey.'

'Adam.' His Christian name seemed to give her infinite pleasure. A smile broke across her face, and she continued, '. . . and we will, Adam.' Then she lowered her long dark lashes. 'And I want you to know that the order in which we deal with things does not indicate priorities. For me, all that we say and do this evening is equally important.'

Then, raising her lashes, she looked at him and slowly opened the two parcels wrapped in oilskin. She removed a series of documents and a black Waterman fountain pen, a stick of red wax and a seal from one, and placed them on the table. From the other she pulled out several maps, and half a dozen computer print-outs.

'You are a clever man, Adam, and I am sure you have figured out by now what I have done?'

'More or less. My guess is that you have changed your financial portfolio. Re-invested huge amounts of capital into long-term projects, guaranteed to render solid and steady profits over about fifty years, in fact. The majority of the investments would be in your own country. You were more or less pushed into becoming my "white knight" by Agristar's attempted takeover-bid for The Corey Trust. You couldn't permit that because you knew that CIA money would filter through Agristar into armaments instead of wheat. That would give the regime not only financial but military power to force their policies on the people.

'All this secrecy is essential for us because the regime does not know that you are my "white knight". When they rumble that their own money was used against their interests, your head will be on the block. But before that they will force you to convert what's left of their foreign investments into arms. That is, if there is anything left. Playing the "white knight" must almost have wiped out your liquid assets. You defected, they hate traitors, you're on the run.'

'Very good, Adam. I believe the expression is, "You got it in one." There is something I would like to make clear to you. They will believe for a long time that I defected. I have not. I am a committed communist, a hard-core Marxist, whose only belief in capitalism is that it is a great way to make money.'

Adam savoured the irony. She was sensational, her realism tinged with wit. She caught his ironic smile.

'We must all sup with the devil sometimes,' she said. 'But, seriously, I want you to know I have done all this because I don't believe that guns and bombs improve nations. People and growth make nations great. Make no mistake, I am not disenchanted with this regime. I am just doing my job investing the country's capital.'

'You are a formidable lady, Tana Dabra Ras Magdala Makoum.'

As Adam voiced the syllables of her name, their eyes met, and in that moment they became friends, and both knew instinctively their vast investment in each other was safe. Tana Dabra had to look away from Adam and clear her throat to regain her composure. Her gamble had worked, and her relief was palpable. Then, after arranging the papers before her, she said, 'A few last details. I am in the process of merging all our investments abroad with those we now fly under The Corey Trust's banner. Here are the documents. In all cases you will see that I have made you Managing Director of the companies, and given the board of The Corey Trust the casting vote and power of attorney. I hope you will accept.' Tana looked at Adam briefly but did not await his answer.

'I know you are going to need all the cash you can lay your hands on. I will do what I can for us in that line. I have a way to release a good part of those thousands of millions of dollars the Emperor stashed away. But, to do so, I will have to be discredited by the present government. They will oblige once they find out I was the "white knight".

'Here are some maps. Ethiopia, Somalia, Kenya, Sudan, all the bordering countries, and Yemen on the other side of the Red Sea. Every name on the map printed in green is a safe place for me, where I will be able to meet you or have gold bullion ready to ship to you. You can invest the gold on my country's behalf in any of my country's companies you see fit to use it in. You will hear from me. Always be cautious. And of course be scrupulously honest, and successful. Make lots of money for us all, because only then will they forgive me and allow me to work openly again for my country. Now sign here, and here.'

Tana Dabra's signature had already been affixed to the documents. Adam signed. He had a great many questions, but in the end he knew they were superfluous, and so he asked none. Tana Dabra lit a candle and used it to melt the sealing wax, which she dripped on to the documents, pressing the seal into the hot, red wax. Adam saw that every paper he signed had been registered with the court in Zug, Switzerland, and had an official seal from the Ethiopian consulates in Paris, London, New York, and Geneva.

He watched her fold them neatly and tie them in their oilskin wraps. She turned to him, handed him the packets and sighed.

'Who says history has to be dull?' she asked. 'If a piece of history is what we have just made, shall we confirm it with a drink?'

'A drink and a kiss, I think,' was his answer.

Chapter 21

Adam was able to contemplate her in the blackness of the African night by the light of the candles flickering in the breeze, and the glow from the dying fire.

There was an atmosphere of sexual suspense about her. That was her charm, the fact that she could create excitement, mystery, not allowing Adam to know what lay beneath the erotic aura around her. Sexual excitement of a type that time cannot wither nor custom stale.

Few words passed between them once their business had been completed and Turhan had poured them crystal tumblers of bourbon and branch water. They listened to the mountain jungle closing up for the night, and the peace of the land entered their hearts, and they became a part of it.

When Turhan had lit the candles they lost themselves in the flicker of the flames. When he had built the fire to take the chill off the night air, their souls danced with the leaping streaks of colour.

She had surprised him when they dined on roasted game, bagged that day, and served with a spiced papaya chutney, relays of warm unleavened bread made on the open fire by Turhan, and drank a memorable best red burgundy, a Chambertin Grand Cru '69. She had placed the pads of her long slender fingers over her lips, kissed them, then slowly and gracefully opened her arms and offered the kiss to the night. She had turned to face him and had smiled at him with her eyes. For a moment he had thought she was about to say something, but the words died on her lips. She shed her inhibiting selfhood, and in that moment he had been made to feel he was the most important man in her life.

The camp was very quiet, Turhan having retreated into the bush to sleep with the others. Adam rose from the canvas chair where he sat next to Tana Dabra and went into his tent pitched behind them. He returned with two horn and silver tumblers of Calvados and placed them on the end of the low table in front of them. Then she took his hands as he offered them to her, and slowly rose from her chair.

He sensed that his physical urge for her was no more than hers for him. His erotic feelings for her were not born of desire, but more from the perception of her beauty. Her beauty appeared to him as the visible form of her immortal soul and revealed itself to him sensually. Adam could actually feel, as their hands touched, the sexual attraction they had for each other converting into lust.

Though she stood very still and silent, her need appeared to draw him to her. He slipped his arms around her and held her close. Adam was acutely aware of her slimness, the strength of her sinewy body and its tense structure. With great tenderness he placed his lips upon hers and kissed her, while stroking her shoulders and her arms. At first there was no response, and then slowly a flicker of arousal stirred in her lips. It was as if she had never been

368

kissed before. Her passivity both surprised and excited him.

Adam sat her down on the batik-covered table in front of his chair and arranged the candles around her. Then, after handing her one of the tumblers of Calvados, he sat down opposite her. They drank in silence, gazing at each other, allowing their feelings to gather strength.

Finally he took the tumbler from her hand and placed it on the earth next to his chair. He took one of her hands in his, turned it over and kissed the palm, opened his mouth and licked it. He was intoxicated by the feel, the taste of her flesh, and when he looked up at her, he saw her eyes flutter closed in answer to the passion of his kiss. Again he was made to feel that she had never been kissed before by a man such as he, and he could feel her waken further to him.

He raised first one of her legs to kiss her on the ankle and remove her sandal, and then the other, before he turned her shift back over her knees and kissed them as well. He went on his knees between her legs and sat back on his haunches, caressing her thighs under the thin shift. Her cool silence dissolved in his hands.

'Open your eyes, Tana Dabra, I want you to watch me making love to you. I want us to experience each other in the full flower of lust.'

He rose and placed a hand on her cheek and caressed her. Only then did she snuggle into his hand and open her eyes. He tilted her chin up, and the fire and passion he saw there inflamed him.

'Oh, look, my love,' she said.

And Adam followed her instructions and looked

up at the night sky that until then had been clouded over and black. The winds high above them had done their work and shifted the clouds, parted them as if they were great black velvet curtains, so that from behind them appeared a multitude of stars, bright silver, and a perfect, white full moon.

She was a black goddess bathed in moon- and candlelight, a unique divine beauty, incomparable. She was a woman outside time and change. And he hungered for her erotic love. His base animal instinct was first to fuck her, make her cry out with pleasure like any female animal being vanquished. His sense of her beauty, his sexual appetite for her, and his general kindness and goodwill toward her appeared inextricably intertwined in the web of desire in which he enfolded her.

She understood, he could sense it in the change of her breathing, in the way her flesh gave in to his hands. The moon was directly overhead and cast them in a moonbeam from above. Never taking her eyes from Adam's she slowly, deliberately swept the candles off the table. They flickered and were extinguished as they fell to the earth.

Adam pulled the pins from the crown of hair on her head and, after undoing the long braid, ran his fingers through her hair again and again. He removed the ivories from her neck and her wrists. He dipped his fingers in the Calvados and wet her lips with it, and then licked it off with his tongue. He did it again and her lips parted. Once more and they opened, and their tongues touched as he pulled her hard into his arms and at last kissed her deeply.

He raised the indigo shift over her head and dropped it in the dust. He kissed and caressed her, lean and lovely in his arms, and felt his penis expand towards her softening vagina, stirring them with overwhelming desire to copulate, to climax again and again.

He helped her onto the table where she stood under the moonlight, and he watched her caress her own body as if surprised by the sensations she was feeling while he undressed before her. For the first time since he had met her he recognized emotion in her face when she saw him naked and rampant. He took both her hands and wrapped them around his cock.

There was lust but fear as well in her eyes and he sensed her urge to back away. She stepped down from the table and was about to speak, beg to be set free from her passion. But he was too quick for her, and crushed her in his arms and kissed her again and again until she whimpered and her arousal was so great it turned her desire into a lust that matched his own.

He yielded as she folded first one leg about him and then the other, and inched her way up around him until they gripped his waist. He tucked his hands under her bottom and fondled her, she was tight and tense and extraordinarily sexy. With deft fingers he probed her vaginal lips and found a well developed clitoris which he delighted her with while he pressed his mouth on her small breasts and delectably erect nipples. Now all reserve was gone, the self was dead for her, animal lust took over. She bit and licked and kissed him, slapped and punched him, as one orgasm after another broke within her. He felt her small tight place relax. He caressed it, it opened like a flower, and he knew she wanted it all. He would not disappoint her.

With fingers of both hands tucked between her vaginal lips, now lusciously moist with come, he pulled her open as wide as he could, and at the same time, away from his body. His desire for her unleashed now, he bit the lips of her mouth as he impaled her on his throbbing cock. He could feel her help him, but to no avail.

He understood at once. This was part of the silence, the distance between them. She had never had a man before. It was unthinkable to him that she should have deprived herself of so much ecstasy. He could only wonder why she had made such a sacrifice. Scarcely penetrating her, Adam remained within and kissed her again with a renewed excitement. He carried her to the table. There she bore the pain of his powerful thrusts again and again until at last he covered her mouth to curb her cries, and he tore her hymen and pushed deep inside her. A few tears trickled from the sides of her eyes. He removed his hand and kissed her with abandon, and then whispered. 'And now the ecstasy.'

And when she felt him withdraw, with difficulty, so tight did she grip him, she begged, 'No, not yet. It feels sublime to have you inside me. Again,' she demanded. 'I have to have more. I want to feel you move in and out of me. More,' she again demanded, and kissed him hungrily.

They were words expressed with passion, words directed by erotic desire, in the heat of clawing sexual need. It was easily recognizable to Adam and inflamed the reprobate in him. All was lost to lust.

He could just reach out to the trestle table. His extended hand sought the butter dish. The cover fell

372

to the ground, but the prize was his.

He withdrew with difficulty, but with freshened carnal enthusiasm at the sight of the rivulet of bright red blood between her open cunt lips, and streaks of it on his still rampant cock. He was too big for her. She needed to be stretched, made wider and more ready to receive him, so he could move in and out of her with ease.

He rubbed the butter up and down her slit, around her clitoris on the inside and outside of her cunt lips. As he did so, he noted something else that made her unique, something about her genitalia that he would never forget, something so barbaric as to stir the barbarism in his soul. He inserted the tip of the large square stick of butter into her, and taking her nipple in his mouth he sucked and bit it, so excited was he by the sight of the butter melting into a phallic form as it passed in and out of this newly-broken virginal place.

He found a white candle still lying on the table, and used it adeptly to assuage their needs. And while he pleasured her with the candle he taught her how to suck his cock. She was a quick and apt pupil and soon her rhythm matched his, and she brought him close to his first peak. They changed positions and he replaced the candle with himself, and was now able to fuck his Abyssinian goddess mightily.

Abandoned to lust, dazzled by the bliss of orgasm, 'the little death', they were reborn again and again through the night, only to die once more in the arms of eros.

He came in her cunt first, and later while sodomizing her, and once more in her mouth. He marvelled at her lust, when she sucked every drop of his semen from him and swallowed it hungrily. And for their last orgasm together, she took him that way again, while he used both candles and vanquished her with them. They were depraved animals revelling in their erotic depravity.

He was worn out, exhausted. They lay in each other's arms, his eyelids feeling heavy. He tried to fight the sleep taking possession of him. It was impossible. He heard her whisper in his ear, 'I've waited so long for you. It has been everything I always imagined it would be with you. I've always wanted you.'

He tried to understand, but he was groggy with sleep. It sort of didn't make sense. He couldn't think about it, it didn't matter now, he would think about it later. His eyes closed and he fell into a deep sleep as he felt her lips touch his in a tender and sweet kiss.

Woodsmoke and the acrid aroma of coffee brewing stirred his senses to the new morning. He opened his eyes to the brightness of an already-warm sun.

Then he remembered Tana Dabra. He sat up. She was gone. He looked around the camp-site. It had been tidied up since the night before. Turhan approached him with a mug of hot coffee. He could hear voices from in back of his tent, but not hers.

He took a sip of the coffee.

'Hungry?' his man asked.

'Famished,' he answered, taxing Turhan's vocabulary.

'Sausages, bacon, eggs, hot biscuits?'

'The lot, whatever is going.'

He put the mug down on the table next to him, and ran his fingers through his hair several times, felt his chin and rubbed the stubble of beard on his cheek. He stood up and wrapped the blanket that had been covering him while he slept, around his nakedness. He picked up the mug again and recognized the bright stain of blood on the black and white batik cloth. He felt again a sharp twinge of the past night's sensuality.

'Turhan, where is she?'

'Princess, she gone.'

'When? Where?' he asked, more concerned than anxious.

'Three hours. Four men come. Not wake you. She said was plan. Leave note on bed.'

'Thanks, plenty of bacon now, I really am hungry. But first, hot water. I want to shave.'

And with that he rose and went towards the tent, hesitated and returned to the make-shift table and swept the batik cloth from it. He brought it to Turhan, who was standing next to the pan of sizzling meat, kneading soda-muffin dough. Adam dropped the cloth to the ground and said, 'You wash this yourself, Turhan, OK? Sorry, better other men not see it. Best for everyone if nothing is said.' He patted the nodding servant on the shoulder.

He saw the note lying on the camp bed, but he chose to leave it there unread for the moment. He picked up towels and went to the make-shift washing area. Only after he had shaved and bathed, adhesive-taped the oilskin-covered documents under his arm, and put on fresh safari clothes did he pick up the note and read it.

Word has come. They know now what I have done, but not yet the details. Leave the highlands in three days' time, and exit through the Sudan. Keep up pretence of hunting. In

375

Khartoum, wait for me at the Grand Hotel. I will try to meet you, at the very least send you a parcel. Until we meet again.

No personal word for him and no signature. Her silence had returned, so did the suspense. They reactivated his sense of her excitement and mystery. Even after a night such as they had created he still had no idea what lay within this erotic Abyssinian goddess.

He sat down at the table, now covered with a different batik of yellow and royal blue. Ravenous, he ate as if for three men. Only then did he ponder the note again. He took out his Zippo lighter, flipped the cover open and struck it with his thumb. The fire leaped and he held the corner of her note over it. In seconds the charred paper fluttered to the earth.

He tried not to think about his carnal savagery with Tana Dabra. Not because he felt guilt or remorse. Rather, because he delighted in it so unashamedly. How far beyond that might a sequel take them?

Adam was a man who lived each day as it came. No agonizing about yesterday or tomorrow. She was gone, it was over. Maybe she would come into his life as a woman again, and maybe she wouldn't. It didn't much matter, either way. What did matter was that he be successful in their business dealings and that he never let her down. In that he could save her as she had saved him and The Corey Trust. So the ribbing he received when he met up with the others in the hunting party made scant impression on Adam. Though they never asked who or what she was, where she had gone, they spoke in terms of her carnal, savage beauty, innuendoes of envy in every phrase.

They avoided the vulgarities of verbal rape charac-
teristic of younger, cruder men, but there was no
missing the implication that they had hoped she
would take them all on, one after the other. They
hinted that Adam had scripted his movie selfishly.
Unused to exclusion, they had all had many women
from different tribes in Africa who would have
obliged them and thought nothing of it, because in
their society promiscuity was not a crime.

On their last night on the mountain, after Rex and
Jock went to bed, Mac and Adam shared a fireside
nightcap, reliving their day of superb sport.

'Was she mutilated?' Mac asked.

Surprised by the question and Mac's interest,
Adam answered, 'Yes.'

'Circumcised?'

'No, that was what was so strange and so cruel. It
was not a tribal circumcision, as is the way in parts of
Africa. She was victim of a different custom. Her cunt
was sewn closed with gold wire, leaving only a small
opening for her to urinate through and one that
allowed her clitoris to be masturbated. She was
checked over every month to make sure she was still
intact, a virgin. When I met her in Samos three weeks
ago, she was still woven with gold wire. A week ago
she had the wires cut away forever.'

'A lover? A jealous father? A sadistic husband?'

'No, none of those. But, in an abstract way, all of
them. You won't get me to fill in all the details, but
the simple answer would be, a favoured child of the
royal house. She was recognized as being very clever
and so was educated to be of assistance to the
Emperor. But financial whizz kids of either sex are
scarce in Ethiopia. She was spotted as one and certain

men invested heavily in her ability.

'They sought to protect their interests, first, because of the Emperor's attentions, and later because of the power she wielded with their money. And even after she renounced her royal connections and became an example to the Marxist regime, those men believed their investment was better protected by a mutilated virgin than a woman who might fall in love and bear children.

'She has been like that since she was thirteen. The power took over, politics took over. It was a sacrifice never seen by her as such, but more as a way of life until she became disenchanted with some of the policies, as of late.'

'An interesting but rather sad story for a beauty such as she. She'll have many lovers now,' Mac said.

'How can you know that?'

'Easy, Adam. You had only to look at her once to know she is a sexual animal, a seductress who will have any man *she* wants. She wore her sexual hunger like a glorious French scent.'

'Mac, let's keep this conversation to ourselves.'

'Okay.'

The men had one more splash of whiskey and went off to bed. Adam was pleased he had levelled with his friends and told them he was carrying important documents of a personal nature for his company. He might be stopped, he had said, from leaving the country. If that did happen, he would make a run for it before he would give the documents up. His own honour and the woman they had met, to whom he was indebted, were involved. And his hunting companions had rallied round him. The meeting with Tana Dabra would simply not figure in their accounts of the expedition. They would be as alert against possible infiltrators during the safari as they were for sightings of game. When they had resolved on this, they settled down to map their journey. Adam appreciated their cool, discreet response to the danger he had involved them in.

It was a week before the cavalcade of jeeps reached Lake Tana and Adam's seaplane, The Lisbon Clipper. A week of high-tension hunting that relegated Tana Dabra, The Corey Trust, his wife and family to the borders of his mind. Only the packet of documents strapped to his side impinged occasionally upon his absorption with stalking the wary animals of the region.

The Lisbon Clipper was a converted 1945 commercial passenger plane. It was a comfortable air-and-sea floating home and office, and for the hunters would be their campsite during the last lap of the safari from Lake Tana over the Blue Nile all the way to Khartoum where the Blue and the White Niles merge into the Nile.

Marked with the exhilaration and the dirt of the trek, the tired men were looking forward to the luxury the clipper offered. They hopped one by one on to the plane from rubber dinghies, after handing up their belongings to the waiting crew. The Captain took a stance at the clipper's door extending a welcoming handshake, and gave a helping hoist to each of them. Adam was the last to come on board, and the Captain gave his hand an extra-hard squeeze that told Adam something was amiss. He was certain of it when the Captain said, 'Welcome aboard, sir.' Years on first-name terms had eliminated all such formality from their relations.

Adam entered the main cabin. His high-backed, fawn-coloured, glove-leather chair slowly swivelled around.

'I have made time to accept your kind invitation to join your party. Unless, of course, you have changed your plans and are in a hurry to leave Ethiopia?' Abebe gave Adam a dangerous, questioning smile.

Chapter 22

It was one of the larger rooms with high ceilings on the second floor. The library of Louis Quinze, pale walnut *boiserie* was filled with sunshine. There were a pair of Boule desks that came from the Palace of Versailles and had been in Adam's family for two hundred years. They were housed at opposite ends of the room, with superb high-back chairs covered in their original tapestry behind them. The large, brown and white marble fireplace, opulent with its heavy yet gracious curves, was flanked by a pair of period walnut chaises facing each other. Their loose down cushions and upholstery were covered with a black and white houndstooth check woven of raw silk and cashmere. Between them was a deep and richly carved, ancient, white marble frieze, once a section of the great ceiling of the temple at Balbec.

Silver discs two inches thick rested on the four corners of the frieze and, on top of them, a thick slab of glass. Adam used it as a coffee table. Each morning newspapers from various parts of the world were placed on it. Hundreds of rare books lined the shelves. Several period French chairs and a set of elegantly-curved library stairs and round reading-tables completed the furnishings of the room.

The large windows affording views onto the

Bosporus and the morning's river-traffic were hung in celadon-green silk taffeta lined with a bright yellow colour of the same material. The luscious, paper-thin draperies were held back with large antique tassels of burnished gold and black and white silk. The carpet, an extremely fine Persian silk, was of a great age, and there were large Ming and Tang bowls filled with full-blown butter-yellow roses. There was but one painting in the room: a large Gauguin from his Tahitian period. So staggeringly beautiful was it that it dominated the room and filled it with rich tropical warmth and colour. It was in this room that Adam kept his favourite photographs of Mirella and they were on the tables everywhere in silver frames.

Mirella was stretched out on one of the chaises, the bundle of Adam's cablegrams still in her hand. She was staring into the fire. The mystery of the passing of time – banal yet unfathomable – occupied her. In the big picture of things time seems irrelevant. But one cannot always look at the big picture, even though one should. She, at least, could not.

It was October. Irrelevant or not, time had made 'alms for oblivion' of significant events in her life. Since that day she and Adam had returned from Samos to here, her new home, his beloved Peramabahçe palace, her new life had been happy and wondrous.

Her work administering her inheritance, the Oujie legacy, was exciting and going well. Her work for the UN was successfully under control. She had eased herself into several different roles: Mrs Adam Corey; Mirella Wingfield Corey, the Oujie heiress; doyenne of a great house; young matriarch of a wooden palace further up the Bosporus, full of her husband's children and the other women in his life; discreet but recognized mistress to Rashid Lala Mustapha.

For weeks now, Mirella had made a habit of walking through the dizzying maze of Istanbul's back streets. She was making their teeming colour and life a part of herself. Often Joshua accompanied her, rarely leaving her side when he was able to steal a day or two from hop-scotching from one Corey Trust office to another. Sometimes she experienced the heart-beat of the old city in company with Giuliana or Aysha or Muhsine, the women of the *yalis*, whom she had grown to admire and had become very fond of. At other times Rashid was her guide. But constantly, wherever she went, she felt the protective presence of Daoud and Fuad, Rashid's bodyguards. There were moments when she would try to recover memories of her life before the Oujie legacy, Adam Corey and Rashid Lala Mustapha.

It was strange to feel those long years of loving and working and learning recede into a kind of blur of a life, a lost decade, that each day became more difficult to recover.

It sometimes felt to Mirella that she had only been born the night Adam Corey and Brindley Ribblesdale had walked into her house in New York. She recalled their shock and disappointment at her indifference then to anything that interfered with the life she had mapped out for herself. Fate and they had forced her to become involved with life and people as she had never been before.

Adam's love for her no longer allowed her to sail through life with tentative feelings and commitments to mere causes and abstract relationships. A woman who hadn't liked getting involved, she was fast learning how to do it yet still to remain her own woman. Whence, she often wondered, had she fetched up the character and strength to carry on? Rich and rewarding as her involvements were, they were paid for with moments of pain, loneliness, and sometimes fear.

Mirella thumbed through the cablegrams in her hand. If Adam had not been able to make contact with her on the telephone, there had been one for each day he had been away from her. Mirella cherished them like icons of their tenderness, religious portraits of a love story.

There was a discreet knock at the door, and it opened. Into the room bounded Adam's three dogs, gentle-looking beasts, nearly as large as sheep dogs, short-haired, and tan in colour, with dark brown on their ears and muzzles. Mirella smiled as they galloped towards her, remembering when she had once accused them of looking like English mastiffs: she had been laughed at because the famed *kurt kopegi* were cunning killers of even the ferocious wolf, with their outsized jaws and their powerful chests.

Then came Moses carrying a heavy silver tray laden with a silver coffee service. Behind him, two of the Turkish house-staff bearing trays of cups and saucers and plates of Moses' home-made tollhouse cookies. Next, in trooped Deena and Brindley with little Alice and Memett, Adam's ten-year-old boy. The room was filled with barking and chatter as the two children and the dogs all tried to crowd on the chaise next to Mirella.

'You really are something, Moses. It seems as if

384

you have conquered the Turks of Istanbul with tollhouse cookies. Mirella, have you been downstairs when he's making them? It's like a factory,' said Deena.

'Well, it is a factory when I bake them. I am feeding this house and the *yalis* and the staff for both houses, and that's a lot of cookies. Have you ever watched Turhan, and Daoud and Fuad eat cookies? What do I mean, eat, I mean devour. They disappear at marathon speed. Some change from cooking for one in New York, and the occasional dinner party. By the way, do you mind if I spend some money revamping the kitchen a bit? I've almost winkled permission out of the regular kitchen-staff.'

'Now, how did you manage that? Tollhouse cookies?' asked a smiling Mirella. This mid-morning coffee-time was like a royal levee, when anyone and everyone was welcome to join her wherever she was in the house or gardens.

'No,' said Moses, handing her a cup of freshly ground American coffee. Then, smiling, he added, 'Would you believe, bagels, cream cheese and lox – they're crazy about it.'

'Now I have heard everything: bagels on the Bosporus,' quipped Deena.

Mirella extricated herself from the children's and the dog's embraces. She went to one of the Boule desks and put her bundle of cables in a drawer. The children and dogs padded after her and, when she returned to the chaise, they all resumed trying to sit around her. So Moses played the pied-piper with his plate of cookies so that the children and dogs followed him out. If they loved anyone more than Adam and Mirella in the Peramabahçe palace, it was

385

Moses. Their endless questions followed him everywhere when they visited, which had become very often.

Amid this scene, Deena's gaze turned to Mirella, as it did often since her arrival in Istanbul several days before. She was astonished by the changes in Mirella, and awed by them as well. Mirella appeared to have blossomed with her sexuality as if it were her very claim on life. As with her famed ancestors, it appeared to bring her everything her heart desired. Deena had always known that Mirella had, in a sense, been trapped in her life until the Oujie legacy offered her a rigorous freedom. Now she seemed to ride on a tidal wave of free will with the responsibility of making constructive and absolute decisions, for herself and her marriage. More, it appeared, than Deena herself was able to do, for she and Brindley had not yet married. Such thoughts prompted Deena to say, 'Mirr, I wonder if you know how remarkable you and Adam are?'

'Oh, dear, what's brought this on, Deena?'

'I think seeing you here in Istanbul, with your home and family around you; tenderness, love, all the things you never used to be able to deal with. It's as if your own release also released the passionate inhibitions of the people closest to you.

'Take Brindley and me, for example. We know it to be true of us. And Lili, you know I am no fan of Lili but she seems to be able to deal better with human relationships. I watched her when we took her to the airport a few days ago. She was positively happy and charming. For the first time since I have known her she appeared to be content and at ease with herself and you, and me, and the world. Why, she had even won Rashid over.'

Mirella's heart skipped a beat when Deena linked her mother with Rashid. Was it jealousy? She had to admit it was – that and fear: seeds of both already planted in her subconscious by Joshua.

He missed no opportunity to discredit Rashid to Mirella, and he was far from subtle about it, in fact downright ruthless. To hear Joshua state, 'He was always interested in stealing the Oujie legacy from you. Isn't it enough that you sold him what he wanted without even opening it up for tender from other interested parties? And for what? The razzmatazz of his jet-setting life, and being made love to by the famous Turkish Don Juan. Famous, that's a laugh. The moment a real man like Papa came along, the baubles and the life-style he offered were shown up as tinsel and dross. And thank God you gave him up for Papa and us. I love you, Mirella, and hate to see you and hear you linked with that bum.'

There was an almost boyish earnestness in his claim. 'Can't you understand it's a sickness with the man? He has to destroy every woman he touches. You've seen it. Papa's seen it. We've all seen it. There was the American heiress from San Francisco, who ended up on a marble slab in Mexico, having died during an orgy on his yacht. The Hollywood starlet on an overdose in his garden. The endless stream of jet-setting beauties who have loved him like crazy and been ditched. Only you never succumbed. But you might just tell your mother how you did it. I saw them together in New York, coming out of Cartier. Stay away, Mirella, he will ruin your marriage. He is out to ruin you and Papa because he can't possess you. That's how I read him.'

Here was a kind of ultimatum that she give up her attachment to Rashid, not see him except in the company of his father or himself. She had had to remind Joshua that what she did had little to do with Joshua or his wants or needs, and they had parted on bad terms – he chastened, and she unhappy about Rashid and Lili, because she knew in her heart Rashid could be evil as well as amoral, and he was not above taking on mother and daughter. The thought had repelled her: it had driven an invisible wedge between them. Along with that went the worry over her stepson: was she about to lose the easy-going relationship she desired with him?

Mirella had to confront for them both the attraction she exercised over Joshua. Tempering frankness with a loving act had brought some success. But the situation disturbed the delicate balance achieved in the love triangle between Mirella, Adam and Rashid, and that was not good for any of them. She was therefore relieved when Joshua sent ten dozen long-stemmed white roses and a note asking her forgiveness. She gladly rewarded a nocturnal phone-call from Paris with just that.

But Joshua's words had goaded Mirella into also confronting Rashid about Lili.

'Tell me it's not true. You are not having an affair with my mother?'

'How very stupid of you to ask me who I sleep with! You don't have the right. You left me for marriage, and I ask you nothing about how, when, where, you make love with your husband. Or indeed if you have taken his son on as a lover. What I do and

388

with whom I do it are no concern of yours. Suffer it like a lady, and in silence. Did you forget I had other women in my life? Were you perhaps under the delusion that you possess me? Not so, my dear. Only partially – no more, no less than I possess you.

'Ah, we know each other's minds too well. I can see that, in your head, you had decided to be magnanimous and allow me the occasional flirtation – good for the gossip columns and to keep the Corey-Lala-Mustapha triangle relatively quiet. All right as long as it was someone anonymous. Or, you would allow me Oda Lala's and my Humayun, a consolation prize because you married Adam. I am going to punish you for that, Mirella, for not being above that.'

His anger had surprised her, but what terrified her was that she saw such cruelty in his face, and such passion. Violent passion that comes with erotic love and knows no bounds.

She had had her answer without a word of admission from him, and she was repulsed by the evil side of his nature he so enjoyed exercising. She had raised her arm and smashed him across the face with the flat of her hand as hard as she could, turned on her heel and stalked to the door of his bedroom. She flung it open, and her eyes fell on the diamond handcuffs around her wrists. They appeared to stop her at the open door, and she began to weep. Mirella was finished with him. She had tried to rip one of the diamond bracelets from her wrist, even though she knew it was impossible to do so.

He had come up behind her, grabbed her by the waist with one arm and pulled her tight to him. With his free hand he had slammed the door and double-locked it. She tried to flail out against him, but he had been too quick for her.

Rashid pushed her flat up against the door and, pinning her there with the weight of his body, he tore her black crêpe de chine dress in half straight down the back. In the tearing at the silk she suddenly felt her defencelessness, and she had tried to wriggle away from him. In vain. He ripped the black panties from between her legs, hurting her, spun her around and slid the dress off her arms and flung it to the floor. Then he slapped her hard across the face.

He violated her nakedness with his gaze, eyeing her long shapely legs in their stockings, whose provocative tops encircled her rounded thighs. He scorned her sensuous-looking feet, shod in tarty high-heeled black satin shoes, yet still the patch of black pubic hair enslaved him. Her breasts, draped in strands of lustrous pearls and diamonds, all his gifts in recognition of his passion for her, were heaving with her sharp and angry breathing. He seized her in a cruel embrace from which she emerged with her hands tied together behind her back. She felt herself being dragged to his bed, picked up and dropped on to it.

He had no need to tie her to the four posts of the bed. Where, after all, could she go, naked and hands strapped together?

He had stood at the foot of the bed and slowly stripped himself naked before her.

'You have been very stupid, Mirella, and have placed a part of our lives in jeopardy by your dumb behaviour. I don't know why. But you are going to have to learn how to handle these occasional crises in our relationship. Better that you learn today.'

'Let me go, Rashid.'

'Never.'

Mirella slowly calmed herself, never taking her eyes from Rashid. His sexual charisma, his male beauty, enthralled her, enslaved her to eros, as it always did. Sexual depravity, the evil that vanquishes the burden of being good, and a kind of base animal love emanated from the very pores of his honey-coloured skin. It reached out and touched a passion in Mirella, drew her back to him.

She knew he was right. He would never let her go because together they represented something rare. Erotic lovers equally matched, one never over-shadowing or stunting the growth of the other. Why be tormented by a desire to escape, to be free? She was free in her erotic love affair with Rashid, and in her real and true-love marriage with Adam. She was a woman doubly blessed. Rashid had been right: she had been stupid, Joshua had almost broken one side of her love triangle.

In the mirror Rashid could glimpse a dark bruise rising on his cheek where she had slapped him. Returning to her on the bed he had announced, yet again, 'You will have to be punished for this, Mirella.'

And punish her he had, in ways much worse for her than violence. He teased her with his hands, had caressed her body with oil of tuberose. Slowly, methodically, Rashid had massaged every inch of her skin with deft fingers, until she mellowed under his hands, and her flesh glistened as if made of slippery satin. And then, naked and rampant, he lay on top of her and stroked her whole body with his until he transferred her lustre to himself.

She was in a passion for him, and he knew it and

391

went further. He used his mouth and his tongue on her clitoris and cunt until he brought her to the edge of orgasm, again and again, only to cease abruptly, cut off the flow of passion ready to burst from her. He tortured her with his body by long denying her the release that he knew his penis alone could grant her. Her humiliating punishment was to have been reduced to beg for this orgasmic release even before his passion for her forced him to concede it.

The sun was well up over Istanbul when he returned her to the Peramabahçe palace, replete and exhausted, and having learned her lesson. Mirella, yet again, yielded to the recognition that, no matter what, she was bound to him, and there could be no leaving him.

That very afternoon he had sent her a letter declaring his love for her. That evening at sunset unannounced he called upon her on his schooner, the *Aziz*, and docked at the Peramabahçe palace. They sailed several miles up the Bosporus to a small deserted inlet with steep, well-wooded hills solid with rich green terebinth and umbrella pine trees, pierced by needle-shaped, dark cypresses, rising tier upon tier high above the river. They walked up the hill through the trees on a narrow, winding dirt path scattered with pine needles, and came upon an eighteenth-century wooden pavilion.

It was a circular love-kiosk with an erotic mosaic for flooring, and white marble fountains, arched floor-to-ceiling doors of glass all around it, that opened on to views of the Bosporus. And from gracefully-curved staircases winding delicately up to a narrow gallery, there were views over the city of

Istanbul, and especially Topkapi Sarayi, rising romantically from what was once the acropolis of the ancient town of Byzantium, the great palace of the Ottoman sultans where Mirella's great-grandmother had once ruled, and whence her grandmother had escaped.

Dazzlingly rich in sensuous charm and opulent privacy, the intimacy insinuated itself everywhere in the room. It was possible to forget the broken panes of glass, the cracks in the mosaic, the fountains deprived of water, the years of dust and decay.

For a moment Mirella experienced a sense of *déjà vu*, and her mind played a trick on her. She saw the room as it had once been, with its silks and its satins, its mirrors everywhere reflecting the play of fountains, and massive bowls of brightly-coloured flowers in full bloom; furnishings in the Oriental manner of the period, a couple in the act of making love.

'My great-grandfather built this hide-away just to make love to your great-grandmother. I am going to restore it just for you. It's my gift to you, a place for our erotic pleasures, for you to delight in the flesh as they did, and with whom you choose. I'll tell Adam I have given it to you because of its history, and because I feel it belongs to both of us. I know Adam well. He will know instinctively never to breach this sanctum. Only if you choose to bring him here will he see it. Just as my great-grandfather granted it as a miniature Taj Mahal to his beloved Roxelana Oujie, whose love at last destroyed him, so I give it to you.'

Mirella had accepted it, but, although it was given in love to her, she did recognize a look in his eye that she had seen before, a certain kind of helpless hatred, and it sent a shiver through her spine. It was a dangerous gift, from a dangerous lover, but she could not help herself, she fell in love with it at once. It was a passionate and thrilling place, now turned a bright golden pink in the setting sun. Echoes of past ecstasies rippled through the ruined love-kiosk on the gentle evening breeze.

Yet again the past reached out and took a part of her life in its ambiguous embrace.

Chapter 23

Deena snapped her fingers. 'Hey presto. Come back from wherever you are, Mirella. You're drifting away from me,' said Deena in her teasing, sing-song voice.

Mirella smiled. Deena always made her smile, and most especially when Deena was in one of her super-organizational moods. At those times everyone had to pay attention to what she had to say.

'Yes, Deena.'

'Right. Mirella, how about Thanksgiving?'

'What about Thanksgiving?'

'What do you mean, what about Thanksgiving? The most important day of my life, and you're asking what about it? My wedding, in your new New York town-house, that's what about Thanksgiving. You haven't heard a word I've said, have you?'

The look of disappointment on Deena's face was too sad. Mirella went and sat next to her, put her arm around her girlfriend and said, 'I'm so sorry. I drifted off, thinking about something you said earlier. Please don't look so sad. Everything is going to be fine. I spoke to Adam last night in Paris, and he assures me the house will be ready long before Thanksgiving. So you're on. Wedding bells and turkey at the Corey house, Fifth Avenue, New York City, three o'clock, *chupeh*, rabbi, and all.'

Deena broke down and began to cry. Brindley went and stood behind her, and passed her a clean white linen handkerchief.

'This is ridiculous, you know, Deena. Getting married is making a wreck of you. I have never heard of so much fuss over two people getting married.'

'Then you have never gotten mixed up in a Jewish wedding?'

'No, never.'

'Oh, my God, how can I do this to you?'

'More to the point is, how can you do this to us?'

'Good question, Brindley. Should we just forget our families and run off and do it in the Istanbul city hall?'

'You're at it again, Deena, dragging me into an unnecessary fuss about a wedding. I warn you, I could get fed up with it.'

'Do you think it's destiny? Are we fated never to marry, but to live in delicious sin?'

'One would have thought so, the way you fix dates for the nuptials with the vicar at Lyttleton Park, and then cancel them. I warn you now, we walk up that aisle on Christmas Eve whether or not we have had a Jewish ceremony in New York for your family. Christ, Deena, I am marrying you, not the Jewish race.'

'That's what you think.'

'Talk to her, Mirella.'

'Leave everything to me and to Adam, Brindley. All you have to do is arrive at the altars on time.'

Deena jumped up from the chaise. 'He's right,' she said. 'I'm making a real *matzos pudding* out of this whole marriage thing. Oh, God, I am as bad as my mother. I don't mean to be. Not another word will I expose you to. I hate myself when I behave like a *yenteh* ranger. Why don't you get on with your work? I can finalize things with Mirella and be done with all the details once and for all, I promise.'

Brindley looked relieved, positively happy. He took his fiancée in his arms and kissed her.

'You mean it?'

'Yes, I mean it.'

'Then I'll see you at lunch time. Until then, I'll be in town at the antiquities department, for the Oujie estate.'

Mirella announced that she would walk Brindley to the car as she had a few things to tell him. She slipped her arm through his and, as they were walking down the main staircase, he said in a whisper, 'What's a *matzos pudding*?'

'I think it's a rather sloppy dessert made of unleavened bread. That's one of her mother's phrases, but I wouldn't quote me on that. Deena would probably call that a WASP's interpretation.'

'And a "*yenteh* ranger"?'

'Well, for one thing, I am sure it is quite the opposite of a Sloane Ranger. Maybe it's a Sloane Ranger, New York Jewish Princess-style. What I do know is that a *yenteh* is a talkative woman, a female blabbermouth.'

'I don't always understand her, but isn't she wonderful, Mirella?'

'Yes, wonderful, Brindley.'

'I do hope she does, in the end, marry me. But it would not entirely surprise me if she left me high and dry at the altar.'

'Never,' laughed Mirella, who was concerned that Brindley might just be right.

Deena was pouring another cup of coffee for herself when Mirella returned. They both began to speak at the same moment. Deena laughingly conceded, 'Okay, it's your house, you go first.'

'Truth games?' asked Mirella.

Both women smiled. 'We're back to that, are we?' responded Deena. Then she appeared to sober up because characteristically they played their truth-twosome for real. They believed in it and worked at it.

The rules were simple. Each was obliged to answer the other's questions with a ruthless honesty. If one of them believed she was being lied to, she would call out 'Nixon'.

Their truth game was their way of helping each other to resolve uncertainties that were causing them conflict. And most of the time it worked. Mirella began.

'Brindley – are you going to marry him?'

'Yes,' answered Deena.

'Are you unsure about being able to handle the marriage?'

'No, not in the least.'

'Then why do you keep cancelling the dates you set for the ceremony? Once might have been acceptable, but three times?'

'I'm not afraid to lose my identity, not afraid of giving up my work, which as you know, I have already done; not afraid of becoming an expatriate – and you know how much I love being an American and living in New York; not afraid I won't fit into Brindley's very English life. Why, I'm not even scared of marrying Church of England-style.'

'Then what are you afraid of?'

'Losing my Jewishness, having a husband and children who will not understand the horrors of a Jewish meal, who will never know what it is to suffer *gefilte fish*, heartburn after a plate of *kishkeh*, chopped liver on rye bread loaded with caraway seeds, that ends up feeling like a hard ball in the pit of your stomach. Having a husband who doesn't understand what it is to be Jewish and over-emotional, and he not knowing how to say *kiddish*.'

'But, Deena, you don't even eat those things, or practise at being Jewish.'

'Don't you think I know that? That I am aware that I have wanted to be more of a WASP than a New York Jewish Princess? But what has that got to do with it? Don't you see? I am Jewish, I know about Jewishness, and now that I'm on the Damascus road and have the chance to trade it in, I don't want to. It's a part of me that I am proud of and don't want to lose. But I will, because I'm going to inter-marry. And because, whatever Jewishness I have, it's mine and I don't particularly want to push it on to anyone else. I never did it to you, did I?'

'Never.'

'And I don't really want to do it to Brindley. I'm not out to turn Lyttleton Park into a Jewish kibbutz, any more than I am out to turn Lady Margaret's beloved village fêtes into B'nai Brith jamborees, or expect Brindley to drop cricket for pinochle games with the boys from the borscht belt.' Then she punctured a little her own earnestness. 'Even this *oi vai is mir* attitude about getting married to a non-Jew is very Jewish.'

'That's all that is worrying you?'

'Absolutely all.'

'Then for God's sake – anybody's God – jut drop it.'

Deena hesitated for a moment and then announced, 'Done, consider my conflict at an end.'

'Nixon,' cried Mirella.

'No. No Nixon.'

'You're sure you're not Nixoning me, Deena?'

'Positive, and to prove it I'll tell you how we will solve the whole thing. Big church wedding at Lyttleton Park on Christmas Eve, as planned. Rabbi and *chupeh* at your house with the whole Corey clan, my mother and father, and Lady Margaret. Strictly a private and personal thing for me on Thanksgiving day. You and I and Brindley and Adam in front of a rabbi, and that's it. I don't want to do another thing about it, or hear another word about it. Except go shopping with you for the dresses to wear, and get a promise that you and Adam will end this odd estrangement you are having and come together in time for my weddings. Okay?'

Mirella nodded her assent, and then said, 'There is no estrangement between Adam and I. You don't know what you're talking about.'

'Nixon,' Deena said somewhat loudly.

'It's not.'

'Oh, it's Nixon all right. Otherwise, why aren't you with him now in New York helping him move into your new house? Why didn't you go to him when he asked you to meet him in Paris last week? Ever since he went on that hunting trip in Ethiopia, you hardly speak about him. Why wasn't he with you for those anniversary ceremonies at the UN, when you were

400

there in N.Y.? Or, for that matter, where were you when the news broke in all the financial papers about that Ethiopian Marxist Princess who turned up trumps for him by becoming his "white knight"? Not estranged? That's a load of Nixon.'

Mirella walked to the window and watched the mid-morning river-traffic, remaining silent. But Deena would not let up.

'Why don't you face up to what's wrong?'

Mirella returned to where Deena was sitting.

'Okay, there is a kind of estrangement.'

'Nixon.'

'We seem to be drifting apart.'

'Nixon.'

'I hesitate to leave Rashid and get more deeply involved in my married life with Adam, because if I do I'm afraid to lose Rashid.'

'That sounds more like it. Jimmy Carter at least. A little off-target, maybe, considering how involved and happy you are with the ready-made family and home Adam has provided you with. Not to mention how fast you have learned to love this palace of his and Turkey the same way he does. The look on your face when a cable from him comes or you hear his voice over the telephone; the way you speak to him – there's a softening of your whole being. You are deeply involved in your intimate married life with Adam. Surely Rashid knows and accepts that? You are not the only married woman in the world to have a lover. It's up to you to keep them in balance.'

'That may be so, but you have no idea how powerful a love exists between my husband and myself. It's so real and so true, and so natural. It overpowers the erotic love I share with Rashid, and

401

all three of us know it. I'm bound to these men, and I don't want to lose Rashid. I am always running away from him to Adam, because our love transcends Rashid's mere sensuality.'

'Mirella, I am asking you not to widen this separation you've created between you and Adam. You're too self-indulgent with Rashid at the moment. And, if I know Adam, he will do nothing until you have worked it out. He'll never help you in this. He is a man as hard as he is soft, and he will simply carry on with his life in the assurance that what you have together will win out. Do it for me, if for the time being you cannot do it for yourself. I need us all to be together. Brindley and I both want to share these times, the happiest of our lives, with you and Rashid and Adam, but we will never be able to unless you get it right.'

Then the two women hugged each other and both knew without speaking another word that the truth game had unloosed a knot for them yet again. Their conflicts dissolved. As soon as Mirella had a few minutes to herself, she picked up the telephone receiver and called Paris, only to find Adam was no longer there.

Adam flew directly from Paris to Cairo with Turhan on a commercial flight, changed to a smaller waiting plane that followed the Nile up to Aswan. There he changed planes once more to a Lear, jet-piloted by Jock Warren-Williams. They took off immediately for Khartoum.

'Thanks for coming to get me, Jock.'

'No problem.'

'Did you book me in at The Grand?'

'Yes.'

'Have you seen anything of Marlo, heard anything of Tana Dabra?'

'Marlo, yes. She's doing a picture-story on the Dinka people and is down there with them now, but she has become the Mahdi's favourite distraction. She's been living with him in one of his mud palaces in the Bayuda Desert. They make some pair. He dark and Oxford-serious, all in sparkling white flowing robes and grandly-wound white turban, with a staff in one hand, a book, usually the Bible or poetry, in the other; while she's in my Abercrombie and Fitch, twenty-two-year-old khaki Bermuda shorts, with my best Turnbull and Asser tie strung through the belt-loops, my best white dress-shirt tied in a knot under her tits, sneakers – I don't know where she found them – and her hair wrapped in a turban the colour of purple figs. And, of course, his whole court of Sudanese officials in their white, white robes padding along after her, hanging on to every word she utters, as she snaps, snaps, snaps away.

'But not a word about your Tana Dabra. Not since your financial wizardry with the Ethiopian government was disclosed in all the papers – along with photographs of her and her telex-statements to the world press from Kampala – two weeks after we all left Khartoum after our hunting expedition.'

Adam sat back and lit one of his cigars. He thought first about Tana Dabra, and how clever she had been with those statements to the press. She had nobbled them all to her will; ruined Agristar for ever in Ethiopia; stopped her government from using the foreign investments under her control for anything but the welfare of the people; used Adam and The

Corey Trust as protectors, manipulated her superiors in the government by making her statements to the world in their name, giving them credit for the entire scheme, 'white knight' and all, and then resigning her position in favour of the Minister of Commerce, Abebe Afeworq Maskal. About the only thing she hadn't done was surface in Paris, New York, or London, where she had a better chance of survival. She had crossed too many people.

Not since he fell asleep in her arms had he heard a word from her, nor had she sent him a sign through anyone that she was safe. Then, in the early hours of the morning, a call, a voice, her voice, speaking in French, 'It is your black princess, come as quickly as possible to where Jock lives.' Then a click, and the whine of a disconnected telephone line.

The two men were sitting on the wide verandah of the Grand Hotel. They had watched the sun set over the Blue and the White Nile where they joined. They had talked with the vendors who come with their wares and spread them out on mats for the tourists to buy, ivory bits and pieces of no great beauty, but of considerable charm, wooden carved animals, primitive and endearing, some wooden instruments of sticks and animal skins, some very good iron work and knives, most of which were made by the craftsmen across the river at Omdurman. There, Jock had an old wooden house where he sometimes lived among the Sudanese, when he was not living in the suite of rooms he kept on the ground floor of the Grand Hotel.

They had known this place for twenty years, and the vendors were always pleased to see Adam. It gave them a chance to exchange gossip and stories with him and he always bought the best of their wares. And they in turn had been very good to Adam, had introduced him to men and places that resulted in several fruitful excavations whose rewards were shared between the Metropolitan in New York and the Museum in Khartoum. They had gone on at length this evening about Mirella, whom they met when she had been in Khartoum to meet him at the end of the Ethiopian safari, anxious to know if they had started a baby as yet.

That had been a surprise, the unexpected arrival of Mirella. Abebe had stayed with the hunting party on board The Lisbon Clipper for a week, as they flew the length of the Blue Nile. Watching, listening all the time. There had been no question about it, he was suspicious about something. Maybe even looking for Tana Dabra. But by the end of a week of excellent hunting, thanks to locations the men had previously chosen, the comfort of The Lisbon Clipper as a camp site, and the camaraderie of the men, Abebe had left them at the border where the Blue Nile flowed from Ethiopia into the Sudan, satisfied he had found nothing out of order.

It was then with some relief that the men had camped twice more before arriving at the Grand Hotel. They had all been in the bar drinking beer from glasses the size of flower vases, trying to quench their thirst in the 110 degree heat and humidity. It had been Rex who saw her first, standing in the doorway. He stood up and all the men's eyes followed his. Adam was the last to reach her, as the men rushed to greet Mirella, he was so taken by surprise. She was the last thing on his mind, but obviously still the first thing in his heart, because the moment he saw her it skipped a beat and he wanted her as he always wanted her when she appeared before him.

However, much as he did want her, for the moment she posed a problem being there where he hoped to see Tana Dabra. He therefore set about to convince her that the heat was too much for her and send her back to Istanbul with Joshua where he promised to be before the week was out.

It was two o'clock in the morning, the heat and humidity still oppressive. The verandah was empty now, except for the Sudanese servant in his white kaftan and neat turban, standing in the dark waiting on them, Turhan lurking not far away. The dim night-lights in the lobby cast patterns of light through the windows, just enough to drink by. Night-sounds reached them, a lonely clickity clack of hooves of horses pulling an open carriage on the road between them and the Nile, whispering palm leaves, frogs croaking.

'Listen, old boy, she's not going to show. No more than she did the last time we waited for her here in Khartoum. It's too dangerous for her here.'

'She'll show, Jock. And when she does, we're going to fly her out. You be ready to leave by eleven in the morning. This cloak-and-dagger stuff is not for me. I have The Corey Trust back on its feet, and a lot of good people in the right places working at it. You know me: "the business" is not my whole life, and it's been enough of Tana Dabra's. I'm going to help her make a life for herself.'

Jock stood up and the two men shook hands. Jock went to the room booked for Adam. They had agreed earlier that, if she did appear, the chances were it would be his room, because it was off the verandah and she could more easily come and go in the night without being seen.

Adam had been right, she arrived in the still of the night. He was lying naked on the bed smoking a cigar, unable to sleep for the heat. He saw her slim, dark figure slip through the French doors leading on to the balcony, a shadow in the dark.

She stood at the foot of his bed, crossed her arms in front of her and raised her dress over her head and dropped it to the floor. He watched her shadowy movements and reached out to crush the cigar in an ashtray on the night-stand. He was enthralled as he watched her glide from the bottom of the bed up between his legs, kissing the inside of his thighs.

She moved like a voluptuous slithering snake. He grabbed her as soon as he could reach her and pulled her on top of him. He abased himself to animal lust, but, before all the reasons he was there for evaporated, he whispered huskily, 'I am never coming for you again. You will leave with me in the morning.'

She whispered back in his ear, 'You will always come when I want you.' She parted her lips again and took his ear between them and sucked and licked it.

In the morning, when he dozed off just for a few seconds, she took her chance and slipped away. This was no longer the virgin he had broken. She had become a fierce lover, fierce and thrilling, dangerous and demanding. By the time he had tamed her, he was left with long deep scratches and bruises and teeth-marks where she bit into his flesh in order to quell her cries of ecstasy. She had been remarkable; but when he and Jock met at breakfast he said, 'She's too dangerous, even for me. My passion for dangerous women hasn't waned, but it has changed since I fell in love with Mirella. You were right about her, Jock. She's a driven, sensual creature, and she won't be coming out of hiding until she's ready.'

The last thing Adam did before leaving the Grand Hotel in Khartoum was to call Mirella in Istanbul. Jock and Adam were half way to Cairo when Adam discovered three cases filled with gold bars tucked under the seats. How had Tana Dabra done it? Jock's plane had been locked, and the lock had not been broken.

Adam called Mirella the next evening from Cairo. They spoke at length about changes Mirella wanted to make in her life, radical changes that would give her more time for them to be together. And they made plans to achieve those ends. From Paris the next day they planned for their future and agreed to meet in New York in two weeks, at which time they would be able to move into their new town-house.

It was Rashid who took Deena and Mirella to Paris to shop for Deena's wedding-dress, his wedding gift to Deena and Brindley. He timed it so that Adam would be in New York and unable to join them.

Deeply in love as he was with Mirella now, his vision was always of her as his erotic mistress-wife of sorts. But of late, since the day he gave her the love pavilion, schemes took shape in his mind that might one day give him the total possession of her that had so far eluded him.

Where once he had shared Mirella with no one there was now the void left in his life by Adam's possession of her in marriage. These days Rashid filled that void with erotic games with several other women, contenting himself with a vacant amusement.

Lili was proving a far more amusing victim than he thought she would be. A fantasy formed of the day he would be successful in manipulating both mother and daughter to join him in an erotic tryst. He promised himself depravity would assume a new look on that day. There were others to fill the void. A seventeen-year-old English beauty, who was completely beguiled by him. A spoiled wealthy American divorcee, who was a perfect masochistic foil to his sadistic whims. And there were others – he picked them up everywhere and enjoyed them all, from the lowest sleazy whore to ladies in society. And, of course, there was always Humayun. The pleasures he gained from sex and intrigue with Humayun were infinite.

Rashid was an intriguer and often he obtained amusement from giving Humayun to other men as a sexual gift. Then he would stand back and watch her transform their sad, often pathetically boring sex-lives. She was the most accomplished enticer of men he had ever come across. She alone matched his ability to draw from men the sexual corruption latent within them. Only once had he regretted his intrigues with her. And how he felt a sympathy for the man involved, and must find a way to save him.

The man was Moses, and it had happened when he wanted to give Moses a gift, sexual delight, in return for all the help Moses had given Rashid with Mirella's wedding preparations. And so he had instructed Humayun to seduce Moses, after Mirella's wedding. This, perhaps the one time Rashid had given Humayun out of a whim born of charity rather than intrigue, was proving to be a problem. How could he have foreseen they would fall hopelessly in love?

409

In the arms of the ravishing and clever Humayun, Moses, who had never been enslaved by anything or anyone, and who believed totally that man must be free, had discovered that sexual fulfilment, so earnestly desired, was paid for by its own kind of enslavement.

With Moses erotically enslaved, Humayun was now using him in the same way that Rashid used her. It disturbed her to have released in him desires that rendered him, however briefly, so abject. In love with Moses in the only way she knew how – through sexual depravity and enslavement – and unable to make Moses understand that the great joy of her life was to please her master Rashid, because of the total pleasure she achieved from belonging to Rashid body and soul, Humayun had appealed to Rashid to destroy the relationship between her and Moses. Not a prospect Rashid was looking forward to, because he had a gut feeling it would start a chain of events he was not ready to deal with. So, for the moment he did nothing. It was, instead, Joshua whom he was about to deal with. Rashid wanted him to stop disturbing the fine balance achieved in his love triangle with Mirella and Adam.

From Paris, Deena flew off to London, ostensibly to begin the re-decorating of Brindley's Mount Street flat, their London home. After three days she gave up, and began to enjoy its English shabbiness, and to enjoy London and Brindley on their own terms, which seemed to suit her admirably. She had never been happier.

Rashid flew on Concorde from Orly in Paris to Kennedy in New York, and then on a private jet to the mid-west of the United States on business. At least that was the route he told the women. He promised to meet them on or before the Thanksgiving family dinner-wedding at Mirella's in New York, and to present himself as an usher at the ceremony at Lyttleton Park, on Christmas Eve.

Mirella boarded Adam's Learjet for Istanbul and the Peramabahçe palace, where she would remain enjoying life with 'the clan' and re-organize for the next six months, before she and Adam would return to New York.

But, before the three parted, they had a bottle of champagne together in the back seat of Rashid's maroon-coloured Rolls on the tarmac close to Mirella's jet plane. It was there that Mirella made her announcement.

She had been discussing with Adam for the last week the new outline she would give to her life now she was married. She decided to resign her position at the UN, and devote more of her time to Adam and his family, whom she had grown to enjoy enormously. Grafted onto it at first, she felt herself growing to be a part of it. As she put it, 'Family present and family past have become the most important things in my life. I have had my career, and I think I have earned the right to retire from one life to begin another. I want to do creative, adventurous things, for myself and my family. I am going to build a small museum in Istanbul, something similar to the Benaki Museum in Athens. It is the Oujie legacy, the archives of generations of remarkable ancestors, whose treasures will be the basis of the collection.'

Deena gave an inward sigh of relief and an outward hug to Mirella. Rashid had kissed her hand gallantly and said, not without awe in his voice, 'When a goddess like you founds a museum, it can only become a shrine to beauty.' But Mirella, her mind earthbound by the practicalities of her task, found something heartless in the vapidity of Rashid's compliment.

What Rashid did not express was his uneasy feeling over her desire for a fuller family commitment. He would have to do something about that.

Chapter 24

They had been physically apart for a considerable time and, although that had not worried either of them unduly, there was a moment of tension before the plane door opened, created by their desire to be together and the hope that time and distance had not changed how they felt about one another. Adam's first sight of Mirella stimulated him on all levels, mental, emotional, sexual. Her desire for union, which was always strong, seemed more acute than ever, and Adam loved that in her. Mirella simply felt weak-kneed.

She was struck dumb with happiness that she was still, at the very sight of Adam, madly in love and overwhelmingly filled with desire. There was an extra dimension to her feelings too, that she could not define but both she and Adam were aware that it emanated from her and it was picked up like an exotic aroma by him. It was something like the scent of love; invisible threads as strong as tempered steel holding them together, or one soul shared by two people.

He wanted to make love to her right there and then, go to extreme sexual lengths to satisfy her, but the time and the place were wrong, even though he knew his desire was right. All the way home in the back of the plum-coloured Rolls, he wanted to

413

express what he was feeling, but it was impossible. Over the heads of Alice and Zhara and Muhsine and Moses, who had all travelled with Mirella from Istanbul and were chattering to him all at the same time, his gaze told Mirella what he was feeling.

The atmosphere between them seemed charged with an extra invisible energy like those sometimes-minute particles of dust in the air that one sees only when the light hits them at the correct angle. Maybe it was just life being lived to the very edge of fullness, yet contained and not spilling over. Neither knew, and neither asked the question.

It was cold, New York cold, and damp, the sort of raw weather that eats into the bones, after the bite of a cruel bitter wind. The windows in the shops along Madison Avenue were lit and gave a warm glow that spilt onto the hard city streets. There was an early-evening bustle of people moving from the cocktail-hour to the dinner-hour – what New Yorkers call the last of the evening rush-hour. It would have been far faster to walk than to ride, but the cold left them no option.

Riding through the streets of Manhattan in the warmth of a luxurious automobile, smothered in furs, alongside a man you are madly attracted to and who is your husband as well, is not a hard thing to take. Mirella was happy.

She window-shopped from the car and listened to him talking with his children, and read the look of desire for her in his eyes when their glances met, and she prayed that she was not reading him wrong. And what if she were? What if he no longer wanted her as she wanted him? How could she face those horrifying moments, the worst fear of all, the dreaded fear of loss? No, she couldn't be reading him wrong, it would be too cruel, too unfair. She put the thought right out of her mind and took up his hand and held it.

The excitement of New York City, and especially from Thanksgiving through to the New Year, would have been enough for any of the people in the car. But for Mirella and Adam that was secondary to their being together again and moving into their new family house. For Moses there was the added joy of returning to what he considered his home town and 165 East 65th Street, Mirella's house, where he hoped to get a better perspective on his love affair with Humayun. For little Alice the excitement of travelling and the promise of seeing Marlo, her mother, was what New York meant. To Muhsine, New York was a frightening adventure, but as always her joy lay in being next to Adam and now his wife Mirella. As for Zhara, moving in with Josh and sharing his fifteen-room apartment at the Dakota for the New York winter social season suited her just fine. Mirella could not but smile at what she was saying to her father.

'You are just like all the New Yorkers who live on the upper East Side. The only good thing they ever condescend to say about the Dakota is that the apartments have great space for little money. They always think there is something second-rate about the West Side, just like New Jersey.'

'Don't be silly, Zhara, I am the one who found the apartment at the Dakota for your brother. It's true, though, what you say. Other East-Side New Yorkers feel the Dakota is on the wrong side of the park. Periodically the West Side has had its time, when it was considered smart and chic to live there, and this is one of those times. However, my beautiful and spoiled Zhara, remember you are an East-Side girl going to live in a more ethnic community.

'It's more a melting-pot over there, more homey, with its little grocer-shops, its Jewish delicatessens, its Italian spaghetti houses, its huge Broadway cafeterias. The West Side is very tolerant in its acceptance of the rich and of the expensive buildings around the corner from the worn-out, cockroach-infested apartments in run-down brownstones.'

Then Adam began to laugh and, putting his arm around his daughter, he teased her. 'Zhara, it will be a change for you, the West Side. It's a place where you will always find a laundry, a cleaners, a shoe-repair shop, and an all-night liquor store. It's a community that rushes around working at life, and I hope you're not too spoiled to appreciate that.'

'That's unfair, Papa, and you know it.'

'Yes, maybe it is unfair. I don't suppose the West Side of Manhattan has any less colour than the streets of Istanbul, and I do know how well you enjoy and take advantage of them. It's just that I brought you up at The Sherry Netherlands, and that's not exactly a neighbourhood where you'll find a *Yeshiveh* next door to an all-Black whore house. Or be exposed to the humiliation of survival. Have you ever seen a pasty-faced ten-year-old boy in a shiny black satin coat, who looks like a forty-year-old man, tucking his long skinny side-curls where his sideburns should be up under his orthodox black felt hat as soon as he gets out of sight of his rabbinical school so that the Puerto Rican kids won't beat him up?

'I saw that once, and I saw the look of terror and

embarrassment on that child's face when the Rabbi came running down the stairs of the *Yeshiveh*, his longer, fatter curls bouncing and his black satin coattails flapping after him as he ran down the street, one hand on top of his head trying to hold down his wide, fur-trimmed hat. He was screaming "revolting, disgusting fellow; evil person, nasty fellow." *Paskudnyak*, that's right, *paskudnyak*, that was the word he kept repeating as he ran after the unfortunate boy, waving a cane I suppose he was going to beat him with. The boy ran away from the teacher as fast as his legs could possibly carry him, only to be trapped at the corner of Amsterdam Avenue by a gang of blacks and Puerto Ricans. No, I think not, you wouldn't see a sight like that. On the east side of the Park, the humiliations are practised behind closed doors.'

'Not always, Papa. Look over there. That bunch of rags piled in the alleyway next to the supermarket cart with the rubbish in it.'

At that moment the rags moved and revealed the haggard, dirt-streaked face of a middle-aged woman. She began screaming as she pounded the damp, ice-cold wall she was leaning against. Several passers-by eyed her, but only for a second. Not one of them stopped. They hardly broke their stride.

New Yorkers are hardened to screamers. On the buses, in the subways, and always on the streets. The Rolls purred past the shrieking bundle of rags. The last they saw of the desperate, homeless creature, was a pair of filthy scrawny bare hands, red and raw from the bitter cold, reaching out of the darkness to drag her back into the alleyway from the glitz and glamour of the Upper East Side avenue.

'The homeless live all over New York now, Papa.

They are the men, women, young people and kids with almost all their options gone. Many of them prefer to suffer in poverty on the streets than endure those shelters the size of football fields packed with row upon row of neatly lined-up cots ... and lots of danger. New York is getting to be more like Bombay or Calcutta. Papa, I'm not blind or insensitive to humiliation. More shocked, I guess. I never dreamed I would see whole families with tiny children living on the streets of New York City.'

'I guess what I was trying to say, dear heart, was that there is a New York street-life out there you have never been exposed to before, but I can see I was wrong about that. Well, just don't be an East-Side girl slumming it on the West Side. If you have chosen to stay there with Josh instead of with us, don't use the Dakota like some East-Side castle-fortress on the wrong side of the park to emerge from in a taxi and return to in a taxi. Take advantage of the richness of the life around you there, and learn from it.'

Zhara looked at Mirella and the two women smiled at each other. Like all of 'the clan' she had become friends with Mirella, so much so as to have taken Mirella into her confidence. They had a secret that Zhara was not yet prepared for the world to know. She was in love, and doing just what her father suggested she should not do, hiding away in the Dakota in the hope that the privacy she got there would give her romance a chance to flourish away from the upper East-Side gossips.

The car at last made some headway and turned onto Fifth Avenue. Central Park seemed to sparkle darkly in the coldness of the evening. Several blocks later they arrived at their new home. All the windows were ablaze with light in the neo-Georgian limestone brick mansion, standing solidly on the corner of Fifth Avenue overlooking Central Park. A forty-room building famous for its elegant architectural restraint and its classy detail, the entrance to it was on the side street rather than the Avenue.

The Rolls purred around the corner of Fifth Avenue and almost immediately through the iron gates onto the horse-shoe-shaped drive up to the impressive front doors.

The excitement of their arrival peaked when they rushed from the cold into the house and were greeted by the warmth of its fine, rich but sedate interiors, and by a pair of huge English mastiffs belonging to Adam, who bounded in from one direction, and four gold-and-white shih-tzus barking and yelping as they ran down the grand staircase with short little feet hardly touching the stairs and hair flying.

All was chaos in the entrance hall, and between the laughter and shouts of 'heel, heel,' the barking, and the chatter, Adam whispered in Mirella's ear, 'Welcome home, my love.'

They only had a second to exchange glances of affection before he gathered up the small dogs from the arms of those around him and placed them in Mirella's arms.

'Here, I bought these for you. This is Misha, Masha, Winnie and Wonkie. Aren't they wonderful? They're small enough to travel with us, and they provide non-stop, in-transit entertainment.'

'Oh God, Papa's gone on an animal spree again,' Zhara said and laughed.

For Zhara and Alice there were pure white, long-haired Persian cats with emerald-green eyes that were produced from the sitting-room off the hall by one of the housemen, even before coats and hats were removed.

They were at last allowed a glass of sherry by an open, wood-burning fire in the sitting-room. Here Josh arrived in time to receive a Kerry Blue Terrier and join a tour of the new New York City family residence, along with everyone else and all the pets.

Mirella felt twinges of loving towards Adam while touring the house, brought on by the fact that he had used nearly every suggestion she had contributed, when together they pored over the plans of the new house, which had already been under way for some time before she ever met Adam Corey.

All were surprised to find several sets of glass doors on the top floor, leading on to a roof garden that Adam declared out of bounds to the clan, announcing it was private territory for Mirella and himself. They might visit by invitation only. Otherwise the run of the house was for all.

They sent Moses and Muhsine down for coats for everyone and, on their return, they all tramped out over the vast roof where Adam had built studios for Mirella and himself. The two studios were divided by gardens and sunken terraces, and sheltered from the wind by trees and shrubs, ornamental pools and an animal shelter, Adam's biggest surprise of all. By the subtle, but adequate lighting they traipsed across the roof-gardens under a light snow flurry to visit Adam's favourite pets, Tao and Chi, his Panda bears.

The family dined on oysters on the half shell and a perfect chilled Chablis, followed by a rack of lamb served pink, with petit pois, roast potatoes, several bottles of Lafite-Rothschild '61, a first-growth of fabulous style and perfume. There was a green salad, and Alice's favourite dessert, banana-cream pie.

The room was very still. A chink of dawn seeped in through the sliver of space made by the parting in the draperies. There was just enough light so one could see shapes in the dark, the objects in the room and the two people cradled together in the huge bed. Mirella lay wrapped in the arms of her husband. The smoothness of his skin, the warmth of his body against hers, and the steady, even breathing that came from his deep and restful sleep took the edge off her anxiety.

Mirella had been surprised when, after Adam had tucked Alice in for the night, he excused himself to her saying he wanted to take Josh and Zhara home to the Dakota. He had something very private to discuss with them. She had been fast asleep when he returned.

Their desires and need to confirm their feeling for each other in sexual bliss had been put aside, and although she understood it, she could not help wishing he had wakened her and made love to her. She watched him sleeping, he was so handsome and big and manly, with none of the delicate yet masculine beauty of Rashid. Different, that was the thing about the two men. They were so completely different it stopped her from making comparisons, and in turn stifled conflicts in her about these two men in her life.

When she woke for the second time that morning, Adam was gone. On his pillow was a note that said, 'good morning' and nothing else. She felt let down, but not for long. When she rang for a breakfast tray, the maid first arrived with an enormous *Revillion* coatbox. Mirella scrambled through the tissue-paper to find a sumptuous chinchilla coat. She rushed to the mirror in her dressing-room and tried it on over her silk night-gown. A note in the pocket said 'I love you, and missed you. See you at teatime.'

As Mirella moved through her day she was amazed at how much she had changed. New York for her had always meant work, career success, and a secret love, the occasional one-night stand, a few good friends, and the opera. And like a good little hamster, she had spent years on that treadmill.

It didn't feel like her New York in the house on Fifth Avenue where she was surrounded by her adopted family and a loving husband. Now that she had had a taste of being in the bosom of family, and had found love, she suddenly wondered how she had survived the life of a single person – all that aloneness.

After lunch she went to *her* room, the room Adam created for her, a space for her use alone. She used a special key in the elevator that took her past the top floor and directly into her room.

The room was more like a pavilion or a green-house. There were eight pairs of fifteen-foot high, leaded glass doors, arched at the tops, that opened out on to the roof garden. The garden was magnificently landscaped with huge shade-trees, flowering shrubs, terraces of grass punctuated with lily ponds filled with large, Chinese fan-tail goldfish. At the far side of the roof she could just see behind a screen of Japanese pines and juniper trees, trained into twisted living sculpture, another pavilion and a large sunken area of tall bamboo trees where Tao and Chi, the pandas, lived.

There were sky-lights in the ceiling flooding the room with light and sky in the daytime, stars at night. What wall space there was was covered from the floor to the ceiling with books. Reference books, atlases, novels, biographies, books of poetry, dictionaries. The honed, white-marble floor had priceless, antique Persian carpets strewn across it, whose patterns and colours were broken here and there by white polar bear and tiger-skin rugs, mounted head and all. There were only three pieces of furniture in the room. A long, four-inch-thick, white marble slab, resting on tall rectangles carved from clay-coloured marble unique to Verona, served as her desk. A Queen Anne wing-chair, covered in its original tapestry, a scene of a unicorn prancing through a wood thick with different shades of green leaves, waited for her behind the desk. On the desk stood the latest equipment in computers and word-processing, and a large Lalique vase, a miracle of crystal, filled with her favourite Regalia lilies.

The third piece of furniture was set in the centre of the room among the date palms, yucca trees, large fan palms, giant papyrus in full flower, and huge pots of orchids, cymbidiums, with stephanatis vines clinging to the tree-trunks and spilling their thick cluster of white blossoms that turned the room into a perfume garden. It was a seventeenth-century four-postered bed with its intricate carved canopy made of pure silver. A love-bed made long ago for a Rajah's favourite mistress. It was covered in lynx furs with many large cushions of hand-woven raw silk.

She wandered around the room touching every-thing. She discovered behind one wall of bookcases a secret door that opened into a perfect white marble bathroom, jacuzzi, sauna, shower and all. Behind the other wall of books another door and a small white marble-and-rosewood kitchen, stocked with food and dinner service for four.

He had thought of everything. When the sun was too bright and disturbed Mirella there was a button to be pushed which adjusted the shields on the roof, cutting off the light to just where she wanted it, and another to adjust the room-temperature. She found the stereo and filled the room with the sound of Rimsky-Korsakov's 'Scheherazade'. She slumped into the chair and listened to Fritz Reiner conducting the Chicago Symphony Orchestra and marvelled at the power they had had to make even the most obvious a new and fresh experience. The ersatz orientalia glowed like the fires of creation, and Mirella blessed the new technology that kept bright this old performance.

The snow that started falling the night before was still coming down heavily, and in the whiteness a stillness fell over the city that made one feel fresh and sparkling. It was like a winter wonderland outside. New York City was having its first crippling blizzard of the season. The kind where offices are closed and young, smart, trendy executives ski down Fifth Avenue to work. The odd car skidded its way up Fifth Avenue because some mad-man knew he could find a parking space.

The trees and lamp-posts wore top hats of heavy snow, and the great city was white-white and pure, and would stay that way until the sand and salt trucks slushed it all up. But, for the moment, the city was undisturbed by man or machines. The cold wind and the snow were etching a miracle of beauty. Mirella adored the heavy, cold whiteness forming outside all around her.

For a long time Mirella sat and listened to the music and watched through the windows the thick snow falling. Then she moved to the silver bed and lay among the cushions and watched it some more. It closed her in from the world, even more than her husband and her privileged life, and she floated mentally out into space, feeling full of joy.

When it stopped snowing and she raised herself from her day-dreaming, there was a late afternoon sun shining. It looked so fresh, cold and invigorating outside. With a sense of sureness, she broke the spell of the snow upon her and made up her mind to go find Adam. She wanted to be near him.

Muhsine brought her a wide belt of black suede, her Tibetan fur boots and her new chinchilla coat. Muhsine helped her lace up her boots, and Mirella stood up to adjust the black cashmere tunic she was wearing over harem trousers of white, paper-thin suede. It had a high collar that buttoned on the side, and great balloon sleeves. It was like a cossack's shirt. She'd worn it all day hanging loose, but now she gathered it under the wide, black-suede belt with its magnificent black opal clasp, around her waist. She bloused the tunic over the belt so that the opal all but vanished, and then adjusted the strands of pearls she was wearing. Slipping her arms into the chinchilla coat, she buttoned it and turned up the collar. She had the habit of touching the large square diamonds on her ears, to make sure they were secure. They were. Mirella tucked her hair under an Adolpho black silver fox cloche and her hands into fine, black

425

calfskin gloves and was ready to brave the weather. She pushed the terrace doors open. When she turned to close them, Muhsine said, 'Adam is with the keeper and the pandas.'

Mirella thanked her and stepped into the deep snow on her Manhattan palace roof-garden. The snow reached almost to the tops of her boots. The cold air was just what she needed. She stomped around in the snow scooping some of it up in her hands and holding it close to her face. The damp cold bit into her skin. She strolled around waving her arms and taking long deep breaths, and walked under the tall evergreen shrubs, the caps of heavy white snow weighing down the boughs; she shook them and they rained down snow all over her.

Two gardeners arrived, greeted her and asked permission to carry on with their work. With shovels and brooms they gently swept the snow away and removed a finely-meshed grid that covered the fish pond with its collection of rare Chinese fan-tail fish swimming in the heat-regulated water.

Mirella walked to the opposite side of the garden and looked down across Central Park. There seemed little activity going on there or anywhere else. She walked through her roof-top snowscape, kicking clumps of snow as she went, sometimes bending down to gather armfuls, tossing the snow high up over her head. She was feeling clean, energized and fresh. She was warm and comfortable all over, except for her face and hands, which were ice-cold.

She discovered while walking through a row of weeping cherry trees, now mere droopy shapes with snow-hats, several curved stone steps leading down to a small observatory, with a domed roof and a powerful 'scope. With her foot she scraped away the snow. A gardener arrived at her side at once to sweep the snow away with his broom, and she was able to descend safely. Once inside, the warmth of the room was welcoming. She pushed a button and the dome slid slowly open; another button, and the telescope began to swivel into place. It wasn't dark as yet and too difficult for her to find the stars. She pressed the buttons again and everything slid back as when she found it.

Mirella left the observatory and walked through the snow-covered rose arbours, stretching, waving her arms about, head back, looking up at the pearly-white sky. She was feeling her body, airing her mind. It was here, out in the cold, in the clear crisp air that she revelled in her happiness and wanted to shout it from the rooftop.

Kicking clumps of snow high into the air with every step she took towards Tao and Chi's enclosure, she looked down at them. Watching the two giant pandas rollicking with Adam and Wing, their keeper, filled her with joy. Adam, dressed from top to toe in racoon, looked like another animal. He was feeding Chi with stalks of bamboo with one hand while rubbing Tao's tummy with the other.

Half an hour had passed and it was twilight. Mirella picked up as much snow as her arms could carry and dropped it into the enclosure. It drifted down like fine white powder. She called to them. The pandas waddled towards her, all the time looking up and making sounds. Carefully she went down the path and joined them. Chi was trying to mount Tao in a haphazard fashion, but he slipped off and rolled in the snow.

Mirella stood up on her toes, reached and put her arms around Adam's shoulders. Their cold lips met and kissed. They rubbed cold wet cheeks together and kissed again. Mirella went all warm inside at the very closeness of her husband, before they had even spoken to each other.

'You are so beautiful, so full of life, I love you. You are always so new and fresh and lovely. When I see you I always want to woo you, win you over, make you love me,' he said huskily, and kissed the tip of her nose and put his arm around her. They walked together making the clucking sounds the pandas liked to hear.

A strange roof-top snow-scene, with the pair of pandas waddling towards them, imitating the clucking sounds and rubbing their heads together. The Coreys spent another half hour playing with the remarkable pets, pretending to eat with them, sitting in their swing. Adam even tried to mount Mirella panda-fashion, and Wing fled from the panda house laughing. Tao tried to mount Adam first and then Mirella, and the Coreys were convulsed with laughter and decided that was the time to leave.

Arm in arm, the Coreys walked to another part of the roof-garden Mirella had not yet seen. There was Adam's hideaway, his lodge. Cold and wet through after entering the lodge Adam rang for Turhan and ordered tea. Standing in front of a roaring fire they began to peel off coats and hats. They seemed unable to get warm, and when Turhan arrived with an enormous silver tray with a tea-service and a delectable-looking cake, they greedily drank, hoping to warm themselves.

Muhsine brought a white cashmere kimono for

Adam and a full-length, white vicuna robe with sleeves of sable for Mirella. Turhan confiscated all the wet furs and boots, while Muhsine brushed Mirella's hair, trying to dry the strands soaked in her winter romp.

Just as Mirella's pavilion was to be her private space, this room, which he called the lodge, was Adam's. It was an enormous and unusual room, on its own; but set floating above Fifth Avenue it was unique.

Panelled in antique *boiserie* of warm rich chestnut taken from his father's château in Perigord, it had magnificent carvings of the hunt as cornices above the doors and windows. There were animal-trophies hung high up on the walls, in several places three tiers high. For the most part they were rare specimens shot in China, Tibet and India. Adam's father and grandfather had shot the best ones, both having been notable big-game hunters of their time.

There were old sepia photographs of locations rarely seen, usually with the game that had recently been killed, and other photographs of large safaris with famous people. The room was a fascinating one, for wherever you looked there was something to attract the eye: animals shot by Adam, antique maps, a superb gun-collection.

The lodge also housed a fine sporting and exploration library. The French doors which opened onto the garden gave a clear view of the panda-enclosure on one side, and an aviary and hawk-house on the other. The walls were mostly lined with books. A snail-shaped staircase in the centre of the room led up to a balcony which circled the inside of the domed roof. The walls of the dome were lined with more shelves of

429

rare volumes, and went as high as possible before the dome was capped by a series of punctured circular windows.

There was a magnificent large desk that had belonged to Louis XV, with a roll top and a gallery of ormolu. The chair used at the desk was of the same period: comfortable, high-backed and covered in a boar-hunt scene of blues and greens. There were deep, inviting chairs everywhere, covered in old, worn leather or suedes, some in antique, hand-woven, bold checks of brown and white. Ottomans covered in crocodile skins, so worn by age they were soft and supple. Writing-tables, map-tables, side-tables, dictionary-stands, all in what appeared to be a haphazard arrangement, but in fact set in half-a-dozen intimate groupings.

Aubusson carpets, allegedly from a king's hunting-lodge in the depths of France's richest hunting-grounds in the late seventeenth century. Amidst all this, the silver bowls of fresh flowers everywhere caused the room to spring into colourful life. Bunches of tall white lilacs near the open fire diffused a heavy scent reminiscent of flowers blooming in a forest. There were lilies, freesia, and on top of the roll-top desk three dozen white tulips, full blown and perfumed. On a long, antique, Spanish oak table there was a baroque silver tray, where antique crystal decanters offered whisky, bourbon, cognac, with large goblets. Sporting-magazines from all over the world declared the occupant's up-to-the-minute involvement with the hunt.

About ten feet from the fireplace and parallel to it was a long, deep Edwardian leather sofa and draped over the back was a large silver fox rug, on one end a polar bear rug, the other a coverlet of white beaver. The stuffed animals – a snow tiger, an enormous grizzly bear, a pair of wild boars – stood around with great presence and a certain authority as if the lodge was their den. A collection of narwhal tusks mounted on wooden bases stood off to one side pretending they were unicorn horns.

Adam kissed Mirella on the cheek and said, 'Let's have tea.'

He and Turhan moved the laden tea-table in front of the fireplace and to one side. Then they placed a pair of dark brown, buffalo-suede-covered Louis XIV chairs opposite each other on either side of the table. There they sat across from each other. The crackling fire cast a light on Mirella, who appeared so young and fresh and with a sparkle of life like the diamonds in her ears and a lustre as rich and rare as her pearls.

Mirella kept studying Adam, who was dressed in a pair of black-and-white houndstooth-check trousers, a black, cashmere turtle-neck sweater and a Saint Laurent jacket of chestnut-coloured leather.

He seemed, in his own very private room, even more rugged and handsome, more a man unto himself. This lodge of his housed the memorabilia of an adventurer, a hunter of animals, a lover of the wild, an explorer of the primitive. Here she felt the rightness of the setting for this man she loved.

It was difficult for her to balance the different sides of her husband's character. Was this then the man who played with panda bears and raised rare birds, who tucked his youngest child into bed as if family was all that mattered to him? Or was he the international manipulator who was reputed since his business coup in Ethiopia to be the next Armand

431

Hammer? Or was the essential man the passionate lover she fell for, who changed her life, her erotic soul-mate? What more was there for her to learn of him? This was her husband, and she hardly knew him when she married him and she hardly knew him now. Yet shamelessly she didn't care. Enough that her body and her heart yearned for him.

Like two nervous lovers they barely spoke, while their desire for each other grew. Over the rims of tea cups they watched Muhsine pull the large, soft cushions from the sofa and lay them on the floor in front of the gigantic fireplace. It looked positively feudal with its five-feet-long logs lighting the entire area where they sat. Turhan covered the cushions with the polar bear skin and laid the silver fox rug near by.

'The man knows me so well he anticipates perfectly,' said Adam, a twinkle in his eye.

They ate small triangular smoked salmon sandwiches of crustless brown bread, paper-thin cucumber sandwiches that melted on the tongue. They ate hungrily after the cold and the romping in the snow. The cake was only five inches in diameter and four inches high. It was covered with hard, thick, white chocolate and looked more like a hand-made, Belgian, cream-filled bon-bon. The white chocolate casing covered thin layers of moist dark cake, and, between them, thick layers of mocha cream.

Turhan heated the silver cake-slicer over the open fire. With a white napkin around its ivory handle he melted a line through the casing and sliced the cake without cracking it.

'A champagne among cakes! Good enough, do you think, to toast absent friends?'

Adam's allusion to Rashid's weakness for chocolate was oblique, but enough momentarily to startle Mirella. For a piquant second, the man's presence troubled the perfect happiness that enveloped her. Yet she felt secure, too, in the mastery and acceptance by her husband that the quick allusion might imply.

Turhan and Muhsine left them to finish their tea. A silence fell over the room except for the crackling of the fire.

'There are so many things I have wanted to say to you since I arrived, but there seem always to be people around and things to do. I haven't even thanked you for the coat. I do thank you, it's so beautiful. And my pavilion, I cannot begin to tell you how much I adore it. But those things amount to very little when it comes to thanking you for the love and understanding you show me. For being the man you are.

'In the fairy tales you would be like the Prince that kissed Sleeping Beauty. You awakened me to a life I missed while I was sleeping, albeit with my eyes open. Do I tell you often enough that I love you? That I always want you, no matter the distance or the people or the time that separate us.'

He gazed into her eyes. He could see the depths of her soul in them, that was enough. He needed, wanted no other words. He stopped her, 'Some things need never be said. If we were to begin that, we would create a barrage of words trying to tell each other how grateful we are for finding real love. Let's just live our love for each other.'

With those words Adam rose from the tea-table,

went around and drew Mirella's chair back. Together they stood before the open fire and watched the flames dance and leap into the air, disappear, die and renew themselves as flames. Silently they turned away from the fire and faced each other. They raised their hands at the same time, and Adam took Mirella's in his, lowered his lips to them and kissed them.

Chemistry, electricity, desire and affection were working for them, as it often did when they were alone together. There was something about the very touch of Adam's skin, his natural body-scent, the very essence of the man, that stirred new life within Mirella. It was the same for Adam.

Still holding hands, Mirella stepped closer and kissed Adam gently, ever so lightly, tenderly. He felt the tremble in her lips and he felt the sheer elation of her kiss. They broke contact and stepped back from each other as if seared by burning desire, and, gazing deeply into each other's eyes, their hearts and souls met.

Slowly, they undressed themselves and let their clothes lie where they fell. Naked in the firelight, love danced between them. Adam finally reached out and touched her cheek with one finger, as if to reassure himself that she was real. He arranged the pearls over her naked breasts and covered her diamond hand-cuffs with his hands. He raised first one hand, then the other to his lips, and turned them over and kissed her palms.

He found her dazzlingly exciting, naked yet adorned with priceless jewels that sparkled in the firelight. Here before him stood the true and natural loving beauty of Mirella combined with her sensual,

434

lascivious soul. This was the Mirella who had captivated him.

Mirella broke the spell between them when she laid hands on her husband and moved them slightly, with tenderness and love, over every inch of his body. His nipples rose under her fingers, his mass of blond pubic hair was combed by them. She held his penis in both hands and caressed it. The weight of it, the life-force she felt pulsating in the long thick phallus, excited the warmth and desire she felt for him. She lowered her lips to his large and beautiful testicles and kissed them, licked them and then ran her hands around the inside of his thighs. Mirella could feel the wetness of her own orgasms, and he had not even touched her as yet. Choked with unblushing desire for him, she said, 'I love you so much, Adam. I want you so much. No matter what happens in our lives, you must always remember that.'

'I do, and I always will, and that's why you are free to do anything you want with your life.'

Mirella had no answer for that.

He reached out and caressed her large, rounded breasts. Her nipples enticed him and, taking them in his mouth, he used his tongue to lick, and his mouth to suck. He pulled her body against his, kissed her. Their lips opened, their tongues repeated the kiss, and they drank their passion from each other.

Adam slipped his hands beneath her arms and moved them lovingly along her sides, resting his hands at her waist. He gripped hard and raised her high above his head. She opened her legs wide and her hands went between her legs. He saw the droplets of her passion glisten on the luscious, dark triangle of hair. With trembling fingers she parted her most intimate lips. Her clitoris was like a tiny, round, pink button, and the satiny wetness of her orgasm lay along her delectable deep pink slit, waiting for his kisses.

She marvelled at his strength and control as he lowered her over his mouth and licked her opening, nibbled at her clitoris, and when she sighed, he pushed his tongue deep inside her, moving it in and out and around. Scooping out her sweet nectar, he drank from the heart of her femininity.

His cunt-kisses sent shiver after shiver of delight through her, and she came with new fresh orgasms. The passion and love they had for each other was infinite. He lowered her still further now and looked into her deep violet eyes and then held her away from his body. She forced her legs and her cunt wider apart and he set her on the tip of his rigid penis. Then with one huge thrust he pulled her all the way onto him. She wrapped her legs around his waist. Now with his free arms he encircled her and with his hands he caressed her hair and kissed her, standing with his penis throbbing deep inside her.

Yet he held himself back and, with her close in his arms again, he slipped down on his knees and laid her on the polar-bear skin. Here the glow of the fire seemed to burnish her flesh, inflaming his passion for her anew. Outside, beyond the room that enfolded their loving, was the chill of the snow. As if to affirm his oneness with the life and warmth of the fire within, Adam continued his love-making until she cried out for them to come together. For a split second, it was as if their hearts stopped on the same beat. For a poised and perfect moment, they encountered oneness.

As Adam draped the silver fox coverlet over them, Mirella tried to compose herself. The calm of her being was not easily restored. Fanciful or not, something seemed to have stirred in the moment that their orgasms mingled ... something that had never stirred, never taken life in previous love-making with Adam or any man. She had felt within her a moment of creation.

Roberta Latow

CHEYNEY FOX

'FIRST LADY OF HANKY-PANKY' *SUNDAY TIMES*

'Genuinely erotic . . . luxurious . . . full of fantasy. It adds a frisson. It sets a hell of a standard.'
Sunday Times

Back in the heady days of the '60s, Cheyney Fox was one of the hottest young art dealers in New York. Her beauty was legendary, her sensuality given free rein. But a crooked colleague forced her into bankruptcy and blackened her reputation, leaving her confidence shattered, her career in ruins.

Fleeing the memory of her failure, Cheyney sought solace in the arms of Kurt Walbrook, an Austrian millionaire. Cheyney became Kurt's wife and gained wealth and position from the marriage, but there was something sinister about her husband, a depravity about his sensuality, that unleashed a dark and disturbing response in her.

Besides, in her heart of hearts, Cheyney Fox had always belonged to someone else . . .

Grant Madigan, globe-trotting, trouble-shooting investigative reporter, was one of the best and brightest of his generation. For him, women were just a decorative but dispensable commodity – until he met Cheyney Fox. Grant was her magnificent obsession, but, recognising instinctively that she was the one woman who could threaten his independence, he brutally rebuffed her, putting cruelty and continents between them.

Cheyney Fox – a woman in a million, an enigmatic beauty whose past contains dark secrets, twisted desires that must not be revealed. She will take on the world, but is the world ready for a woman like . . . Cheyney Fox?

FICTION / GENERAL 0 7472 3490 6

ROBERTA LATOW

HER HUNGRY HEART

'*A sunshine sizzler, packed with non-stop sex*'
People Magazine

He was handsome, tall and slender, with bedroom eyes
that devoured women. She was a tall willowy blonde
with the looks of a showgirl, wealthy, cultivated and
intelligent, an enchantress who knew how to tame men
and, once they were tamed, clever enough to keep them.
They met on New Year's Eve 1943 at a chic party in
New York's fashionable Stork Club. Their erotic
attraction was immediate and mutual. Their love affair
would last a lifetime. But Karel Stefanik was not free to
love Barbara Dunmellyn. He had Mimi, whom he had
abandoned in the cruel chaos of war, a child whose fate
becomes inextricably entangled with that of her father
and the woman he loves.

This, then, is the story of their hungry hearts, the lovers
that fuel their lives; and finally of their own all-
encompassing love.

'The first lady of hanky panky. Her books are solidly
about sex . . . it adds a frisson. It sets a hell of a standard'
The Sunday Times

'Naughty, certainly . . . the sex is larded with dollops of
exoticism and luxury' *Observer*

FICTION / GENERAL 0 7472 3884 7

A selection of bestsellers from Headline

LAND OF YOUR POSSESSION	Wendy Robertson	£5.99	☐
TRADERS	Andrew MacAllen	£5.99	☐
SEASONS OF HER LIFE	Fern Michaels	£5.99	☐
CHILD OF SHADOWS	Elizabeth Walker	£5.99	☐
A RAGE TO LIVE	Roberta Latow	£5.99	☐
GOING TOO FAR	Catherine Alliott	£5.99	☐
HANNAH OF HOPE STREET	Dee Williams	£4.99	☐
THE WILLOW GIRLS	Pamela Evans	£5.99	☐
MORE THAN RICHES	Josephine Cox	£5.99	☐
FOR MY DAUGHTERS	Barbara Delinsky	£4.99	☐
BLISS	Claudia Crawford	£5.99	☐
PLEASANT VICES	Laura Daniels	£5.99	☐
QUEENIE	Harry Cole	£5.99	☐

All Headline books are available at your local bookshop or newsagent, or can be ordered direct from the publisher. Just tick the titles you want and fill in the form below. Prices and availability subject to change without notice.

Headline Book Publishing, Cash Sales Department, Bookpoint, 39 Milton Park, Abingdon, OXON, OX14 4TD, UK. If you have a credit card you may order by telephone – 01235 400400.

Please enclose a cheque or postal order made payable to Bookpoint Ltd to the value of the cover price and allow the following for postage and packing:

UK & BFPO: £1.00 for the first book, 50p for the second book and 30p for each additional book ordered up to a maximum charge of £3.00.
OVERSEAS & EIRE: £2.00 for the first book, £1.00 for the second book and 50p for each additional book.

Name ....

Address ....

....

....

If you would prefer to pay by credit card, please complete:
Please debit my Visa/Access/Diner's Card/American Express (delete as applicable) card no:

Signature .... Expiry Date ....